The Importance of Joseph Ross

The Headless Trilogy

Headless
The Barabbas Choice
The Importance of Joseph Ross

BOOK 3 OF THE HEADLESS TRILOGY

The Importance of Joseph Ross

When justice meets pity ...

ROBERT BLAIR

THE CLOISTER HOUSE PRESS

To my wife Helen

Foreword

This is the third in a trilogy of novels. It follows on the first two, Headless and The Barabbas Choice. In it the themes of the earlier works are developed and, to some extent, synthesised. Many of the characters of the previous novels make a re-appearance here. There is also continuity in terms of the narrative. The central theme of the first two novels, justice in its traditional form, is plunged into the world of politics where it is required to compete for survival (or to be more accurate, revival) against the competing forces at work in modern society.

Among these is the received wisdom that the institutions charged with serving justice have the patent on it, confining it within parameters defined solely by them. It thus becomes no more and no less than what they say it is. Within these institutions the established view of justice is narrowed to a preoccupation with the legal processes of its implementation. Any insistence on it having to demonstrate fairness to justify its authority is rejected as subversive and deemed not the pursuit of decent men. This view is so deeply enshrined that it is seldom challenged and portrayed as what it is, a bizarre incidence of the means being used to justify the end. The legal apparatus of law is just that, a method of ensuring that justice is done. But even when it is clear that it is failing to do so – anything from procedural niceties to witness intimidation can be allowed to decide cases – the outcome is sacrificed on the altar of due process. There are certainly competing interests in play here, each with a claim to legitimacy, but, astonishingly, conventional wisdom invariably picks out the same winner – due process. This is the issue that is central to the theme of the second novel, The Barabbas Choice.

It is interesting to note that a degree of wriggle room is on occasion accorded to certain forms of political activism. When deemed to be acting in furtherance of views in tune with the prevailing Zeitgeist, activists come to be seen as honourable operatives. Popular drama and literature look kindly on activists who break the law in pursuit of causes that tick the right boxes, challenging the corruption of the rich for example or standing up for the interests of the oppressed. If, however, the challenge comes from other less favoured quarters, the nightmare of anarchy is evoked in all its horror and the full force of the law is deployed without compunction. This is to some extent understandable. Any political agenda that can lay claim, either genuinely or cynically, to be in the service of feeling for one's fellow man is a winner. By extension, any policy that falls short on cosy emotional impact is damned. In the world of generalised perception, when hard reason takes on soft sentiment it invariably loses. It's much easier, for example, to approve of aid being sent to the starving of a third world country than to oppose it on the strength of evidence that it is being used to line the pockets of the oppressors. Curiously though, when we move from the public to the private sphere the outcome is less predictable: This for the simple reason that in close-up the price of ignoring the head is easier to see and harder to pay. This is the source of one of the great divides in politics. Those in the business of deciding social policy and drafting legislation operate largely in the sphere of generalised perception, while those who live in the realities reconfigured by the politicians are left to confront consequences that have hard, and in some cases very sharp edges. In the specific case of the criminal law, the governing class tends to pride itself on its capacity for mercy and leniency and favours them over the emotional asceticism of justice. Our cultural evolution from Victorian times has seen a marked shift from one to the other, to such an extent that many in positions of influence and authority have come to see the idea of justice as interchangeable with the notion of mercy. As a result the 'justice' they dispense is subjected to all sorts of constraints and requirements that properly belong in the job description of mercy. The emotional differs from the rational in many ways, but the one that is particularly salient here is its susceptibility to immediacy. When a dastardly crime is committed the public's feelings are incensed; there is an impassioned call for justice. But by the time the system gets round to dealing with the case, the initial emotional surge has lost much of its momentum and the culprit eventually gets to fill the empathy gap. The same compassion that swelled up at the outset for the victim of the crime is now bestowed on the felon, who is recast as a prey of the justice system. It is not without significance that those advocating mercy show little sign of shame when, in compliance with their demands, a murderer or a rapist is released prematurely and then goes on to destroy other innocent lives.* Distance seemingly makes the heart grow fainter.

There is a disturbing volatility at the very core of justice. If not inspired by compassion, Justice would be a poor and potentially cruel thing. But when it allows itself to be subsumed by compassion and runs scared of being labelled 'vengeance in disguise' it is not worthy of its name and betrays the duty it has to society. How to maintain the tension without caving in to one side or the other is a problem that confronts all western societies. What makes matters worse, we are living in an age soaked in sentimentality where people find it increasingly difficult to separate feeling in the first degree from the warm glow of feeling about feeling. (The faux grief on display at Princess Diana's obsequies is only the most cringe-worthy in a long line of examples). One thing is certain; our society will not come up with any intelligent accommodation if it fails to

---

* According to recent statistics almost 20% of murders in Britain are committed by prisoners out on remand or parole.

diagnose the problem. It is not a question of finding a magic formula. Indeed, one of the main reasons for the present state of affairs is the delusion that a perfect system can be devised, a system so perfect as to preclude the need for good men to act on their judgement.

It is the self-imposed task of the New Prometheans of the novel to find a way of getting the criminal justice system and the culture that surrounds it back to doing its bread-and-butter job of balancing crime and punishment. Modern day culture has become so embedded in hollow feeling that the notion of justice, even in the rare moments that it can differentiate itself from mercy, is impregnated with the vacuity of emotionalism. It is one thing to decide that justice should be imposed; it is quite another thing to get down to the messy business of carrying it through. It's the difference between simply pressing a button to terminate the bad guy and plunging a dagger into living flesh. Conservative sections of the public are on the whole in favour of harsher punishment, most notably the death penalty, for dangerous criminals, but strange though it may seem, their support bears the very same stamp of sentimentality as you get with the liberals who are horrified by it. At the first execution whole swathes of support would swing back to the liberal orthodoxy when the public is confronted with the predictable press reaction, stories about the deprived past of the criminal, the impact on his wife and children, the trauma of those forced to witness the execution.

It is very difficult to break from the ethos of the group in any area of culture, but it is particularly hard in matters of morality. To prise people away from group-thinking and group-feeling and to get them rooted in the particular is to run counter to the mentality of society, especially one steeped in consumerism and fixated on on-line reality. There is an inherent instability in the basic mechanisms of moral thinking. To gain a moral perspective you have to move out of your normal egocentric take on reality and try to see the world from the vantage point of another person. That gets you as far as sympathy, but it is only a first step. To decide on the question of moral rightness or wrongness, you must be able, in Kant's phrase, to universalise the perspective. That is where trouble can arise. In choosing an alternative perspective from which to look upon your own action you expose yourself to the risk of hijack. If you are in the orbit a person with a more forceful personality than yourself or if you belong to a social, religious or political set, it is very easy to allow yourself to fall under their spell, so that the whole attempt to think morally can easily turn into an attempt to win approval. It's easy to see this process at work when looking from the outside – it explains for example the phenomena of a morally conscientious country like Germany falling under the spell of the Nazis – but it is not at all obvious if viewed from within the group. If I chose to operate in a group of like-minded people, where is the line between what I think and feel and what the group thinks and feels? The most that can reasonably be expected from the average individual is a little shuffling away from the epicentre of the group. Anyone who can make a radical break from the mindset of those with whom he identifies without the encouragement of an alternative support base is rare indeed. As an unconventional young man of outstanding intellect and deep sensitivity, Joseph Ross, the eponymous hero of the tale, is the perfect guinea pig for the pilot scheme that Robert Snoddy sets up. He has an intellect more free than most of conventional thought patterns. That creates almost labora-tory-style conditions for Snoddy and his fellow Prometheans to observe the human sympathy and propensity for mercy that comes with the warmth of Joseph's nature going head to head with the strong intellectual conviction he has of justice, in order to determine if any kind of synthesis is achievable.

The secondary issue, namely what degree of shuffle it is reasonable to expect the man-in-the-street to make from the epicentre of the prevailing wisdom, is also extensively explored. The plot centres round the efforts of the New Prometheans to secure a parliamentary seat. No attempt has been made to provide an accurate account of party procedures. The interest is not in the party as such, in this case the Labour Party, but on the contemporary political forces for which the contest provides a battleground. This could almost just as easily have been filtered through a narrative involving the Tory Party, but the allegiance Labour supposedly has to the traditional working class culture is more clearly established in most people's minds. It is the divergence between the cultural conservatism of the people the party purports to represent and the cosmopolitan liberalism that it actually promotes that provides the general thrust of the political narrative. This complements the main theme. The plausibility of some of the events described in the story in the context of a real-life selection process for a parliamentary candidate is a matter of lesser importance. The reader is asked to believe that, in spite of mounting evidence to the contrary, modern politics has retained its traditional tolerance for intellectual debate and grant the author some poetic licence in the cause of exposing what are perhaps more fundamental truths about the present state of the political landscape.

Finally, it must be stressed that, despite the emphasis that has been placed here on the philosophical and political themes that run through the narrative, this is first and foremost a novel and it asks to be judged as such. Like all members of the genre it stands or falls on the convergence of plot and theme and on its ability to engage the reader in a story involving characters that come to life on the page. I leave it to the reader to decide whether it passes that test.

Robert Blair

Robert Blair is a retired teacher who was born and grew up in Northern Ireland. He studied modern languages at Queens University in the 1960s and at the University of Ulster in the 1970s where he took a masters degree in German twentieth century literature. His concerns with matters educational come from a teaching and examining career that spanned four decades. His interest in politics is coloured by his study of literature and philosophy, his experience growing up in a Labour supporting family and the effects of the Ulster troubles on the Enlightenment values he had been taught to respect. None of his novels to date are set in Ulster, but some of the issues are aired, minus their Irish accretions, in this and his two earlier novels.

Chapter 1

"What the hell are they going to do to me?" The question never came to full articulation; it remained embryonic but shot like a bolt up through the man's consciousness. In its wake came little whimperings from within that ebbed and flowed from terror to outrage. His cheekbone ached from the blow it had received and at the back of his throat he could taste the blood from his nose. They had clapped a hood over his head; he could breath, but air was filtering wet and clammy through the fluffy hem of the aperture that had been cut for his mouth. The cloth of the hood was thick; he was in total blackness. His hands were clamped in cuffs behind his back. In the twenty minutes or so he had been here he had already been assailed by multiple crescendos of compulsion to break free, see light and breathe cool air. The panic soared higher in urgency each time, deepening further the pit he fell into when the energy-burst was spent. Back down in the depths, he gradually came to feel the consolation of simple despair; there was solace to be had in its embalmment.

Gradually the terror of the what-next was nudged off centre by an urgency to fathom the why of what was going on. Had he pushed them too hard? Did they see the favour he had called in as some kind of blackmail – did they think he'd been threatening to grass them up if they didn't get him off? That wasn't on his agenda at all. He had done a job for them. Okay, he'd been paid, but you look out for your mates, don't you, and you expect them to look out for you. That was all there was to it. But maybe they didn't see it that way; maybe they thought he was trying to put the screws on them. And now they were scaring him off, teaching him a lesson, warning him not to mess them about.

1

They were just trying to scare him – that was it – put the fear of God in him. They didn't actually need to hurt him. No, threatening would be enough. They were just showing him what they could do to him if he didn't play ball. They were putting the frighteners on, that's all. Sure, if they were intending to kill him, why would they stick this hood over his head? It was just so he couldn't identify them. That meant they didn't intend to top him. No, he'd come through this.

A warm wave of assurance swept over him. Things weren't so bad. They weren't going to bump him off. But the wave did not linger. As it passed, it trailed in its wake the chilling thought that being spared a death sentence was no guarantee they weren't going to get seriously vicious. They weren't just going to give him a good talking-to and leave it at that, were they? They were going to give him a taste of what to expect if he mucked them about again. Yeah, they were going to hurt him. He needed to face it, that's what *he'd* do if he were in their shoes. But what were they going to do to him? He'd heard of IRA punishments where they used power drills on the victim's knee caps. He suddenly became uncomfortably conscious of his own knee caps. And then there was his eyes – he could never bear anyone going anywhere near his eyes. No, they weren't thinking of doing anything to his eyes – they'd hardly have needed the hood if they were going to blind him, would they? Chainsaws, he'd seen a movie where they'd used a chainsaw to cut the arm off a guy who had grassed them up. God Almighty! Could they really be that vicious? He needed to get them to listen to him. He could offer them some sort of deal. There was bound to be something he could trade. He could do another job for them. That's it – and he wouldn't ask for payment. There must be somebody they'd like to put the screws on. He could do that. He had never knocked anyone off before, but if it came to it he could. That was the answer. They wouldn't say no to an offer like that. No way. Yeah, and if he did knock somebody off for them, he wouldn't be able to blab to the police, would he? – He'd be in too deep. They'd know they could trust him then. It was a no-brainer.

No sooner had his thoughts slotted into this little hatch than they flared up all over again. His mind was in a kind of symphonic loop. Every time it was drawn back to the drill and the chainsaw; the whine became more piercing, the bit blunter and more biting, the blade more jagged. It was with increasing desperation that he reached out for the calm that came at the end of each wave. But repetition produced a diminishing return. In the end he lost the last dregs of the faith he had in his ability to cut himself a deal. There was no escaping the terrifying threat of those diabolical tools of torture.

He remained in the swelter of this fever for what might have been hours on end. It was only when he heard the lock being turned on the door that he re-entered the world of definite time. He was strangely grateful for being pulled out of himself. He couldn't see anything of course, but the sounds told him that two people had entered the room. They helped him to his feet, roughly but not with any obvious intention to inflict pain, and frog-marched him in similar fashion outside into the open air along uneven ground before ushering him into another building with a rough stone floor. He was then impelled into a sitting position – to his relief there was something there for his backside to settle on, a hard wooden object, probably a stool. He was aware of further presences and had the feeling of being surrounded on all sides. Not a word had been said, but he could hear chairs being moved into position and creaks as they took the weight of occupants. Then there was a shuffling of papers and the unmistakeable sound of a pencil being dropped on a wooden surface. Then came the voice; it was a posh voice, the kind you'd expect from someone like an army officer. It whisked up the hope that its owner wasn't brutish, that he'd be a type that would take no pleasure in inflicting pain.

"You've been a very naughty boy, haven't you, David?"

3

Only his mother called him David. More hope. He wouldn't muck this man about; he'd show him he was someone you could cut a deal with. He took the initiative.

"Look. I didn't mean no harm. I knew Schinski had political connections that go right up to the top. I'm not into politics, but I know he knows very powerful people. All I was asking him to do was get them to pull a few strings with the fuzz and make it all go away for me. It was no big deal for him. I done a good job for him. I got that little snitch off his back, didn't I? There's no way he'll be going to go to the papers now that I've fixed him. So, you see, I thought it would be no big deal for him to help me out with my little problem. I wasn't saying he had to. I wasn't threatening him or anything like that. I wouldn't have done nothing if he'd said no, straight up. I'm not one to let my mates down. You tell me what you want me to do and I'm your man. Any other little snitch that needs shutting up . . . I'll even top him for you if that's what you want."

There was an almost audible intake of breath from the three men on the other side of the table. Glances of incomprehension were exchanged. Eventually the man on the right of the group beckoned to the others that he would take over. His voice was deeper, polished but not quite as 'posh' as the first speaker's.

"You seem to be good at making promises, David, but how good are you at keeping them?"

'David' was slightly taken aback by the change of voice, but this only inflamed his anxiety to press home his case.

"I clobbered Cooper for you, didn't I? You wanted me to put the fear of God in him. I did that, didn't I? He won't be telling nobody nothing. You're in the clear. I done my job. I played it straight with you. What more proof do you need?"

There was a long pause while the new speaker considered his options. When he finally spoke his tone was warmer than before.

4

"We'll need to think about that, David. We'd like to be able to trust you, but we'll need some kind of assurance that any trust we show you will not be misplaced. For the moment, you'll go back to your room. We'll have to keep you in the dark, but we'll remove your cuffs and the hood and someone will bring you something to eat."

As soon as the prisoner had been ushered out of the room, still hooded and hand-cuffed, the three men gave full vent to the surprise they had been suppressing.

"I think we've struck some kind of seam, gentlemen. The question is: what kind of nuggets have we hit on and how are we going to dig them out?"

The voice belonged to the eldest of the three, the one who had taken over the interrogation. He looked at the other two. Both made that slight tilt of the head and raise of the eyebrows that comes only slightly short of a full-blown admission of cluelessness.

"That name Schinski, does it mean anything to you? Clearly he's someone with considerable clout that seems to extend as far as the police."

The owner of the 'posh' voice eventually broke the silence that this had been met with.

"I think we're dealing with some kind of cover-up. This man Cooper must have known something that *Mr Schinski*, whoever he is, wanted kept quiet. They got our friend on the job and he put the frighteners on Cooper. But how does this tie in with his assault on Hill? Oh, hang on a minute ... When the police didn't charge him, we assumed that was down to the old story of legal niceties clogging up the system. But it looks like we were wrong. It looks as if these people put pressure on the police to drop the case. It was down to a word in the right ear. And that word came from this mysterious *Schinski*."

"So our friend here thinks we're acting for Schinski. He thinks the Schinski crowd didn't appreciate being pressured into helping him over his assault on Hill and we've been sent to teach him a lesson."

This was the first contribution from the third member of the group, a tall, youthful man with blond, wavy hair and a pointed chin. There was a distinct northern strain in the voice that contrasted sharply with the plush tones of the response.

"I think we're on to something bigger than we thought. We'll need to go upstairs and get advice on how to proceed. I'll get on to HQ right away."

Chapter 2

As he squared up to the mirror, razor in hand, Justin took in the image that confronted him. He had never liked his face; it was too ... He paused for a moment to think what was wrong with it. It was too *familiar*; it betrayed too much of the goings-on behind it. It wasn't like other people's faces; it provided no privacy, no inscrutable screen to trespassers. But then again, maybe other people felt the same way about their faces. It wasn't his face itself that was the problem; it was his ownership of it. He tried to see himself as others might see him – Mr Justin Wright, Oxford graduate and up-and-coming journalist ... no, nothing so grand – humble newspaper hack ... recently married to Miss Lizzie, Oxford graduate and probationer teacher. He could envisage himself encapsulated in pen portrait in a short story written by some future Maupassant or Somerset Maugham, with his potted past history and the assurance that comes with such histories that there was a tale waiting to be told of what lay ahead. He did indeed have a history, but whether there was a tale worth the telling lurking in his future was another matter. Dullness and routine are the moss that pristine life inevitably gets clogged up with. And this morning, for some reason, he was acutely aware of the dampness it thrived in.

When he got to the kitchen the whiff of fresh coffee gave promise of a tangent out of the loop he was in. Lizzie was on the hoof nibbling toast and stuffing papers into the satchel, still redolent of new leather, that he had bought her to mark her first teaching job. He could not share in her dynamism, but he was glad all the same to be in its presence.

"Did I tell you? Simpson's coming to supervise me this morning. It's the Year 12s. Why the hell did it have to be that class? They're such a shower. I hope to God Willy Green is sick. The others are prepared to settle for a bit of common or garden disruption, but for him nothing short of havoc will do, the little puke."

Justin smiled. Of course she had told him. "I'm sure you'll be able to handle him. Don't let Simpson cramp your style. You could always ask him for advice. From what you've told me, he'll be more than happy to share his platitudes with you. Remember, it's all about background – don't for God's sake let the foreground get in the way!"

She laughed. "You're such a cynic. The family background does matter, you know. But I'd dearly like to see Simpson's face if Willy came off with one of his smelly body noises to back up his signature tune, '*Fiche-moi le camp*'.[1] It's the only French idiom he's ever bothered to learn – I wonder how enlightened Simpson's nose is. Will Willy's deprived background help it to filter out the stink?"

A final quick sip of coffee and she was away. Justin had had a latish evening the night before covering a very tedious council meeting and felt within his rights to make a late start at the office. He could of course write up the report here at home, but the thought of having something to warrant a delay in tackling it – the journey to work, a confab with Michael, his news editor, and maybe even a snippet of office gossip – was too inviting to resist. He finished his corn flakes with an ear half cocked to the *Today Programme*. As usual, his frustration levels built up as the interviewers asked the *wrong* questions and the interviewees answered what they thought the questions ought to have been. It was just the usual exercise in political musaic, just a more pretentious version of what was on offer on Radio 2 or Radio 1 for that matter … No, Classic FM was nearer the mark, the channel that reduces the treasures of musical exploration to a bottomless

---

[1]   F... off

8

source of ease and relaxation. Frustration was edging towards stupefaction when he became vaguely aware of the distant jingle of his mobile. The usual pantomime ensued before he tracked it down in the pocket of the jacket he had been wearing the night before. He expected it would be Lizzie asking him to bring her some vital piece of Gallic back-up material she had forgotten, but no, the name beaming at him from the screen was *Rob Snoddy*.

The opening "Hello, Justin. How are you?" was followed up without even the hint of a pause for reply: "I need to see you. It's urgent. Can you come round?"

Justin was not insensitive to the robotic style. In fact he welcomed it. In his dealings with him Robert Snoddy had always swung wildly between a coldness that bordered on hostility and an intensity of common interest that held out the prospect of intimacy. Justin was tempted by the intimacy, but its starkness against the background of the more prevalent chill made him wary. He was much more at ease in the shallower waters of the Snoddy experience.

His pride suffered no offence in agreeing to drop all and answer the call. This was a better distraction than an editorial confab or office chit-chat. His curiosity was whetted. What could Snoddy want to see him about? When given its own space however the question started to emit sinister vibrations. Could it be the old business with Dwayne Rodgers? That surely had been put to bed. Burrows and Wilson were safely in prison. Had something come up – some new evidence that proved their innocence? But even if the truth came out, he had nothing to fear; it was someone from the organisation who had killed Rodgers – Justin had never really been given all the details. The bottom line was: it wasn't him. He'd fired the gun, but it was only blanks he'd fired. That was all he'd done. An undercover policeman showing willing to execute a murderer that the authorities had failed to bring to justice isn't technically a criminal offence. No physical harm had been done.

9

The curiosity that the call had provoked was gradually morphing into anxiety. He finished his coffee in determinedly robotic calm and even washed up the breakfast dishes before returning to the bedroom and taking more trouble with his dressing than was usual with him. The black polo-neck always looked good under his grey tweed jacket – very nineteen-sixties. It provided an air of suavity that his mounting disquiet needed as cover for its rawness. He wouldn't take the car – too much trouble, besides the walk would do him good. And it would take longer.

As he made his way along the wet pavements his apprehension fastened on to previous bouts suffered in the lead-in to encounters with Rob Snoddy. On several occasions during his time undercover he'd had the distinct feeling that he'd been sussed, especially the time he'd been summoned to take part in the mock trial. He was sure that he was the one that was for the chop. And he wasn't wrong to be worried. They had actually sussed him; they knew he was a cop. But they were prepared to believe that he had jumped ship and come over to them. They still needed to be sure. The trial and the sham execution that followed was their way of testing him. Stuart Stranaghan was a bonus. Snoddy had spotted a chance to get the Inspector to compromise himself. He was a master at controlling people and he guessed how Stranaghan would react if he was forced into choosing between justice and the law. The 'Barabbas Choice' he called it. Stranaghan did not disappoint. It cost the poor man his career.

The door was opened by Naomi, Snoddy's better-bred half. She looked at her beautiful best, but the effect was forever tainted for Justin by the cynical tag that Lizzie had pinned on her – *the lovely Naomi*. The warm smile she gave him and the general effusiveness of her greeting clashed markedly with Snoddy's perfunctory acknowledgement of his arrival. He was ushered out of the warmth of Naomi's presence into the little room that served as the Snoddy den.

"Something has come up. A few of our people were dealing with a low-life called Craig who had assaulted a man called Hill. It was pretty nasty. Hill was left in a bad way – the doctors doubt he'll ever be able to walk again. Craig was charged, but the case never came to court – some procedural nicety, the usual story. Anyway, we thought we should step in. We picked Craig up and interrogated him, but out of the blue he started going on about a completely different assault – on a guy called Cooper. Apparently he'd been acting as a hit man for somebody going by the name of Schinski. It looks as if it was Schinski who pulled the strings and got the police to drop the charges in the Hill case. Craig seemed to think we were Schinski's men. He assumed that Schinski and his crowd, whoever they were, hadn't taken kindly to being dragooned into helping him. He thought they had read it as blackmail: *Get me off this charge or I'll blow the whistle on you,* that kind of thing. The bastard was shit-scared, he really thought he was for the chop."

All this was said with a minimum of tonal variation, information proffered as food to sustain the body rather than titillate the palate. When eventually he did pause it was as if he had been called away to another thought. Justin certainly got no impression of being given time to take in what had been said. It felt almost like an act of boldness when he asked what it all had to do with him.

"We're not sure how to play it. If we go in heavy without knowing what we're dealing with, Craig might well be more scared of Schinski and his crew than he is of us and clam up. We're playing along and letting him think he's right about us acting for Schinski. For the moment we're letting him stew. But we're working in the dark. We need to know who exactly this *Schinski* is, who *Cooper* is and what information he has that Schinski wants no-one to know about. That's where you come in. You want to be a top newspaper man. Now's your chance."

Justin felt abruptly uprooted from the ground he had been

so comfortably embedded in. He had complained bitterly of the boredom of it, but now he was assailed by the sudden revelation of how unappreciative he'd been of the safety of his rut. *What about his report on the council meeting? He couldn't just drop all and follow the clarion call, could he?*

"I've spoken to Eardley and he has squared it with your editor. You're free to go sniffing and find the fox."

Snoddy smiled. His smiles were offered so sparingly that you felt specially favoured when one was conferred on you.

"Okay. Where do I start?"

"Craig hails from Manchester. You could start from there."

Justin was handed a print-out of all the gen they had on Craig. He was reminded of the need for haste and was summarily despatched.

Chapter 3

Manchester slipped into the same slot in Justin's mind as the one it occupies in the national consciousness. It was the industrial past incarnate. His father's father had worked there all his life in a small engineering firm and his father too had served his time as a fitter's apprentice before getting married and heading south. His imagination had been fired by a treasury of stories he had heard from his father of blows dealt and blows received in the relentless skirmishing with the Bosses. Most of the wrangles involved his grandfather who had been a shop steward and stout defender of the comrades' interests. In Justin's youthful imagination the bosses always took the form of men of indeterminate age dressed in trench coats and wearing wide-brimmed hats. They would sometimes be smoking cigarettes like the workers, but more often they would appear with modest cigars wedged between nicotine-stained fingers. There would be no waistcoat-and-braces style ostentation in the smoking, quite the opposite; it would be done almost furtively, an attempt, he supposed, to underplay their connections with the bigger boys above them, the ones that really pulled their strings, the 'owners'. Black funeral-type cars would deposit these anonyms at the factory gates. But this only happened when things got really bad. On such occasions they would do their business, give their orders and then have themselves whisked away back into the bosom of their caucus. His father's efforts to imitate the clipped accents of these aliens in the stories he told had set down a marker that had become for him a touchstone of falsity and hypocrisy. Puppets and puppeteers were held in equal contempt; for the young listener they were the two faces of Capital at its evil work.

His last visit to Manchester had been to attend his grand-mother's funeral. He'd have been about thirteen at the time. His grandfather had passed away many years before, too soon for the grandson to separate the man from the mythological creature that had taken the good fight to the forces of injustice and oppression. The thing that struck Justin most at the funeral was that there had been a lot more talk of his grandfather than of the deceased woman. All of the stories were recounted ostensibly to honour the lady who had been at the great man's side, but Justin had misgivings; he sensed that his granny was being sold short. The love that she showed to everyone, even to the daughter-in-law that had taken her beloved son down south and away from her, did not make for tales of daring-do; it was just what it was. The extent of its suffusion deprived it of definition.

He still had some relatives living in the city, but this was not the time to take them up on the pledges of keeping-in-touch that funerals inspire. After a train journey where it was the past rather than the countryside that seemed to whisk by, he booked himself into a Holiday Inn near the centre and considered his strategy. He had one contact in the Manchester police, Nigel Best. They had roomed together at the police academy and become quite close friends. Justin had taken it for granted that their friendship would span the whole of their lives, but, as is inevitably the case, the proximity that had given rise to the friendship proved also to be the arbiter of its duration. Contact petered out. Justin wasn't even sure if his friend was still based in Manchester. He had tried his old mobile number on the journey up, but had been put straight through to voicemail. He'd left a message; he assumed that meant the number was still active – he really ought to get to know things like that, he felt such a fool always having to ask. If he got no answer in the next hour or so, he'd make enquiries at a police station. Even if they wouldn't give him Nigel's number, they could contact him and get him to him call back. In the event it wasn't necessary; just as he was unpacking the little overnight bag he had hastily stuffed with necessities, his mobile rang. It was Nigel.

There was a swapping of the usual salutatory information, done less for enlightenment, more to offer reassurance of continued interest in the friendship. The catching-up drink, an essential element of such re-launches, was arranged for that evening. Nigel would be off duty at eight o'clock and gave directions to a pub not far from Justin's hotel. There was ample time for Justin to catch his breath and make a call to Lizzie. He hadn't called her earlier; he knew she'd probably be locked in battle with a class of ... what did she call them? ... *languor slugs*. It had never really occurred to him, but she was right: adolescents do cling to their boredom, they hate it, they rail against it, they blame all the world for it, but they won't let go of it for love nor money.

There was of course another reason why he hadn't called her: She wouldn't approve of what he was doing. The very mention of Snoddy's name was a red rag to a bull to her. She completely ignored the fact that it was through his involvement with The New Prometheans that Justin had got this newspaper job in the first place. The paper was part of the Matthew Eardley press empire and it had been clearly understood that he was being given the chance to learn the ropes in order to be in a position to promote the views of the organisation. He had no problem with that. He believed in what the organisation stood for. He had after all been prepared to kill ... he stopped himself from adding 'for it'. No, It wasn't 'for it' that he had been willing to shoot Rodgers; it was for the belief he shared with it in the need to step up when justice was being short-changed by the system. He started the conversation with Lizzie with every intention of coming clean about his trip to Manchester, but when it came to it he ducked out; he ventured nothing more damning than that he had been sent to cover a story.

Nigel hadn't changed a bit. It's strange the way you can

15

remember what people did, what they said, how they looked, but you can never quite keep hold of the aura they generate, that look, that turn of phrase, that bag of quirks they carry around with them like a knapsack. That is the magic of the person or conversely, in the case of those with whom you've resolved to make a fresh start and let bygones be bygones, the sore that resists the balm. The first couple of pints oiled the catching-up process. Nigel had done well in Manchester. He had hit it off with his DI and was quietly confident of an early promotion. The money would be useful as he had met 'this stunning woman'; she had moved in with him and they were expecting a child in the autumn. Justin was much more frugal in the biographical tit-for-tat. He made much of his awakening to the world of ideas at Oxford, omitting of course to mention the shape those ideas had taken, but it was his relationship with Lizzie that he offered as the main reason for his decision to give up the police and finish the mod langs degree.

By the third pint Justin decided it was time to grasp the nettle.

"Listen, Nigel. I need a favour. I've been sent up here to cover a story. We've come on some information that suggests there's some funny business going on in high places. We've been given a name of a potential whistle-blower. We've heard that he's been got at. Somebody gave him a kicking. Our problem is, we don't know anything about this guy, except that his name is Cooper. We need to find him and persuade him to talk to us."

Nigel gave him a distinctly policeman's look.

"You want me to help you? You're an old friend, Justin, but don't you think you're pushing it a bit? It would be more than my job's worth if I were caught helping a journalist friend get himself a scoop."

"That's not what this is about, Nigel. Okay, we might get a good story out of it, that's true, but, what's more important, we'd expose this thing, whatever it is. All I want you to do is to check the Manchester hospitals to see if they've treated any patients called Cooper for assault-type injuries in the last six months. You could tell your boss, if he asked you, that you were following a tip-off. And that's the truth. That's exactly what you'd be doing, isn't it?"

The police stare softened to a reflective frown. Justin saw a gap in the fence.

"Come on, Nigel. There's no hidden agenda here. I'm not asking you to do anything bent ... And just to prove there's no bribery and corruption going on, I'll keep my hands in my pocket and let you buy the next pint."

The wrapping seemed to sell the package. Nigel got up and went to the bar. When he came back, pints in hand, he nodded his head by way of a belated acknowledgement of what had been said.

"Okay, Justin, I'll see what I can do."

Chapter 4

It was late morning when Justin got a text from his friend asking him to meet him back at the pub they had been at the previous night.

"I phoned around and I think I've come up with a couple of possibilities. The Royal Infirmary had had two Cooper cases. One was a man in his thirties suffering from head injuries and two broken ribs – that was four months ago. The other was an older man, a 57-year-old who had bruising to the face and severe abdominal damage – that was a bit longer ago than you asked me to check, eight months to be precise. Computers can be wonderful at times; it's no extra work for them to check a few thousand more records . . . and no moaning about it not being their job. Trafford General also had a case, but I doubt if he'd be your man; he was in his seventies and said he had fallen from a ladder. I got all three addresses and checked them against the electoral role; they all checked out."

Nigel was anxious to get away. As he edged towards the door he was less than profuse in the conventional calls and pledges for keeping in touch. Justin was left with the uncomfortable feeling of having been set down and left like an untouchable in the back of beyond. Still, he had got what he was looking for. He'd start with the 57-year-old. Men of his age were less likely to be involved in a casual punch-up.

The taxi driver was very familiar with *Olden Place*. It had been quite posh, he said, when he was a boy. His father's boss had lived there, but the large terrace houses, Victorian, had now all been converted into flats and the gardens concreted over to accommodate residents' cars. The life had gone out of the place. 28b was at the end of its terrace. The concrete that had been laid in the erstwhile garden had been crudely ridged and with little regard to consistency of line. There was only one car in attendance to cover its barren look. Justin mounted the little perron and pressed the Cooper buzzer. It took two more presses before it sparked into amplification producing that distinctive drone that precurses a humanoid voice. Even through the static it was possible to detect a weariness and indifference in the humanoid that answered.

"Who's there? What do you want?"

"I've a package for you, Mr Cooper. It needs to be signed for."

It wasn't the most original of approaches, but it was guaranteed to produce a face-to-face. There was a long delay before a very suspicious '*What kind of package?*' came back.

"It's just an ordinary parcel, nothing special-looking about it. It's quite heavy."

Another long delay, followed eventually by an '*Okay, bring it up*'. The buzzer buzzed its instructions to the door, and Justin was in.

When on reporter duties, Justin always carried a little shoulder bag that contained his i-pad, a small dictaphone and a few other more basic reporting items. This he could now pass off as the repository of the imaginary package.

When he got to the landing the door to 28b was open. On the threshold stood a man whom Justin would have taken for much older than 57. He looked small and emaciated with a bald crown and two tufts of brown hair sitting like muffs above his ears. There was a cigarette smoking from his right hand. He fitted in a hurried puff as Justin approached.

"Where's this package, then?"

The unamplified voice had even less energy to it than the earlier version.

"It's in the bag. But before I hand it over, I'd need some identification. Do you have anything to prove you are Mr Terence Cooper?"

The man looked surprised, but showed no sign of challenge. After a weary '*Wait there*', he turned and made his way down the little hallway. Justin followed. The man got into the living room before he became aware of the presence behind him. He was clearly startled, but there was more fear than surprise in his eyes. It came out as bluster.

"What the hell do mean by coming into my house? I told you to wait at the door, didn't I?"

Justin played innocence.

"I'm sorry. I thought you wanted to show me a document. I'll go back again and wait outside if you want."

The relief that the docile tone produced did the trick. The removal of the threat had a more positive effect than if it hadn't been posed it in the first place.

"No, it doesn't matter. Here's my driving licence. Will that do?"

Justin made a great show of examining the document.

"That seems to be in order, Mr Cooper. I just need you to confirm your last place of work."

Suspicion made an immediate return to Cooper's eyes.

"What is this? Why do you need to know that? Who sent you here?"

Justin needed to gamble. He put all his money on his ability to reassure this man. If he could reproduce the relief he had induced earlier, there was a fair chance that he could get him to talk. He had little doubt that this was the Cooper he was looking for.

"I'll be perfectly honest with you, Mr Cooper. I don't have a package for you. I'm afraid that was only a ploy. I have reason to believe you to have been the victim of some very unscrupulous men. I'd like to help."

Cooper looked at him with open eyes. He was clearly

struggling to decide which direction to run in. Fear and mistrust tugged one way, indignation and aggression another. Could there be any opening in-between for a willingness to believe?

"Look, Mr Cooper. I can understand why you'd be suspicious of someone who knocks on your door, tells you a blatant lie and then says he wants to be your friend. I'd be too, anyone would. But just hear me out. I am a journalist and I think that something pretty nasty has been going on. I believe that you found out about it and threatened to expose it. That cost you a beating and, I suspect, your job. That tells me that you're an honest man. You tried to do the right thing. But in the end you were up against more dangerous people than you could cope with. You've kept shtumm ever since. I don't blame you. You did your best. But now I'm offering you the chance to fight back. You'll not be on your own this time. I know people who will be able to protect you, people, you'll find, who have a lot more clout than the crowd that had you beaten up."

Cooper was quick to latch on to this last remark.

"You don't know what you're talking about. The people that got at me have seats at the top table. You think your mates have more clout than a member of her Majesty's Parliament?"

A sneer accompanied this challenge, but it was a sneer inspired by the flow of the words; it lacked the venom of the heart-felt. Justin was more affected by the revelation than by the gauntlet flung in his face. His shocked surprise made a large puncture hole in the aura of control he was trying to convey.

"So it's an MP that's involved, is it?"

As soon as the words came out he could feel the naivety of them. He took a moment to regain his poise. He urgently needed to inspire confidence.

"I see what you mean. But just think about it: being an MP might make him powerful; it also makes him more vulnerable. If you expose him he'll be a spent force. There's nothing weaker than the weakness that comes when power is taken away."

He drew breath. Cooper didn't fill the gap.

"Another thing: If you spread the truth, you spread the threat. You'll be off the hook. You're only a target while you keep it to yourself. It's me and my people that he'll be dealing with and, believe me, he'll find us a lot harder to push around than you."

"That may be, but it wouldn't stop them taking it out on me if I cross them. Do you think they'd just forgive and forget?"

There had been the slightest of hesitations before Cooper came back at him. Some kind of traction had evidently been gained.

"They wouldn't dare. Believe me – we'll put the fear of God into them. Listen, we won't publish anything without asking you first. You will have the final say. You have my word on that."

"What good is your word to me? I don't know you. You could be anybody. You might even be working for them, testing me out."

It was hard to answer that. Offering assurance of assurance is never convincing. A change of tactic was required.

"Okay, Mr Cooper. You win. Well actually, *they* win. If you're prepared to let them away with the beating they gave you, so be it. I would have thought though that the man who stood up to them in the first place would've been prepared to have another go when he got the chance at a more even contest. Have they killed all the fight in you, man?"

There was a further, more marked hesitation before Cooper replied. This time the hesitation infiltrated his words. It wasn't Justin, it was his own thoughts that he was battling with now.

"It's true, there's no fight left in me. It was the fight that I had in me that did all the damage. I'm a widower, you know. My Ellie, she's gone now, passed away. If I'd kept my head down she might still be alive today. Maybe, maybe not. She was already very ill, but all that grief those bastards gave me didn't do her any good. She might've got another year or two."

Hesitation petered out to silence. Justin resisted the temptation to fill it; it was better left to itself. When Cooper finally got words back, they had a distinctly different tone to them.

"What you said is right. They shouldn't be allowed to get away with what they did to me and Ellie. Can you promise me that you'll really go for them?"

"I promise you we'll do everything we can to expose this MP. But you'll need to give me all the facts, and if you've any documentation. You realise we can't just print a lot of accusations. We need to be able to back up what we write."

"They think they're safe. They took all the written records, but there's more, stuff they don't know about.

"Okay, fire away. Tell me the whole story, starting from the beginning."

Before he started Cooper went over to an old sideboard and fetched the bottle of Johnnie Walker that Justin had noticed earlier sitting on it. Without a word he disappeared with it into the kitchen. There was a clatter of kitchen cupboards being opened and closed before he re-emerged with two very full glasses, offering one to his guest.

"Sorry, I forgot to ask if you take water in your whiskey. I don't, but I'll get you some if you like."

The offer was clearly rhetorical; he had already sat down on one of the well-worn armchairs before Justin had time to accept.

"I was the Union's accountant, the Amalgamated Industrial Workers. My boss was Derek Schinski. He's a big noise in the local branch of the Labour Party, very pally with Reggie Whitehouse, our MP. The two of them play a lot of golf together. The Union makes an annual contribution to Party funds. The amount each member pays is stipulated in the Union constitution, unless of course they opt out. All the money goes directly to party headquarters. Schinski and Whitehouse concocted a scam to increase the membership contributions. They established a fund to combat poverty – perfectly legally, a ballot of the members was held. The levy was modest, just under a pound per member per month – but when you consider the size of our membership, that makes for a very tidy sum. It was left to the discretion of the Union Executive Committee as to how this money was to be spent. There's an obscure third world charity called The Florence Nightingale Trust. It's based in Nairobi and just uses a PO box in this country. They were our chosen charity. The money was sent, not as a lump sum but in instalments at irregular intervals, ranging from hundreds to many thousands of pounds. When I was countersigning the cheques I noticed that the payee on some of them was simply written as Florence Trust while others were Florence Nightingale Trust. This just struck me as a simple curiosity at first, especially the omission of the 'the'. But there was a pattern. The ones addressed to Florence Trust consistently involved considerably larger sums than the others. I asked Schinski about this, but he simply laughed it off. There was something over-egged about the way he did it though that made me suspicious. The whole payment process was complicated, he said. Corruption is a big problem in Africa. The money couldn't be paid directly; it had to be filtered through channels. If the Kenyan government officials got wind of the payments there would be many hands in the till. When I thought about it, this was an ideal set-up for Schinski. It would be extremely difficult to follow the paper trail.

"I decided to make my own inquiries. After a lot of getting passed around from one agency to another, I managed to contact the charity. Sure enough, they had only received the smaller sums. I got talking to a Scotsman from Perth who was very open with me. Clearly, he wasn't aware that any funny business was going on. I didn't enlighten him. I got him to send me a statement of all the payments they had received from us. I made an excuse about building work at the office and he didn't object when I asked him to send it to my home address.

"I wondered what the other Florence Trust could be. I scoured the internet but I could find nothing. Then it occurred to me that it might just be a made-up name of an individual. I went to Somerset House and checked the records. It wasn't hard. A woman by the name of Adele Beaumont had changed her name by deed pole to Florence Trust a couple of years previously. When I dug further I discovered that Ms Beaumont was a business associate of Mrs Reggie Whitehouse."

"What did you do then?"

"I did nothing at first. I thought about going to the police. But I didn't think I should. It would have been cowardly going behind Schinski's back like that. I thought the manly thing to do was to confront him and give him a chance to explain himself. How naive can you get?"

"Did he threaten you?"

"No, he tried to soft-soap me. He could see that there was no point in denying it. He told me that the money was being used for good; it was helping the fight against poverty in this country. That counted as political for it was to be channelled through the Party. Because of stupid restrictions on political funding the union wasn't allowed to raise more than the amount stipulated in its constitution. There could be no change without a full vote of the membership. That would cost money, money that was needed elsewhere. Where was the harm, he said.

"He almost managed to persuade me. He said that government cuts to the welfare budget were making life very hard for poor families. It was important for the Party to do something. The funds he had raised were helping to provide food banks in Manchester. Without them a lot of people would go hungry."

Cooper took a large sip of his whiskey. A smile that seemed to have come from some distance away crossed his face.

"It's funny, isn't it, the way people oversell everything these days? I suppose it comes from all those stupid ads they see on the telly. If they had left it at that, I'd probably have let it drop. I'm an accountant, okay. I'm programmed to go by the book. But I've been a human being for a lot longer than I've been an accountant. But no, they just had to add a sweetener. The next day Whitehouse appeared in the office. He was unusually pally; normally he treated me like office furniture. He took me aside and told me he would see me right if I kept shtumm. When I asked him what he meant by that, he said some of the money could be 'redirected'. There was enough to go round. I would find that virtue didn't have to be its own reward, those were his exact words. It was clear to me that I was dealing with a crook. Those weren't the words of someone bending the rules to get the right thing done."

"So how did he react when you turned him down?"

"I didn't turn him down. I played along with him. I needed some hard evidence before I went to the police."

"And did you get it?"

"Yes, I went to a solicitor and made a statement covering everything that had happened. I got him to witness it. Then when the promised payment was made – it was in cash of course – I lodged that with the solicitor as well. He also had the statement I'd got from Nairobi. I thought I had enough now to take to the police. I went along to the station in St Anne Street and asked to speak to the most senior officer.

"I had to wait, but eventually I was taken to see Chief Superintendent Bailey. He was quite sympathetic, but – quite understandably – cautious. He told me he'd need to see the evidence and arranged a second interview for the next day. He was very keen for me not to talk to anyone about it. The second interview never took place. The next morning I had just left the solicitor's, having collected my documents, when two men fell in with me on the street, flanking me on either side. They were primitive types, shaven heads, mean looks – animals in clothes.

The one on my right grabbed hold of my arm and the other elbowed me in the ribs. It was really hard and knocked all the breath out of me. If it hadn't been for the one holding me up I'd have hit the ground. There was no power left in my legs. The two of them swept me along. They told me that I had had a change of heart and that I would have no further need of the contents of my briefcase. I was to phone the solicitor later that day and tell him that the matter had been resolved to my satisfaction and that I no longer needed his services. By this time we were in the little park at the end of the street. They ripped the briefcase from me. I tried to resist, but it was quite useless. They plonked me on a bench and left me to lick my wounds. It was all so matter-of-fact."

"But according to the hospital report your injuries were more severe than a couple of cracked ribs."

"No, that wasn't the end of it. Stupidly enough, I decided to keep my appointment with Bailey. I felt so humiliated, sprawled there on the bench. It wasn't an image of myself that I wanted to be stuck with. However, when I got to the police station I was told that Chief Superintendent Bailey was in a meeting and that my name wasn't on his appointments diary. That took the wind out of my sales, but I persisted and said that I wanted to report a crime. The desk sergeant started to take down details, but then the penny dropped. I was wasting my time. The Chief Superintendent was the only person who knew that I would be at the solicitor's – he had shown great interest in finding out which solicitor I had used. He had to be in on it. I told the sergeant I'd changed my mind and went home.

"Ellie wasn't at all well that night. Rather than make dinner for myself I decided to get a carry-out from the Chinese in Hope Street. It was dark and to get there you have to go down a walkway. It was there that I was set upon. It was the same two. I couldn't see them this time, but the voices were the same. This time they really laid into me. You've seen the hospital report, you say – they punched me in the stomach and when I was on the ground they kicked me repeatedly, again in the stomach. I thought they were going to kill me. It sounds funny, but it came as a great relief to me when they told me that next time they would finish the job, and if I breathed a word of this to anyone, there *would be* a next time. I managed to make it back home and phone for an ambulance. I was kept in hospital for three days. One of the neighbours looked after Ellie."

"So you decided to call it quits at that? I must say, I don't blame you."

"Yeah, it took me a couple of weeks before I could go back to work. When I did, Schinski came into my office and told me to clear my desk. He wasn't threatening or anything. In fact I got the impression he was simply following orders and took no pleasure in what he was having to do. He said that I could always take my dismissal to a tribunal, but he would seriously advise me not to. Again, this came over more like genuine advice than a threat, but certainly I was left in no doubt that there would be consequences."

"Well, now's your chance to turn the tables. Whitehouse, you said, spoke to you directly. Have you any hard proof of his involvement apart from the cheques that were written to his wife's friend?"

Cooper swallowed down the last of the whiskey in his glass. A smile like a sunrise swept across his face – it was the first time Justin had seen him smile.

"Oh yes, that I have and then some. I knew I'd need something more on him than the Florence cheques. I have a friend. He's a wizard when it comes to technology. I got him to rig up a recording device in my office. It operates automatically in response to sound and it shuts itself down once the talking stops. That way it can last for weeks. I knew that Schinski sometimes used my office when I wasn't there. The little gem was there working the whole time I was off. I did exactly what

Schinski told me and cleared my desk. The recording device came up trumps. I have the whole of a conversation between him and Whitehouse, discussing how they were going to deal with me. It was Whitehouse's idea to send the heavies in to give me the second kicking. Schinski tries to dissuade him. He says he knows me and that I am a bit of a wimp. But Whiteside insists. If I'd been stupid enough, he says, to carry on after the warning I'd been given when my documents were snatched– I did after all try to go through with the interview with Bailey – I'd need to be given a more *robust* message. As far as the rest was concerned, they had secured the evidence in the briefcase; that was out of the way and they'd cover their tracks by moving the fund to a different account. A few backdated cheques would camouflage the payments that Nairobi hadn't received and they'd replace me with someone *more willing to be creative in his accounting.*"

Justin stared at him open-mouthed.

"You mean you had all that and you did nothing?"

"You saw what happened when I went to the police. Who could I trust? I didn't think those heavies were bluffing. If I got it wrong I was a dead man. And then there was Ellie. She went downhill very quickly. She was taken into hospital the week after I was shown the door. I had a couple of weeks of toing and froing between home and the hospital before she was admitted to the hospice. I visited her there every day until the end. After that I just felt nothing. I couldn't see the point of doing anything, so I just drifted into doing nothing."

Cooper's eyes welled up as he said this, but the deep sadness that Justin had seen in them when he first talked of his late wife now harboured distinct traces of defiance.

Chapter 5

Robert Snoddy always took pleasure in his visits to Stoneyford. He was especially fond of the library with its magnificent stained-glass window that flooded the room in cyan-blue sunlight, a holy air that bestowed freshness on the antique solemnity that otherwise dominated. The magnificent eighteenth-century mansion was the 'seat' of Matthew Eardley. He liked to tease his wealthy friend with that word. The rejoinder always came back along the lines that the Eardley family had only just arrived and had not had time to take their coats off let alone take a seat. Eardley was indeed a nouveau riche; he had made his money in advertising, had expanded his empire into the media and now enjoyed the dubious title of press baron. It had often occurred to Snoddy how history was updating itself with Eardley. The old aristocracy had elbowed its way to the top in mediaeval times using the weapons of the day; refinement had come generations later, and by the time it did come it had of course forgotten the struggle it had had to get there. Eardley was a man of considerable refinement; he was well educated and had a taste for fine things, but he did not need to draw on the folk memory to appreciate the vulnerability of his position. He knew that the privilege he enjoyed to indulge in gentility depended for its continuance on the blood and guts that is inevitably spilled in the battle of life. What made the man better than most was his ability to appreciate that the same applied to all sections of society – even the most lowly – the dread of being dragged back into the mud. He was keenly aware that goodness had no innate right to survive; it couldn't just parade its virtues and expect immunity from the teeth and claws of reality.

Stoneyford was the ideal setting for these Council meetings.

It lent solemnity, but, more important, it bestowed historical resonance. It sounded very grand and overinflated to use words like that, but Robert Snoddy was in no doubt that he and his little band of New Prometheans were taking on nothing less than the massed forces of intellectual orthodoxy. The perspective amplified their triumphs, yet kept them from spilling over into expectations of a definitive breakthrough. *Macte lente puer,* a phrase he had picked up from his old mentor Dr Greenfield, invariably came to mind when he thought of this and just as invariably he found himself translating it as 'Take each game as it comes' – so much for historical register!

The others had already assembled as he was ushered into the library. The 'usher' was Eardley's Jeeves, a Mr Robson, a man in his early fifties who had been a sergeant major in the Royal Engineers. He always commanded his full title; *Robson* would have slipped effortlessly off the tongue, but it would have done less than justice to the particular form of gravitas that the ex-sergeant major exuded. The four men who had been standing by the fire that was blazing in the imposing fireplace came over to greet him. As well as Eardley there was Greenfield, Compton and Andrews. Peters hadn't been able to make it – he was in America on business – and Levy was going to be late, if he got there at all. Amid all the hand-shaking, Snoddy was distracted by the figure of a woman slowly emerging from behind one of the wing-backed armchairs by the fireplace. Set against the backdrop of the blaze the figure was visible only in outline, the features of her face finally appearing as she extended her hand to him in greeting. It was the handsome face of a woman in her mid thirties. It was attractively womanly, yet at the same time modestly dismissive of its feminine appeal.

The men, apart from Eardley and Greenfield, ran the various departments: Compton was in charge of information gathering, Andrews recruitment, Peters security and Levy procurement. Francesca Bergman was the first woman to be asked on to the Council. Eardley had long been an admirer of her writings. He had first met her in person at a conference when she was working as a political columnist in The New York Times and had been impressed enough to lure her over to England as political editor of his flagship broadsheet. Snoddy had been equally impressed; she knew the American scene inside out, but not only that, her European hinterland was extensive. She had grown up in France with a Spanish mother and a Swedish father and spoke five languages, although she was quick to insist that her Swedish and German caused her frustration whenever she had to fight her political corner in them. She was the ideal choice when the decision was taken to appoint a political adviser to the Council.

"Glad you were able to make it." Snoddy said. A wan smile allowed the remark to hover between sincerity and sarcasm. He had in fact insisted on her being present at the meeting. She responded with a grin of similar ilk. "It's always politic to obey urgings, provided the provenance is sound."

Snoddy was anxious to get down to business. He had a great aversion to preliminaries, the chat in little cabals of twos and threes whose false intimacy is both a refuge from exclusion and an agency of it. It made him think of the squeaking and tweaking of orchestras tuning up for a performance. The truth of the matter was: he was always more conscious of the risk of exclusion than of the opportunity to fraternise. He felt distinctly more secure when the meeting was called to order. The dulcet tones of Eardley duly obliged. They were all invited to seat themselves round the large conference table that occupied the far corner of the room. Even the choice of where you should sit pained Snoddy. He would have much preferred it for everyone to be allocated a place. He made a point of getting to the table first so that he wouldn't have to impose himself as someone's companion. It was Greenfield who took the chair beside him.

"Gentlemen ... and lady," Eardley began, "Welcome to you

all. This meeting has been convened at Robert's request. There has been a development, he tells me, that has opened up a set of possibilities that he is anxious we give serious consideration to. It all sounds very exciting. At this point I'm as much in the dark as you are, but I'm sure Robert will be able to cast light into our darkness."

Snoddy didn't follow Eardley's example and stand. He disliked that kind of formality and began his address as if he was already in mid flow.

"Some of you will be familiar with the Craig case. He's the thug who beat up a fellow called Hill and left him in a wheelchair. He was arrested and then released without charge. So we stepped in, but when we were interrogating him he started going on about an attack he had carried out on another man, someone called Cooper. He had done this at the behest of a certain Mr Schinski. Cooper apparently had some gen on Schinski that Schinski didn't want to come to light. Craig was hired to put the frighteners on him. There was mention of Schinski having friends in high places. Craig had obviously persuaded him to use these friends to get the police to quash the charges against him for the assault on Hill. It looked as if we had stumbled on something pretty big, so I sent Justin Wright up to Manchester to follow up on it. Justin came back yesterday with a very interesting tale to tell.

"He quickly tracked Cooper down. It turned out he was an accountant with the Amalgamated Industrial Workers Union. He had discovered that union funds were being misappropriated by the General Secretary Derek Schinski and the local MP, Reginald Whitehouse. When Cooper threatened to expose them they tried to buy his silence, and when that didn't work, they set Craig on him.

"Justin did very well. Cooper was scared sh.., silly, but Justin managed to talk him round and got the whole story out of him. Cooper is a meticulous bookkeeper and kept detailed records. But when he tried to present this evidence to the police, he was intercepted by a couple of thugs who made off with all his documents. The only person who knew enough to set this up was the high-ranking police officer he had confided in. The plot thickens! But the best news is: Cooper managed to make a recording of Schinski and Whitehouse discussing intimate details of the case. We've got the two of them bang to rights!"

The beam of delight with which Snoddy accompanied this last remark was met with lukewarm smiles on faces that were obviously trying to do better. It was Andrews who stepped up as spokesman for the disappointing reaction.

"That's good news certainly, Rob, but surely we didn't need an extraordinary meeting to discuss anything of this nature. You don't need our approval to follow it through. If the evidence is as clear as you say, then just go on and publish it. It'll cause a scandal, the two clowns will be prosecuted and the union and the Labour party will be well rid – I take it that Whitehouse *is* a Labour MP, coming from that part of the world?"

A look of impatience perilously close to the edge of disdain passed across the Snoddy face. No sooner had it appeared than it was retrieved, but with evident signs of effort.

"We could of course follow that line. It's the straightforward thing to do. But let's use a bit of imagination here, gentlemen … and Francesca. We have been exercised for some time by the question of upgrading our operation and bringing it into the political arena. We can't change hearts and minds on a national scale by just plodding on with what we're doing. It's all very well bringing justice back to the people, but the only people who know about our work, the only people we can allow to know, are the people who are directly involved. We fill in for the courts when they let the law get in the way of justice. We have been doing that outside the law, but our ultimate aim is to get the law back into line with the justice it's meant to serve. This is surely a heaven-sent opportunity for us to take a first step in that direction."

He looked around the table for signs of assent. The minds of all were clearly busy at work, but there was nothing to suggest they were close to the completion of their business. Snoddy had never grown out of the naive belief that what was clear to him must be clear to everyone else, in spite of multiple experiences to the contrary.

"What I am proposing is that we use the information we have to put pressure on Whitehouse to give up his seat ... and stand down in favour of a candidate of our choosing!"

Apprehension following on the heels of comprehension passed domino-like from face to face. It fell again to Andrews to give voice to the communal speechlessness.

"You mean to use what we have on Whitehouse to blackmail him?"

"That's exactly what I mean. If we print what we know, he'll lose his seat anyway. His political career will be over. And he'll certainly do time. If he agrees to our demands he can step quietly aside and walk into any number of cushy directorships on the board of this and the council of that. Westminster looks after its own ... provided of course you pose no threat to the gravy train. A prison sentence is a no-no. If you are incompetent enough to fall foul of the courts, the Establishment is adept at passing itself off as the tragic victim of its own misplaced decency."

"Yes, but Whitehouse is a Labour politician, isn't he? You can't seriously see Labour as a party that's ever likely to accept the kind of things we stand for."

"As a matter of fact I do. We're exactly the kind of medicine the Labour Party has needed for years."

"Well, you can say that. But even if you're right, that's not the point. The point is: does it know that?"

Snoddy affected the grin of a combatant who had been dealt a feeble blow.

35

"Of course it doesn't. That's precisely why the medicine is required."

Andrews had no ready answer to this. The delay, as he searched for one, lent credibility to what Snoddy was proposing; the idea might possibly not be quite as preposterous as it ought to be. Compton intervened.

"What you are proposing is utterly absurd, Robert. We all know you like to think outside the box, but this time you're in outer space. The Labour Party is, in principle at least, a party of the Left. In the eyes of the world we count as being of the Right. You might say that's wrong, but the fact remains that's the way it is. There isn't a cat in hell's chance of them accepting one of ours to represent them in Parliament."

This was a more serious blow, but before Snoddy could hit back Greenfield came in. When Bruce Greenfield spoke everyone listened. He had no portfolio on the council; he was there merely for his good sense and sound judgement. This afforded him the luxury of never having to add an urging edge to what he said.

"Let's not be too hasty. Robert may have a point. What we want is radical change and the party that is most comfortable with that must surely be the Labour Party. Rightness and Leftness have long been a sham in British politics. Every since I can remember the two main parties have been shadow-boxing against each other round and round the ring of orthodoxy. They treat each skirmish like a title fight, but neither side is champion of a cause that has any substance to it.

"The Right is seen as the champion of the badlands, ruthless, self-centred and money-crazy. So to avoid the boos and win over the crowd, it plays to its weakness instead of its strength. It reminds me of one of my colleagues. Before he came into teaching he had been an industrial chemist. He spent years on a project to develop a soap that wouldn't leave any scum in the washbasin. However when he eventually succeeded, the sales department ruled it out on the grounds that 'scum' was an unacceptable concept in the advertising world.

"The Left on the other hand sees its good name as its birthright. This has led it into self-righteous arrogance; it really has come to believe that it can do no wrong and should be given carte blanche in turning taxpayers' money into testimonials to its socialist compassion. Every now and then, usually after a full term of 'progressive economics', there is a need for a reality check and it has to promise to apply a modicum of 'head' to its 'heart'. So, however undeserving of the prize, the Left has acquired the exclusive rights to moral self-confidence. But don't you see? That puts it in a much stronger position to go out on a limb and embrace a more robust form of morality, all the more so if it is one that will resonate more with its core supporters than the fashionable fetishes of its Fabian wing. As for the Tories, they would run a mile from anything that their core supporters would be likely to support. They wallow in moral self-loathing and need the approval of the Left before they would dream of extending a foot outside the corral they have allowed themselves to be herded into. In fact I'd go further. For most of the top brass in the party the Conservative label is merely a flag of convenience. They are Liberals at heart, but they know they'd never get into power if they openly admitted it."

Compton observed a respectful pause before countering.

"If we want to go down this road, why don't we just simply start up our own party? That way we wouldn't have to make ourselves acceptable to anyone other than the electorate. Surely our vision of how things should be done is so radically different from any of the existing parties that it needs a new party to promote it. I had the impression that was why we asked Francesca here on to the Council. I thought she was to be our political guru."

All eyes turned to Francesca. Although this was the third meeting she had attended, her input to date had been minimal.

She had apologised for this in advance saying that she wanted to observe and get the feel of things before allowing herself to be heard from. That period of grace was now clearly at an end. Her first remarks were addressed to Compton.

"I'm afraid I can't agree with you, David. If you look at the history of new parties, it's not an encouraging picture. They all start off with a bang. Phrases like 'new dawn', 'watershed', 'crossroads in history' get bandied about. Hope believes its own fantasies. But then gradually the 'must happen' becomes the 'should happen', then the 'might happen', finally, whimpering and with much pain, the 'won't happen'. Hindsight then puts the knife in and delivers the ultimate verdict, the 'couldn't have happened'. No, if we are to get political we can't do it on foot; we have to hitch a ride. And the only two buses available belong to the Tories and Labour. The Liberals of course are our natural enemy."

"Okay, but don't you think we'd do better with the Tories? They've always been the party of law and order. And law and order is what we're principally about, isn't it?"

"It would seem so, wouldn't it? But I think I see where Robert is coming from. The perception of the Tories as a law-and-order party is tarnished. It comes over as the great and the good trampling down the worthy poor. There's a whole forest of old chestnuts embedding that image in the national consciousness. What we are proposing is the complete obverse of that. We want to take the power away from the great and the good and hand it back ... perhaps not so much to the poor as to the worthy. I think that sits better with the image the Labour party has of itself than the image the public has of the Tories. Bruce hit the nail on the head. The Tories are scared stiff of the slightest association with nastiness. Labour on the other hand has whole shelves of righteous antitoxins in its perfumery. No, when all is said and done, I'd go along with Robert and try and hitch a ride on the Labour bus."

David Compton was not an obstinate man, but his normal willingness to concede to the flow was under severe pressure. He had always simply assumed the Conservative Party to be the natural home of their political cause. He had watched as the socialist conscience had gone soft on everything, with the honourable exception of course of 'the evil rich'. He could not bring himself to believe that the Left could be persuaded to accept the existence of evil in any other form. He looked over to John Andrews to see if there was any support for further resistance. Andrew's face gave nothing away. He essayed a rather forlorn 'What do you think, John?' anyway. The question did not meet with a welcome. The answer came with reluctance and on the hoof.

"I'm not sure. My first instinct is scepticism. But having listened to what Bruce and Francesca have had to say, I can see that it just might work. Francesca is here because she knows her politics better than the rest of us. I don't see the logic of asking someone on to the Council to advise us on political strategy and then disregarding what they tell us. Let's give it a go. It'll not be the end of the world if it doesn't work."

"It won't be the end of the world, but we'll have burned our boats with the Tories."

Compton knew he had lost, but he was glad to have something better than 'On your heads be it' to offer as a parting shot.

Eardley had let the discussion take it own course but now, in consummate 'chairmanic' fashion, he dipped his oars in the water.

"Well, it looks as if you have the Council's backing, Robert. It's worth a punt, or maybe a drop kick from inside our own half would be a more apt term. The big question that now faces us is: who is to be given the ball to make that drop?"

Nomination requests, like explosive devices, are usually followed by a hiatus of several seconds during which those with opinions try not to appear too eager and those with no thoughts on the subject wait in anticipation of the imminent rush. Eardley's little *jeu de mots* had lightened the mood and given the dissenting Compton the chance to rejoin the fold. He was glad to take it.

"Since the whole thing has been his idea in the first place, I think it only appropriate that Robert should take it on."

Snoddy knew better than to rush to accept. He glanced sideways towards Greenfield, but his old teacher, perhaps feeling the same reluctance to declare his hand, merely passed the parcel on to Francesca, who was more than happy to take it.

"As I see it, the situation invites one of two approaches. The candidate we choose could keep his head down until he is selected and only then gradually reveal himself in his true colours, which we know are unlikely to pass off as Labour Party red. This strategy has the distinct advantage of increasing his chances of being selected. The downside is that it makes his next moves extremely difficult. Complete u-turns don't go down well in political circles. There's an argument for him to start off facing in the direction he wants ultimately to take. You used a rugby analogy, Matt. You'll hardly be surprised to hear that I've never played rugby, but I do play golf. So let me use a golfing one. We're faced with the choice between taking on a difficult drive from the tee, giving ourselves an easy high iron to the green, or playing safe, steering clear of the bunkers but leaving ourselves a very tricky second shot.

"If we play safe we will need a candidate who has no track record, someone with no political past that could cast doubt on his socialist credentials. I'm new here, so I wouldn't know what kind of pool we'd be dipping into for that. The rest of you are in a better position to know than me. If, however, we take the bolder shot on, then Robert is certainly the kind of candidate we'd be looking for. I'll spare his blushes. Suffice it to say he has the intellectual armoury not to be asphyxiated by all the red feathers he is certain to ruffle. Having said that, I don't think he should go in with all guns blazing – that would be foolhardy. There are whole tracts of Labour Party policy that are best left untouched. Home truths are like prophets: the closer they are to home, the more honour they forfeit. Economics is a case in point. It's absolutely vital to steer clear. The Labour Party will simply not be lectured to on tax and spend; its compulsion to find ways of spending other people's money invariably goes through the same cycle as mumps and measles; the spots are only acknowledged when it's too late to avoid election defeat. There's simply no help for it."

This sparked off a litany of corroborative instances and examples from those around the table. In the end Eardley had to bring the meeting back to the business at hand. Compton formalised his nomination of Snoddy, Peters seconded it and the motion was passed unanimously. Mr Robson was summoned and celebratory drinks were served.

Chapter 6

"You mean to say they aren't going to use my stuff?"

Justin was affronted. The pride he felt in the job he had done, previously content to lurk smugly backstage of his consciousness, suddenly surged forward and voiced its grievance. This was to be his first big story, his breakthrough into journalism proper. And here was Snoddy telling him that his piece would not be going into print. Frustratingly however, the flame of his indignation could find nothing to set ablaze on the stony surface of Robert Snoddy's impassive response. As far as Snoddy was concerned, Justin had been given the task of ascertaining certain facts, he had been told the circumstances of the need to know these facts, it was not up to him to determine the use that the information should be put to, end of.

"What am I to say to Terence Cooper? I told him we'd expose Schinski and Whitehouse. He trusted me. Now you want me to go and tell him, 'Thanks very much for sticking your neck out. Sorry there's nothing in it for you, but don't worry, we'll make sure we do very well out of it.' Or should I just come clean and laugh in his face?"

This was a too great a departure from logical clarity for Snoddy to keep up the restraint he imposed on his natural impatience. How was he to argue with someone who couldn't see that analytical judgements have nothing to do with the amount of emotional grace they attract? He had sensed a tendency to 'flakiness' in Justin right from the outset, but he thought he had got over it. The man had surprised him; he had come through and shown that he was prepared to go out on a limb for what his brain told him was right. That had enhanced him in Snoddy's eyes, but now here he was going all fluffy and sentimental and ignoring the hard bones of the issue.

"What does it matter to Cooper how we deal with Whitehouse? The bottom line is the Honourable Member is being dumped in the *merde*. He's going to lose his beloved seat. Okay, he'll avoid public disgrace, and doors will still be open to him that would be shut in his face if we exposed him. But we'll get that trade union shyster too and that bent policeman. And don't forget, we also dealt with Craig. Mephisto's little helper will not be beating people up any more. He's a changed man, didn't take to the whip at all, I hear. On the whole I think Cooper has every reason to be grateful to us, we've done a fair job for him."

Justin could see all this, but he found it difficult to quell the strong sense of frustration he felt, not so much at the less than ruthless comeuppance that the felled Goliath would get, more that Cooper would be denied his chance to stand over the body and plant his foot on its head. He had been Cooper's champion, he had provided the sling and he had achieved a victory, but it was not to be a glorious one. He would have to accept Snoddy's directive, but he would not add good grace to his compliance. Sensing this, Snoddy moved on.

"You can explain to Cooper that the first priority is to force Whitehouse to give up his seat and you can tell him that this is best achieved by threatening to publish rather than by actually doing it. I'm sure you can find some way of getting him to see that. It's important we keep him onside. We'll see to Schinski and Whitehouse. I know the perfect man for that job. If things go to plan, your job will be to go up to Manchester and make sure I get a good press."

The sweetener he was being offered was mouth-watering indeed. Political journalism was rainbow's end for Justin, but that didn't stop him from feeling he was acting out of weakness, a feeling that always descended when he complied with the

Snoddy will. He could never quite persuade himself that it was the reasonable rightness of it, not the sheer force of it that he was acceding to. The meeting with Cooper would be painful to him, but *'twere better it were done quickly.* He booked a seat on the 7.15 the following morning.

Chapter 7

Derek Schinski was at his desk sipping his coffee and poring over his tattered copy of 'Health and Safety at the Workplace'. It was not his favourite reading, but over the years it had armed him with a veneer of plausibility in the multiple claims for industrial damages he made for his members. The bigger boys didn't bother to contest them as long as they weren't too extravagant, and the smaller concerns were invariably too much in fear of the unpredictability of the legal brain and the rapacity of the legal pocket to trust to the courts. All he needed was a magic phrase, an abracadabra that would open cheque books, and this little volume abounded in them. His current search centred on 'the duty of care' of firms for employees suffering from stress induced by family trauma. One of his members had caused severe damage to the machine he was operating. When it emerged that he had been drinking, he was dismissed. The question Schinski was looking to raise was the responsibility of the firm to ascertain if the man had been in a fit state to work at the outset and if there was any counselling mechanism in place to deal with the situation if it had been found that he wasn't. Section 117c was beginning to produce some promising verbal contortions when the telephone rang. It was Sylvia, his secretary.

"I have a Mr J F Blogs on the line wishing to speak to you, Derek. He won't tell me what it's about, but he says it's urgent."

"Okay, Sylvia, put him through."

Schinski was more than willing to be prised away from this rather tedious dig for litigants' bones.

"Mr Schinski, good of you to find time to speak to me."

The voice was plummy, the type Derek Schinski instinctively winced at. He associated it with everything he had been schooled in taking offence at, Eton and Harrow, silver spoon, haughty mirth. His first impulse was to counter it with raw vulgarity, but he had tried that once and had come off badly. Ever since then he acted with less ambition, content to wait for opportunities to pierce little holes and effect a more gradual deflation of the ego behind the voice.

"Yes, I am a busy man, Mr ... Blogs, is it? What can I do for you?"

"Well, as a matter of fact, Mr Schinski, I have a plan that would make you a less busy man. More time for the golf course ... you are a keen golfer, I hear. And more time for all those things that make life all that it's cracked up to be."

All that Schinski could manage in response was a very lame 'What are you talking about?'

"I can be with you in ten minutes, if that's convenient, and all will be revealed."

This was Schinski's opportunity to assert himself.

"I'm afraid it *isn't* convenient. I've some very pressing matters to attend to."

There was a deep sigh at the other end of the line and a hint of mock apology for the impatience in the tone of the impending response.

"I don't think you quite understand, Mr Schinski. I'm offering you a get-out-of-jail card. It's not quite free, but it's on special offer. I really think you should ponder the priorities of your morning. You can't seriously want to go to jail?"

The abandonment of metaphor chilled Schinski to the bone. It was followed by a surge of wattage in his head. He tried to bluster, but it met only with a very calm and very withering 'I'll see you in ten minutes'.

The ten minutes served their intended purpose. Questions forged themselves in a burning caldron of panic. The mind made frantic sorties into its memory banks but came back with nothing to link this Blogs with the Cooper business. And it had

46

to be that. He certainly hadn't been squeaky clean, but the scam with Whitehouse was his only real venture into what would count as criminality. He shouldn't have listened to that bloody man Whitehouse. He'd been managing quite nicely doing a bit of fiddling with expenses and contriving the odd bonus; he didn't need to get involved in anything really heavy. And that episode with Cooper ... it was nasty and it was over the top. Whitehouse was adamant that they'd no other choice. He doubted that. Cooper had a streak of honesty in him that seemed resistant to anything he had thrown at it. That was true sure enough, but experience told him there's always a way. It's only a question of honing in on it. It had been a huge mistake for Whitehouse to offer to fund private treatment for the man's wife.

When Sylvia buzzed through to announce the arrival of Mr Blogs it occurred to him that he had made no attempt to put a face to the man. The voice on the phone had remained a voice. As Sylvia ushered the stranger in he was almost surprised to be confronted with a standard human. Particular characteristics like the extravagant hairstyle and the Grecian nose only came through in a second wave.

He was spared the decision of how to react to the intruding presence by the intruder himself, who stepped forward and held out his hand, beaming the smile of a friend.

"So glad you could fit me in, Mr Schinski. I'll not waste your time. In fact you might say I'm here to save you time, so to speak."

The mischievous smile that accompanied this remark came across more as a token of good humour than a harbinger of ill intent. Schinski was almost tempted to fall for it.

"Please state your business, Mr Blogs. As I told you before, I'm a busy man."

"Please, please, call me JFB. My friends call me that. Blogs is such an anonymous name ... No, you can't say that, can you? It's an oxymoron."

47

'*What the hell is he on about?*' Irritation didn't get as far as verbal expression, just a frown on the Schinski brow, before JFB continued.

"You have a reputation, I believe, as a very successful claims litigator. You come highly recommended. That's why I've come to you. The case I bring you could well prove to be the glorious climax of your illustrious career. And, as I indicated, you will be in a position to retire at the end of it."

'*Is he selling something? Could I have got the wrong end of the stick? Maybe this has nothing to do with Cooper after all. Maybe I've been adding two and two and getting five.*'

The whole Cooper thing had unbalanced him. It was putting demons in his head. He needed to buck up and pull himself together. But when you don't know where to jump, it's better to stay where you are. Silence offers the best cover for confusion. The visitor had a free platform.

"To pull this off you'll need more than your redoubtable negotiating skills; you'll need help, help from on-high. But I'm told you have friends in high places, so that shouldn't be a problem. How important an ear can you come up with to whisper into? We don't need to go theological on this, political will do. How about an MP? Could you book the ear of the Honourable Member for … say, this constituency? What's his name? … oh yes, Reginald Whitehouse, but I suppose you're allowed to call him Reggie, are you? Yes, he would do very nicely. Could you arrange for the three of us to meet … here, tomorrow at eleven o'clock? He, like your good self, would be in line to hear something to his lesser disadvantage."

Ill intent had now openly abandoned the disguise of good humour. The 'Here, tomorrow at eleven o'clock' had been enunciated with an imperiousness that brooked no quibble. He had been right; it really was Cooper come to haunt him. But he would quibble. It would only be for show, but it was the only act of resistance to indignity he could muster.

"I don't know who you think you are coming in here and giving orders. But if you think I'm going to summon Mr Whitehouse on your say-so, you've another think coming. I think you should leave my office."

This was greeted with the same deep sigh he had heard on the telephone and a quasi-brave grimace that showed the effort that patience was making to impose itself.

"My dear Derek ... sorry to be so informal ... we three simply must meet. Don't you see that? The only question is whether it's to be in thunder, lightning or in rain. A terrible concoction is the only remedy for what ails you both, and I have the formula. Neither of you will like the medicine, but what naughty boys do?"

Pausing to identify the degree of disquiet showing in his quarry's eyes, he reverted to the imperious tone, only this time it had crossed over to the menacing.

"Be here tomorrow and be here with your friend."

Chapter 8

Justin's meeting with Terry Cooper went off more smoothly than he had anticipated. The accountant was satisfied with the assurance that measures were in place to put right the wrong he had suffered. The whole nasty business had exhausted him emotionally and he wanted no active part in its denouement. Justin had come up with a line highlighting the risk of provoking a libel suit and promoting the easier option of using the evidence they had against Whitehouse and Schinski as a lever to force their resignations. But Cooper showed little curiosity. A dressing had been put on his wound, that's all that mattered to him. He was anxious to talk of other things, offering snippets of information about his late wife and inquiring as to Justin's circumstances. This had the effect of making Justin feel even more of a fraud than if he'd been required to elaborate on his phoney explanation. The two men drank tea and parted ostensibly as friends. But the sense of relief Justin felt as he left was a poor counterweight to the guilt.

Partly in response to this and partly out of frustration at having himself been sidelined from the main action, he decided to take the opportunity, while in Manchester, to make some more inquiries about Chief Superintendent Bailey. All the focus had been on Schinski and Whitehouse, but in many ways Bailey's part in the affair was even more unsavoury. Snoddy had made no mention of how he was to be dealt with. Justin suspected that the political opportunities Whitehouse's criminal behaviour had opened up had blurred the issue of crime and punishment, which, it shouldn't be forgotten, was at the very core of the Promethean agenda. He didn't for a moment imagine that there was any thought of ignoring Bailey's crime and letting it go unpunished. Snoddy had said they would get him, and he believed him, but there was an obvious problem. If they did a deal with the other two, their leverage on Bailey would be limited; they couldn't expose him without exposing them. They could of course try to bluff him, but if he was as good a politician as to get himself up the greasy pole as far as Chief Superintendent he would surely see that they would be loath to compromise the political opportunity that had fallen into their lap. If he picked up on this he might turn the tables on them and threaten *them* with a public confession. It was highly implausible that he'd be prepared to up the ante to that extent, about as unlikely as one nuclear power attacking another. But the threat of mutual destruction did after all produce an international stand-off that has been successful for more than half a century. They might be well-advised to establish a second front and get him for something completely unrelated to the Cooper case. If he was in the thick of this mud, there were likely to be other troughs he had his hands in.

Having conceived the idea, he spent some time dragging his feet with a series of diversionary must-dos before getting round to making the dreaded phone call. How do you get boats that have been burned sailing again? That was the question that exercised him as he looked up Nigel Best on his contacts list. When the dialling tone was replaced by a voice at the other end it was a voice that smacked of disinclination to renew acquaintance with any sort of by-gone, immediately denting the modest hopes Justin had that his dinner invitation would be accepted *as* a thank-you for the help his friend had given him. It took several more acknowledgements of his indebtedness along with multiple assurances that no more credit would be sought, before the hesitation that presaged a polite refusal turned ungracefully into less than half-hearted acceptance.

When they met up at the restaurant Nigel obviously had had time to collect his feelings and station them in a more sheltered spot, close to wariness but not out of earshot of friendliness. Small talk was no longer on special offer; they had covered most of the ground from cruising altitude last time and had not forged any connections nitty or gritty enough to promote tittle-tattle below tree level. The Cooper case was the one subject that could have been plugged the gap, but it was the one that must be avoided. The weather is traditionally called on to lubricate the workings of social intercourse. This is now an outdated cliché; among modern British males the role has passed to sport. Justin and Nigel had been back-row partners in the police academy second XV, so in the end the threat of silence was effectively, if self-consciously, thwarted.

In the course of this chat, which neither participant was fully committed to, Justin steered them towards the question of leadership on the field, the specific qualities required of a team captain as opposed to a pack leader.

"The difference is you want a pack leader to be someone like yourself, but braver, stronger, more determined, whereas the captain should be someone who goes about his business in a different way to you, and still gets to courage, strength and determination, but taking a different route. The pack leader helps you to look up by looking up with you; the captain gives you something to look up to by earning the right to look down at you."

"You make that sound very patronising."

"No, not at all. 'Looking down' is not the same thing as 'Looking down your nose'. I know it sounds that way. It's looking down in the way a father looks down to encourage a child to do something more grown up than it's done before, jump a ditch, climb a stile – that kind of thing."

"Yes, I see what you mean. When you put it like that, you'd have to say there's not much proper leadership about these days – plenty of pack leaders, but not many captains. The trouble is, some of the good pack leaders get made captains, and instead of becoming good captains, they just stop being good pack leaders. The rule book takes over and they turn into line managers, God help us."

"You're talking about the police? You're right, our leaders didn't impress me much either, although there is the odd dinosaur still about. I had one, an Inspector. His name is Stranaghan. He's Irish. Now there's a man I really admired. You knew with him that if there was flak going you wouldn't be left to take it by yourself – a dying breed."

There was an opening here for a follow-through. He seized it.

"Listen, Nigel. I didn't mean to talk shop tonight. But there's something you should know. I would watch out for your Chief Super if I were you. During my inquiries I've discovered that he's not squeaky clean. In fact he's up to eyes in very murky water."

A look of policeman's caution returned to Best's eyes. An instant block was put on any inclination to follow up with a question. A self-imposed silence was left to do the job. Justin felt the pressure of it.

"That man Cooper I got you to make inquiries about, he was beaten up . . . and that Chief Super of yours was behind it."

The sceptical silence was overtaken by a very curt "You have proof of that, do you?"

This was tricky territory. If he said that he did, the obvious follow-up would be 'What's stopping you from acting on it?' and if he said that he didn't, his allegation would be dismissed as a malicious fantasy.

"Not the kind of proof that would stand up in court, but proof nonetheless. Cooper had gone to see Bailey and provided him with information about a crime that was on-going at his place of work. It was a serious case of fraud. No one apart from Bailey was privy to that information, so no one else could have known that Cooper was a threat to them. On his way to Bailey's office for a second meeting to supply the documentation he'd collected to back up his allegation, he was mugged and his briefcase and all the evidence it contained was seized."

Best hammed a facial expression of serious puzzlement.

"Let me get this straight. If you can prove that, why do you say it wouldn't stand up in court?"

Justin was being taken where he didn't want to go.

"The reason is simple: Cooper is unwilling to testify. He's scared. He told me, but he just wants to put the whole business behind him and move on."

It was the only line open to him, but it risked exposure if his friend decided to check it out.

"Okay then, but why are you telling me this?"

Justin was beginning to regret having embarked on his fishing expedition. He had been far from clear from the outset as to where it would take him. He had simply trusted to his ability to muddle through. It was a talent that always served him well and generally got better results than over-elaborate plans worked out in advance. This time the signs weren't good. He decided to cut and run.

"I just thought you should know. Forewarned is forearmed. You did me a favour and I considered I owed you one."

This was met with the studied coolness of a customs official in that elongated moment he takes to check your passport before giving you the nod and allowing normal human interaction to resume.

Chapter 9

It was approaching the eleventh hour the following morning as two figures, one perched on the desk, the other pacing the room, impatiently bided time. The old-fashioned pendulum clock on the wall above the door, exceeding its role as a nostalgic relic of glory days-gone-by, was in clear command of the field of attention. No words were exchanged between the two. Everything that could be asked and answered had worn itself out and come to a speechless junction. Time had taken on the mantle of fate. The clock's hands slowly homed in on their portentous points … and still nothing, no knock at the door, no buzz from Sylvia. The big hand dallied for its allotted time and then simply moved on. As is inevitably the case, relief from anxiety came encumbered with anger at it for having wormed its way in on false pretences. Relief was gradually metamorphosing to a faint chimera of hope when, at ten minutes past, the awaited buzz did at last come through from Sylvia. Now it was the turn of those embryos of hopefulness to take the hit from their annoyance.

JFB was extravagantly dressed, his lime green jacket competing for attention with his lemon waistcoat and his Cambridge blue trousers. The vibrancy of the colour was matched by the ebullience of his movement.

"It's a pleasure to see you both here, gentlemen. And what a pleasant day! I'd expected us to be meeting in thunder, lightning or in rain, but perhaps the sun will lighten the darkness of the deeds and the hurly-burly will be more hurly and less burly … or should that be the other way round?"

Schinski exchanged a glance with Whitehouse that seemed to solicit confirmation of how he had described the intruder. Whitehouse was in no mood to delay his offensive.

"Just sit down and state your business, Mr whatever-your-name-is – you don't really expect us to believe that it's Blogs."

JFB was not to be put off his stride.

"I'm quite prepared to answer to 'Whatever-your-name-is', but then that would be confusing, for me it would need to be 'Whatever-my-name-is', which of course is Blogs. I think we're going nowhere here. Tell you what – I'll refer to you as 'Gentlemen'. That's no greater a diversion from the truth than for you to call me Mr Blogs."

This was too much for the Whitehouse patience. The honourable member had acquired only the merest patina of refinement in his years in the House and was prone to revert to the *moeurs* of his more humble origins. He moved towards JFB as if to lay hands on him, but was restrained by Schinski. JFB stood his ground and waited calmly until restraint had been unequivocally established in the MP's intent, before seating himself on the chair that had been strategically placed facing the desk. The other two followed his example and took their seats behind the desk.

"Now that the nomenclature has been sorted out, gentlemen, ('Gentlemen' came with particular emphasis) I will begin.

"It appears that the two of you have been up to very bad things. You have been putting on your own production of Robin Hood, but you seem to have missed the rather important point that it's the rich our hero should be stealing from and the poor he should be giving to. The casting has also been weak – I haven't been able to figure out is which of you is Robin and which is Friar Tuck. I know of course who Maid Marion is, but you went and messed that up and gave her the wrong name – why on earth did you get Adele to change her name to Florence? It pains me to say it, but the whole production has been a lamentable cock-up. It's simply not in the spirit of progressive redistribution."

Whitehouse flared up at this, but again Schinski interposed.

"Okay, Mr Blogs, cut the crap. Spell it out in plain English. Why are we all here?"

"Fair enough. I'll give you the bottom line. We want you both to depart the scene, to don your slippers and betake yourselves to a happy isle where, to misquote Tennyson, you can rust unburnished and no longer shine in abuse."

"You mean you want us to resign? Are you mad? Why the hell should we do that?"

"Well, you do have an alternative. You could choose to sail to an unhappy isle where teeth are required to be gnashed and left-leaning Furies fume wrath from the salt of the earth. Put more simply, you could opt for prison and disgrace."

"And what makes you think that we've done anything that would bring that on us?"

"It's not a question of what I think; it's a question of what I know. I know that, with the evidence that we have to put before a court, no jury would have any alternative but to convict you both for fraud and grievous bodily harm. You would both be disgraced and you would face lengthy jail sentences."

"And where is this evidence you're talking about?"

"There are quite a few bits and pieces – Terence Cooper's testimony, the corroboration of his solicitor of the submission he made to him, the letter from the Nigerian headquarters of the Florence Nightingale Trust."

Whitehouse gave a triumphant laugh.

"That's nothing. You'll need to do better than that. Get out of here before I throw you out."

In a gesture of disdain for the challenge JFB slouched further down in his chair and stretched his legs full out in front of him.

"I do apologise, gentlemen. I have saved the choicest titbits for the end. A bad habit of mine, I know. But Mummy always told me not to gulp my food. I should have mentioned the confession we have from Mr Craig. It covers quite a lot of sordid ground. Mind you, a judge mightn't like it; it's full of bad grammar and spelling mistakes. And then there's the little matter of the recording we have of a discussion on the subject of how to be rid of a turbulent bishop of the books. Remarkably, the two voices on the recording bear a striking resemblance to yours, gentlemen."

From the look that passed between Schinski and Whitehouse you could see that the light had dawned that further bluster would be futile.

"What recording?"

This, from Whitehouse, was more of a gasp than a question; it spelt the complete surrender of bravado.

"People small-minded enough to be accountants are noted for their attention to detail, are they not? In Terry Cooper you had a molecular gem in your midst, and you didn't even suspect it. The tenacious Terence had a recording device installed in his office – he knew you liked using his cubby hole to get away from nosey ears in the front office – and you, my friends, came up trumps and did a most fortuitous audition. You don't know how happy that made him, rare birdsong to a twitcher's ear it was."

Whitehouse could contain himself no longer. He stormed out of his seat and made straight for his tormenter. He was a robust man. In his youth he had had a few games in the second row for Hull Kingston Rovers. Before JFB could react he was lifted by the lapels of his garish jacket out of his chair and hurled to the ground. Whitehouse made to pick him up again with the clear intention of delivering a punch, but as he moved he suddenly let out a yelp of pain and clutched his back. The exertion had been too much for the sixty-three year-old vertebra. Using the back of JFB's now empty chair as a crutch, he eased himself down on to it and took uneasy breaths. Schinski stood back, aghast at what had happened, not knowing whether to focus on his enemy or his ally. In the end he opted for his ally.

Ignoring the stricken foe, he went over to the filing cabinet, extracted a glass and a bottle of finest malt and poured Whitehouse a generous measure.

As this was happening JFB got back to his feet. The smile, which had momentarily departed, returned to his face. In such circumstances smiles are often drafted in to cover for embarrassment, but not this one. Nor did it give any hint of triumphalism at the discomfiture of his assailant. It was simple bemusement at the absurdity of the MP's sense of his own integrity managing to survive and assert itself in the midst of all the evidence of its decease. Somehow this man had been keeping his truths and his fictions from interfering with each other. The smile turned to a laugh as he caught Schinski's eye.

"You couldn't spare another glass of that stuff?"

Schinski was taken aback at the mildness of the victim's reaction but was glad of the defusion. He went back to the cabinet and collected two fresh glasses. The whiskey was poured in silence, but there was hope in the air that better things would come of its drinking. With Whitehouse preoccupied with the spasm in his back the configuration of the group had switched; JFB and Schinski were now an odd kind of faction. There seemed to be an understanding that it was up to the two of them to produce an outcome. JFB was quick to sense this.

"We have no desire to rub your faces in the mud, Mr Schinski. What you did, particularly to Terry Cooper, was very wrong. You put that man through hell; you had him beaten up and then you threw him on to the streets. And you knew the problems he was having coping with his wife's health. You can't have any complaint when the tables are turned on you, can you now?"

Schinski picked up on the change of tone. He thought before he answered.

"I'm really sorry for what was done to Terry. He's a decent bloke and he didn't deserve that. If only he had listened to reason. To be fair to Reggie, he did try to avoid violence. The money he offered him wasn't peanuts. But Cooper would have none of it. He had this daft notion of keeping things above board – everything by the book."

This acted like an on-switch to the Whitehouse mindset. Pain was momentarily forgotten.

"Yes, exactly, what can you do with people like that? That type makes me sick. They think the world is all balance sheets and memos. I've come across a lot of fancy boys in my time. Put them in the back streets where I grew up in and you'd see what good all their little bits of paper would do them – sweet Fanny Adams.

"Anyway, what great harm were we doing? What's it to our members if we cream a little off the top – a couple of bob a week it cost them, not enough to buy you a pint of beer. When I see what the big boys at Westminster get up to – a backhander here, a consultancy fee there, not to mention all the freebies – what we did was no big deal; it would hardly pay for a week's bed and breakfast at the Savoy."

JFB turned to his attacker. The anger that he had held in check was let off the lease.

"You see it as a kind of game, do you? Fiddling with union funds is one thing, but what you did to Terry Cooper is another thing altogether. You deserve the same kind of hiding you gave him."

"And you would be for giving that to me, would you?"

Whitehouse had straightened up, but still kept one hand for support on the back of the chair. JFB moved towards him and looked threateningly into his face before turning and setting his empty glass on the desk. It was as if he had merely taken a deviation on his way. It was Schinski that he addressed himself to.

"I have a proposal to make to you both: Number 1: I want our honourable friend here to resign his seat – he can cite ill-health, overwork, family commitments, whatever he likes. Number 2: I want you both to secure the appointment of a successor of my choosing. Number 3: I want you, Mr Schinski, to stay in post until the successor has been appointed. After that you too will develop reasons to call time on your trade-unionising. If you comply with these demands you will avoid prison, your pensions will be secure and you will be free to take up any appointments that your distinguished and unblemished records will open up for you. The choice is yours. Take it or leave it."

The silence with which this was greeted was like a penny sinking slowly to the depths before landing on the ocean bed. The absence of instant outrage was a grudging admission of understanding. Whitehouse's was the greater silence. Eventually Schinski managed an utterance.

"This 'successor of your choosing', who is that to be? And what makes you think *we* can get him endorsed by the Executive Committee?"

"You don't need to know who he is at this stage. All I can tell you is that it will be someone who will be up to the job; he'll be able to impress your Committee, you can take that from me. As for getting him endorsed, that's your problem, gentlemen, but I have every confidence that fear will see you through. In my experience frighteners move mountains better than sweeteners. You were just a bit unlucky with Cooper."

Schinski looked to Whitehouse who had slumped back into the chair. There were no reinforcements forthcoming from that quarter, just an empty stare in the direction of anything other than the other two.

"We'll meet here again at the same hour in two days time and iron out some details. I'll leave you to it, gentlemen. You have a lot to discuss."

With that JFB left the room making great play of closing the door gently behind him.

Chapter 10

There was indeed much to discuss. The pain in Whitehouse's lower back set in like a winter frost now that there was nothing left to distract it. It added octane to his ranting against the low cunning of *that little wart* Cooper and the arrogance of this *ridiculous JFB clown*. Ideas were in short supply. He had given no thought to defeat; it was just a matter of coming up with a way to win, and a way there must be. Another whiskey was poured in shared silence, but not, as he assumed, in a communion of anger. It came as a cruel betrayal of their supposed fraternity when Schinski revealed where he was at in his thinking.

"You must be in with a good shout at a peerage, Reggie. The party could do with a few more good Northern voices like yours in the upper chamber. God knows, they've enough of the other sort, all shit and no bull. You never know, you might be able to put in a word for me some time."

The look on Whitehouse's face turned thunderous.

"What the hell are you talking about? You don't think I'm going to give in to that little prick? I'll see him in hell first."

Schinski had known better than expect anything other than this from his partner in crime. Reggie Whitehouse wasn't the sharpest pencil in the drawer. He had got to where he was by being rough and gruff, the trophy working-class, plain-speaking curio, to be wheeled out on display as a reminder to the party faithful of the Party's cloth cap provenance. In his early years he had been everything the cliché demanded of him, honest, hard-working and devout in his belief in the heaven-on-earth that victory in the class war would bring. But as the years went by he had seen too much career ambition unbridled, too many deals done, too few promises kept. The light went out of his eyes and his instinctive aversion to falling out of step took over. The maxim 'If you can't beat 'em, join 'em' found a safe cranny in the whys and wherefores of his doings. Yet even after all the disillusionment and his blatant betrayal of his office he was still immensely proud of being an MP. He would refuse to loosen his bite; better to die like a rat with its teeth in its killer. The only way forward would be to get him something grander to bite into. But first Schinski needed to calm him down.

"Come on now, Reggie. You know me, I'm not one to run away from a scrap, but there comes a time when you have to back off, live to fight another day. That's what we must focus on. We've got to set up that other day."

In the absence of the expected torrent of indignation, he felt encouraged to continue.

"How long is it you've been an MP? Thirty-five years is it?"

"Thirty-seven"

"There aren't many could better that. I'd say you must be in with a good shout. We've just got to play our cards right. Have a word in Jack Bradshaw's ear. He's very pally with George Mason in the Whip's office. Say that you're thinking of packing it in and you were wondering what they could do for you. You don't need to commit to anything. Just fly the kite."

He knew that Whitehouse's retirement would go down very well with the Party's top brass. He had served his purpose well as a Party mascot, but his work in the constituency and his contributions in the House did little for the Party's reputation. They would be very glad to be shot of him. In the Lords he could still do the mascot thing at a safe distance from the front line.

Self-knowledge needs a thin skin, and Reggie had spent too much time in the sun. As far as he was concerned, his feelings for the Party were one and the same as his value to the Party. But as the clouds of his outrage started to break up, the red benches began to seem an appropriate forum for him to display his political acumen. If truth be told, thoughts of elevation to the

Upper House were no novelty to his imagination. Okay, he could live with swapping his seat in the Commons for one in the Lords, but his dignity demanded that he hold on to his resentment.

"That's all very well and good, but how do we go about getting the Executive Committee to accept the bugger these people are trying to push through? If we can't manage that there'll be no deal anyway."

Schinski had no answer for that. He would have a better idea once he had met the man. For the present he was content to have cleared the first hurdle.

Chapter 11

The two handshakes were very different. When he shook Schinski's hand JFB had an impression of collusion being ratified. With Whitehouse it was more a kind of Christmas truce.

"Well, what's it to be, gentlemen? Are we in business?"

The smile that accompanied the questions gave no hint of ill will. It was much too pleasant for Whitehouse's taste and met with a darker scowl than open aggression might have elicited. Schinski in contrast showed willing to reciprocate.

"We are open to persuasion, Mr Blogs, but there's one point that needs to be cleared up: What's to stop you from reporting us to the authorities once you've got what you want from us?"

"You can rest easy on that score. How could we betray you without betraying ourselves? If it became known that our candidate had been selected on the basis of ... shall we say pressure of an unworthy kind, how long would he be allowed to remain in the House? The same applies to you. You can't betray us without betraying yourselves. We're both locked in a compact of eternal trust."

Schinski was already aware of this logic, but wanted assurance that the other side was equally clear on it.

"Okay, so where do we go from here?"

All three men had been standing, but JFB took the initiative and sat down. The others followed suit. It was a gesture that epitomised the idiom; it was time to get down to business.

"I have our candidate with me today. He's waiting in the car. There's one thing I'd like to clear up before I go and fetch him. I want you to treat him as an innocent party in all this. As far as you are concerned, he knows nothing about the circumstances of this meeting. You have asked him along because you have read some of his stuff and think that he would be an ideal person to get the Party out of the rut it's been in for years."

Whitehouse looked scornful.

"And what's the point tell me of this charade? I'm too long in the tooth to be playing buck-stupid games."

"The point is you'll make a better fist of persuading the Committee if you're consistent. If you treat him one way in private and another way in public you'll be straining your theatrical abilities. Besides, let him put his arguments to you and you'll be able to relay them with more conviction to the people that need persuading."

"He has a point, Reggie. He wants us to ... what's the name for it? ... Method acting that's what they call it, isn't it? I suspect you do a bit of it yourself, Mr Blogs?"

JFB returned Schinski's smile. It was a seal on their collusion. He opened his briefcase and took out two folders which he handed to the other two, the receptive Schinski and a determinedly dog-in-the-manger Whitehouse.

"There's some reading for you, gentlemen – some articles that Mr Snoddy has published. They should make interesting reading. If you have any issues with them you can get him to explain them when I bring him to meet you. I think an hour should do the job. Until then, gentlemen."

The door was closed behind him with the same solicitude as on the previous occasion. Left alone, the two men found themselves in the mode of pupils left with work by the teacher. Whitehouse eyed the file of papers in front of him with distaste bordering on disgust. He had spent most of his career ducking papers; they were fodder for minions to digest for him – secretaries, advisers, drones from the whips' office. People, they're what mattered. He knew about bullying and obeying, and when you got down to it, that's what politics was all about. You bullied who you could and you obeyed who you had to. Fancy ideas came and went; they were like snazzy greasepaint that can't weather the scrutiny of ordinary light.

Schinski was a different animal. He hadn't made it to university. He was more than bright enough, but he'd had a father who divided the world into those who were in heaven and should be in hell, and those who were in hell but deserved to be in heaven. All toffs belonged to the former category, and if you had either money or education, you were a toff. The son challenged the father many times on this, but any battles he won in words were pyrrhic victories, serving only to confirm for the older man the chicanery of the educated classes. All thoughts of reading for the law had to be abandoned; the foundry doors swallowed him whole. It was only after years of dogged determination that he'd worked his way up the union hierarchy. He would tackle the forms and endless pages of regulations with all their sections and subsections that no one else could bear to look at, let alone master. Not surprisingly then, it was he rather than the aspirant lord of the realm that settled to his work.

In the hour or so between JFB's departure and return Schinski had time to read the documents through several times. There was a lot to digest, some of it bordering on the unpalatable. He made detailed notes and formulated a few questions he felt he needed to put to the mystery candidate – this despite numerous interruptions and protestations from his colleague, who had recourse to a couple of visits to the filing cabinet to sustain him. When finally he had waded through the papers, Whitehouse felt at liberty to seek corroboration for his misgivings about anyone capable of writing 'such guff'. Schinski was in no mind to comply.

"Listen to me, Reggie, and listen good, we're not here to pick holes; we're here to see where this guy is in danger of ruling himself out with the Committee and it's up to us to reel him back in. Our future – your place in the Lords – depends on us getting him past the Committee. That's the business we need to be addressing. Nothing else matters a damn."

Whitehouse gave a grudging grunt, but before he could follow it with a litany of face-saving yes-buts Sylvia's buzz signalled the arrival of the intruders.

Chapter 12

The tall shaven-headed figure that Sylvia ushered in along with the garish JFB arrested the attention of the two hosts. He was wearing a three-piece suit of grey tweed with an open-necked shirt. The absence of a tie somehow authenticated the quality of the tweed and suggested a preference in the wearer of substance over style. The smile on his face similarly denied any role as a front for nervousness or a desire to please; it was the smile of a man at ease with the situation. Whitehouse took the instant dislike to him he had already budgeted for.

The introductory formalities would have done credit to the best aspirants of RADA. No outsider could possibly have suspected the ignoble bloodline of the encounter. The charm exuding from the three active participants had a convincing authenticity to it, which Whitehouse's militant reticence did nothing to undermine. Coffee was brought in by Sylvia who seemed more anxious to please than had been evident before, and the meeting eased into session with Schinski in the chair.

"You have a very impressive academic record, Mr Snoddy – a first from Oxford in modern languages and then a Masters cum laude. The subject of your thesis was Friedrich Nietzsche I see. Is that not a strange subject for someone wanting to represent a socialist party in Parliament? I don't know much about philosophy, but as I understand it, Nietzsche is a figure associated with the far Right?"

An involuntary flicker of disapproval appeared on the Snoddy smile.

"That's a common misconception, Mr Schinski. This is not the time or the place to go into detail, but Nietzsche believed in men reaching their potential and he felt that the main forces of

Western civilisation had combined to stunt that potential. Christianity is his great *bête noire*. She saw it as an encouragement to the weak to wallow in their weakness and the strong to indulge them. Anyone who thinks that that's what socialism should be about is more of a social worker than a working socialist in my book."

This was deep water for Schinski. He had done a good job of educating himself, but he was not up to crossing swords with an Oxford scholar. He did however have a deep confidence in his practical intelligence. When he kept his feet on the ground he was a match for anyone.

"You say that's not what socialism should be about. Let me change the question slightly. Do you think that that's what it *has* been about?"

This produced another flicker, this time of approval.

"That's an excellent question, Mr Schinski. You've hit the nail right on the head. I believe that that is precisely where the Party has lost its way. It's time for a change of direction and I see it as my job to help steer it back to being a true party of labour."

"Don't you think that's a very big ask? How do you propose to convince the membership that they've been getting it wrong all these years? People don't like being told they're wrong. They resent it and they're not going to take kindly to ... if you will forgive me... an upstart like you asking for their endorsement and patronising them at the same time."

This brought Whitehouse to life. This was a band wagon he hadn't dreamt would come his way.

"The Party represents the people that the banks and the big concerns treat like shit and have always treated like shit. I've been in this game before you were out of nappies. And now you come along here and tell us we've been getting it all wrong, we should listen to you because you know best. Who the hell do you think you are?"

The smile on Snoddy's face was instantly replaced by a look

of cold intensity. His chair had been facing forwards towards the two men seated on the other side of Schinski's desk. He half stood up and, clutching the two armrests, angled the chair round so as to face directly at Whitehouse. The wilfulness of the operation made for a disconcerting prelude to what he was about to say.

"Mr Whitehouse, I never met you when you were a young man. I've read what I could about your early career and what I read reminded me of my father. My father was a man I loved and admired. He was a good man. He had, as they say, his heart in the right place. If someone needed a loan of a few quid to get them through to pay day, he'd put his hand in his pocket. If someone was being harassed by the town hall or the landlord, he'd take up their case and try and get them justice. He was a Party member. He'd take the day off work, and lose his day's pay, to canvas at the elections. His kind was what the Party was all about. He gave help when he could and in return he expected help when he needed it. What he did not do was to treat his fellow man, or allow himself to be treated, as an inveterate basket case. When he saw that the Party had become more interested in looking in the mirror to see how well it was playing the Good Samaritan than looking at the reality to see what was happening to the traveller, it was no longer the party for him.

"I know, Mr Whitehouse, how difficult it is going to be to get the Party back to a party that my father, and people like yourself, would be proud of. If you were a younger man I'd want you there beside me fighting for its soul. As it is, I would hope to be able to tap into your vast experience. Any help and advice you could give me would be greatly appreciated."

Whitehouse stared open-mouthed. It was as if a cramp had loosened in his brain. He had been bracing himself against this dastardly act of senicide that was being perpetrated on him and showing defiance by embracing the very failings he was being axed for. It was perverse. He still had a brain that could service

71

his purposes and he hadn't been using it. His head might be old, but here were young shoulders willing, seemingly, to have it put on them.

"You won't find it easy, young man. People are not easy to handle."

As soon as the words came out he wanted them back. What was he thinking of? Had he forgotten what this was all about? This man was here to take his seat in Parliament away from him, to rob him, to leave him without the thing that had boosted the image he had of himself in his and everyone else's eyes. He was about to fall back on the comfort of his self-pity when a voice in his head called on him to remember his shame. It was his own father's voice. Yes, there was truth in what this young pup had said. His father too would have deplored the way he had gone and the way the Party had gone. Maybe it wasn't too late for him to do something about it. And certainly, at his stage of life, the Lords was the place to do it. His thoughts were interrupted by Schinski who was eager to keep things businesslike.

"I've read your piece on law and order. It's a bit radical, don't you think? . . . a major overhaul of the justice system, a complete rethink of penal arrangements and the scrapping of all human rights legislation?"

Snoddy displayed a degree of reluctance at being redirected away from Whitehouse.

"Yes, it certainly is radical. But doesn't the Party see itself any more as a radical party? That's exactly the problem; the Party stopped being radical a long time ago. It has become an historical society that sees it as its mission to preserve all the noble pronouncements of radical antiquity. Maybe it should change its name and call itself the Preservative Party. The Tories wouldn't know what had hit them."

"But didn't you just say that the Party had lost its way? Surely that means that it has lost touch with its origins? How could it be a slave to them then?"

"A good point, Mr Schinski, but there's a big difference between staying true to concepts and becoming enslaved to magic word potions. It hasn't been so much a question of throwing the baby out with the bath water, more a case of throwing the baby out and keeping the bath water."

This was getting too philosophical for Schinski. He was keen to return to safer ground.

"Let's get back to what you are proposing. You challenge the whole notion of human rights. Are you seriously suggesting we should get back to allowing people to be treated like animals? I don't think you'll get many takers for that in the Party."

"Why does everyone assume that? It's the kind of thinking ban-the-bomb campaigners go in for. *If you don't agree with us you are secretly hoping for World War III, you'd like to see the end of human civilisation and the complete extinction of all life forms on the planet.* Strangely, none of us who are against banning the bomb are aware that that's what we're hoping. Only the good guys know, and they've a duty to make us war-mongers look our own wickedness in the eye. It's a classic case of confusing ends and means. The righteous bang on about their righteous ends; it follows, doesn't it, that any means they propose to get to these ends must have angel dust sprinkled all over them? No, sorry, wrong, it doesn't follow!

"The problem with human rights is that they are unconditional, they treat human beings as objects. It's all one-way traffic and the traffic is allowed to flow with no regard to where it is taking us ... and very often that's over the cliff and into the sea. Human beings are not passive recipients of some immutable moral plasma; they find themselves in the ethical equivalent of a magnetic field and their presence, their actions, play a significant part in giving that field its particular character. Moral fields don't come from a big ethics factory in the metaphysical ether, they're not mass produced; they are brought into being by each individual as he goes about his doings and un-doings."

The look of incomprehension on the two faces on the other side of the desk brought the would-be candidate up short. He had told himself not to do this. He was well aware of his weakness for well-dressed abstractions and he knew full well that they were not the stuff of politics. How often had he told himself that? Stick to folksy ballads. Keep wisdom homespun. Still . . . no real harm done; it was better to get it wrong here than before a selection panel.

"I'm sorry, gentlemen. I got carried away. What I'm saying is quite simple really. The rights that people have should depend on what they do. If they behave well, they should expect to be treated well. If they behave badly, they should expect to be treated badly. The only 'right' they can call on is that their ill-treatment should be proportionate. Notice I say 'ill-treatment'. My moral betters would be appalled. They see it as society's job to administer 'treatment', just like a doctor. Of course, if the treatment fails, the fault lies with the physician, not the patient. I don't say that the question of what is proportionate is a straightforward one. It's problematic, but it is at the very heart of the justice debate. Strangely though, it's not the question that gets asked nowadays. It has long since been drowned out in the babble of all the bogus concerns that are closer to the hearts of liberal intellectuals."

There was a nod of approval from Whitehouse. He knew exactly what it felt like to be 'drowned out' by these 'lady boys' who he had watched take over the Party. Maybe this young pup would be a match for them. He could certainly trade words with them, and words were their thing, their only thing. Schinski was less enthusiastic. This man was proposing to open up a whole can of worms. Some of the old guard would certainly be sympathetic to what he was saying, but the people that counted were too fond of their polite cucumber sandwiches to swallow rough stuff like this.

"But surely you realise, Mr Snoddy, that the Party is

committed to the human rights movement. It would take a lot of persuading to throw it over. How would you set about that?"

Snoddy's face forged an uncharacteristic grin.

"I've a friend in the Samaritans. I'll take some lessons from him."

"I don't follow."

"The Samaritans specialise in steering people away from suicide. That's what I'll be doing. If the Party doesn't link up again with the working class people in this country it will be signing its own death warrant."

Schinski gave a chuckle. It was a cheeky answer, cheeky enough to win over enough on the Committee? The man might just have a fighting chance. The constituency was weary of having a sitting MP who the times had left behind. If they picked this man he would certainly get them out of the backwater. The question is: would they be prepared to ride the white water he would plunge them into? For the present the important thing was that a possible strategy had emerged; he would try to sell Snoddy to them as a kind of Moses figure. They were sick of the devil they knew, and it was just possible that they mightn't recognise him as the devil they didn't know.

Chapter 13

Curiosity is the quintessence of addiction. It powers the host onwards and drowns the cry of caution in the roar of its thrust. PC Best knew he should let the matter drop, but the itch insisted on being scratched. He had to find out more. It would do no harm to look up Cooper's address. It didn't commit him to anything. He would have it and he could use it or just leave it lying around until the fever had passed. Of course, once the information was there, it was conspicuously there. What possible harm would it do to check it out? When he'd heard Cooper's story he'd know what to do. He wouldn't *have* to do anything. He could just listen and allow things to develop, but only if they were heading in a direction he approved of. Such were the thoughts that pin-balled around his mind until they worked up enough energy to generate action.

He didn't want Cooper to know he was a policeman, so he introduced himself as a friend of Justin Wright's who had come at his friend's bidding to see if any progress could be made in the case without requiring direct evidence from the victim. Cooper blinked at this.

"But why do you not want me to give evidence? I don't see how that would make things worse. Surely we've plenty to back up anything I would tell the court. I know how tricky the law can be and how things can get twisted into shapes they never had, but I must say it really took me by surprise when Justin said there was a risk of them taking a libel action against us."

This was a bolt from the blue. Justin had told him Cooper wasn't prepared to give evidence. Why had he lied to him? What the hell was going on?

"Oh, nothing has been decided. It's just a question of

exploring possibilities. Justin's a very cautious man and he wants to be sure you're not exposed to any threat. You've suffered quite enough already."

The spontaneous non-committal of his response came as second nature to one used to getting the public to keep their noses out of police business. It plugged the hole. He was the one who should be asking the questions. Steering a delicate course between his need to know and an ignorance that would betray his lack of involvement with the case, he managed to get the bookkeeper to take him on a tour of the evidence. Cooper was a willing narrator and when he had finished his tale, it was clear to Best that there was more than enough to convict Whitehouse and Schinski. There was every chance that Bailey too would go down. There was certainly more than enough evidence for a charge to be brought against the Chief Super, and the charge in itself, even if it didn't stick, would be enough to end his career. But why hadn't Justin acted on this? What was his game?

The earlier assurances he had given himself that the new knowledge was sure to show him the way forward were now exposed as a siren call. He had simply traded the nagging of a small uncertainty for the bullying of a greater one. Justin had not been lying about Bailey – he was sure about that now – but what had stopped him from taking things further? Was he scared? Had he been got at? How much did Bailey know about it? Could that be the reason why Justin had told him to be wary? If the Chief Super ever got wind of the fact that he had been helping Justin, he'd be in the firing line. Maybe Bailey did know and Justin was just going through the motions. That was it! Justin couldn't bring himself to come clean and admit he had landed his friend in the shit. That vague warning he gave him was probably just a sop to his conscience.

Justin had left Manchester the day before, so the only means of contact was his mobile. He made several attempts, but it went through to voicemail each time. Infuriation courted paranoia.

Was Justin doing a hit-and-run and shutting his eyes to the road-kill he had left behind him? But then gradually the shadows would lighten and thoughts of a brighter hue would push themselves through. At the end of the day, what could Bailey do to him? Surely *he* was the one holding the axe; it was the Chief's head, not his, that was on the block. But then again ... there must be something preventing Justin from wielding that axe.

His thoughts circled around his anxiety, whipping it up, and then dampening it down, only to go back and repeat the cycle. If only Justin would answer his bloody mobile! When he got off duty he headed for The Red Lion. It was the pub in the next street to the station where everyone went after a hard shift to help them slacken back into the rhythm of domestic humdrum. He spotted Charlie and Andy, two mates of his, at the bar. He went over to join them, but he could see that they were already in the throes of leaving; their pints were being downed at a more acute angle than early pints would warrant and their conversation was consciously working up to a definitive full stop. He ordered himself a pint as they left and looked around. The only hospitable face he could pick out belonged to Jack Bull. Sergeant Bull was one of those people who you can't imagine having gone through any phases to become what they are, in Bull's case a strong, fatherly figure possessed of a wisdom that kept the feeble efforts of youthful intelligence at arm's length. The old-fashioned air he had about him gave the impression of a steady ship holding its course on an ever-changing sea.

He was on his own. Best went over and sat down at his table. They were not particular friends, in fact Best couldn't remember them ever having had a proper conversation, but the team bond is its own thing and no stickler for personal intimacy. Within minutes the chat flowed like the beer and within an hour Best was homing in on the old boy's thoughts on the subject of Chief Superintendant Bailey.

"A complete shit, the type who'd sell his granny if it would help him get another rung up the ladder. I've seen pushy bastards in my day, but that one takes the biscuit. You'd think any bugger would be satisfied at making Chief Super. Not him, he won't stop until he's our next Chief Constable."

This was said in a tone more of amusement than outrage, as if it was the way of the world that was being cited, not the rogue behaviour of a lone maverick. Encouraged by the candour, Best pushed further.

"What did he do to make it up to Chief Super? You're not going to tell me it was talent."

Bull took a sip of his pint.

"No, don't be fooled. He's a clever bastard, not just wheeler-dealer clever. He knows his job and he gets things done. Of course, as we both know, that's not enough. You need to kiss the right arses, and he has kissed plenty."

"Any in particular?"

This was a blunder. The easy intimacy that had grown up between the men suddenly developed a fault line. The question wasn't one to find a home in casual gossip; it smacked too much of the interview room. Bull took a slow and deliberate sip of his drink, as he scoured his young colleague's expression for clues. Best tried to put his face on casual. He feared the worst, but luck was with him; he was spared a judgement. Out of the blue a beer tray was plonked on to the table; it had three pints on it. The two men looked up. Towering over them was the smiling face of Chris Corry, another sergeant who Best knew only by sight. The thread was broken as the pints and the donor were given their welcome to the table. But once the biddings and greetings were out of the way, Bull seemed eager to draw the conversation back to where it had been left.

"Nigel here and I have been discussing our esteemed Chief. I was telling him what a wonderful guy he is. But what was it now you wanted to know, Nigel? Oh yes, you wanted to know what friends he had in high places. Chris here is a better man to answer that than me. He and the Chief are quite pally, aren't you, Chris?"

There was clear sarcasm in this, but the problem was to know where it was being directed. Which combination was at work? Were Bull and Corry ganging up against him or had he been drafted in by Bull to have a go at Corry? Corry's reaction tilted him towards the latter – a knowing smile directed at Bull, then a switch to a more earnest, straight-laced look in Best's direction.

"Jack's always been jealous of me and my 'special' friends. He thinks I do a bit of match-fixing, don't you Jack? But I tell you, Nigel, the smart money isn't on me, it's on him for the Inspector job."

This was news to Best. He hadn't realised the two of them were rivals for promotion. The two men were using him to talk at each other.

"Come on now, Chris," Bull retorted, "I know that any friend of yours is a friend of mine, so it's just as much in my interests as it is in yours for you to have good connections. The question Nigel here wants an answer to is, how good are the connections that your connections are connected to?"

This produced a hearty laugh from Corry, but again it was to Best that he addressed himself.

"The truth of the matter is that the Super and I are both members of the Masonic Order. Jack thinks that that means I'll walk into the Inspector job. He's got it all wrong of course. If anything, it increases *his* chances. The last thing Bailey can afford is to be seen showing any favouritism towards a fellow Mason. Anyway, why are you interested in Bailey?"

A few pints had been drunk, not enough to block danger signals, but enough to boost confidence that threat could be managed. He could duck the question, but that wouldn't get him anywhere. If he took it on, he might be able to get where he wanted to go. He just needed to be careful.

"I heard that he was very chummy with our local MP – Whitehouse isn't it? -and that the said gentleman is well known for his, shall we say, shortcuts to getting what he wants. I was just wondering if our Super was of a similar persuasion."

The question acted like a touch on a limpet. Corry visibly stiffened. But he let only a glimpse be caught of the effect; companionable chatter was almost instantly resumed. The effort however was counterproductive; the affected lightness only served to highlight the impact the question had made.

"Whitehouse, I know of him of course, although I don't know him personally. From what I hear the old boy is no great shakes in the brains' department. He's not daft enough not to be aware of it though. That's why he cultivates this image of the crooked old fox in the smoke-filled room. It's all an act, I'm told, a cover-up. Better to be taken for a bit of a villain than a bit of a fool. As for George Bailey, he's not above a bit of wheeling and dealing sure, but that's the height of it. If you're asking me, I'd say that, when you really get down to it, our Chief Super is as straight as they come. That is, of course," he added, looking pointedly at Best, "unless you've any reason to think otherwise ...Another pint?"

Chapter 14

In most constituencies it was standard practice for a selection panel to be set up to put forward a candidate for the Executive Committee to rubberstamp. In his capacity as representative of the local trade unions Schinski was bound to be on this panel as was Whitehouse as the out-going MP. The Chairman, Trevor Windsor and the Honorary Secretary, Hugh Savage, would also be there. There would have to be a woman of course, and that would inevitably be Margaret Millership. The dreaded Maggie was a formidable beast whom no other woman, and certainly no man, would oppose. That left another four places. These would probably be decided at the next meeting of the Executive, the one where Reggie would drop his bombshell. If they could keep it quiet until then they might take the Executive unawares and get a couple of the *right* people elected, or at least keep a couple of the *wrong* people off.

Schinski had already thought it through. There were two main camps in the Party. There were the old die-hards, the ones who beatified the memory of the Tolpuddle Martyrs and for whom the word 'Miner' was spoken with a reverend tremor in the larynx. For them the metaphysical reality of nationalisation was clearer and sharper and more compelling than all the miserably botched efforts that mere history had had the ineptitude to come up with. Scargill was a fallen hero; he had taken on the dragon and died in his failed attempt to slay it, the dragon being of course all things *Thatcherite*. That name, when it had to be spoken, was spat out as from an inferno of fury, fire on fire. Such unlovely malevolence notwithstanding, these were for the most part decent men who desperately wanted to keep the faith of their fathers and forefathers whom they fondly remembered,

82

like the troubadours of old telling tales of derring-do in the great war of the classes.

The other rampart was manned by people like Windsor and Savage. They didn't see the world through the prism of socialist myth, although that didn't stop them milking the security it offered. Fluidity was their watchword. Anything that laid claim to permanence or even longevity had to be exposed as a traitor to the future. The only rule that they respected was that there should be tolerance to everything that showed tolerance to everything. By the same logic, all who condemned must themselves be condemned. They were in fact middleclass liberals catching a free ride on the working man's bandwagon. They piled on, brandishing their sincerity passes when election time came round. Between elections they did their best to pretend that their unsophisticated brethren simply weren't there or, alternatively, were away undergoing treatment – but not to worry, they would soon get *better*.

Schinski was a professional; he was in neither camp. If he had to choose, his heart was with the cloth-cap brigade. The liberals were cleverer. He found their arguments harder to refute, not that he tried, except in his own head. The power within the Party was with them, so they were the ones that he had had to please. But now, if he was to get Snoddy nominated, it was the cloth-caps that he must look to for support. He must get as many of them as possible on to the Panel. It would not be easy. In fact it might prove to be the greatest challenge his Machiavellian skills had yet to meet.

As things stood he was on a hiding to nothing. The only member of the Committee outside the progressive caucus was George Maxwell. George had no time for what he sneeringly referred to as these 'namby-pamby' crusades, that his intellectual brothers on the progressive left went in for. The trouble was he was too far on the other side. He had visited George at his home once. The house was a shrine to the glorious socialist past;

pictures of Kier Hardie, Clement Atlee, Nye Bevan and Tony Benn filled the walls. In pride of place, above the mantelpiece, was a photograph of him dining with Michael Foot and beneath it a letter from Foot thanking him for his hospitality. When Schinski had asked him why his gallery did not include the likes of Harold Wilson or Tony Blair he was taken to the loo and shown a rogue's gallery of caricatures of the said gentlemen along with Jim Callaghan and Dennis Healy, all dangling at the end of a hangman's noose. Still, there was something about Snoddy that suggested he might touch some nerve in the traditionalist psyche. He had been impressed by the way he had handled Whitehouse. More of the same might well do the trick.

There were a couple of others who might be amenable. Johnnie Taylor was young and had ambitions in the party. His youthful enthusiasm was perfect cover for his crass pragmatism; he would put his shoulder to any wheel that was moving freely. If he could be persuaded that Snoddy was a winner he would back him. The one member of the progressive camp that might be won over was Max Fischer. Max was the most intellectual of the intellectuals. His German background – his father was German and his mother English – had provided him with an arsenal of conceptual abstractions which he used to great effect in dazzling those who crossed swords with him in debate. He took particular pleasure in shooting down anyone who attempted to dig in and hold ground. He was fluidity personified. It would be interesting to see how he would react to Snoddy. It could go either way, but Snoddy just might be the man to get him to turn his guns on his own side, if for no other reason than to demonstrate the firepower of his intellect.

These were the people he would work at getting on the Panel. It was unlikely he would be totally successful. Max Fischer would be a shoe-in, but he would settle for one out of the other two. And there was another strategy open to him: he could press for some representation outside the Executive. The progressives would be so confident of securing the nomination for one of their ilk that they wouldn't see any danger in it. Declarations of loyalty to 'democracy', 'the grass roots', committing to 'the voice of the rank and file', they'd think, could be wallowed in at no expense to the wallowers. And he knew just the man on whom all that democratic fervour would best be showered.

Chapter 15

'Unless you have any reason to think otherwise'. The words got played over and over in Nigel Best's head. They didn't change. What did change was the tone. It was like one of those images that you see reproduced in infinite variations of psychedelic colours. Depending on the recording he played, the line came over either as idle banter, dismissive irony or thinly veiled menace. The trouble was he had no longer access to the original recording; the replays had overwritten it. Whatever the truth of it, he resolved to give up this foolishness. If Bailey was bent, it was not his problem; he'd leave the task of outing him to others. The standard sophist argument against religious non-belief came to mind: if the believer is wrong about there being a heaven and a hell, he loses nothing, but if the atheist is wrong he stands to face an eternity of damnation. He would muster what faith he could in the propriety of his boss and get on with it. Justin Wright and Terence Cooper were to be dismissed as chimerical devils tempting him to err.

After a few days the recordings in his mind faded and matter-of-factness took hold again of his thinking. He was working on a burglary case, nothing special, a routine exercise with little hope of an arrest, when Sergeant Bull popped into the office with a message, delivered in full I'm-sorry-to-have-to-tell-you modulation, that the Chief Super wanted to see him. The meaningfulness of the tone and of the look that followed was impossible to dismiss. Dread rose as from its grave. He gulped down the rest of the coffee he had been drinking, placed the mug carefully on the table and headed up the stairs like a moth towards the light of revelation.

With his heavy spectacles and thinning hair, still remarkably black despite the ruin that fifty odd years had wrought on it, Chief Superintendent Bailey had always reminded Best of a comic book he had read when he was a boy telling the story of a mild-mannered florist in nineteen-twenties Chicago who turned out to be the brains behind the St Valentine's Day massacre. It had been one of those silly associations that the mind throws up for its own amusement. But recent developments had emboldened it, and now as he stood in the doorway waiting for direction, he had the eye to pick out the sinister curve on the Bailey smile as he beckoned his underling to take a seat.

"I was just about to have a coffee sent up. Would you like one?"

A polite refusal was probably expected, so it was made. Bailey picked up the phone and ordered the coffee. The whole exercise was performed with a focus of attention that denied it being a mere preliminary to the main, much weightier business on the agenda. With the phone out of the way, the Chief Superintendent spread his elbows on the desk and clasped his hands together completing the form of a triangle, all the time fixing the constable with his gaze. It was the first hint of anything other than friendliness, but it made no overt disclosure of hostile intent.

"You've been with us for a year or so now, isn't that right? How would you say you've been getting on?"

Was this an invitation to stick his neck out and have it chopped off?

"Pretty well, I reckon, sir, but that's really for others to say. All I can say is that I've been happy here and I don't think I've given any cause for complaint."

That was further than the head should have been advanced. Surprisingly, the chop didn't come.

"No, you've done better than that. Inspector Turner has sung your praises to me more than once. He has high hopes for you. He tells me you have an inquiring mind. That's a good thing in an officer, but he also tells me you have a tendency to go off at tangents. That's not so good. Independent thinking within the team is to be welcomed, but it's important not to lose touch, you must keep everyone in the loop."

At this he paused. His gaze became more fixed. Best felt under pressure from a question not yet asked, but looming. Sensing this perhaps, Bailey became more leisurely in his preamble.

"The first thing we look for in an officer is a capacity for teamwork. That's what the service is all about. Those who know the value of corporate loyalty are the ones who pick themselves out as future leaders. You can't lead men if you don't buy into the force that unites them."

The question still didn't come. Another pause allowed for another disingenuous gaze.

"I'm sure you understand what I'm saying."

There was a sudden switch of body language. Bailey looked down and busied himself with some papers on his desk. The silence this was done in gradually impacted itself as more than a mere pause; the interview was at an end! Best rose from his chair, but when he got to the door Bailey's voice came back to life.

"Oh, there's something I forgot. I'm told you made it your business to interview a Terence Cooper a few days ago. May I ask why?"

Coming from behind him like that, the voice was like a stab in the back. He was unable to resist his first reaction and spluttered out an unguarded "How do you know that?"

"It's my job to keep my ear to the ground. Remember what I said? If you're not in the mix you can't lead the pack. I have had dealings myself with Mr Cooper. He's a bit of a fantasist . . . came to me with a cock-and-bull story about trade union corruption. I had it investigated of course. Load of cobblers. He hasn't been spinning you more of his yarns, has he?"

There was nowhere but the truth to run to, or the least of it he could get away with.

"Yes, he told me he had been assaulted and wanted me to look into it."

"Did you?"

Quick thinking was needed; he was damned if he did and damned if he didn't.

"I couldn't decide. There was nothing to go on. I didn't think I could get anywhere with it."

"Is that why you made no record of the interview?"

Bailey was offering him a lifeline. He grasped it in both hands.

"Yes, sir, but now that you've put me right, I think I'll just leave it at that."

"What put you on to him in the first place? Did he contact you directly?"

"No, it was through a friend of mine. He's a journalist – actually he used to be in the force. He had spoken to Cooper and had given him my name."

The image of a snivelling collaborator he had seen in an old war film flashed up in his mind. But he *wasn't* a collaborator; he hadn't made any promises, had he? Besides Justin had broad shoulders; he could take the strain. It couldn't do *his* career any harm after all, could it?

"A journalist, you say, and an ex-copper? That's interesting. Would I know him? What's his name?"

"No, you wouldn't know him. We met at the Academy. He went off to do some undercover work and that's the last I saw of him until he turned up a week or so ago."

"Try me. What's his name?"

The question was mild in expression but it bristled with compulsion. He could lie of course, but that would only make things worse.

"Justin Wright."

He was unable to form a sentence to put the name in. In isolation like that, it sounded like a forced confession. Bailey couldn't have failed to notice, but he made light of its starkness.

"No, you're right. The name doesn't ring a bell. But anyway, remember what I said, Constable Best: The team maketh the man, but only if the man shows fealty to the team."

Chapter 16

It was announced yesterday that Reginald Whitehouse is stepping down after thirty-seven years as Member of Parliament for Bury West. In his press statement the veteran MP said he had not lost his appetite for politics and hopes to continue to serve the Party in other capacities, but the everyday demands of representing his constituents were putting a strain on him that his advancing years could no longer bear. It was time, he said, to make way for younger blood, someone who would stay true to the best traditions of the Labour movement and at the same time hone them to the much changed world of post-industrial Britain.

Reginald Whitehouse, Reggie as he is known to his friends, leaves Westminster with a solid record of political integrity. Closely associated with the Unions, he campaigned in the early days for a statutory minimum wage and backed the miners when they challenged the Heath government in the 1970s. He came to the notice of the wider public in March 1990 when he was arrested during the protest against the Poll Tax that resulted in whole scale rioting in Manchester. He was not charged, but in a press conference covered by the world's media he declared his willingness to face prison rather than submit to what he called 'the dark forces of capitalist greed'. He became a vociferous supporter of Neil Kinnock but took a back seat after successive election defeats and the arrival of Tony Blair. During the Blair years he was a much subdued figure in the Party; he never openly opposed the leader and kept his own counsel in the Blair-Brown rivalries, although there was little doubt where his sympathies lay. In the subsequent years of opposition his has been a voice of calm in a Party that has been on the verge of pulling itself apart. It is widely expected that a seat in the House of Lords will be found for a man who has served the Party so loyally and has so much experience to draw on.

The immediate question arises as to his successor. Will the Party opt for a candidate of the traditional Left or will it choose a moderniser? Ideally, the successful candidate would be someone capable of bringing the two strands of the Party together. The candidate will be selected by a Selection Panel drawn from members of the constituency Executive Committee. The final appointment is in the gift of the Committee, but in the past this has been little more than a formality; the Panel's choice is invariably rubber-stamped. One distinguished source expressed the hope that a member of the general party be co-opted on to this Panel. This, he claimed, would help to reflect the views of the wider party and extend the democratic legitimacy of the process of selection, a move rendered all the more important in the light of the dubious insider dealings rumoured to have determined such decisions elsewhere in the country. The source was concerned that the public might draw dark conclusions should such an initiative fail to materialise.

The above article appeared in the *Manchester Herald* the day before the Bury West Constituency Committee was due to meet to consider its reaction to the Whitehouse resignation. The subsequent flurry of phone calls between the Chairman and other trusted members of the Committee produced a circuitry of indignation and anger: *Who exactly was this 'distinguished source' and what right had he to tie the Committee's hands?* The most wounded voice belonged to Derek Schinski; he was one hundred percent behind the Chairman and he would draw on his contacts at the Herald to flush this meddler out.

The opening quarter hour of the meeting did no more than light up the same circuitry. The Chairman waved the paper in the air and called on the 'Judas' to own up. Secretary Savage, while sharing the Chairman's outrage, pointed out that the traitor was not likely to come from within their ranks: it was surely more reasonable to expect that someone pushing for an outsider would himself be an outsider. This received a begrudging nod from the Chairman. Schinski followed up saying that his inquiries within the reporting staff had revealed that the article had not been written by one of them; it had come from someone sent up by the London office, a young reporter by the name of

Wright. As far as anyone there knew, Wright had no local contacts and it was quite possible that he had just made the whole thing up himself. The blatant dishonesty of such reporting immediately allowed credibility to ride on the shoulders of outrage. Heads nodded, hypothesis hardened into fact and the meeting moved on.

It was agreed that apart from the ex-officio appointments, the Chairman, the Honorary Secretary and the outgoing MP, the Panel should include Schinski and Margaret Millership. Discussion as to whether or not to include an outsider took up little time. No other option: The genie was out of the bottle and had to be accommodated. The only issue was whether to include him in the Panel of nine or to add him as a tenth member. In the end they opted to keep the Panel to nine, which meant there were only three more places open. As expected, Max Fischer's contribution to the internationalist and intellectual kudos of the group proved irresistible as did the Adonic dynamism of Johnnie Taylor. George Maxwell, in spite of Whitehouse's advocacy, was turned down in favour of Nathan Roberts. This was not a welcome development. Roberts was an out-and-out Marxist who saw everything in terms of class warfare; he was most certainly not the type who would be open to any breach of socialist orthodoxy. Schinski could see a head-on collision coming.

The curse did however produce a blessing. Emboldened by his success, Roberts pushed for his candidate for the outsider spot, a known firebrand by the name of Sweeny, who, among other things, had campaigned for votes for prisoners and a strict quota system for all public offices based on ethnicity, sexual orientation and economic status. This had not gone down well with the Executive and there was strong resistance to his candidature. At this point Whitehouse proposed Willy Topping. This, unbeknown to the others, was at Schinski's prompting. Willy was the kindest of creatures for whom socialism was nothing short of God's special plan for mankind, a political precursor to Heaven. There was no hate in him, even for the nasty capitalists who took the food from the mouths of the poor. They were to be stopped certainly, but once weaned off their exploitative proclivities, they would see the error of their ways and rejoin the brotherhood of man. Willy was liked, but in the manner that children are liked. It was unthinkable that a bird of such limited brain should have a seat on the Panel.

The time was ripe for Schinski to make his move.

"As I see it, brothers, there are two candidates worth considering. The first is Gregory McDaid. Gregory has done a lot of good work for the Party. When elections come round you don't have to ask him twice; he knocks on the doors and talks the talk. Just ask our Secretary here: 'Who gets through the biggest pile of leaflets, Hugh?' And as far as Party meetings are concerned, have you ever known Gregory to miss one? If it were a Sunday school, he'd get a Bible for attendance. I know there's been a bit of a cloud over him lately, that sad business in the gents at *The Red Rooster*. But remember, he wasn't charged, and in our country a man is innocent until proven guilty. This might be a good moment for us to show some solidarity with a man who has been a good servant of the Party. It would be a brave and honourable choice."

There was a general rumble of dissent around the table to which the Chairman was quick to give voice.

"I admire your loyalty to this man, Derek, it does you credit, but I think you've let your feelings cloud your judgement on this one. The Press are on side when it comes to liberalist rhetoric, but they'd hang us out to dry if we stepped in a real muddy puddle. You'll forgive us if we pass up on bravery this time. What's the other choice you think we have?"

Schinski gave enough time for the blow to be seen to hurt.

"You have a point, Trevor. You'll forgive me for letting my

heart run away with my head. But of course you're right – tongues would wag. Okay then, if I stop listening to my heart and start listening to my head, I'd find it hard to go past Freddie Douglas. When you come to think of it, he's the stand-out candidate."

He stopped and let this sink in. An immediate follow-up would have weakened the impact of the proposal. Freddie was the man he really wanted on that Panel. He was a young man still in his early thirties, but he was perfectly at home in the philobabble of the ideological set and could swim in the nostalgia of the folk tribe like a duck in a pond. To the one group he was a like-mind, to the other he was a kindred spirit. To Schinski, he was a clever manipulator with ambitions of one day running his own puppet show. Both men had recognised themselves in the other and had come close to a declaration of mutuality in a whiskey session one evening after a triumph at a constituency meeting. Quite apart from serving his own purposes on this occasion, it would do Schinski no harm to give a leg-up to a man who one day might well go right to the top. With such misshapen bridesmaids lined up at the altar, the beauty of the bride shone clearly through and Frederick Douglas was unanimously accepted on to the Panel.

Chapter 17

It had been some time now since Stuart Stranaghan's retirement from the force. The first excitements of a life gloriously free from the routine of work had gradually faded, but he could still remember the initial zeal with which he had guarded his deliverance. In the first months he had been loath to make any kind of commitment, even ones that promised pleasure. He hadn't wanted any marks made on the pristine pages of the week ahead; he just loved being left to wallow in the unlimited potential that their blankness offered. With time, of course, the spring wound down and what had seemed like an infinity of possibilities in waiting gradually turned into a continuous stream of vacuity that threatened to wash over him. The early sense of open vista had been accompanied by a glorious feeling of having come to a kind of mystical terminus where the major figures of his past, many long since dead, had been awaiting his arrival. Memories of times spent with his father and mother and especially his long lost grandfather came teeming in; he even 'remembered' times and incidents before he was born, drawn from stories he had been told as a boy. Such memories of things remembered were as vividly textured as experiences he had lived through himself. He wondered if this could be the true inspiration for the notion of Heaven, this linking up with souls lost to death and the special dispensation to access their memories and see with their eyes. Sadly, as in due course the present filled up, the dominion of time was restored, the past receded, the ghosts took their leave and Heaven gave way again to Earth.

He was in the garden enjoying the sunlight as it filtered through the hazy autumnal air. Gardening wasn't really his thing, but he did enjoy the occasional project. He was especially proud of a little low wall he had built using old square sets; they were more forgiving than bricks; they revelled in irregularity and that was something which his limited bricklaying skills could supply in abundance. Today there was nothing more interesting on the agenda than the Sisyphean task of mowing the lawn. He did appreciate the miraculous beatification that the ordered lines brought to the garden, but he could never get away from the sense of how short-lived the transformation would be. Next week he would be at it again; it was no better than washing dishes. He was just about to start up his cantankerous mower when he heard footsteps on the front driveway followed by the two-toned chime of the doorbell. His wife Heather was out, so he nipped round the side of the house and found someone he would have described in the witness box as a slightly built male figure in his early thirties, just about to engage a second time with the bell.

"Bloody Jehovah's witness!" he thought. The judgement was reinforced by the expression on the man's face when he turned and caught sight of Stuart – a smile of the sort that is determined to see the positive in any negative and insist that all is for the best in a world that the good Lord designed. But then the smile morphed into a don't-you-recognise-me look, the type that Stuart dreaded, for almost invariably he had to disappoint. On this occasion however the light dawned and he was able to beat the actual 'Don't you know me?' to it.

"Myles! Detective Sergeant Myles!"

He was painfully conscious of the shame of not being able to come up with a Christian name; after all the two men had spent many weeks working together on the first Snoddy case. Myles however seemed not to notice.

"Well as a matter of fact it's now Detective Inspector, sir. I got my promotion last July."

Stuart's congratulations were received with awkward humility. Stuart was genuinely pleased; he had always liked

Myles with his rather gauche boyishness and that seriousness he brought to his intent to do the right thing. Surprise and pleasure at seeing former colleagues fuelled the chat as the two men entered the kitchen and coffee was brewed. Stuart's curiosity started to nag as to the reason behind the young man's visit but it did not behove the host to ask outright, it would demean the welcome. It wasn't long however before Myles got to it himself.

"I've been given a rather curious assignment, sir. (He couldn't bring himself to take up Stuart's invitation to call him by his first name) I've been asked to reopen your last case. There seems to be some unanswered questions over the conduct of your undercover man, DC Wright. Could I ask you why you decided to pull the operation? Did you have some doubts about him yourself?"

The question hit Stuart with a thud. It was like a cancer patient being told that his 'recovery' was just a remission. He had hoped that his Super's increasing frustration with the case and all the man-hours it was clocking up would allow him to bury it with a minimum of explanation. And it looked as if that's what had happened, but now … after all this time? Why would anyone want to drag it up again? Stuart had few attributes as an actor, but he knew enough to cash in on what he was actually feeling. His surprise was acutely genuine; the problem was to hide the fear sticking on to it.

"Justin Wright? You can't be serious! Justin was a very inexperienced officer. In fact he hadn't even completed his training when he took on the job. It was my fault; I shouldn't have asked him to take on such a difficult assignment in the first place. Chief Superintendent Matthews was against the whole thing from the start and in the end I had to admit he had a point. But there was never any question of young Wright getting up to any funny business if that's what you're getting at."

"Didn't you think it odd that he resigned from the force and went on with his studies at Oxford? Does that not suggest that he got too involved in the case and maybe even that he changed his loyalties? I see that he is now working as a journalist. And did you know that the newspaper he works for is owned by Matthew Eardley, one of the men he was investigating?"

"That's hardly surprising. Matthew Eardley owns a large chunk of the press in this country. If you want to work as a journalist the odds are you'd end up working for one of his papers. No, I don't see any problem with that. And as to his resignation, that's hardly surprising either. If you spent months on what turned out to be a wild goose chase, do you not think you'd be a bit disillusioned? Don't forget, that was his first and only experience of police work."

Myles, in true Myles' fashion, gave this time to sink in before he went panning for plausibility. This was something Stuart had always liked about Myles; he was an excellent listener.

"So you don't think there's any cause for concern then? I'm sure you're right, sir, but I'll need to speak to Wright. I've studied the files and there are a few questions I want to put to him. I just thought I'd get your thoughts on him first."

The pressure was off for the moment at least, enough for Stuart to go on the front foot.

"I hope you don't mind me asking, Graham," (the name had come at last) "but what's this all about? Why has the case been reopened? Has something come to light that I hadn't spotted?"

The question evoked not the slightest sign of caginess in the respondent.

"I couldn't honestly tell you. The order came from the top, that's all I know. And I was picked to lead the investigation because of my familiarity with the Snoddy case. I know how keen you were to get Snoddy and how disappointed you must have been when the undercover operation you set up fell through. It's strictly against the rules now that you're no longer in the force, but, don't worry, I'll keep you posted. Call it a quid pro quo – you see, you did teach me something, I can manage the odd Latin phrase now. I might well need your advice if I do turn anything up."

'Oh thee of total faith!' The phrase came unbidden into Stuart's head when Myles had taken his leave. It was not, as might be supposed, inspired by smugness. Quite the contrary, it was an expression of fear of impending doom. The trouble with too much of anything is that it invites the act of shedding the surplus, and once underway, the process would more than likely develop a momentum of its own.

Chapter 18

The day after the ads appeared in the press asking for applicants to contest the constituency of Bury West for the Labour Party, the following piece entitled 'Whither Socialism?' made the lead in a prominent political magazine.

Socialism is a word in search of meaning. It used to mean something, if not clearly defined, at least with parameters not beyond the pull of a central core. That core was the welfare of the working class in the various theatres of life. The theatre that saw the main action was the world of work with the drama centring on the traditional struggle between labour and capital.

The Marxist thesis, embraced in large part by the British Labour Party, was to end the conflict by abolishing capitalism itself; the means of production were to be wrested out of the private grasp and put in the hands of the State, the direct representatives of the people. This was the dream on which all socialists pinned their hopes. Alas, the dream proved a poor match for the intricacies and foibles of reality. Wherever it was tested, it was found wanting. The mainstream Left was eventually forced into a strategic retreat; it jettisoned direct state interference in wealth-creation and regrouped around the axis of redistribution. The abandonment of this tandem of wealth creation and wealth disposal has in turn thrown up issues that socialism has found very hard to deal with. It is the old problem of trying to face two directions at once. The need to juggle the fundamentally contradictory claims has been the irritant that has caused the Labour Party to itch and to scratch so hard that it has drawn its own blood.

Broadly speaking, the left wing of the Party has focused myopically on the redistribution agenda — needs before must. The right wing hasn't gone as far as to invert this and put 'must' unequivocally before 'needs', but it has on occasion shown willing to make an accommodation with the interests of wealth creation, usually however after it has strayed too far down the other road and serious damage has been done. Invariably the addictive appeal of philanthropy proves too strong to resist. Gordon Brown was a classic case. Everyone will remember his courtship with Prudence; the pair was right up there with Charles and Diana as the nation's favourite couple, but then disaster struck, Brown went off in an orgy of spending and poor old Prudence was left without a penny to her name.

The same story plays itself out at inter-party level. Every decade or so the country gets bored with the Tories and re-elects a Labour government. It is largely a question of renewed forgiveness for the Prodigal Son who comes back promising to mend his ways and be a good boy. The promise is only half believed; everyone knows that sooner or later he will be back to his old habits, but they love him for it, until of course things get too serious and then it's back to the pin-striped medics for another dose of economic castor oil.

On this basis is there any reason for persisting with our two-party system? The Labour Party could give up and become the left wing of the Tory Party, or vice versa, it wouldn't matter which. It would of course be a terrible blow to the whole pantomime of political spectacle. The masses would be left with soccer as the only outlet for their tribal loyalties and the political class would be without a mass audience to show off their verbal-chess skills to. Can things really have come to such a pass? If politics had only to do with economics the sad answer might well be yes, but politics has to do with a lot more besides. This alas is something our politicians seem to have forgotten. To paraphrase Tennyson, there are 'works of nobler note that may yet be done'. Making life better for people, or at least making it easier for people to lead better lives — that surely has to be at the core of every politician's intent. In this the Labour Party has a distinct edge over the Tories. It has its roots in the ordinary people and is better placed to empathise with their instincts and their sense of what is right and decent.

But instead of making this the foundation of a worthy vision of society, the Party has decided to follow the moral compass of the metropolitan elite and gone off in a very different direction. The only interest it has shown in the welfare of the class it is pledged to champion has been crudely material-istic (the redistribution agenda). Its moral dimension has shifted away from the visions of the founding fathers to the fashionable obsessions of the environmentalists, the multiculturalists and the new wave 'moralists' who interpret nearly every antisocial act perpetrated by anyone with earnings less than the average wage as residual contamination from the big bang of capitalist society. This reflex is patronising, it is worse than that, it is totally dismissive of the hoi palloi as moral beings. Not only are they considered incapable of taking responsibility in their own lives, their views are at best ignored, at worst held up to ridicule when it comes to setting the moral compass for the political agenda.

This is at the heart of the rot that has set in on the Left. It has come down to a metaphysical plea to forgive the lower classes since they know not what they think. The intellectual Left has in all but name taken power of attorney over the white working class. It sees it as its duty of care to ensure the poor fools are treated with compassion; it makes sure they don't go short in the monetary stakes, but it is equally determined to save them from themselves when it comes to wider social issues; no way are the dear creatures to be allowed to indulge their unfortunate tendency to be unenlightened. Look at the record of the Blair-Brown government — benefits for all, extended open hours for pubs and clubs, big push on the expansion of gambling, a softly-softly approach to drug pedalling. Contrast this with the constant chipping-away at the meaning and status of all things conventional, not to mention the mass immigration they encouraged that put such a squeeze on jobs, housing, schooling and social services for those at the lower end of the social ladder.

Were these not the actions of a political mindset that regarded the lower orders as children to be amused and indulged and given pocket money to play with while the grown-ups got on with the serious business of serving the greater good? This 'greater good' was of course something only perceivable by those who inhabited the moral uplands. The bitter truth is that the party whose entire raison d'être should have been to serve the needs of the ordinary people was deeply ashamed of the tastes and views of those very people. The money it strove to redirect towards them was clearly little more than a sweetener for them to keep their mouths shut and leave the Party to press on with its highbrow progressive agenda. The big question is: Will the dreary assembly line of Blair-Milliband Doppelgangers with their Guardian-approved lists of things thinkable and things unconscionable ever give way to a new generation endowed with the wit and insight to reconfigure the working-class ethos in a form robust enough for it to regain its rightful place as the centrepiece of socialist philosophy?

The article finished with a seemingly casual reference to the impending West Bury by-election and speculated on the possibility of the emergence of a new voice for 'this old and venerable party.' As a gesture to the hope that West Bury might pick up 'the call of a party lost in the wild', complimentary copies of the magazine were to be posted to all paid-up members in the constituency.

Chapter 19

"There's a *gentleman* here to see you, Derek. He says his name is Lord Dooley. Mind you, he doesn't look much like a lord to me. Anyway, he insists that it's urgent. Shall I let him in?"

It was unusual for Sylvia to come in and announce callers like that. Normally she just used the intercom. Presumably it was to give vent to her scepticism as to the man's credentials. She was wrong of course. Schinski had heard of Lord Dooley, although the two men had never met. He had earned his peerage as a whip in the last Labour administration and was known for a belligerence that belied his diminished stature.

When the visitor entered the room he did so in a manner that somehow belittled the act of crossing a threshold. There was no question of Schinski being accorded his proprietorial due. Handshakes and conventional greetings were endured with indulgent impatience before the peer took the seat that was just about to be offered him.

"I've been advised that you're the man I need to talk to."

There was a brief pause, but not long enough for Schinski's curiosity to establish itself.

"This peerage business with old Reggie, I'm not sure it's on. He may have to settle for a knighthood."

Schinski had long ago learned that steamrollers are better diverted than resisted. It was important that the impulse to confront should not be allowed to muddy the mind and impede him from mastering the controls. So he simply stood up, went to the door and called in to Sylvia to bring in a coffee for one, having ascertained that the 'good lord' was not desirous of joining him. Dooley, clearly put out by the diversionary manoeuvre, resorted to a rehash of his opening salvo.

"No, it can't be done. It's a knighthood or nothing."

Schinski resumed his seat and affected an air of curious indifference.

"That's all very interesting and I am flattered that you have honoured me with the information, but can I just ask just why you are telling this to me and not to Reggie? I would have thought it was his news more than mine."

Dooley made a face that clearly showed pleasure in the scowl that it produced.

"Don't be coy with me, Schinski. It's common knowledge that old Reggie hasn't been with it for years. Everyone knows that you do all his thinking for him."

Schinski was not totally impervious to the compliment despite its unholy origin, but, more to the point, it provided him with an opening.

"Are you telling me then that thinking is required? If the decision is as done and dusted as you claim, what is there to think about?"

This time the Dooley scowl showed less pleasure.

"You're trying to twist my words. I was warned that you were a tricky bugger. I'm telling you because the stupid old fart needs someone to whisper some sense in his ear when he gets the news. You know what he's like; he's likely to do something stupid."

"You think he might do a Samson and bring the house crashing down around him? Is that what you mean? Well I dare say, he might do just that very thing."

Reggie was indeed what Schinski's old Glasgow granny would have described as a 'right thrawn bisum.' He had never really weighed up his personal feelings about Reggie, but when he came to think about it, he couldn't say he liked him. He tended to like people with a bit of creative devil in them, and Reggie could never be described as that. The thing that irked Schinski most was the man's utter predictability; you knew the kind of thing he was going to say before he came out with it. Of course this was what made Reggie the perfect conduit for his own ambitions; it was so easy to get your halfpence worth of like-mindedness in before he voiced his opinion – it produced a much more ego-enhancing effect than an approval-seeking echo would do. In the early days Reggie had opened many doors for him. But for this he felt little gratitude and certainly no sense of indebtedness. With his prodding and prompting Reggie had come to see him as an adjunct to himself. In promoting the younger man's career the old boy was merely expanding his own boundaries. If truth be told, Reggie's time was up – he had outlived his usefulness to him and to the Party. He should take the knighthood and sail away into the sunset. And yet, and yet … there was something that grated. He had 'promised' Reggie a peerage and it would be an affront to his professional pride to give up on it so easily. By publicly announcing his decision to stand down as an MP they had parted with their money before the job was done. They had no come-back over shoddy workmanship. And yet, and yet … Wouldn't he just love to take that smug look off Dooley's podgy face! He would press a few buttons and see what it produced.

"You were quite right to come to me. Reggie is dead set on this peerage. He told me that if the Party mucked him around he'd make sure there was enough shit flying around to make the Party stink in the public nostrils. It's up to you of course, but I'd think twice if I were you before I'd invite that kind of reaction."

Dooley, who had been lying back in the manner of one in command of the tidings he was bestowing, suddenly lurched forward in his seat, losing at least a decade in his seniority and a full rung in his loftiness.

"What the hell are you talking about? What could he do to the Party, apart from make a complete fool of himself and make us look bad for having had such a pathetic specimen to represent us in the Commons?"

The question was framed as rhetorical, but Dooley's eyes betrayed it as genuine.

"He wouldn't tell me, but I know he has something. He has referred to it from time to time over the years, always when some of the top brass were hassling him – no details, just that little smile he gives, a bit like a child with its comfort blanket. What's it he calls it? ... 'my little mannequin from the Pru', that's it."

Schinski watched as concern spread like a rash across Dooley's face. There were clear signs of emergency deliberation getting underway. The man continued to bluster, but Schinski could see that the real action was taking place in camera behind the voice. Eventually a reconnection was authorised.

"Okay, maybe, just maybe, the peerage could be put back on the table, but only on one condition. We'd need Reggie to endorse our choice of his successor. If you and Reggie can get our man elected, the peerage could be his."

Was he hearing this right? Do buses always come in twos? Schinski found himself grinning when he should have been wincing. But almost immediately the wince did succeed the grin. The ruling out of the peerage was only an opening gambit then, it was a bargaining chip. Dooley was put out merely because he hadn't been able to introduce the offer on his own terms – as an act of magnanimity deserving of a reciprocal response. As it was, it had more of the air of a hastily drawn line in the sand. Schinski made a show of deliberating, laboured enough to convince his adversary that he was fully aware that the power to accept or reject the offer was greater than the power to make it. And that power was in his hands.

"So you have someone you're keen to foist on us? May I ask who that is?"

"I'm not prepared to tell you that until you agree to the arrangement."

This was said with relished belligerence. Schinski readily responded.

"Now let me be clear on this, your Lordship: You wanted shot of doddery old Reggie and to encourage him you were prepared to offer him a peerage. The fish takes the bait and announces his resignation. Job done! But once he's in the net you say to him, 'Sorry, Reggie, when we said a peerage, didn't you realise we couldn't have meant a peerage? Come on now, you must have known that. But we do have some good news for you: if you really want us to have meant a peerage, we've a little thing we'd like you to do. This time we will of course mean what we say.' . . . I need a bit of help here. Can you suggest any way of explaining to Reggie how he should have known that last time you didn't mean what you said, but this time you do? He's a bit slow, as you know, and my teaching skills aren't what they ought to be."

"That's your problem. If Reggie knows what side his bread is buttered on, he'll do what we ask. If he doesn't, then we'll find someone else who will."

"Now that, if I may say so, your Lordship, is not a strategy worthy of your celebrated intelligence. If I were to tell Reggie what you've just said, he'd lose it and all hell would break loose. I know him and I know what he's like. If someone hits him a dig in the face, he doesn't complain to the referee, he goes in with the boot. You might get someone else to speak up for your man, fine, okay, but who are you going to get who can spare you the grief that Reggie will give you?"

There was a hint of concession in the bitter grin that replaced the aggression in Dooley's face, an acknowledgment that a man-of-the-world had met his match.

"Yes, you might have a point, Derek. You have my word on this. If you get our man nominated, Reggie will get his seat on the green benches. I can't do fairer than that. I've my reputation to think of. I do a lot of wheeling and dealing as it's called, and if it got out that I didn't keep my promises I'd lose the ability to do my job. Remember, it wasn't me who promised Reggie the peerage."

There was sense and substance in this, but he needed Dooley to give him something that he could hold over him, for he was now quite set on beating this man. Reggie was going to have his cake and eat it.

"I'm sorry, but once bitten, twice shy. I'll want something in writing."

Seeing the look of horror that this touched off, he was quick to add, "It needs to be something that would damage both sides if it came out. That way it would be in neither side's interest to pull the plug on the other. That's the best way… in fact it's the only way of ensuring that both sides keep to their word."

Horror seemed to take time out for reflection, but only the briefest of moments; it made a swift return as outrage. The visitor sprang to his feet.

"What the hell do you take me for? Look at me. Do I look like someone daft enough to leave his prints all over a murder weapon? Think again, Mr Schinski. And when you've got back to your senses, call me on this number."

He plonked a card on the desk and treated his assumedly vanquished adversary to a masterly performance of stomping out.

Chapter 20

The visit – it felt more like a visitation – of DI Myles had reopened a whole chest of anxieties for Stuart Stranaghan. He had done wrong but he had acted with the best of intentions. At the time he'd really believed that Snoddy was prepared to let Justin take the rap for the Rodgers' murder. He saw himself faced with a straight choice between allowing an innocent man to go to jail for it or bastards like Burrows and Wilson, who, morally if not legally, deserved everything that was coming to them. He had no regrets about that bit. As far as it touched them, justice had been done, albeit in a roundabout way. There was no real doubt that Rodgers had committed the murder that had sparked the whole thing off – and it had been a vicious, sadistic killing. And Burrows and Wilson as members of the Rodgers gang had undoubtedly been party to it. And the legal system had let them all get away with it. Where was the justice in that? Something needed doing. He hadn't done it, but he had acquiesced in the doing of it, at the expense of allowing Rodgers' real killer to get away with it. There was no doubt about who the killer was; it had to be Snoddy or, more probably, one of his cronies acting on his orders.

That he found hard to live with. Not a day had gone by in which he had not felt the ache of regret for what he had done. It had been wrong ... but then again, it would also have been wrong *not* to have done what he did. He had hoped that resigning from the police force would square things with his conscience – he was not betraying the law as a servant of the law. That was something at least. But it wasn't enough. The instincts he had built up over a lifetime could not be so easily dismissed;

they gnawed and gnawed, impervious to the rationalisations he tried to blanket them in. His sense of shame was strongest under the gaze of his wife Heather. She didn't know the whole story of course. She knew that his resignation had been prompted by him needing to break the rules to save a young colleague who had got out of his depth, but the actual details he had kept from her. He wasn't at all sure she would disapprove of the morality of his collusion with Snoddy's crowd, but he was sure she would damn its foolhardiness. He had stepped outside the social enclosure and exposed them both to the vicissitudes of the moral wilderness.

He would of course have to warn Justin. He had no contact number; that provided him with an excuse to phone his old friend Bruce Greenfield. As always, he found the good doctor in mid-enthusiasm for his latest project, in this case the draft of a presentation he was making to persuade the Board of St Judes to re-think modern languages provision in the school. Nothing could have been further removed from Stuart's current concerns, but before he knew it, he found himself taking the side of Russian over Chinese and agreeing that Spanish offered little to justify its place on the curriculum. When he finally got round to announcing the reason for his call, Greenfield showed no signs of alarm, assuring him that 'young Justin was sound in defence and would be sure to leave no gaps between bat and pad'. Conviction does not always convince, but Greenfield had a knack of getting it to punch above its weight. This – and an invitation to dinner the following Saturday – did much to revive Stuart's flagging spirits and quell the tone of anxiety in his voice when, having obtained the mobile number from Greenfield, he left a voicemail for Justin alerting him to the impending visitation.

Chapter 21

The trawl for applicants for the soon to be vacated Commons seat produced an unmanageable list of twenty-three. The task before the Panel in its opening session was to whittle this down to twelve from which a further shortlist of five would be drawn up at its second session. The interval would give the members the opportunity to study the applications in greater detail and to make their own inquiries about any individuals who aroused either interest or suspicion.

Schinski left it to the beginning of the week of the meeting before he called the number that Dooley had given him. He had thought the matter through and settled on a strategy. If Reggie didn't show willing, Dooley would be sure to nobble other members of the committee. In fact he was almost certain to have at least one other member in his pocket already. But Reggie's compliance would give him two votes for the price of one, for he naturally assumed that Schinski's vote would come with Reggie's. If he thought he had these two votes, plus a third or fourth that he was likely to have secured, he might become complacent and not trouble himself overly with canvassing further votes, at least not to the extent of offering sweeteners. An abject climb-down was what was called for. He could do a credible '*abject*'. Dooley would be at his peacock finest savouring the sorry surrender he would put on for him. But he would enjoy it just as much as the almighty lord would; the pride that would puff those jowls and tilt that chin up to 'haughty' would make the forthcoming fall all the sweeter. The telephone conversation was brief; a clear hint of compliance, but insistence that the matter should not discussed over the phone – security and all that. If Dooley wanted him to lick his master's fingers he would have to meet him here at his office. He expressed himself rather more delicately, but was quite firm in his resistance to Dooley's attempts to send a junior in his place. If a deal was to be done, the main man needed to be there.

When, a significantly short time afterwards, the great man arrived, Schinski gave every appearance of being impressed by the visual fanfare of self-importance. He had given the matter a great deal of thought, he said, and had realised he was asking the impossible in insisting on some kind of written undertaking. He would take Lord Dooley's word as a gentleman that he would honour their agreement. He just wanted to be clear on the exact terms of that agreement. *He and Reggie Whitehouse would do all in their power to ensure the nomination of ...?* It was with obvious aversion that Dooley filled in the gap – Cameron Brown. *He and Reggie Whitehouse would do all in their power to ensure the nomination of Cameron Brown as the candidate for Bury West.* Schinski spoke as if repeating words that had been set out for him to recite. The scene had all the hallmarks of a public occasion, a kind of ceremonial pledge of fealty to the party machine. Dooley seemed to pick up on the register and delivered his word of lordly honour in a like tone of solemnity. When the thing was done speech resumed to the less formal as Dooley sketched a few details of the MP-to-be for Bury West.

It was in fact *the* Cameron Brown, the big star of stage and screen. He was from an acting background; both parents had successful careers in the West End and his mother made a decent chunk of the family fortune doing television commercials. Young Cameron followed his parents on to the stage, but his extreme good looks marked him out for higher things. He soon came to the notice of the wider public as an action hero in blockbusters where he went around killing villains and seducing women; he was currently in line to take over the role of James Bond when existing contracts expired. As for his political experience, he had a distinguished record of support for left-wing causes but was best known for his anti-nuclear stance and his staunch internationalism. He'd been a paid-up member of the Party since his earliest days and in recent years had been more than generous with his donations. Getting a few MPs with that kind of profile was just what the party needed to win back public confidence after the disastrous years of ideological blindness. At this point Dooley became quite lyrical; the man obviously believed in something, even if it was only successfulness.

When the triumphant peer had left, Schinski returned to the humdrum routine of clerical chores. He went doggedly through his mail, which consisted mainly of correspondence relating to claims against employers, Sylvia having triaged the junk. There was however one letter that instantly brought a smile to his face – an invoice from a firm of electrical fitters specialising in electronic security systems. As he read it, he could see an image of good old Terry Cooper nodding in approval: 'Now there's a man who knew a thing of two about embarrassing indiscretions!'

Chapter 22

There were only two musicals Justin could summon any enthusiasm for, My Fair Lady and Calamity Jane. As far as he was concerned all the others came in varying degrees of staginess with songs that screamed self-satisfied membership of the genre. 'I'm a proper little gem of a musical song, aren't I just?' was what they all seemed so proud to establish. But Lizzie insisted on going. They had seen very little of each other over the past few weeks, so the least he could do was grin and bear it. He had even managed not to be ungracious; at least he thought he had. The pub afterwards was his reward for a good deed done. But the effort was not over even then; he still had to stifle his censorious promptings as Lizzie waxed lyrical about this and that.

When she went to the loo he checked his mobile – a voicemail and a text. The text was from Rob Snoddy; he was to dig up what he could on Cameron Brown. Cameron Brown? Why on earth would Snoddy want him to do that? Did he want him to go through another hoop and turn himself into a gossip columnist now? His immediate impulse was to phone Snoddy and ask for an explanation, but it was late and all the good work he had done to make the evening a 'shop-free' zone would be undone; it could wait until the morning. The voicemail was from a number that was vaguely familiar. When he played it, he instantly recognised the unmistakeably Ulster tones of Stuart Stranaghan. There was urgency in the voice. "Something has come up. You'll need to be prepared for an unwelcome visit. Get back to me as soon as you get this."

When Lizzie came back he made a joke about the guardians of the table relieving each other and made his way to the loo. The signal there was weak, so he went out into the street. As his former boss brought him up to speed, he felt a resurgence in the pit of his stomach of that chill of angst he for so long had had to live with at that time. He had forgotten the reality of it and now suddenly it was as if he had never been free of it. It was with supreme effort that he saw out the evening with Lizzie without giving in to the temptation to share his load with her.

When he got to bed sleep was hard to find. He had no trouble finding channels of drowsiness, but they were taking him just under the waves of consciousness, and before long he would be jolted back to the surface. Anxiety was reacting to the anaesthetic. In the end there was nothing for it but to get up and meet it head-on. He had to be clear on how much he could tell this police Inspector without pointing him in dangerous directions. He could tell him all about the mock trial and execution, no problem there. He would claim of course that he knew all along that it was a sham, a test the Prometheans had set for him to prove his bona fides. The earlier incident where he had had to carry out the flogging? Okay, that wasn't strictly what an undercover policeman should be doing, but, for Christ's sake, how else was he to gain any credibility? A policeman pretending to be a villain has to be allowed to do some villainy. As for his resignation, that was easy; he had fallen in love with Lizzie and besides he'd developed a liking for the whole experience of being a student at Oxford. Apart from anything else that was the truth, clearly, though, not the whole truth.

No, the more he thought about it, the safer he felt or, more accurately, the safer he thought he should feel. The messy bit was the bit that involved Stranaghan. How could Stranaghan explain his presence at the murder scene? An anonymous tip-off? Yes, but then how did he get on to Burrows? Another anonymous tip-off? And why were they given to *him*? *He* wasn't involved in the Rodgers' case. The tips surely had to have come from someone in Snoddy's crowd, if not from Snoddy himself, and yet the Inspector hadn't followed up on this. In fact it didn't even get a mention in his final report. That would hardly look good, would it, considering the whole point of the undercover operation was to collect evidence against Snoddy? That was bad enough, but even more damaging was the remarkable coincidence of the Prometheans conducting a mock execution of Rodgers and then the body of the very same man turning up immediately afterwards and in a location remarkably similar to the one where the role play had been enacted. If you were of a fanciful nature you might look on this as one of the ironies that chance throws up, but anyone rooted to common sense would be bound to conclude that the Prometheans were the ones behind it; they had simply followed through on their self-appointed mission of ridding the world of a vicious criminal ... Yes, it all hinged on that; this man Myles mustn't on any account find out that it was Rodgers' trial and execution they had faked. If that were kept from him, he would have no reason to doubt the innocence of the charade.

Chapter 23

When Myles presented himself, shortly after breakfast the following morning, Justin made a passable show of surprise.

"So Inspector Stranaghan hasn't been in touch? You didn't know I was coming?"

The question demanded a step-up in feigned bafflement and an awakening of curiosity.

"Inspector Stranaghan? Why on earth would Inspector Stranaghan be telling me to expect you?"

"I've come to ask you about the undercover investigation you made into Robert Snoddy and his crowd."

Justin found it hard to gauge whether Myles had not addressed his question out of scepticism or as an acceptance of its validity. He knew he mustn't overcook his incredulity, so he plumped for getting the wrong end of the stick.

"Are you telling me the case has been reopened? Well, all I can say is 'Good luck with that.' I'll do anything I can do to help, of course. I must say, I'm surprised. Snoddy's lot don't keep within the law – they're keen on their punishment floggings. I'm sure you've read my report. You'll know that I had to pitch in myself. Nasty business! However we found no evidence of anything more sinister. We'd thought they might go as far as murder, but it was all smoke and mirrors. They played at it, but they didn't go the whole hog. When this became clear, we pulled the operation. Getting hard evidence against them for the flogging would have taken a lot of time and resources; it simply wasn't worth the effort."

Myles was happy to play along with Justin's seemingly mistaken assumption that it was Snoddy rather than himself that was the focus of the new inquiry. He got Justin to take him

119

through the whole operation from the beginning: his early experiences of playing the role of an undergraduate, the people he met, how he managed to infiltrate the organisation, details of the operations he was involved in and, finally, that mock trial and execution.

"At what point did you realise that it wasn't for real?"

Justin knew that this question would be coming. He had come up with several stories he might spin, none of them totally convincing. In the end he had had to pick the best of a bad lot.

"I recognised the fellow who was playing the part of the prisoner. He had been one of my so-called 'facilitators'. He was heavily disguised and he's a professional actor, but there was something in his manner that clicked with me, and once you get an inkling the whole illusion falls apart."

"So you're telling me that it was only when you got to the barn where the execution was to take place that you realised that it wasn't for real? How then were you proposing to get yourself out of the situation? There you were in a firing squad with a rifle in your hand about to shoot someone dead – I just don't see how you were going to avoid going through with it!"

"To be perfectly honest, Inspector, I realised that I was totally out of my depth. When I was summoned to the trial I thought they were on to me and that I was the one they were targeting. I was mightily relieved, I can tell you, when I realised that I'd got it wrong. I had to go along with them. It wasn't just a case of staying in character – I thought my life was on the line. I knew that there was nothing I could do to save the prisoner. The only thing I could do was to make sure my bullet would miss – if this poor bugger was going to die it wouldn't be any of my doing."

He could see that this answer was distasteful to the Inspector; it was messy, but the very messiness of it was what would surely sell it as authentic. There was a long pause before the Inspector continued. Clearly, time was needed for the unpalatable nugget to clear the digestion.

"You were a bit vague in your report about the details of the mock trial. You gave a detailed account of the nuts and bolts, but you didn't have much to say about the actual case against the accused. What was the actual crime that the accused was being charged with?"

The change of tack was disconcerting. This was the area he needed to protect. Even without mentioning Rodgers by name, if he told the Inspector that it was about the abduction and sadistic murder of a young man who had crossed a gang of thugs by standing up for a defenceless victim it would be immediately obvious that it was Rodgers that had been in the dock. He had to come up with a different narrative.

"It was the type of case the Prometheans specialise in, one of those where the Law decides to pussyfoot around rather than do the job it's there to do."

"Yes, but what exactly was the case that was being tried?"

"It was a murder case. The accused had killed his girlfriend because he thought she was going to report him to the police for selling drugs, and he had got off because all his mates swore he was with them when the murder took place."

"What made you so sure he was guilty? If the prosecution couldn't break the alibi at the real trial, how were you able to do it?"

He was getting dragged into too much detail. The whole skill about telling lies is in keeping them simple.

"We had the testimony of a witness who was a close friend of the girl. She told us the girl had threatened to inform the police after an incident when a user had died after.... her abusive boyfriend ... had supplied him with bad stuff. He had beaten her up and she feared for her life."

"What was the name of this 'abusive boyfriend' by the way?"

Myles had been quick to spot the hesitation. Justin had come very close to saying 'Rodgers' and had just in time corrected it to the rather clumsy 'her abusive boyfriend'.

121

"Robinson . . . Jack Robinson, that was it, I think."

Myles grinned incredulously.

"Really? You'd have thought they could have come up with a more convincing name."

"Yes, you would, wouldn't you?"

A way of turning his gaffe to his advantage suddenly suggested itself. He seized on it.

"Yes, that was one of the things that made me a bit sceptical."

As soon as this came out he became painfully aware of how much of a nonsense this made of his feigned uncertainty over remembering the name in the first place. Fortunately Myles failed to pick up on it.

"But you must have had more than that surely."

"Yes, Maggie – that was the victim's name – was on the phone to our witness – I can't remember her name – when Robinson caught her and accused her of snitching on him to the police. As she was talking Robinson came into the room and demanded to know who she was talking to. He seized the phone from her and asked who he was talking to. Our witness didn't know what to do. She just yelled at him to leave Maggie alone and then foolishly told him that Maggie was going to pack her bags and make a new life for herself away from him and his scuzzy friends. This produced a torrent of abuse and then she heard repeated screams and the sound of blows being landed. After that the phone went dead. When the police found Maggie's body there was no sign of her phone; it was never found, even though she was known never to go anywhere without it."

"So why didn't your witness come forward? With her evidence the police were almost certain to get a conviction."

"She did. She told the police exactly what I've just told you. They had her signed statement. But then she was got at. One of Robinson's mates, who also happened to be one of the ones who swore he was with them at the time of the murder, came round and made threats against her family. She was in no doubt that he meant what he said. She withdrew her statement and refused to appear as a witness. The prosecution had to drop the charges."

Justin was pleased with himself. He had been a very convincing liar. The story had tripped off his tongue. The Inspector obviously believed him. But then an uncomfortable truth dawned; the reason he had been able to make it up so seamlessly was that he had been following the main threads of the real story. He had taken the Inspector far too close to the Rodgers' case.

"So you had no doubts about Robinson's guilt. How did Snoddy take it from there? How did you convince him that you had become a convert?"

"He asked the three of us if we thought the death penalty was appropriate in this case. The others answered they did and in theory I had no problem with it either. I thought it was all hypothetical, so it didn't matter. In any case, I've always felt that the law lets murder victims down. So, no problem – I agreed. But then the bolt from the blue! Snoddy asked us if we were just spouting cheap pub talk. Were we prepared to put our money where our mouth was and do the deed ourselves? I got the distinct feeling that I was as much a target as Robinson was, he was testing me out. And so later, when I recognised the supposed prisoner, the whole thing fell into place"

"You say this was based on a real case. Can you give me the details of the trial? I'd like to have a look at the transcript myself."

Justin had seen this coming.

"We thought at the time that we were dealing with an actual miscarriage of justice. And that was the basis we worked on, but Snoddy later told me they had made it all up. So it was just as phoney as everything else."

Myles was clearly disappointed.

"So what happened after the phoney execution? Did you all just pack up and go on your merry ways?"

"No, we went to chill out at one of Eardley's lodges."

"I noticed you didn't give any names to the others in your report. Were they not known to you? Hadn't you come across them before?"

This was another danger zone. He had been careful to keep Joseph's out of his report. Joseph was the last person he wanted this Inspector to be talking to. It was a risk not admitting that he was there, but it would be an even greater risk letting the Inspector loose on him. He was out of the picture now and there was no reason to think that Myles would get on to him. So, like a man escaping from a bear and running towards a wolf pack, he committed himself to a denial of any knowledge of the identity of his fellow jurors-come-executioners. Myles expressed surprise at this, given that Justin's job had been to collect information. But he seemed to be satisfied with the explanation that open curiosity about his fellow jurors would have aroused suspicion, the last thing Justin needed at a time when he thought he was already in their sights. Myles moved on. He was curious as to why Justin had decided to abandon a police career that had barely begun. This was easy meat, the tension wound down and the interview ended amicably with the two men comparing notes on the experience of working with Inspector Stranaghan, a man, they both agreed, made of the right stuff.

Chapter 24

When the Panel met to select the twelve from which the shortlist was to be drawn up the task did not prove onerous. There were a couple of marginal decisions to be taken at the thin end of the list, but Snoddy and Brown were comfortable inclusions. There was one other name that stood out from the rest, George Sinclair. Sinclair had constantly featured in the national headlines thirty-odd years previously as a militant Glasgow councillor. His face had been the darling of newspaper cartoonists and his voice, a no-prisoners-taken, Celtic-warrior *basso profundo* had inspired mimicry both hammy and professional throughout the land. He had the title deeds to a whole swathe of anti-Tory invectives and could lay claim to the most vicious enunciation of 'Thatcher' and 'Tory cuts' of anyone to the left of the Tory wets. He had done all he could at local level, he said in his application, and now it was time for him to enter the wider world of national politics. He could certainly pose a problem for Snoddy's selection. There were still many in the Party who preferred the familiarity of hard-rock protest to the wussy discipline of *realpolitik*. But, then again, there might be mileage in that for Snoddy. In any case there was nothing to be done to block Sinclair's progress at this stage.

Schinski had decided for the time being not to share the burden of Lord Dooley's intervention with Whitehouse. When Reggie's emotions were off the leash there was no knowing what follies they might commit. Much easier to confine him to the rational sector of his brain, however lacking that might be. There he was less likely to come up with anything robust enough to resist Schinski's promptings. Schinski as yet had no master plan in place to shape these 'promptings', but at least he'd have a blank sheet to work on when the time came.

Meetings were Schinski's pasture lands. The babble of half thought-out ideas, wrong-headed convictions and misplaced questions produced a sense of urgency in his brain to create order, any kind of order. In the process ideas would invariably pop up, some of them indistinguishable from the babble, but some worthy of more elaboration. In the course of this meeting one such idea did present itself. He decided to run with it. He proposed that each member of the Panel be assigned a name from the list, do all the necessary research on that particular candidate and report back to the next meeting. He didn't want to pre-empt in any way the final decisions the Panel might make, but it seemed fairly clear that there were three applicants that stood out and would therefore require more rigorous investigation than the rest. When asked to identify these three, he feigned an air of embarrassed surprise, one of those coy looks that drip regret for exposing the fact that there are people present not sharp enough to be spared an explanation.

"Well, there's George Sinclair for a start. The man's a legend. We'd need a very good reason indeed not to give him a full run. Secondly, there's Cameron Brown, another name that the public will instantly recognise. He's a certain vote-winner. We couldn't possibly rule him out."

He paused long enough to allow himself to be prompted to name the third 'no-brainer'. In the act of replying the words came out intermittently; it was clear they were being distracted by thought.

"Well, I suppose, on reflection, the third candidate is not so obvious. Indeed, on reflection, I don't think it would be fair to name him. As it looks to me he might even be the pick of the bunch, but clearly I've jumped the gun. Let's wait and see. Let him sink or swim in the mix with the others. If I'm right about him, he'll emerge. If not, no harm done."

Despite the predictable attempts to get him to identify this 'third man', Schinski stuck to his guns. It wasn't the curiosity of his co-panellists that he wished to excite so much as to sow an ambition in them to come up independently with 'the right answer'. His proposal was adopted and the remainder of the meeting was spent allocating candidates to panellists. As the sitting member Reggie was given first pick. Schinski suggested he should take one of the two front runners and, knowing the history between Whitehouse and Sinclair, he had no doubt that it would be Brown he would choose. Sinclair was snapped up by Roberts. The two men were longstanding friends and allies, comrades in arms in the holy war against Thatcherism and all things Thatcherite. Apart from the lone female candidate, a Ms Willoughby, pre-emptively bagged by Maggie Millership, the rest of the list was gone through alphabetically. When Snoddy's name came up, Freddie Douglas expressed casual interest and faced no competition in securing his lot. This produced a wry smile from his mentor. A judicious word had passed between them at the coffee break. The mentor himself was of course at pains to keep his carefully prepared powder dry and stay clear of association with any of the names on the list. In the end he was allocated a couple of candidates whom no one else felt moved to volunteer for.

Chapter 25

When they met for a much needed drink after the Panel meeting Reggie Whitehouse gave full vent to his feelings on the '*honour*' conferred on him of having his pick of candidates to investigate.

"What the f . . . do I want with that? Do they think I'm some kind of hack?"

Schinski's face took on a broad grin. He knew exactly how the aspiring peer would look on the prospect of putting in hours of tedium in the pursuit of God-knows-what. For the likes of Reggie empirical knowledge came cooked and served; it wasn't something you had to hunt and kill and skin for yourself. But Derek Schinski knew otherwise. He knew the difference between a mass-produced ready-meal and a chef's special. Those little details that hide themselves away beneath the common knowledge, they are the ones that have the kind of energy that can be turned into power.

"Don't worry, Reggie. I'll do the work. All you'll have to do is present it. . . with bright-eyed enthusiasm. I'd like maximum brightness by the way."

Reggie didn't know whether he was party to this cynicism or the object of it. He never quite knew with Schinski. He inclined on the side of taking offence.

"Why the hell should I show any enthusiasm for a nancy boy like Cameron Brown?"

"Listen, Reggie. I'm not asking you to *have* enthusiasm, I'm just asking you to *show* it. The powers-that-be are keen on our bold boy becoming the next MP for Bury West. And they want us to cooperate. So we must be seen to cooperate. If you're serious about wanting that seat on the green benches, you'll need to do your best John-the-Baptist impression and tell the Panel all about the new Jesus Christ."

"But what about the deal we have with the Snoddy crowd?"

"Let me worry about that. We don't have to get Brown nominated; we only have to do our best. And it's up to us to do our best to ensure that our best isn't good enough, isn't it?"

Next on the Schinski agenda was a meet with Freddie Douglas. He had managed a quick word during the coffee break at the Panel meeting, but he hadn't been able to go into his reasons for getting him to take on the research on Snoddy. He had decided to be frank with Freddie, or at least as frank as he needed to be. Freddie knew how important it was for him to have a man like Schinski as a sponsor and would be more than willing to earn the privilege. As long as he was assured that his time would come he would be content for the moment to put in a good stint on the Schinski team. That aside, Schinski really liked Freddie. He reminded him of the image he had of himself when he was Freddie's age. It was the nearest thing a bachelor with no parental ambitions could have to fatherly feelings. He savoured the thought that at some time in the future he would be in a position to make the what-might-have-been for himself become a reality for his protégé.

The Welcoming Arms was the venue of choice for the confab. It was one of those old Victorian pubs that curled up its lip at all the kitsch inflicted on it over the years by its various proprietors in their efforts to modernise; it was shoddy certainly, but in its very shoddiness it somehow exposed the indignity of the compulsion to fashion. In this setting Schinski could see himself as the successor to a long line of forebears, cloth-capped shop stewards who in premises such as these had triumphed over, smooth-talking management in the relentless struggle for a better deal for the working man. Every time he was seated here with a pint before him he could catch in his mind's ear distant strains of the great proletarian folk theme; it's the closest brush he ever had with idealism.

Freddie greeted his arrival with his usual matter-of-factness. Freddie always seemed to put him down as a 'pint man'. If truth be told, Schinski was not a drinker and, if anything, preferred cider, but he was perfectly happy to 'get into character' here in The Welcoming Arms and drink the drink of the glory days. His pint was already waiting for him on the table next to the gin and tonic that Freddie had ordered for himself.

"Okay. Why am I so anxious to do the report on this Snoddy fellow then?"

"You are anxious because it will give you the opportunity to be the man who was the first to pick the winner. There's as much kudos to be had these days from spotting genius as there is to having it yourself."

"So this Snoddy's a genius, is he?"

"Well, maybe not a genius, more I'd say a genie. If we can get him out of the bottle and into the House he could do us a lot of good, and I don't know about you, but I have a wish or two that I wouldn't say no to him granting."

"He'd be able to do that, would he?"

"I'd *say* he would. He has a lot of powerful friends in high places. I think it would be very much to our advantage to make him owe us a biggish favour. He's hell bent on becoming an MP and he's willing to do what it takes."

"Yes, but will he be willing to do what it has already taken? Once he's elected, he won't need us anymore. What makes you think he'll settle his debt?"

"You know me; I only see the good in people. The history of mankind is a fantastic tale of noble deeds and men whose word was their bond. Well, I'm not much of a romantic, you can keep the fantasy, but I do like deeds and I do like bonds; it's the failed lawyer in me I suppose."

It took a second or two of mental readjustment for the penny to drop. When it did Freddie let out a guffaw.

"So what kind of bond do you have in mind?"

"You can leave that to me, Freddie. You concentrate on producing a glowing report, one that will have the Panel eating out of Snoddy's hands. I'll see what I can do about coming up with something that will have our future MP eating out of ours."

"But what makes you think there will be something to come up with?"

"I've done a bit of research myself and I think there are a few dark secrets lurking not too far beneath the surface. He was tried for murder you know. He was accused of killing the headmaster of the posh school he went to. He got off; in fact the judge threw out the case, it should never have got to court, he said. Snoddy wrote a book about it, a novel. I've just read it. The odd thing is: in the novel at least, it's perfectly obvious that Snoddy was as guilty as hell even though the evidence he produces in court proves beyond doubt that he wasn't. He went on and got a first at Oxford and ever since he has been involved in an organisation calling itself The New Prometheans. They claim – what is it they say? – Oh yes, they claim that 'the light of reason has been hijacked by the professional classes' and it is time it was handed over to the people. You can see how that ties in with his determination to be a Labour MP. You'll need to make the most of that in your report for the Panel. But this Prometheans thing, I think there's more to it than meets the eye. It all looks very dodgy. We've someone on it. When he's finished his digging I'll be surprised if he doesn't unearth a few nuggets that our Mr Snoddy will be very anxious to keep below ground."

The 'someone' referred to was of course Graham Myles. George Bailey had contacted Schinski when he had got wind of Justin Wright sniffing around. That's when the decision was taken to set Myles to work. The two men had vulnerabilities in common, but that is as far as their association went. Schinski had never liked Bailey. He couldn't fault him for being as calcu-

131

lating as himself, but he found him much too cold a fish. Cold fish always gave such predictably one-dimensional briefs to their ingenuity; they gave the noble art of manipulating fellow humans a bad name.

Chapter 26

Robert Snoddy was what most people would call 'a loner'. He liked his own company better than most of what was on offer on the outside. There were a few exceptions – Bruce Greenfield, his old German teacher, Matthew Eardley, the man with the money behind his great project and, although it took him a long time to realise it, Stuart Stranaghan, the police Inspector who had made it his business to get him locked up. He felt the same way about Stranaghan as boxers seem to feel about a worthy opponent who has shown courage and dignity in defeat. When Stranaghan lived up to the expectations he had of him and showed willing to sacrifice his own career in an act of loyalty to his junior officer, he achieved identity in Snoddy's eyes; amid all the cant thought and cheap feeling that swirl in the social waters, here was a man who was prepared to be a man, someone who forged his own rule book out of his own life experience.

Of course there was also Naomi . . . and Justin, Justin Wright, the young officer who Stranaghan thought he was rescuing from his clutches. He didn't quite know what to make of Justin's conversion to the cause. Was he to be admired for having the guts to fly in the face of the conventional social code? Or was his change of heart simply evidence of a weak-minded unwilling-ness to resist the pressures of the immediate moral landscape? He was inclined to give him the benefit of the doubt, but recently the man had started to go flaky. That had to be down to the influence of Lizzie Partridge. He had come under her thumb. Lizzie was a bright girl, but she was far too afraid of her own brightness; her brain was under strict orders: 'Never allow your thoughts a free run lest they get ahead of group-think and group-feel.' He had had a fling with Lizzie himself, but he'd never been able to prise her away from her barnacle grip on orthodoxy. With most people he would put this down to simple witlessness, but what was galling about Lizzie was that she was more than capable of appreciating, even savouring the subtlety of sophisticated argument. You'd think you had convinced her and then she would turn round and dismiss your entire line of reasoning. What did she call reasoned debate? ... a clever little game for clever little boys, but a complete waste of time when it comes to the grown-up business of living a life. Her take on thought was utterly demoralising. It conjured up an image of a wheel spinning furiously, generating heat and even smoke, and yet somehow failing to achieve any traction. Justin was welcome to the bitch. Maybe *he* would find an antidote to her damned witchery, but somehow he doubted it.

He had been told to expect a Frederick Douglas to call on him at 11 o'clock. He felt just as he had done the morning of his viva. Would he get a fool to impress or a brain to battle with? In academe the two are not mutually exclusive; in fact one is the horse to the other's carriage. Directionless intellectuality is just as bad as mindless rigidity. How many academic papers had he read and ended up asking himself why the hell the authors had bothered. Maybe that's the way Lizzie saw him? Bitch! According to Schinski, Douglas was there to find praises to sing to the Selection Panel, but he'd need to suss out the man before he'd know what praises to supply him with. The song must suit the singer if it is to please the audience. When he had asked Schinski what to expect he had been told to expect a sharp wit operating at ground level and focused on only one thing, how to get where he wanted to go. That was clearly true of Schinski himself. Maybe he was merely crediting to others what he would credit to himself.

The first thing that stood out about Douglas when Naomi ushered him into his study was the sartorial splendour of the man – three-piece suit of obvious quality, silk tie, and cuffs that protruded just enough from the sleeves to reveal their stiffness. His hair was got up in a web of sophistication; it was clearly a coiffure that had never been snipped under a barber's pole. The shoes, dark grey matching his suit, had a lacquered shine reminiscent of tap-dancing footwear of the Fred Astaire era. Snoddy had no idea whether this represented the height of businessman chic or if he was projecting himself as a one-off dandy. In any case he was not one for an eye to miss. The ear too was almost instantly engaged. The *assessor* spoke with a formality that belied his age. He couldn't be any older than Snoddy and yet he spoke in a bizarre blend of working class proper and anachronistic posh. Snoddy immediately recognised the phenomenon; he himself was similarly prone, but took the more conventional route of calling on vulgarism to offset it.

There was chat of this and that before Naomi brought in the coffee. First name terms were rather clumsily established as were the roles of interviewer and interviewee as the tit-for-tat sharing of biographical detail gradually gave way to one-sided questioning. Douglas did not take long to cut to the chase.

"Tell me Robert, what makes you think that someone who has been tried for murder would make a suitable parliamentary candidate?"

"Someone who had been *convicted* of murder certainly wouldn't. But someone who had been completely exonerated, and whom the judge was angry about even having to try, is surely in the same position as someone who hasn't been accused in the first place."

"Well hardly. Mud does stick, does it not?"

"Mud that has been falsely imported, do you mean? Isn't that what is known as a smear campaign? Surely when mud gets thrown, those who throw it are just as likely to be smeared as those who are targeted. Anybody who throws mud is bound to get it on his hands, but it's far from certain that he'll land it on his intended target."

"There's some truth in that, but I'm curious, why did you allow it to come to trial at all? You had all the evidence you needed to prove your innocence well in advance of the trial. You saw the reaction of the judge; as you said, he was very put out with you for wasting the court's time."

"Simple. I had been wrongly accused and I wanted my day in court. The establishment had messed up. If they'd got it right and I'd been guilty, they would have made a public spectacle of me. Well, I wanted to make a public spectacle of them. It was my humble little version of 'J'accuse'."[2]

"But what exactly was it you were accusing them of?"

"I was accusing them of what I call professional narcissism. The professional class has no appetite for the messy chaotic scenarios that reality throws up for them to deal with. So they re-work them, sanitise them and shape them into more ordered, more tractable narratives and take it from there. They then dose themselves with amnesia pills and convince themselves they have addressed the original problem. It's a bit like the algebra problems you get at school. You know the answer will always come out in whole numbers. If it doesn't, you know you've got it wrong. Social professionals – lawyers, teachers, politicians – that's their stock-in-trade, that's how they clear their in-boxes. It wouldn't be so bad, if they didn't have the effrontery to tell the people at the sharp end that everything has been sorted. If anyone has the temerity to point out that actually everything isn't sorted, they're dismissed as obsessives, bigots or idiots. Plebs, you see, don't have the brains to follow the subtle intricacies of professional 'solutions', so how can they expect their opinions to be taken seriously? Well, I think it's high time an institution like the Labour Party weighed in on the side of the little people."

---

[2] Reference to the trial of Dreyfus, a Jewish officer in the French army wrongly accused of being a spy. The trial was a public scandal and let to a major shakeup of the French establishment.

Douglas leaned back in his chair and placed his hands behind his head. The smile on his face registered appreciation of what had been said, but the look he was directing towards the ceiling suggested a flaw had been spotted.

"That sounds all very worthy, Robert, but do you really think the Panel will buy it? They're not a stupid lot, far from it in fact, but they're not the sort to be going in for Oxford debates. You'll need to give them something a bit more concrete than that to work with."

"Okay, let's get down to brass tacks. On education, let's liberate the working class from the drivel that the educational establishment feeds to them – no more Mickey Mouse studies, no more our-customers-are-always-right exam boards, no more failure paranoia: fewer heart procedures, more brain surgery. On the law, let's protect the public from the low life that pollutes their lives – the restoration of the concept of punishment for crimes, trials that deal in sensible reasoning and not Cartesian proofs. On politics, let's use a moral compass that is approved by ordinary people, not a decadent metropolitan elite drowning in moral agnosticism."

The wince that this produced was playfully exaggerated. Douglas' hands were removed from the back of his head and he leaned forward.

"That's quite a bagful, Robert. Do you have any more sacred party-cows lurking in it ready for the slaughter? It seems to me you don't so much want to represent the Labour Party. You want the Labour Party to represent you."

"No. I want the Labour Party to represent itself, and put an end to its longstanding indulgence in humbug and bad faith. Let's shock the Guardianista of Primrose Hill; let's start looking out for the upwardly mobile in places like Bolton and Hartlepool."

"Why only the upwardly mobile? Surely, it's the poor we socialists should be concerned with, whether they're upwardly mobile or not?"

"The instant 'No' that this evoked from Snoddy was shorn of the playful, slightly impish tone that had accompanied his discourse up till now.

"No! There's no merit in being poor, just as there's nothing to be ashamed about it either. Apart from the very young, the sick and the elderly, people should be encouraged and helped in proportion to the efforts they make. Those who make little or no effort don't deserve to reap what they haven't sown. That's one of the most pivotal blunders the Party has been making. They've bought into the most saccharin elements of the New Testament and swallowed them whole. The Labour Party is not a woolly Christian sect; it's an organisation that aspires to run the economy of a major country and should be driven by an ethic that is rooted in the hard reality of survival, not floating in some airy-fairy sentimental vapour. You ask honest people, people who live at the coal face of survival, what they mean by morality and you'll get a very different list of priorities from what you'll hear at high table. More important – crucially important – the people who espouse that unsophisticated morality actually live by it. In the most literal sense, they keep body and soul together. That's a hell of a lot more than can be said of the moral high fliers, who come crashing to the ground the moment morality comes calling on their own personal lives and they're asked to put their money where their mouth is. They're quite prepared of course to put in government money; they'll find homes for the feckless, next door not to them of course, but to the very people whose morality they despise; they'll forgive and forget rapists and murderers and let them loose on the social services of the lower classes. For them morality is all about making virtuous decisions about what other people should do."

Douglas was visibly impressed, but there was an element of reluctance in his admiration which was not to be swept aside.

"I assume that is the moral base for this organisation of yours, The New Prometheans, I believe you call yourselves? I'll be frank. I'm disturbed about what I've heard about it. I'm told it's been the subject of police investigations. Some kind of vigilantism, I believe?"

"You've heard wrong. Vigilantism is an ugly thing that puts the outrage at the crime above the cold facts of the case. We don't advocate that. It's the job of the Law to focus on the facts and sift out the truth; that's what confers legitimacy on the punishment that follows a guilty verdict. Most people assume that it is the state's ownership of the law that confers this legitimacy, but that's not true. If it were, what's to stop a regime like Hitler's Nazis or some tin-pot dictator claiming the legitimacy to pursue a programme of genocide? If a case goes through the courts and is conducted in accordance with the due process, should the sentence command respect, no matter what? Clearly not. You might argue that such regimes are not democratic and therefore not reflective of the will of the people, they are consequently disqualified from conferring legitimacy on their courts. It sounds vaguely plausible; but how should we react to those same courts imposing punishments on rapists or child killers? Would we say that since the courts lacked legitimacy, those criminals should walk free, at least until such time as a legitimate regime is put in place? Of course we wouldn't. And what does this tell us? It tells us that our judgements are based on what we perceive as justice, and not on the principle of state backing."

Snoddy paused to test for attention. He had been told time and again by Naomi and others not to overestimate the attention span of his audience. If he was to be successful in politics he must learn to curb his intellectual enthusiasm. For God's sake, most people read tabloids, if they read at all. Books with sentences that consort with a second subordinate clause or, Heaven forbid, a sub-subordinate clause, come with a public warning as being dangerously outside civic wavelengths. Douglas' failure to come in at this point was a sign either that he had totally lost the thread or that he was following the argument and didn't feel any need to escape. The busy look in his eyes tipped the balance towards the latter assumption and Snoddy continued.

"In this country we don't have the problem of dealing with despotic or racist government, thank God. But we do have a problem. We have allowed a professional class to take over the law and tell the rest of us that they know best. It's very similar to the mediaeval church conducting its affairs in Latin and shutting down any challenge from the laity. It's a common enough phenomenon. Given enough time, detail inevitably smothers the big picture and process takes over. Over time many of the rules and practices which the law has evolved have become enshrined as holy writ even when it can be shown that they are inimical to the ends they are supposed to be serving. The truth that dares not speak its name is that our courts are not holy places; they are simple workshops and they are to be judged on their ability to get that work done."

"So you set up your own courts and dispense justice according to your own lights? Is that what The New Prometheans is all about?"

Douglas had indeed been following him very well.

"No, that's not what we do; that's what the police thought we did. The New Prometheans want to carry the light of the law and the fire that goes with that light back to the people. The Foundation investigates and logs cases that the courts have been too mealy-minded to think through, but it does more than that. If the people are to take back possession of the Law from the professionals they must shown themselves to be up to the job. It's one thing to express support for harsh punishments, especially the death penalty, when you are standing safely behind a pint in the pub and sharing your thoughts with like-minded buddies. It's quite another thing to engage in the sordid business of implementing such punishments. That's the other side to our programme; we set up realistic simulations of punishment scenarios and monitor how people respond to the reality of the punishment they advocate. We hope to build up a picture of the psychology of moral decision-making. If there was a referendum tomorrow on the death penalty it would probably go through with an overwhelming majority. The trouble is that within a year of its implementation, after the press had had a few field days supplying graphic accounts of the prisoners' last hours and the pain and anguish caused to their nearest-and-dearest, there would be a clamour for a second referendum and the first one would be reversed. Each result would be as meaningless as the other. Both would be based on a childish take on the world. The New Prometheans are concerned with finding out how much grown-up morality modern people are capable of."

A moment of silence followed that came over as somehow Snoddy's due. Douglas gave a substantive nod of the head, rose from his chair, reached forward and shook Snoddy by the hand. There was a broad smile on his face as he asked a parting question; the smile had an innocence that seemed at the same time to acknowledge and disavow an undertone of sarcasm.

"I have your assurance, do I, Mr Snoddy, that your organisation ... sorry, your foundation ... has never indulged in any activities that the CPS might feel obliged to involve itself in?"

Snoddy's reply took its cue from the spirit of the question.

"Never, Mr Douglas, never."

"I will quote you on that."

Mutual understanding had been registered and sealed.

Chapter 27

"What have you come up with? Please don't tell me that Cameron Brown is the goody-two-shoes that his PR people would have us believe."

The question was from Derek Schinski to Justin Wright.

"No, he's not a goody-two-shoes, but he's boringly ordinary, which is almost as bad, isn't it?"

"You found nothing?"

"Well, the usual things. His looks have taken him a long way. When I say 'looks', I don't just mean he's handsome. He goes in for *significant* looks as well; he does them very well and he has the wit not to spoil them by doing too much talking. Mind you, that's as far as his wit goes. He's not the clearest of thinkers. He has a few little set pieces about Tories and capitalism and he does a good line on compassion, not all gushy like most of his crowd – understated, he does it in negative, a couple of words of sympathy scattered here and there, then a quick switch to venom at the bad guys, the ones he puts down for all the dark matter in the moral universe. You know the kind of thing. It works a treat."

"What does he do with his money? Can we get him there?"

"No, I don't think so; he has his fast cars, of course, and the mansion. That's in fact where I interviewed him, all the latest gadgetry, and the obligatory swimming pool – that goes without saying. All the rooms are minimalist; you get the impression of being in a film set. I think the man's constantly on show for himself. But apart from all that, he's been quite generous. There's his big charity, Acting for Action. He has pumped quite a lot of his own money into that and he has got a lot of his cronies to sign up. They insert a paragraph into the theatre programmes and they do a spiel at the end of the performance appealing for donations, and then there's all the publicity they get in the press – it doesn't do the charity, nor for that matter their careers, any harm. To date the charity has accumulated a sum in excess of four million pounds."

"And where does the money go? No dark secrets there?"

"Not as far as I can tell. It's all above board. They work with bigger charities and fund projects in the Third World."

"What about the donations he has made to the Party? Where does that money come from?"

"That seems to come directly out of his own personal funds. No, I think you're flogging a dead horse there."

Schinski took a sip of the coffee Sylvia had brought in and pondered the situation. JFB had offered him Wright when he told him he needed someone to do some digging on Cameron. He supposed Wright knew his business. But even if he didn't it was too late to engage another sleuth. A change of tack was what was needed.

"You say our theatrical hero is not the sharpest cookie. He hasn't done too badly considering. There's got to be someone pulling his strings. Do you have any idea who that might be?"

"No problem there. His father died when he was just a boy and his uncle has been his guiding light ever since. You might have heard of the uncle – Gary Adamson? He was a rising star himself in the TUC way back in the eighties, but he backed the wrong horse. He was one of Scargill's henchmen. After that, he faded into the background – local council, that kind of thing. But he has done a good job grooming his nephew and he's having the time of his life with this second bite of the cherry."

Schinski's face suddenly brightened.

"So, that's the way of it; he writes the scripts and his thespian nephew performs them. Now there's something we can work on. Let's put our heads together and see if we can come up with a few cherries for Comrade Adamson to chew on. And then we'll see how well the nephew gets on spewing it all out."

Chapter 28

Inspector Myles' inquiries were not proving productive. The explanation Justin Wright had offered for his actions had seemed convincing enough, but then experience told the Inspector that it is only when you hear an account of events from a second or third angle that you are able to get a reliable fix on the truth. It's the basic principle of navigation. What he needed was to talk to some of the minor figures in the drama. The name that kept popping up was Lizzie Partridge. He knew that she and Justin had got married, so it was a question of calling on her when Justin wasn't at home. It was Saturday morning; Lizzie would not be at school and Justin was more than likely out doing what reporters do. He phoned the landline. Sure enough, it was Lizzie who answered. *Mr Wright was not there and he wasn't interested in a timeshare in Cyprus.*

The Lizzie that a few minutes later answered the doorbell threatened to be just as frosty. Maybe there had been other cold callers that morning or maybe it was resentment at not being the person in demand, but Myles' inquiry as to whether Mr Wright was at home met with a very petulant 'No, he's out!'.

"Well then, maybe you can help me. Elizabeth Partridge isn't it? Or have you taken your husband's name?"

Impatience gave way to suspicion at the mention of her name, but before she could come out with the indignant 'What's that to you?' that was on her lips, Myles followed up.

"My name is Graham Myles. I'm a police officer and I'm making some inquiries that your husband has been helping me with."

Suspicion remained, but it changed hue.

"You're not a friend of Justin's then, an old colleague of his?"

"No, I have just recently met him. As I said, he's filling in a few details for me about a case he was involved in."

In order to avoid opening up old wounds Justin had not mentioned Myles' visit to her, so this came somewhat as a shock. Since Justin's brief police career had only amounted to the one operation, there could be no doubt as to what case was being referred to. Clearly she needed to be on her guard.

"Your in-put would be very welcome, Miss Partridge or I should say, Mrs Wright. I'm trying to build up a picture of the scene at Oxford. You knew Robert Snoddy, didn't you?"

She knew that if she answered, she would be accepting engagement, but it was impossible not to reply.

"Partridge is fine. Yes, I did know Robert Snoddy, but I think you'd best talk to Justin. He didn't take me into his confidence. I had no idea he was an undercover policeman As far as I was concerned, he was just a fellow undergraduate trying to get a decent degree."

"I understand that, Ms Partridge. That's not what I'm concerned with. I'd just like you to fill me in on what kind of things went on, who were the other personalities involved. No more than that."

She could hardly refuse such a reasonable request without seeming over-defensive.

"You'd better come in."

She led Myles into the kitchen where there were telltale signs on the table that some form of border dispute was in progress. Crumby plates, sticky knives, a corn flakes packet and a marmalade jar minus its lid were lined up against two determined little piles of exercise books, one open, one closed. Reciprocal havoc had been wreaked.

"I'm just having a coffee. Would you like one?"

The two of them sat down after the table had been cleared of things properly breakfasty and the exercise books had been relocated to one of the counters. Myles' observation on the undoubted tedium of marking was met with a shrug of the shoulders.

"You teach your lesson and then you have to face all the kaleidoscopic distortions of what you said, or thought you said. It's worse than boring; it's an exercise in self-flagellation."

"Did you always have it in mind to be a teacher when you were at Oxford?"

"No, it's something that just suddenly put its hand up." She chuckled. "There, you see, I can't get away from the classroom. No, it was the last thing I saw myself doing. At Oxford I got terribly sick seeing all those grand intellectuals prancing about with their pet theories and their absurd political recipes, trying to tell the world what it should be doing, most of them totally ignoring human nature and some of them even trying to reinvent it. Quacks, the lot of them, I thought. Plodding along familiar paths with a few individuals at your coattails is as ambitious as anyone should be allowed to get, and teaching is the ultimate exercise in plodding."

She laughed. Myles was making progress.

"And what about the others on your course? There was Justin of course. Did any of the others turn into mad professors?"

"There were a couple who decided to take on PhDs. One of them, Peter Osborne, is struggling his way through the works of Hermann Broch. He's very welcome to it. Broch's main work is 'The Sleepwalkers'; that says it all for me. Petra Walker, she's doing research on Rimbaud, not the macho one, the French poet who spent most of his time in a drug-induced trance and then told us all about it and helped make hallucination the thing that every serious student should aspire to. Now there's something worth devoting three years of your life to!"

She didn't follow this up with the expected complementary chuckle, but seemed rather to be in throe to her memories.

"Then there was Joseph. Poor old Joseph! He allowed his

146

head to get so screwed up worrying about... what was it he called it? ... *the existential authenticity of rationality,* that's it. He couldn't cope with it, so he packed up and left and never finished his degree."

"*The existential authenticity of rationality?* What on earth is that?"

"You'd need to ask him – something about living out your ideals, putting your life where your head is. I was extremely fond of Joseph. He had an endearing gentleness about him. But to be honest, he was a bit of a fruitcake."

"How did Justin get on with him? Were they friends?"

"Not exactly: It was a funny kind of relationship they had. It was a bit one-sided. Joseph thought the world of Justin. He really looked up to him. He was scared stiff of Rob Snoddy and I think he saw Justin as some kind of buffer. I don't know."

"Why would he be afraid of Robert Snoddy? Did Snoddy do anything to him? Did he threaten him in any way? Would that have had anything to do with him packing up his studies?"

Suddenly Lizzie checked herself. The conversation had started so casually; she had been talking about people who had nothing to do with anything that needed to be kept from this Inspector. There seemed no harm even in mentioning Joseph, but now the whole nature of the policeman's questions had moved beyond the casual, conversational sphere. She instantly knew that she had said too much.

"No, it was just one of those dominance things that men go in for. Rob is what is called these days an alpha male and Joseph is way down the pecking order. There wasn't any more to it than that."

"You say Joseph dropped out. Have you kept in touch? Do you know where he is now?"

How could she have been so stupid? Joseph was as flaky as a snowdrop. If this Inspector gets to him, who knows what he might say? But she mustn't panic; she mustn't make the Inspector any more curious than he was already.

"No, we haven't heard from him lately. I wouldn't put it past him to have headed off to Tibet or somewhere just as absurd, somewhere to get his head sorted out. It's the type of thing he'd do."

"Would Justin be likely to know anything about his present whereabouts?"

"I wouldn't think so, but you could always ask him."

Myles produced a rather tatty notebook from his pocket. He didn't actually lick his pencil, but it felt as if he had.

"Could you give me Joseph's full name?"

The question, innocuous though it was, seemed somehow to require a handing-over of jurisdiction. Once the Inspector had his full name Joseph would be out in the open and irretrievably out of her and Justin's control. It was a silly thought, for clearly the Inspector had other sources available to him for the information. Yet as she answered she had an uncanny feeling that she was committing an act of betrayal.

"His name is Ross – Joseph Alyn Ross."

Chapter 29

The Panel met the following Friday. Reports were heard on each of the candidates in alphabetical order. Cameron was second on the list. Schinski had penned a glowing account for Whitehouse of the actor's charitable works and his generosity to party funds. The main emphasis was on his rhetorical prowess, his ability to move audiences as well of course as his appeal to the female voter. Whitehouse was reluctant at first to embrace the eulogistic spirit – it went against the grain of his political egoism to heap praise on a fellow politician – but once he had an audience in front of him, he forgot about the message and focused on the delivery, and, for all his shortcomings, he was a consummate crowd-pleaser. Schinski had two reports to deliver himself. The candidates he was reporting on were not seriously in the running, but he avoided any hint of negativity and was careful to be seen to be digging for nuggets of merit. In doing so of course he succeeded in exposing to full view the mediocrity of the material available to him, at the same time establishing his credentials as someone with no axe to grind.

While the reports were being delivered interest bobbed up and down among the Panel like the heads of swimmers doing the breaststroke. Some heads remained longer at the waterline than others. The one exception was the head of Nathan Roberts. It remained fixed. Roberts was clearly neither interested nor bored; he was simply intent on getting to his report. When he finally got to his feet, he surveyed the table with a look that said that the real business of the meeting was at last about to be done.

"What we've been hearing so far, comrades, is just so much claptrap – half-baked socialism from full-baked mummy's boys. What's the point of filling the commons with that type of individual – Reggie's luvvie, for example? What does he know about working class life? Sweet Fanny Adams! It's all about him and the little bourgeois party games that keep him and his ilk from feeling too guilty about all the money they've squeezed out of the rest of us. They're just like the wealthy merchants in the middle ages buying themselves time off purgatory. Well, I don't think the Labour Party should be peddling such rubbish. We don't want fellow travellers; we want people who understand the socialist dynamic and are prepared to see out the logic of the class struggle. That means ridding society of the very class that Cameron and all those poncey liberals who call themselves socialists belong to. We can do without them and their bourgeois notions; they spend their time agonising over the colour and design of the deckchairs when what we want is proper ship builders."

He then proceeded to wade through George Sinclair's impressive record of socialist engagement. He had fought the good fight against the forces of oppression on all fronts except in the House itself; it was now time, Roberts declaimed, for an infusion of real red blood from someone who would not just flap around anaemically on the backbenches; this was a man who would walk straight on to a seat on the Labour front bench. When he had finished his speech Roberts sat down with an air of assumed modesty of the kind that insists that the speaker is deserving of no special praise; he is merely a messenger telling it as it is. The look on some of the faces around the table suggested however that maybe there were other reasons for him not to expect their plaudits.

After Sinclair it was Snoddy's turn. On the Chairman's invitation Freddie Douglas rose slowly to his feet, his eyes trained on Roberts.

"I'm sure," he began, "we are all grateful to Nathan for reminding us of our party's common roots with international communism. And it is good that the candidature offers us a name that provides a link with that past. However it is the future we should surely be concerned with and I'm not sure that George Sinclair is the man for that. I think I might have found that man. Nathan is quite right when he talks about the way our party has moved away from the concerns of the common man and how it has been cosying up to the liberal establishment and wedding itself to the social concerns of a decadent elite that wallows in self-indulgence. The Labour Party rose to power because it wanted a better life for the ordinary people of this country. That meant a fairer wage, better working conditions and an equal chance to learn to appreciate the finer things in life. It also meant protection from those elements in society that would deny them this. Historically, such elements were identified with the capitalist class – and quite rightly so since unscrupulous employers were a major source of the misery that our forebears had to endure. But what we need to do now is to look afresh at the working man's lot. Things have changed considerably since the early years; we might find that we need to reassess our diagnosis. We might even find that some of the things we have been doing to help have in fact had the effect of hindering. Our policies, or at least some of them, may well be part of the problem.

"When I talked to Robert Snoddy my eyes were opened. Here is someone with a very clear awareness of where we are at and an inspiring vision of where we should be going. He is old working-class in body and soul and he has an outstanding intellect that is both analytical and imaginative. I must say, comrades, when I interviewed him, I felt the way I imagine a football scout feels when he discovers a George Best or a Paul Gascoigne. It will be for you to judge whether I've gone over the top, but at the very least you mustn't pass up on the opportunity."

It was a performance out of the top drawer. Schinski would have liked to indulge in a show of that's-my-boy approval, but restricted himself to a thoughtful nod.

The final candidate was Maggie Millership's adoptive contestant, a Ms Agnes Willoughby QC. Millership pressed hard, but as she worked through the list of her candidate's achievements, Schinski had the distinct impression of hearing one of those stories that rely entirely on name-dropping for its interest, the type of thing that theatrical types go in for, unnecessary verbatim renderings of banal conversations and accounts of commonplace incidents that the socially unconnected would never get away with. In this case the name that constantly fell from the lips was the strangely sanctified word 'woman'. He himself had never had a moment's doubt that women were just as capable – or incapable – as men, but why the hell did we have to put up with this kind of thing every time there's a choice to be made between male and female candidates? When the ode to feminine virtues was over Schinski made a point of having his voice heard.

"Thank you for that, Maggie. I can't speak for everyone, but you've certainly convinced me that Ms Willoughby has to be one of our chosen candidates. She is clearly a very able woman and would bring qualities that are greatly needed to the job of representing this constituency in Parliament. I was particularly impressed by that incident you related where she got T Smith & Co to admit responsibility for unfair dismissal against that unmarried mother. That was sterling work."

Another meaningful nod and he sat down.

Deliberations did not prove overtaxing. Cameron, Sinclair and Snoddy went through without objection and Ms Willoughby, being the only female candidate, was a moral imperative. The Panel did however feel obliged to justify its formation by engaging in a prolonged discussion over the fifth name to be added to the shortlist. In the end, after eloquent but measured advocacy from Schinski (which had all the more impact since he was not one of the candidates that the union secretary had reported on) it was decided that Francis Meadows would provide the best addendum to the choice they wished to make available to the Committee. Mr Meadows was a postgraduate student doing an internship at Party headquarters and was by some distance the least inspiring candidate that Schinski could pick out.

Chapter 30

The five successful candidates were informed of the favour they had found with the Panel and invited to attend a session of the full Executive Committee on the last Friday of the month. Each would be allocated half-an-hour during which they would be required to make a ten-minute presentation followed by questions which would be put to them in response to the points they had made. When all five candidates had been heard, a further session would take place the following day. Here they would each be required to answer an identical set of questions which the Panel would compile. After that, two candidates would be chosen to proceed to the final stage of the selection process. No details were given of the timing or of the form that should take. Since the job of compiling the set of common questions had been passed over to it, the Selection Panel needed to be reconvened. But time was short and it proved difficult to find a date that was acceptable to everyone. In the light of this Schinski sent out a circular proposing that the task be delegated to a sub-committee made up of the five members responsible for the initial reports on the successful contenders. Schinski offered his union offices as a venue and the meeting was set for the following Saturday morning.

Schinski was not in the habit of calling at the Whitehouse residence. He had attended a few dinner parties there, but that was business. Apart from the odd round of golf his personal relationship with Reggie had been strangely one-dimensional. When he was a boy he had read an old-fashioned boys'-own yarn set in a public school between the wars. The hero had been the captain of the house who, in addition to his feats on the sports field and his general sir-gallahading around the school, had taken on

154

himself to protect his likeable relic of a housemaster from the mean cunning of the overbearing headmaster. In doing so he had won the respect and affection of the relic's much younger wife. There had been no follow-up on that in the story line; it was probably deemed to be outside the interest range of the young readership of the day. It was only in later years that he began to imagine the juicy riches that that path might have offered. The realisation came to him as he gradually began to cast Reggie in the relic's role. In terms of character Reggie was far removed from the likable Mr Chips figure of the story, but his wife Gladys was a woman who combined intelligence, beauty and warmth. He could easily have been tempted into unchartered territories.

When he appeared at her doorstep she was mildly surprised that, despite her husband's absence, he accepted her invitation to come in. The conversation skirted around the reason for his visit. Schinski took pleasure in denying her politely suppressed curiosity. He commented on the pictures on the wall, inquired about her latest project (Mrs Whitehouse was a well known writer of children's books) and responded to inquiries about his latest feats at the bridge table. They shared a passion for bridge, but despite frequently declared intentions, they had never got round to entering a tournament together. Finally, when he felt that the elasticity had gone out of the suspended enlightenment, he broached the subject.

"I have a rather odd request to make to you, Gladys. I'd like you to call Reggie on his mobile on Saturday morning and insist that he come home immediately. You can make any excuse you like, but it must be something he can't say no to."
An eyebrow rose to this, but only as a complement to a smile.

"Should I suddenly acquire a broken leg? Or would it be better if Blanco here bit the bullet and choked on a bone? I tell you what: I could say that I've crashed his precious Harley. No, that wouldn't work; he'd never believe I'd go near that awful contraption."

Schinski joined in.

"You could always tell him you've met an irresistible foreign billionaire who wants to whisk you away, but you'd like Reggie to run his eye over him for you before you decide."

They both laughed, but it wasn't just the joke they were sharing, it was the value they both put on the fact that Gladys had not immediately demanded to know the reason behind this bizarre request. This created a certain intimacy between them. It remained unspoken but nonetheless acknowledged.

"It doesn't matter what you come up with as long as it can be substantiated afterwards. That's important. So unless you really do break your leg or decide that poor old Blanco's days are numbered, don't use that as a pretext. Of course, you could use that wealthy suitor I'm sure you do have in the wings, but be sure not to claim he has billions if he only has multi-millions. The timing, that's important. I'll text you. That will be the signal for you to call him."

He had intended to offer a complete explanation, but he couldn't bring himself to destroy the intimacy that leaving the unasked question unanswered had created between them. No doubt she had her own reason for not asking. She was a determinedly independent woman and much of that independence had been maintained by keeping her distance from the small print of her husband's interests even though she was always quite happy to countersign them.

His next appointment was a work session with Freddie Douglas. They needed to do some homework on the questions that the subcommittee had been tasked with drafting for the candidates. He had been at pains to keep himself off the subcommittee, but that was only so that he would have a free and invisible hand. Freddie had been impressed with Snoddy and was well placed to come up with questions that would allow his man to present himself in a favourable light to the committee. The emphasis must be on what Snoddy had called

156

the *deracination* of the Party – Freddie admitted that he had had to look the word up when he got home. As regards policy, they needed to focus the questions on the topics of education and the justice system. Those were the themes that brought Snoddy to life. Economics seemed to hold little interest for their man; discussion of it couldn't be avoided, but it would be best to play it down. This would be where Sinclair would feel most at home; it was important therefore to come up with wording that would encourage him to expose his true Marxist leanings. A 'Do you agree …?' format seldom fails to entice intimacies out from darkened corners.

The drafting took nearly two hours, but it was work that Schinski relished. His grandfather had immigrated from Eastern Europe as a young man and as a non-native speaker had an appreciation of *the flexible beauty* of the English language, which he passed on to his grandson. English could shadow the eccentricities of the real world, he said, much better than either German or Polish, the two languages he had spoken as a child. "Learn to take orders from it and it will take orders from you." It was advice that it had taken him some time to absorb, but as he got older he had come to appreciate the value of the wisdom the old man had passed on.

When they had done, they had constructed several versions of the five questions they wished to promote. It was vital to be flexible; the last thing they wanted was for the others to feel they were being railroaded. They even produced as camouflage a couple of very badly constructed questions which were bound to be dismissed. With Freddie's meeting-handling skills to push the right questions through, there was every chance that Robert Snoddy would get to play on his home turf.

Chapter 31

Schinski was in his office to greet the subcommittee members as they arrived. Margaret Millership was the first to appear. She was a stout lady, given to wearing copious amounts of jewellery. It always intrigued Schinski as to how she could seek to impress the world with baubles while doing nothing to reduce her more than ample waistline. He concluded that the premises of his reasoning must be wrong and left the question as one of those adult-type things that young children take on trust. She was an intelligent woman, but her thought processes circled round her central concerns in such uniform orbits that he felt compelled to image the horror of what it would be like to be trapped inside her head. He was sure that she was aware that he was on to her and they both observed a polite, but uncompromising no-fly zone in the space between them. They shared the fear that any outbreak of open hostility would cause mutual damage on too great a scale – showpiece acts of reciprocal consideration had become the order of the day.

Next to arrive was Max Fischer. Because they shared names clearly rooted east of the Rhine, Fischer had always presumed an affinity with him. Schinski could not return any sense of like-mindedness with Fischer's Teutonic infatuation with abstraction, but he found it served his interests to fake it. There was moreover fascination to be felt at the way Fischer could take a down-to-earth series of incidents and spin it into a spiral of speculation that answered to whatever ideological claptrap he was courting at the time. The way he did it was so much more entertaining than the predictable route that Maggie Millership took to her particular idée fixe.

The 'blatant male chauvinism' of a distinguished physicist

who had lost his job for making a joke about female lab assistants was the latest incarnation of the Millership obsession. It was in all the papers, but some of them apparently 'had the effrontery to excuse the embedded sexism of post-industrial society.' Fischer showed somewhat underpowered alacrity in support of this outrage, but did manage to come up with an allusion to 'the false consciousness of the masses', epitomised by the popularity of rags such as The Daily Mail. Consensus having been achieved – smiles and nods being Schinski's sole contribution – the conversation groped around for somewhere to move on to. Fortunately the other three arrived and spared them the indignity of having to settle for silence. As they arrived, Reggie was in full flow, treating the others to his latest irritations with the bankers and all things 'usurerish'.

Sylvia didn't work on Saturdays, so it was down to Schinski as host to serve the coffee. This removed him from the general chat. Reggie, for all his faults, was a great talker; he never allowed himself to be daunted by the inattention of those he was speaking to, one of his undoubted strengths as a politician. The odd thing is that when a dominant talker leaves a gathering, after a short hiatus, the others always seem to be left with lots to talk about. Thus it was when Reggie got the call from Gladys. He disappeared into the back office and returned a few minutes later, ashen-faced.

"I'm sorry. You'll have to manage without me this morning. I've just had a call from my wife. There's an emergency at home. I'm needed there."

The reference to 'an emergency' was a clear warning against any further inquiry. Schinski would dearly have liked to know what fiction Gladys had fabricated, but naturally forbore to ask. Reggie's departure was dramatically unceremonious. His concerns were clearly elsewhere and his interest in events here dissipated in the same puff of smoke that signalled his exit.

When the smoke had settled, Schinski announced his own

departure. There were suggestions that he should stand in for the indisposed MP, but he rejected them claiming that as he had not been appointed by the Panel it would be presumptuous of him to push his preferences. He was sure that they wouldn't need any help from him to come up with questions that would leave the candidates nowhere to hide. So, in a manner reminiscent of an old manservant, he withdrew and left his betters to it.

Schinski had his reasons for turning down the invitation. It was important to his strategy not to be privy to the questions that the subcommittee would draft. There could be no question of him staying around and being present at the birth. But if truth be told, there was another, less worthy, but equally compelling reason: it was Saturday and Saturday afternoons meant only one thing for him – the magic of the beautiful game. From the age of three he had been taken religiously by his old grandfather to watch. It became to Saturday what to the churchgoer worship is to Sunday. In the early days, too young to follow the game, his eyes would be focused on the antics of the goalkeeper regardless of where the ball was on the field; he would absorb all the moves he witnessed, from the trivial depositing of the cap at the corner of the net to the flamboyant diving saves and the daring headlong lunges at the feet of raiding forwards. After every game these feats would be re-enacted in front of the sofa at home. A ball of wool from his mother's knitting would be pressed into service. The sofa would be defended against all-comers. Occasionally, for he did feel the need to give a nod to realism, he would let one in, but only when a heroic string of saves allowed for an honourable failure. Before the matches, as he tracked to the ground he would marvel at the indifference of the civilian population – for that's how he thought of them – all those going about their everyday business, oblivious to the great event about to take place on their doorstep. When he first heard the words 'Forgive them, Lord, for they know not what they do' it immediately resonated in association with this phenomenon. The old magic was now long gone, but that didn't stop him trying to rekindle it from the expectation that every Saturday morning brought. A few years ago he had been invited on to the board of a junior club just outside Manchester; it was a chance to combine his professional talents with his longstanding love of the game. In fact it was his first pet project in the club – the building of a modest social centre – that had tempted him against his better judgement into joining in on Reggie's hare-brained scheme to re-direct the union subscriptions. The club had ambitions to move up in the football world and Schinski saw himself as the man to bring that about. His regular pre-match lunch date with his fellow board members was an appointment that brooked no interference. There was talk of him taking over eventually as chairman, but he still needed to offer them something more substantial by way of investment to demonstrate that there was money where his mouth was. However that was for another day. For the moment it was time off – a hearty lunch, football talk and then the match.

The celebrations that followed a well earned draw against the league leaders began to pall about seven o'clock. Schinski wasn't a drinker and could see no good reason why anyone should want to dull his joy – sorrow was another matter – in a fog of indiscriminate positivity when there was something real and substantial to be happy about. He left the revellers to it and met up with Freddie. Had things gone to plan?

"More or less. Maggie was predictably insistent on a question about female quotas. There was no talking her out of it. So I went along. You see, I've learnt from the master: 'Give, but never more than you can take back'. Sure enough, she then backed me over the law-and-order and the schools questions. As you thought, Fischer wanted a question about socialist economics and I managed to get them to frame it the way we discussed. Yes, I think you'll be pleased with what we came up with. I'll email you and Reggie a copy."

"No, don't do that. That's the last thing I want. I don't want to know and I certainly don't want Reggie to know. Why else do you think I arranged for him to be called away from the meeting?"

Schinski then produced a folded sheet of paper from his inside pocket and handed it to Douglas.

"Here, take a look at that."

Douglas unfolded it and started to read, but he got only as far as the first couple of lines before looking up in surprise.

"What is this? Why are you giving me a set of questions? You surely don't expect me to swap these for the ones the committee came up with?"

Schinski took a moment to enjoy the confusion he had caused before replying.

"Well, not exactly. Or, more precisely, yes and no. Snoddy is your man, right? You'd be prepared to go to any lengths, or depths, to get him elected? Of course you would. If push came to shove, you'd even be prepared to drop Reggie and me in the shit?"

The Douglas mind was racing to keep bafflement at bay. But Schinski had had his fun; it was time to enlighten.

"I want you to email Reggie a copy of those questions for him to pass on to Brown. That'll give our little star celebrity time to get his scriptwriters on the job and learn the lines they feed him."

A beam of comprehension slowly spread across the younger man's face. His eyes returned to the sheet.

As he read through the list, the light that had just dawned deepened into full blooded appreciation.

"You know, Derek, you're a right bastard."

162

Chapter 32

'Did he know anything about Joseph Alyn Ross?' was the question Inspector Graham Myles had just put to ex-Inspector Stuart Stranaghan. It was one of those questions that tempt you to lie, but at the same time offer opportunity to postpone full-blown mendacity until a more immediate threat comes calling on your guilty secret.

"Justin mentioned him in his reports. He was one of the Snoddy crowd. It was he who introduced Justin to Snoddy, wasn't it? But that's all in the reports. I don't think there's anything more I can add."

"Did you ever meet him personally?"

Was this the moment to lie? . . . no, there was a way out.

"I saw him once at a meeting. It was the launch of Snoddy's book. I was invited. Bruce Greenfield asked me. I half expected to see you there. I must say, Myles, I don't think Snoddy did you justice in that book. He made you seem like a man-from-the-ministry, all rules and regulations, no feel for the unpredictable weathers of life. Maybe that's why you weren't invited."

It was a crude effort at distraction, but Myles seemed up for it.

"I read the book. You're right. I came over like a right prat. But then, maybe I was. Snoddy is no fool. I can't say I like the man, but he does have a sharp eye as well as a sharp tongue. I think I've become a bit more three-dimensional since then. I learned a lot from you, you know, not just the Latin phrases."

If only he could believe that! Would he really be three-dimensional enough to understand why Stuart had broken all the rules, why he had aided and abetted the conviction of an innocent man? No, the Myles he knew would never be able to get that far into that third dimension. He resisted the momentary temptation to delve further into what had changed in his take on the world – better to keep things in shallower waters even if it meant that they would the sooner get back to the matter in hand.

"So you never actually talked to Joseph?"

There was no way out of this one. Unequivocal denial was the sole option. However it was a very crude 'Not that I recall' that involuntarily came out, smacking of the very caginess he had been so anxious to disguise. The former Sergeant Myles would haven't have been able to hide his incredulity, had he picked up on this, but the more mature Inspector Myles might well have learned the art of concealment. The spirit of bonhomie remained unchallenged between the two men and Myles went off in search of a whereabouts for the lost Joseph.

Chapter 33

The search for Joseph Ross was not as straightforward as it had first appeared. Myles checked the tax office records, but both the home address and the place of employment were out of date and no one at either place could provide any information as to his present whereabouts. All Myles could gather from the garden centre where he had been employed was that he was 'away with the fairies' and that the Inspector could do worse than check all the nearest mental asylums. When pressed about what he meant by that, the manager recited a number of instances of 'the little weirdo' talking to himself and writing stuff in some kind of dairy he carried everywhere with him ... 'when he should have been working!'

"It wasn't that he was workshy, mind. When his mind was on the job he was a good little worker. That's why I kept him on, but one day he just went too far. I sent him off in the van to deliver some euonymus plants. It should have taken him less than an hour, but he didn't show again until the following morning. We had to get by the entire day without that van. When I tackled him about it, all he had to say for himself was that he had got into 'a deep discussion' with the guy that took the delivery. He invited him to come to a meeting of some group or other – I can't remember the name. I ask you – what can you do with somebody like that? I'd no option; I had to show him the door. I was sorry, mind. There was something likeable about the guy. He was ... gentle, like. You know what I mean?"

"Did you ever hear from him again? He never applied to you for a reference or anything like that?"

"No, the last I saw of him was that day. He didn't argue or try to get me to change my mind. He just got his things together and left. To be honest, it made me feel a right heel. But what could I do?"

"How about that delivery he made? Could you check you records and get me the address?"

The Church of the Resurrection had seen better days. There was something about it that suggested it had come down in the world. It was not in a state of neglect. Quite the contrary, it looked to have been infused with a new found prosperity – the brightly painted door, the garish banner announcing that 'Jesus Saves All Who Repent', not least the impressive array of roses and dahlias and, of course, the tints of gold of the euonymus bushes, now well established. Myles could not help but feel that the old gravestones and the lichened slabs that formed the path might have found weeds and moss more compatible company.

There was no one around the old building, but to the side, behind a little copse of scraggly Scots pines, he could see the gaunt outline of a large Victorian building, presumably the rectory. He walked over and rang the bell. It was one of those fossilised bell buttons that you don't expect to work, but it did, emphatically so, emitting a tune worthy of any jaunty ice cream van. It took a third ring to bring anyone to the door. The 'anyone' was a middle-aged man in a dog collar, a flabby nylon thing at the top end of a shiny black T-shirt that looked as if it should have a Guinness logo emblazoned on the front. The smile on the middle-aged face had an air of perpetualness about it; it certainly did not give the impression of being tailor-made for Myles. The mention of Joseph Ross was enough to produce an instant invitation to enter the portals. Myles was ushered into the large sitting room where a teenage girl was squatting on a very tatty sofa, legs tucked up under her, listening intently to whatever was coming through her earphones. Myles expected her to be introduced and then presumably dispatched to some other corner of the family abode, but the good Reverend simply

166

ignored her presence and directed the visitor to a substantial table at the window.

"Joseph! Why do you want to speak to Joseph? The poor boy has been through a lot. When he came to us he was a soul in torment. He has made great progress towards the light, I'm pleased to say, but his spiritual wounds are far from healed."

As he said this the smile had not gone, it had merely taken on a sadder hue. Myles pressed him for clarification.

"Joseph had made the mistake that so many clever people make. He believed that it was given to him to understand the condition that the Lord has chosen to place us humans in. He has had to pay for his vanity. It's as simple, and as complicated, as that. We children have been given brains to deal with the world of physical things. We have become masters of technology; we can send men to the moon, we can plot a course to the most distant planets, we can play around in nature's most minute workings, but when it comes to deeper things, things that touch the heart and the soul, we must cast our braininess aside and call on our own hearts and souls to make their kind of sense of them. That is the journey that Joseph is on."

"So where is he at the moment?"

For the first time a chink developed in the smile. The eyes seemed to switch functions from radiating out to filtering in.

"You didn't tell me what you wanted with Joseph."

The Reverend was insisting on a trade.

"It's a matter I want him to clear up for me. When he was at Oxford he got involved with some dangerous people. I need certain information about these people and I've reason to believe Joseph will be able to help me with that."

This time the clergyman's face really did change. The smile was banished and a dark cloud passed over his eyes.

"I know all about Joseph's past. He has told me everything and I would beg you not to open up those wounds again. It could set him right back to the pit we found him in."

There was a weightiness about this man that demanded respect. It ran counter to the distrust Myles had acquired of those who peddled the gospel with its saccharine 'good news' for all those willing 'to be washed in the blood of the lamb'. The husband of an aunt of his had been a lay preacher and had droned on with the same monotonous recipe for dealing with all evils, from warts to the Third World War. For those willing to receive his message he had a smile that logged shared superiority; for those who weren't the very same smile was retained to service pity and contempt.

"I'm sorry, but I simply must speak to Joseph. How would it be if you were present at the interview? You being there might help him to get through it. He mightn't feel quite so exposed."

The idea had come to him out of the blue. It certainly wasn't standard police practice, but then again, juveniles have to be interviewed in the presence of a responsible adult, don't they? He was likely to get more from the interview if Joseph had moral support. The Inspector however couldn't be sure if the idea had arisen from this sober calculation or if it was the strength of this clergyman's personality that had prompted it.

"That would be kind, Inspector. However, there is a slight problem. Joseph is presently spending a week at a retreat in Yorkshire. He's not due back until Friday. Can I suggest you come back on Saturday morning? In the meantime I will pray for us all. I will ask the good Lord for guidance. May He grant us the wisdom not to treat literal truth as a graven image."

Chapter 34

Derek Schinski's view of politics was like a filmmaker's take on special effects. He was fascinated by the technical skills involved. It was a constant source of amusement to him to observe how one piece of verbal trickery would succeed while another failed. On him personally they all failed. How the public could not see through the linguistic ploys of political practitioners, even those applied with skill and subtlety, was something that inspired admiration and contempt in equal measure. He looked forward to the occasion of the candidates making their submissions as a critic might look forward to a drama premiere. Would there be any novelty to admire or would the same tired old spells and potions be called up again to conjure their tarnished magic?

Cameron Brown was first up. Chairman Windsor threw in some chatty preliminaries before firing off the opening question: "How would you suggest we stiffen Party policy on law and order to make it resonate with our wider membership?" It was clear to Schinski from the satisfied look on his face that the candidate had heard only what he thought he was going to hear. The far-away look he produced as he strained to summon his thoughts and cobble together a pattern for their delivery was a tribute to his histrionic prowess. No one could have suspected that the oration he was about to deliver was pre-packed, ready-made and had been honed to perfection in front of the sitting-room mirror.

He began with an acknowledgement of the present poor state of enlightenment amongst the lower classes. This he laid firmly at the door of the gutter press. He took great delight in his own gusto in doing so. He then moved into more reflective mode as he proceeded to analyse the *true* reasons for antisocial behaviour. How were we to expect ordinary citizens to behave other than badly when they see the bankers, the fat cats of industry and the whole capitalist class feathering their own nests at the expense of the public purse? The public needed reassurance that the standards demanded of ordinary citizens would be applied just as rigorously to their so-called elders and betters. There was also a clear requirement for better education. In the twenty-first century how could we allow people to be left in a state of such abject ignorance? How could we tolerate an antiquated form of judgementalism that allows us to condemn the people we choose to call criminals in isolation from the economic and cultural deprivation into which they have been cast? We must change the terms of the debate and move away from a culture of blame.

The rhetorical graph he had traced had been flamboyant in its undulations and had contrived to terminate dramatically at a cliff edge. The failure of the audience to supply the finishing touch by applauding had however the unfortunate effect of leaving the speaker high and dry. Brown was unabashed; his facial expression showed generous acknowledgement of the applause that there ought to have been.

Next came Nathan Roberts' question; it amounted to little more than an invitation to endorse the virtues of state ownership of the means of production. This time there could be no mistaking the fact that this was not one of the questions he had been told to expect. His theatrical experience stepped up to the mark and prevented his full horror from exposing itself – only Schinski and Freddie Douglas could see behind the facial scenery. He asked for the question to be repeated and then offered a paraphrase, a device Schinski had often seen used to claim ownership of a question and credibility for the answer. It was obvious to Schinski that he was buying time to decide which of his prepared responses would best fill in the void that had suddenly opened up. He started off along the route he had obviously plotted to deal with the issue of industrial action. It was going quite well until Roberts interrupted and demanded that he 'stop waffling and answer the bloody question'. Chairman Windsor glowered at his colleague for this unacceptable breach of etiquette and apologized to the candidate, urging him to answer the question in whatever way he saw fit. The interruption had provided more thinking time, but damage had been done. Brown clearly now felt compelled to give something that could at least pass for a straight answer to the question and conceded that public ownership of the means of production 'should not be excluded from the economic armoury of a socialist government.' Again Roberts interrupted and, running the gauntlet of the Chairman's ire, required the hapless candidate to specify which industries he would target initially. A more quick-witted candidate, Schinski felt, would have fallen back on a call for some kind of inquiry or study to make recommendations to the Executive Party, but Brown's mind went blank and he simply dried. In good chairing fashion Windsor covered the cringe-making hiatus with a further rebuke to Roberts and then moved swiftly on to the next question.

It was on education. This Brown was well prepared for, but he again failed to take in the nicety of the wording of the question. Freddie Douglas had worked hard to push through the wording that he and Schinski had formulated. It was tilted so as to invite criticism of the status quo, asking for new thinking on historical policies of the Party. This was lost on Brown who took his cue instead from the question he had been fed and launched into a diatribe against Tory attempts to lift the more able working class children out of the class they could usefully serve and turn them into little bourgeois stooges. He did exactly what Schinski had hoped he would do; he went into patronising mode and left the Panel to wonder if he saw the sons and daughters of workers as individuals at all or simply conscripts for dispatch to the front line of the class struggle. Volunteering didn't come into it. He didn't realise it, but the whole verbal armoury of the First World War – cannon fodder, lambs to the slaughter, '*dulce et decorum est*' – could now be lined up against him.

Although it didn't feature in the list he had been issued with and so could not have been rehearsed, the final question, Maggie Millership's summons to a rant on the iniquities of male dominance, produced some fine rhetoric from Brown. It was clearly a subject close to his heart. Ms Millership positively purred as she listened to him dripping with empathy for the plight of her gender. The chalice of indignation was passed to and fro between questioner and responder and supped with such intimacy that the others felt uncomfortable at being privy to it. Could it really be that Maggie Millership was contemplating an extra-sororal political affair?

The next candidate to appear before the committee was Agnes Willoughby, Maggie Millership's own runner. Schinski had never met her, but he had somehow formed an image of her as a dumpy thirty-something-year-old with frizzy hair of the kind that defies any attempts to get it to fall into line; he was quite convinced that she would be wearing a beany and one of those long thin woolly scarves that get wrapped back around the neck every time the wearer feels the need to show that a debating point has been scored. He was quite wrong. She was a tall, elegant woman, well-dressed in a sea blue skirt and jacket. She could well have passed for a candidate for the leadership of the Conservative party. Her performance over the questions was patchy. She had obviously been well coached on how to lace what she said with large dollops of empathy and concern. She 'felt for' everyone to whom she could attribute any kind of plight, problems were invariably described as 'issues' and the remedies she offered always came accompanied by variations on the word 'challenge'. She also showed great liking for the notions 'radical' and 'progressive', and broke with her commitment to empathy only when words such as 'Tory', 'reactionary' and 'middleclass male' entered the sentence. The only problem was that she could not be tempted away from noble aims and worthy sentiments; when it came to policy she would *look again at* this and *question the wisdom of* that, she was even prepared to *radically rethink* some strategies and, of course, to *invest* in the NHS and *work for better understanding of issues* such as educational underachievement, criminality and the problems associated with long term unemployment. All in all she name-dropped her way to a good score on Schinski's what's-what tick list. When she got on to her chosen ground, gender inequality, she finally came up with specific proposals – huge swathes of positive discrimination with strict quotas to back them. She gave quite a convincing performance, but to Schinski's mind this late show of naked clarity only served to highlight the cotton-woolly cloudiness of her earlier performance. This could not have been lost on her patron whose conversion to the Cameron Brown fan club was now surely a distinct possibility.

Chapter 35

There was no formal discussion of the respective merits of the two candidates before the Panel broke up. This was at the behest of the Chairman who considered it best practice to delay such deliberations until the remaining three candidates were heard the following day. This of course did not prevent private exchanges.

Before the meeting Schinski had casually invited Max Fischer to join him for a nightcap. The two men were not close despite having known each other for several years. Schinski was aware that his German colleague considered him an intellectual lightweight, but had reason to suspect that he did not think him a fool. Although the invitation had come from him he insisted on Fischer choosing the venue. He knew of course what that would be; there was only one pub that Fischer was ever seen in – the Excelsior, an Alsatian establishment where good chess was played and great quantities of *Weizenbier* consumed in litre steins. A litre of strong German beer was the last thing Schinski wanted, but he would probably get away with a few sips of the stuff.

Fischer, like most men of ideas, was a talker rather than a listener and showed no diffidence in sharing his thoughts on the performance of the two candidates they had heard. Brown he considered a typical example of his profession – large ego, tiny self.

"What makes these people think that by playing a character you can lay claim to its soul? That's just what the cannibals felt they were doing where they ate their victims. 'I am part of all that I have ate.' Sorry about the grammar, but it scans better."

He gave a loud belly laugh. Schinski had a deep aversion to

all things Teutonic – his family background had encouraged him in this – and there was something markedly Teutonic about the particular way the laughter was laboured; it denied all kinship with good humour. Fischer, oblivious to his companion's misgivings, warmed to his subject.

"I saw Brown once on stage. It was in 'Julius Caesar' at the Savoy. He played Brutus. After the performance he stepped forward and treated the audience to his thoughts on the relevance of the play to the modern political scene. He saw the whole thing as a pre-enactment of the demise of Margaret Thatcher. Sooner or later, he said, the forces of moderation contrive to combine together and root out the cancerous growth of extremism. Such twaddle! But then the English Left have never been up to much when it comes to identifying the key elements of dialectical process."

A change of subject was called for. Teutonic wading in the bogs of political metaphysics, or whatever other grand name Fischer and his clan might choose to give it, was decidedly not Schinski's cup of tea. What did Fischer think of Ms Willoughby?

Fischer showed a flicker of irritation at being deflected from his course, but he soon warmed to the digression.

"*Ein Zauberlehrling!* A sorcerer's apprentice! She knows a few magic words that she has picked up from her masters, but I wouldn't bet on her being able to convert them into anything approaching meaningful syntax. Words are not to be trusted when they are off the leash; they combine and conspire and set themselves up as reality-makers. But we mustn't be hard on poor Ms Willoughby; she is treading a well-worn path. Modern politics is more about saying than about doing, which of course is logical given our acceptance of the verbal as the prime element of political reality. If our ambitions go no higher than the floor of the House, then Ms Willoughby is as good a candidate as any. She will huff and puff and blow no more houses down than the wind would have done anyway. The real damage she and her ilk will do is as unpredictable as the configurations of the words they release into the air. I wonder how many ex-prime ministers or cabinet ministers come to see themselves as victims of the very buzz words and jingles that helped them to power in the first place.

> *Ach, das Wort, worauf am Ende*
> *Er das wird, was er gewesen.*"[3]

The German was lost on Schinski, but then much of the English had been as well. Fischer paused, possibly realising he had lost his audience. But before he could resume, Schinski became aware of a voice from behind him unmistakably echoing Fischer's German tones.

> *Ach, er läuft und bringt behende!*
> *Wärst du doch der alte Besen!*[4]

Fischer was startled. He looked up to see an elderly gentleman in a tweed suit with, if he wasn't mistaken, the chain of a pocket watch dangling between two pockets of the waistcoat. The man was smiling, clearly enjoying the advantage he had over his fellow recitationist.

"Max Fischer, isn't it? You obviously don't remember, but we met a couple of years ago at a Goethe-Institut gathering in Cambridge."

Fischer thought for a moment and then, springing to his feet, he seized the newcomer by the hand and shook it vigorously.

---

[3]   Oh for the word to change him back
      To what he was before
[4]   How he runs and keeps on going!
      Wish you'd be the broom once more!

"Greenfield! Bruce Greenfield! Of course! We had a great chat about … what was it now? … Nietzsche, wasn't it? Come. Sit down. Let me get you a drink."

While the waiter was summoned to fetch a single malt, Fischer made the introductions.

"Bruce here is one of a rare breed, a Germanist who understands both the German and the English mind. He has kindred spirits in both camps. Can you imagine someone who is equally at home with John Stuart Mill and Friedrich Hegel?"

Then, turning to the newcomer …

"May I introduce Derek Schinski. Don't be fooled by the name, Bruce. Derek is British through and through. Pragmatism, that's the name of the game, isn't it, Derek? None of this high-faluting nonsense about the dialectical convulsions of the *Zeitgeist*, a waste of a good brain that could be better employed buying and selling, ducking and weaving, eh Derek?"

Fischer obviously took more of the personal stuff in than Schinski had ever credited him with. Strange how you are always trying to indent yourself on others and yet are just as surprised when you succeed as when they show no sign of cognizance of your being. He would have to show this Teuton more respect in future. Greenfield and Schinski had never actually met – they had of course spoken on the phone when Schinski had set up this 'chance encounter' – so neither man's thespian talents were overtaxed.

"What are you doing here, Bruce? A bit off your migratory paths, isn't it?"

"As a matter of fact I'm here with a former pupil of mine. He's taking a rather important viva tomorrow and I thought I'd lend him a bit of moral support. He's having an early night, so why not try this place out, I thought. I've been told it's the nearest thing in England to the *Hofbräuhaus*."

"A viva, you say. I'm intrigued. What's his subject?"

"Oh no, nothing like that, it's not an academic thing. He's being interviewed tomorrow as a prospective Labour Party candidate. Anyway, enough about him, what are you up to these days? Still trying to persuade the world that Wieland deserves a seat at the top table alongside Orwell and Huxley?"

The inquiry was lost on Fischer as was the bantering tone.

"You mean to say you've a candidate in for tomorrow's interview? That's amazing. I'm on the Selection Panel! What's your candidate's name?"

Schinski had been impressed with the acting skills the schoolmaster had displayed in affecting casualness, but now the more difficult art of simulating surprise without hamming was to come under scrutiny. Greenfield was equal to the task; the facial expression he contrived was incredulity incarnate.

"Really? You can't be serious!"

He took a few seconds, ostensibly to savour his wonderment, a sort of inner 'well, well'. Then, in a noticeably quieter voice, he changed tack.

"You know, Max. What you have just told me makes complete nonsense of the advice I've been giving him. I've been telling him to keep things simple, not to expect too much from his audience. They're likely to be, shall we say, slightly limited in their ability to absorb a full *German breakfast* – I actually used that expression, can you believe? – a full helping of philosophical abstractions. Now that I know that you're on the Panel, I'll have to get him to revise his strategy."

"No, Bruce, don't do that. Abstract thinking is not something the Panel would warm to. You're quite right; it would be above their heads."

As soon as the words were out he seemed suddenly to realise that he had just insulted his colleague.

"Sorry, Derek, I don't mean to imply that my fellow panellists are stupid. As I said earlier, it's just not the English way of thinking."

Re-addressing Greenfield, he added "Derek is on the Panel too."

When pressed for more information on his candidate, Greenfield affected reluctance on the grounds of leaving himself open to charges of exerting undue influence. These were swept aside by Fischer whose curiosity had been thoroughly whetted.

"His name is Robert Snoddy. He is the most gifted pupil I have taught in my entire career. He came to us as a scholarship boy; his background is working class through and through. The Labour party is in his blood. His father was a lifelong trade unionist and supporter of the Party. I met him a few times. I felt privileged. He was the ghost of Socialist past and a reminder to everyone that there might still be a home for radicalism once the snivellers and complainers and offence-seekers have been driven from the temple. Robert lacks his father's dignity, but his heart is at one with his head and, believe me, that makes for a powerful combination."

Despite repeated urgings, Greenfield smilingly refused to be drawn on policy issues. That would be a step too far in the abuse of privilege, he maintained. Snoddy would speak for himself the following day before the whole Panel and the two men would see for themselves a talent that the Party could ill afford to pass up. Fuelled by copious rounds of single malt and German beer, the conversation broadened out. The great questions were explored, not least the *Quo Vadis* of socialism in the aftermath of the revelation of what Greenfield insisted on calling its 'economic dysfunctionalism'. Schinski purred quietly in the corner but made his exit early in the proceedings, happy to leave the other two to the pleasures of transacting in their erudition.

Chapter 36

Before Schinski set off for the afternoon interviews he received the call he had been expecting from a very agitated Lord Dooley.

"What the hell are you and Whitehouse playing at? Those questions you passed on to us were complete duds. I thought we had a deal."

Schinski savoured the moment; taking the wind out of an opponent's sails is always a pleasurable experience, but not as pleasurable as making off with the sails.

"Yes, I know; we're as unhappy about it as you are. It was that bastard Fred Douglas. He fed Reggie the wrong questions. He never let on, but I think he's pushing for George Sinclair. Not to worry though. We'll make bloody sure his man doesn't get in."

"I don't give a fig about his man. It's our man that I'm concerned about. Anyway, I don't understand. What's this about Reggie being fed the wrong questions? Surely he knew what the questions were? Why did he need to be fed them?"

"No, that's just it. Reggie wasn't at the meeting. He got an urgent phone call from his wife just before the meeting started and had to leave. He got a copy of the questions from Douglas afterwards. He had no reason to think they were anything other than the real McCoy."

A tirade of invective was unleashed from the other end.

"Listen to me, Schinski. You put this right. You find some way of getting Brown the nomination or you can kiss goodbye to Reggie's peerage. I don't care how you do it, but do it. Understood?"

"Hold on a minute, Lord Dooley. Reggie and I have been let down just as much as you were. We've acted in good faith. We had a deal, sure, but that deal didn't involve us actually *securing*

Brown's nomination; the promise we made, and the only promise we could make, was to *use our best offices*. It was a question of trying; we gave no guarantees about succeeding."

"You call that trying! When I engage a plumber I don't pay him for *trying*! I pay him for doing the job! Stop buggering me about, Schinski! Just get the job done."

"We'll certainly do our best for Brown. There's still a chance, but you've been in this game long enough, my lord, to know we can't guarantee anything. One thing's for sure though, we'll see to it that Sinclair doesn't get in. Freddie Douglas has messed us about and we're not going to let the bugger away with that."

An anger shared is an anger halved. Well, perhaps not quite halved, at any rate lessened. There was more than enough bile left seething in the Dooley cauldron to necessitate the catharsis of an ultimatum.

"Okay, if that's the way you want to play it; I will keep to our agreement and I'll put as much effort into getting Reggie his precious ermine as you put into getting Brown nominated. But you can be sure of one thing: there's no way I'll be outperforming you. If you fail, you can count on me failing too."

The little snigger that accompanied this was quite intolerable. Schinski was tempted to swap threats with the man, but he thought better of it. Why play an ace to beat a five or a six? He'd wait until Dooley came out with his king. For the moment he'd settle for a bland acknowledgement of his opponent's strength.

"I don't doubt for a moment, my lord, that you will do whatever you can in pursuance of your own best interests. I respect that and I would expect nothing less from you. And nor would you expect anything less from me, would you? I think we understand each other."

181

Chapter 37

Thoroughness is a virtue that every good policeman must honour and cherish. But it is a deity that shuns the sunnier slopes of Olympus where all the fantastical and inventive sprites cavort; it favours the quiet of the shadier foothills to sip its nectar in company with soul mates, honesty, fidelity and sweet reason. Inspector Myles was, like many of his profession, averse to over-exposure to the sun.

There was no obvious line for his inquiries to follow, not least because he was not at all clear what he was trying to find out beyond following through on a vague suspicion that Justin Wright had in some way compromised himself in the course of the undercover operation. In his report Wright had admitted to assisting at punishment beatings, but he had never admitted to taking an active part himself. He had described his role in luring victims and had once been present when the actual beatings had taken place. It was pretty obvious that his part had not been merely that of spectator, but, quite sensibly, he had stopped short of putting his specific input on record. Surely that couldn't be what he, Myles, was being asked to find evidence for? How could anyone in Myles' position be expected not to get some dirt on his hands? There had to be more to it; anything short of murder surely had to go down as collateral damage. The only case in his report where murder was an issue was that mock trial where Wright had to be seen to condone a death sentence. He had subsequently been dragooned into forming part of the firing squad, but he knew the whole thing was a sham. He had recognised the man playing the part of the accused as one of the so-called facilitators who worked for the organisation. So he was aware that it was blanks he was firing and not real bullets. He claimed not to have recognised any of the other members of the squad. So apart from Snoddy who directed operations, there was nobody he could test Wright's account against. Snoddy would of course know who the others were. It would be hard for Snoddy to refuse to supply that information, but, knowing Snoddy, he was far from sanguine.

The prospect of an interview with Snoddy filled Myles with a feeling which he was unwilling to acknowledge as dread. He remembered the barbed hostility that the man exuded. As a junior policeman he had been completely at a loss to counter the fusillade of taunts directed at him for his supposed slow wittedness and lack of erudition. Looking back, he could see how easy a target he had offered Snoddy, but he had acquired layers since then; he was older and wiser and more solidly fortified. He would surely now be more of a match for his nemesis. It was a pity though to have to test the waters; his nascent self-belief might not yet be quite impermeable.

Disappointment and relief are more frequent bedfellows than convention chooses to acknowledge. They were certainly an item when Myles learned that Snoddy was not at home. The news was delivered on Snoddy's doorstep by an intimidatingly beautiful creature in a masculine looking dressing gown looking down on him over a pair of heavy-rimmed spectacles. As is often the case with beautiful women, they look at their best in aesthetic adversity.

"No, he's gone up north on business. I'm not sure exactly when he'll be back, but it won't be for a day or two at least. Who should I tell him called?"

When he gave his name, the standard reaction was interrupted in midstream by a sudden dawning of light on the lovely face.

"Inspector Myles! You wouldn't by any chance be the Sergeant Myles that Robby sometimes talks about?"

So Snoddy had talked to her about him. The two of them

must have had a good laugh. He could just imagine Snoddy in full flight turning him into an even more abject figure of fun than he had actually been. When he confessed to the charge, her face lit up even more.

"Do come in and join me. I'm having a coffee. I've always wanted to meet you. My name's Naomi Ballintyne by the way. Robbie and I are together."

Before he knew it the Inspector was sitting in the kitchen with a mug of coffee in his hand. He did of course know about Naomi Ballintyne. She had popped up several times in Wright's reports. It had been as a result of her investigations that his cover had been blown; she had gone up and interviewed his father and in the course of digging around had uncovered the fact that he was a student at the police academy.

"What is it you wanted to see Robbie about?"

The question had an air of casualness about it that made it sound more like a gesture of conviviality than a request for information. Myles was tempted to allow himself to be taken in.

"I am interested in the mock trial he organised, the one where he pretended to get the jurors to execute the prisoner after they'd come up with a guilty verdict."

Naomi gave out a seamlessly good-natured laugh.

"But he does that kind of thing all the time. I imagine you mean the one that your man took part in?"

There was something slightly smug about the way she said 'your man'.

"Yes, I need Mr Snoddy to supply me with a list of the names and the details of all the people who took part."

"I'm not sure if he'll be able to accommodate you there, Inspector Myles. But you can always ask him when he gets back."

"You say he does that kind of thing all the time. Why?"

Naomi had been shuffling around tidying things away, but suddenly she stopped and sat down at the table.

"Do you want the pocket version or the full-blown, hobby-horse version of my answer to that?"

She didn't give Myles time to answer before continuing.

"Our field of interest, Robbie's and mine that is, is in the way the rational and the emotional jockey for position in the human psyche. When reason tells us to do one thing and our emotions tell us not to, what factors come into play to determine which side wins? That's the question we are trying to find some kind of answers for. Most people deep down subscribe to the principle of retribution. If justice means anything, it means achieving an equitable balance between the wrong that's been done and the wrong that needs doing to cancel it; the punishment should fit the crime. If anyone takes the life of another human being – not on the spur of the moment, but coldly and with clear intent – the only rational response is to require that person to forfeit their own life. Anything less is a denial of the value of the life that has been taken. If, out of compassion or simple distaste, we choose to depart from that principle, we abandon any meaningful attachment to the core principle of justice. And yet that is precisely what our judicial system does, and takes pride in doing. What we still persist in calling our criminal justice system is a confused set of procedures designed to produce a mixed bag of goodies. Our punitive system has three ostensible objectives: deterrence, protection for society and rehabilitation. The success rate for all three is pitifully low. In any other field failure on the scale we are witnessing would lead to a clear-out of the entire directorate and a complete rethink of the so-called reforms that have been introduced in the name of progress. But no one that matters in the legal world really gives a toss. What *they're* exercised about is their own holy rituals and their moral passivism. See no evil. Do no evil. They are so obsessed with avoiding doing the wrong thing that they shirk the responsibility they have to do the right thing. Where would we be if surgeons took the same view? The legal profession has talked itself into believing that its first duty is to its own squeaky clean innocence – a thing of beauty that must be kept safe and dry from the bloody business of getting the scales of justice to balance. Purely coincidently of course, this worthy commitment to moral conservation does no harm at all to the bank balance of its devotees. The more legal sophistry generated in court, the fatter the fees. Any thought of cutting down on the crap is met with the indignation of the righteous and dismissed as a dastardly assault on noble Justitia herself."

She smiled. Myles could not be sure if she was trying to solicit his approval or to pour scorn on the need for it.

"If the public were allowed any say in the matter, which of course is totally out of the question, there would be a landslide in favour of punishment being restored as the cornerstone of our justice system. This would mean the courts stopping playing clever buggers and taking all the evidence into account, not just the stuff that gets through the loopholes. It would also mean longer sentences and of course, where appropriate, the death penalty. The public would be subject to a torrent of abuse from the great and the good. They would be told that they were too stupid and too ignorant to make such decisions. Their humanity and decency would be impugned. Yet in spite of all those pressures I think they would follow their instincts. What I'm more dubious about is their ability to resist the guilt they would experience when the first execution was carried out. The old Catholic guilt that kept the Church in business for centuries would re-emerge as the weapon of choice of the liberal establishment that has replaced it. Every organ of the liberal orthodoxy would be put to work to swamp the common but inarticulate instinct for justice in a torrent of self-disgust."

Another smile. This time Myles was in no doubt that he was being patronised. His pride was smarting. But for the time being at least he would let it smart.

"So if you think that, what purpose is served by championing the cause of hard-line justice? For that, from what I understand, is what you do, isn't it?"

His question made an instant impression. There was an obvious re-adjustment of register in her reply.

"You've hit the problem bang on the head, Inspector Myles. There would be absolutely no point in campaigning for hard-line justice, as you call it, only to see it swept away at the first sight of blood. That's precisely the point of our research. What conditions are required before ordinary human beings can be expected to follow through on justice while retaining the healthy human emotions which inspire their aspirations in the first place? These mock trials are experiments in that field. It's easy to condemn some of the monsters we put on trial, but it's not so easy to confront the reality of putting them down."

"Yes, but you don't just conduct fantasy trials and executions, do you? You carry out real punishments, you actually flog criminals, don't you, the ones you think the courts have failed to deal with?"

"Hand on heart, Inspector, I have never wielded a whip in my life."

The smile broadened out into a laugh as she dared Myles to imagine this elegant woman brandishing a whip. She didn't wait for him to acknowledge his failure.

"Advanced society has a chance it has never had before. We can look after the poor, we can heal most of the sick, we can provide educational and cultural opportunities of all kinds. There is no excuse for people to resort to criminality. We have the means and it is our duty to be as kind a society as has ever been on earth, but by the same token we have every right to be a society that shows zero tolerance to those who choose to reject it. Rich families tend to produce spoilt children and that is for the simple reason that the usual disciplines of need and necessity are not in play. When the parents fail to make up for this deficit, their offspring are encouraged to think that the

187

world centres around their needs and to hell with everyone else. Previously this was a problem largely confined to the leisured classes. Nowadays the very poorest lead lives that in terms of ease and comfort would have been unimaginable even to royalty in the past. So we are not just dealing with a class of individuals, we are dealing with people right across the board. On this scale we can't afford to buy into the redemption thing, and it's not a question of being cruel to be kind; it's a question of being hard and being soft at the same time. That's something that's difficult to get the heart round – hence our researches."

It all sounded plausible enough and he'd have been tempted to believe every word of it had he known nothing about Snoddy. There was also of course the business of the beatings; she had had precious little to say on that score. He hadn't got the information he had come looking for, but at least now he had a better understanding of what the Snoddy connection was all about. The added bonus was: he had had a much more charming tutor.

Chapter 38

'Respectful' would be a fit word to describe the manner in which Francis Meadows took his seat before the Panel, but he was having to work too hard to conceal the swagger that had so obviously been put on hold. It was precisely the way youthful waiters or fitness coaches adopt a persona of courteous tolerance to elderly clients; both parties recognise the 'respect' on show as a mere function of the occasion. The details of his CV were confirmed with a modesty that protested too despairingly. Pride was allowed to breach the confinement of its cloister only to acknowledge plaudits for the grand gesture of repentance the young Francis had made in his sixth form year when, as a matter of principal, he had expelled himself from his public school and donned the sackcloth and ashes of his local comprehensive. He did not of course reveal that his place at Cambridge had at that stage already been guaranteed and that the 'local comprehensive' was in fashionable Hampstead. At Cambridge he had joined the Party, a turning point in his life that he was pleased to liken unto a 'coming out'. He had campaigned vigorously for all the causes that 'mattered' – peace, sexual equality, trade union rights – and had been mentioned in dispatches (not the phrase he used) in skirmishes with the Tories, the Military, Northern Irish unionists, Christian fundamentalism and all forms of *bigoted* opposition to mass immigration and the EU. He 'made no apology' for his radicalism; he was sure there were decent Tories, even decent fundamentalists – he stopped short of what was clearly for him the oxymoron of a decent Unionist – but he was a man of principle and those who harboured twisted principles or no principles at all had to be confronted, and that's exactly what he would continue to do if elected to the House of Commons.

There was a complete change of tone when he started to work his way through the set questions. Here detail came in large dollops, detail, that is, on the operations and manoeuvrings that any policy changes would need to go through before emerging as new-born legislation. A sharp brain was proudly allowed to go through its paces. Who, the proud owner of the brain was clearly asking, could fail to be impressed by its mastery of detail and knowledge of how politics worked? Make me your MP and this miserably insignificant constituency will be at the forefront of a radical programme of reform.

What exactly that programme of reform should be gave less opportunity for ingenuity. Little after all was required. It should be obvious to anyone free of the poison of the Daily Mail and that 'cabal of panderers to red-necks' that the drive for social equality is the only licit pursuit of a civilised legislature. The hounding, root and branch, of all forms of sexual discrimination he declared as the sine qua non of twenty-first century membership. (His appreciation of the impishness of the Chairman's inquiry as to whether this would include the scrapping of the BBC's 'Woman's Hour' unfortunately dawned too slowly to earn him credit for self-abasement). State ownership of major industry was at the heart of the socialist vision as was the continued control of education – he took unrepentant pride in sharing the offendedness of those forced to look on as the capitalist progeny prepared for a life of privilege in their public schools. Law and order – that old fixation of the blue-rinse brigade – could only be tackled from behind. Better education, better living conditions, more community involvement – those, along with penal reform, were the areas where the remedy was to be found. Take away the reasons for crime and you take away the crime – simple as that.

George Sinclair cut a very different figure when he clonked into the room. No false modesty here – his every gesture bespoke achievement and distinction. You could see that in his own mind this man was God's most trusted servant, not a whisperer in the divine ear, an adjutant for bouncing ideas off, no, just the humble henchman always on hand when dire deeds needed doing in service of the sacred will. As he looked around the table you had the feeling that he didn't consider the Panel quite worthy of the surrogate presence that he was bringing into their midst. He pre-empted the conventional welcome by the Chairman with a breezy 'How's Trevor?', and, ignoring the answer, called over to Nathan to confirm the venue of an address they were jointly to give to a coyly unspecified workers' group. He seemed to be at pains to create the impression right from the outset that he was not there to impress the Panel; it would be up to them to prove themselves worthy of his attention.

'Direct Action' was the star he lived by. All the niceties and all the nit-picking that went with the high-faluting posturing of parliamentary windbags would be swept away by a huge tidal surge of popular outrage if the clowns at Westminster didn't get their act together and look out for the interests of the people who elected them in the first place. It would be his job, if he was elected, to apprise them of that fact. He made no apology for citing Marx:

'The democratic petty bourgeois only aspire to make the existing society as tolerable for themselves as possible . . . The rule of capital is to be further counteracted, partly by a curtailment of the right of inheritance, and partly by the transference of as much employment as possible to the state. As far as the workers are concerned, one thing, above all, is definite: they are to remain wage labourers as before. However, the democratic petty bourgeois want better wages and security for the workers; in short, they hope to bribe them into accepting their place.'

He quoted this with the passionate clumsiness that an auto-didact might bring to ideas expressed in language just beyond his level of competence. When he had finished and had retrieved his own voice, he became again the master of his message.

"That, comrades, hits the nail bang on the head. The Labour party has become the whore of the middle class twerps that prattle about in their fancy London suburbs. Patronising pricks, the lot of them! What the hell do they know about the problems that ordinary folk have to put up with, many of them caused by the very people who are supposed to stick up for them. Take the view the top brass took of the EU. It used to be the Labour party saw it for the capitalist quango it is – capital talking to capital without the inconvenience of having to make concessions to national parliaments who suffer from the handicap of needing to get themselves elected every few years – it's a sure-fire way of cutting down on the trinkets and baubles they have to feed to the masses. And as for labour, what a set-up! The entire populations of Europe at Capital's beck and call; at the whim of big business they can be shunted round the continent undercutting the local workers and under-mining the Unions. To hell with the housing problems, the strain on social services, the burden on schooling. Not since Victorian times have the English working classes been subject to this level of control by the ruling classes. The movement of labour we have just witnessed continent wide is an exact rerun of what happened on a national scale during the Industrial Revolution when the workforce was cleared out of the countryside and packed like sardines into the slums of the new factory cities. And what, this time round, did our esteemed Party, the so-called workers' party, have to say about it? Can you believe it? They couldn't tell their arse from their elbow; they couldn't see the difference between globalism and international socialism, and in the name of internationalism the bloody fools – I've another word for them, but there's a lady present – the bloody fools sided with Big Business!"

The look that accompanied this tirade would have befitted the face of a cross old schoolmaster returning to class to find the boys flouting the authority of the work he had set them. These particular 'boys' might have thought the storm had reached its height, but there was more to come.

"I ask you why, comrades. Why does a party bloodied in the class struggle sell out like that? I'll tell you, comrades. It's simple; the Party has lost its soul. It has become a bloody gentleman's club. Can you not smell the stench of liberalism? Let's keep out of the mucky fields, gentlemen, it whispers, no nasty vulgar sports for us, leave that to the roughnecks with all their bigoted views on the great social issues. Let us keep the perfume bottle close to our noses and get on with our tea dance, prancing around deodorising the world with our candles of sweetness and light. Let's give the masses the freedom they crave to drink themselves to death, gamble twenty-four seven and get high on the drugs of their choice. And, if that doesn't mind-alter them enough, compulsory education for primary school kids on gay marriage, transsexuality and respect for every culture and every land, except of course their own. But the most important lesson of all, the one that the masses absolutely must absorb, is to learn to love the shame they need to feel if anything that's not on our prissy little list of political correctness, anything at all, should pop up in their hearts or in their heads. The common working man should get on with 'enjoying' life and give the Party power of attorney over his conscience. He should be grateful for being liberated from the drab ordinariness of leading a normal sober, drug-free life, saving up his money in his piggy bank to improve the living standards of his female wife, his boy sons and his girl daughters. I bet Marx never thought the day would come when this kind of false consciousness would be met with approval by a socialist party and not seen as proof positive of membership of the *Lumpenproletariat*."

This was said before the Chairman had a chance to start on the set questions. When he did get to ask them they seemed flat and formulaic, lacking the historical dimensionality that Sinclair had conjured up like a lion and a witch from the wardrobe. His answers patronised the questions with a string of 'Of courses'. *Of course* he would control the press – rags like the Daily Mail wouldn't be allowed to publish their lies. *Of course* there would be no question of promoting such rubbish as gay rights and multiculturalism; there would be no witch hunt either, but people should be allowed to form their own views, free of the pernicious propaganda of the liberal media. *Of course* criminals should be held responsible for their actions and pay for what they have done – the real victims of the liberal fantasy that there are no criminals, only crimes, were the ordinary decent folk who are forced to share their streets with these low-lifes.

The final two questions answered themselves.

"Just look at the present membership of the Labour Party", he said, "and ask yourself where the greatest traitors to the working class movement got their education. Where are the fitters and plumbers, the bus drivers and traffic wardens? No, you won't find any. What you'll find are lawyers and media people, teachers and all the arty-and-farty set. These are the people who have come out of our sewer of an education system smelling of roses and primed to spout the bourgeois cant that passes for progressivism. Just look at what they say and then look at what they do. They are living proof that lies can't live in the real world."

In response to the question of direct action he recalled his experience with Scargill's miners. It had taught him one thing about direct action, he said: you need to think like a military commander.

"It's not just a question of winning the propaganda battle; you've got to have the weight of economic power on your side. That's why Thatcher won; she had built up enough coal reserves to see off the strike. It was a question of who would crack first, the miners or the government, and she saw to it that the government was in a position to outlast the strikers. Isn't it strange that the lesson had not been learned by someone like Scargill, who of all people should have known his Marx?"

When the Chairman thanked him for sharing his thoughts with the Panel, Schinski took it on himself to endorse the Chairman's remarks. It was not something he had planned to do and no last minute thought of strategic gain had entered his head. He was quite simply and quite naively impressed by the glimpse he had had of character in this man, the joining-up of thought and feeling with the way he had led his life. The question of whether he actually agreed or disagreed with the man was strangely irrelevant.

Chapter 39

A much needed break was taken after Sinclair's departure and before the final interview with Robert Snoddy. Nathan Roberts positively glowed with the self-satisfaction that a proud father of a bright sixth former would struggle not to let show at a school prize night. He made a bee-line for Schinski, the most obvious of his fellow admirers. Schinski was practised in the art of using praise as a lubricant for breaking down resistance. But this time he exercised it pro bono, taking a bizarre pleasure in taking his feet off the pedals and allowing the slope to carry him where it would. It came to him only as an after-thought that his un-programmed magnanimity might nonetheless serve the cause of pragmatism. If he scratched Roberts' back, Roberts would surely scratch his. Besides, a lot of what Sinclair said would chime quite well with what he knew of Snoddy's views. His feet went quickly back on to the pedals.

"You know, Nathan, up till now I'd have been inclined to give my first-choice vote to this fellow Snoddy who's just coming up. To be honest, none of the others are much cop, don't you think, especially that prat Brown. But now I'm not so sure. Snoddy might well have to make do with my second preference vote."

Coffee downed and whisperings over, the Panel took their seats for the entrance of the final candidate. After the bluster of the grand old man of the Left, Snoddy's youth was the first thing to impress itself, and with this, understandably, came anticipation of a similar disparity in self-possession. Any such thoughts were immediately dispelled by the sonority of the voice that he produced in response to the Chairman's invitation to outline the main details of his career to date. The Panel heard how, having taken a first in modern languages at Oxford, he had pursued his interest in the question of justice in society and had been fortunate enough to acquire the sponsorship to set up a research foundation. His interest in the subject had been sparked by a series of events when he was in the sixth form at school. The headmaster had been attacked and killed and, for reasons best known to the authorities, *he* had been charged with the murder. Naturally he had been acquitted. Indeed, the trial judge had been furious that the case had even got to court. He had subsequently written a novel based loosely on what had happened, in which he developed in fictionalised form some of the thoughts and impressions it had evoked in him, particularly the way justice and fairness are constantly being neutered by the professional classes. That's why he had used the name The New Prometheans for his research foundation, its principle focus being to explore what it would mean, in both psychological and political terms, to return justice to the people.

In view of what he had said the Chairman deemed it appropriate to start with the question of how to dispel the popular notion that people should be held responsible for crimes that the system has backed them into. Judging from the collaborative tone in which the question was posed, he clearly expected the candidate to go along with the assumption behind it. His expectation was withered instantly to a crisp. Snoddy simply stared at him and asked for the question to be repeated. It was a rhetorical request but it nonetheless required the question to trot out a second time and in doing so look thoroughly ashamed of itself. The ground had been sufficiently readied for Snoddy to implant his thoughts.

"I'm sorry, but I thought this was a Labour Party interview. Have I got it wrong? Is this the point where everyone takes off their masks and exposes themselves as liberal heart-warmers? How can a party that has a proud history of calling a spade a spade sign up for this liberal twaddle? Of course grown men and women must be held responsible for their actions. What's the alternative? If man is no more than the product of the forces that act upon him, nothing any individual does can be subject to censure. That's the same as saying: anything goes. So what would be the point of having any moral code, including the heart-warming liberalism that promoted the idea in the first place? I would put the question on its head. How can we wean the public off this Disneyland version of reality? Fantasy should neither be the inhibitor of action, nor should it be the instigator. On the one hand we have the gatherings of fashionable progressives having their narcissistic love-ins with their beautiful selves, on the other we get ugly pub talk of hanging and flogging and nuking the evil out of the world. What we need is to infuse some reality into the mix. That's what we are about in The New Prometheans. If someone really thinks that murderers and terrorists should be free to walk the streets after they have served their liberally diluted sentences, then they should put their money where their mouth is and take responsibility for the deaths that their leniency sponsors day and daily. Equally, if the pub bore wants to hang and flog, then, provided it can be established that he's not using this as a front for sadistic urges, he should be asked to carry it out himself. A society that had to confront the realities of dispensing justice would be more likely to make the right decisions about it. As things stand at the moment, it is the liberal establishment that is making all the running and the people at the bottom of the social heap, the very people the Labour Party is supposed to represent, that are picking up the tab."

"Could you put some flesh on the bone here, Mr Snoddy? Where exactly are you going with this?"

The interruption came from Hugh Savage. Everyone was quite taken aback. Savage rarely contributed; he was an inveterate note-taker, just like those ubiquitous Japanese tourists who don't do first-hand experience; everything has to go through the lens of a camera. The rarity value of this was of course lost on Snoddy who one could see was eager to respond.

"I would like to see a complete shake-up of our very complacent criminal justice system. I'd start with the trial. How is it that we have a government committee – isn't it called 'Nice'? – tasked with deciding on what life-saving drugs the NHS can afford to dispense, in other words which categories of patient they are prepared to throw to the wolves. Yet not a peep is raised against the extravagent wastefullness of criminal trials. The possibility of an innocent man being convicted obviously carries greater weight than the virtual certainty that huge numbers of patient lives will be lost by default. Does that not strike you as curious? Apart from the expense of such trials, there is also the question of the ability of juries to take in the splurges of facts they are bombarded with, most of them of dubious relevance. Any teacher will tell you that concentration levels, even among the brightest, have thresholds well below the levels we fantasise juries are capable of. I have quite a few ideas as to how to deal with this problem, but I don't think this is the appropriate forum for me to go into detail.

"On the question of penal reform, why is it, I ask, that 'penal reform' always implies further steps in the direction of liberalisation? Anything that would tighten controls on prisoners, make prison a place of punishment, a place no one would ever want to return to is regarded as horrifying and not suitable celebral content for anyone in polite society. It's interesting to watch the liberal mind at work. On the one hand it picks away at all existing controls and then, having done so, makes a great show of being scandalised by the subversive forces that the resultant laxity allows to thrive. It seizes on this as further proof that prisons don't work and concludes that genuine penal reform is only a staging post on the way to the ultimate goal of abolishing the entire practice of incarceration. A drug culture has been allowed to develop in our prisons. Therefore, so the argument goes, if you lock people up there is a real risk that you'll be turning them into drug addicts. This invites the obvious conclusion: it's pure folly to lock people up. The question that's never asked is why a drug culture has been allowed to develop in the first place. Could it not possibly have anything to do with the great liberal leaps of faith into the unenlightened dark: freedom of movement, prison visits, internet access, availability of mobile phones etc., etc.? You have to give it to these reformers; they don't just go up and murder the opposition, they drip-feed it a poisonous diet and then after turning it into a retching basket case they consent to do the decent thing and put it out of its misery."

This was too much for Secretary Savage. The inveterate scribbler had put down his pen. He was clearly agitated.

"I'm sorry, Mr Snoddy, but you sound like someone on the other side of the political divide. What is a hanger-and-flogger doing applying for a Labour nomination? We are the party of compassion and understanding."

Snoddy's face betrayed a glimpse of a sneer, but it was instantly stifled and an obviously forced-fed expression of the compassion and understanding he had been accused of lacking substituted.

"I'm sorry too, Mr ... Savage isn't it? But the people I am sorry for, the people who I think have the first claim to the Party's compassion and understanding are the victims of crime, not the perpetrators. You know, we used to think of evil as something so obviously ugly as to be self-identifying – the devil and his gargoyles with all those horns and that. Then we got enlightened and realised that evil didn't always come in wolf's clothing. We were so proud of our cleverness at making this discovery that we went to town on the good and turned a blind eye and a very deaf ear to the bad and the ugly. Everybody was seen in God's image; the face of Satan was sanctimoniously banned from every mirror in the land. The truth of course is that people are neither good nor bad; they have both goodness and badness in them and they must take blame as well as credit for the scope they allow each of these forces to operate through them. Contrary to what the fairytale morality that has taken hold of our infantilized society would have us all believe, the good in men doesn't wipe out the bad."

The answer had not come in a register Savage was expecting. He was taken unawares and needed time to reconfigure before fashioning a response. This was denied him by the Chairman who was anxious to move on to the next question.

"How do you react, Mr Snoddy, to the notion that the Tory elitism in education is a deliberate ploy to deprive the working class of its most able members?"

This was the one Snoddy had decided should be his big gamble. The answer he had prepared would shock them, he knew, but he was counting on Schinski having done enough in the background to keep him in the hunt amid the fury it was sure to cause. To go back to the golfing analogy, he was dicing with danger now and running the risk of hitting the ball out of bounds; it was the only way he could see to give himself any chance of reaching the green with his second.

"I don't do conspiracy theory. The Tories are opportunists; they improvise as they go along. The notion of a grand conspiracy to deplete the working class and cream off the best of them is Machiavellian on a scale that is well beyond their very narrow ideological horizons. But even if it were, it wouldn't matter. The whole concept of the class struggle is well past its sell-by date. It was an excellent analytical tool for dealing with the social and economic reality of the nineteenth and early twentieth centuries, but it no longer corresponds to the reality before us. There are still working class people, yes, millions of them, but their interests can no longer be served by grouping them together and treating them as a single entity. It is considered as racism – a word, by the way, which has been liberally abused, and mainly by liberals... Shall we say it is not seen as acceptable to treat people exclusively in terms of their ethnicity, religion or nationality? Why then is it legitimate to treat the working class as an amorphous social block? Go to any working class area and you'll find the people there differentiate among themselves using criteria that social engineers would most certainly frown upon. They actually use old-fashioned moral judgements, and show no shame in doing so. They judge their neighbours on scales of such things as cleanliness, decency, industry, thrift, self-improvement – sometimes even the old-fashioned notion of good taste. Look down any working class street and you'll see houses that are well kept and clearly loved and others that have the shame of neglect peeping out from the weeds and litter in the garden, the peeling paint on the doors and the grime on the windows. It all shouts out: you see what the council is *not* doing for me... I think it's time our Party started to tell these people 'We don't care! We are here to look after the victims, but you're not the victims, you're the enemy! The Labour Party is there to help those who try to help themselves. When *you* start to care, *we'll* start to care, but not until then.'

"Education is the greatest agent of self-help; it is something that gets inside the person. Yet all the Labour party seems to be content to do is to turn the lower orders into patients in need of its first-aid, and that first-aid always amounts to getting the state to provide them with the toys of their choice and as much pocket money as can be screwed out of the relatively better-off. Asking the low-paid to fork out for important things such as housing, education or health is not considered an appropriate use of this pocket money; such grown-up things are seen as the obligation of the state which is obligated to act *in loco parentis*. No serious in-put is expected from the underclass beyond the obligation to remain within the bounds of non-criminality. It's demeaning, for it just about matches the expectations one would have of a five-year-old!

202

"I think it's time for a radical change of heart. Our Party has played a shameful part in the process of allowing education to nose-dive into a form of naked consumerism that operates on the principle of the customer always being right. Selling is all. To hell with the product. If the customer finds the course you're offering too demanding, change it, but keep the name of the course. The punter must continue to think he's getting the real McCoy; he's not to know it's a pig in a poke. You can't expect the modern quasi-student to be prepared to put in long, frustrating hours confronting his own limitations. Yet that's precisely what true education demands of those who genuinely want to acquire it. Water it all down; declare a state of parity of esteem for all branches of study from rocket science to lace-tying; hand out wads of diplomas and degrees and make every consumer happy, reinforced in his cocky assurance of being the measure of all things. The founding fathers of our Party must be turning in their graves as they look on and see how the Party has not only acquiesced, but in fact has led the way in turning one of the kingpins of socialist progressivism into a tawdry exercise in capitalist-style deceit."

An inaudible gasp went up from the Panel members – it could not be heard, but it could be seen on their faces as they looked to each other to confirm the impact of what they were hearing. It was a moment Schinski knew he had to seize. He had not expected Snoddy to ruffle feathers. He had assumed he would have told the Panel what he thought the Panel would want to hear. That's what most MPs did after all. Once they got themselves nominated and then elected, they could say and do what they pleased, citing the received wisdom that they were not mere delegates but men chosen for the soundness of their judgement and answerable in the first instance to their own conscience. It was a tried and trusted method of keeping democracy at a safe distance from the voters and from selection panels such as this.

Why the hell did Snoddy feel the need to blurt out what he thought? He couldn't seriously believe – could he? – that in politics of all places honesty is the best policy. It was too late for an exercise in watering down what had been said. The thing had to be brazened out. With histrionic solemnity Schinski got to his feet, made great show of wonderment at the candidate's audacity and then took on the collective chin the chastening blow that had been struck to the Panel's sensibilities.

"Comrades, I have attended many gatherings such as this. Normally what we hear is music to the ear – not good music, certainly not horrible music, just mood music to soothe and reassure that all's right with the world, or more important, all's right with the Party. Well, today we've heard something different, something many of us found not exactly melodic. But you know what they say: true friends are the only ones with the right to tell home truths. I'd like to thank you, Mr Snoddy, for being so frank with us. You have given us much to ponder and you have shown confidence in us not to follow the line of least resistance. As we all know, insecure employers have a track record of turning down able candidates if they sniff the theat of being shown up."

This met with a very mixed response, but it went down well with the Chairman who was relieved to have had the burden of appraisal lifted from him. The remaining questions were worked through. They produced little in the way of feather-ruffling answers and Snoddy was accorded all the conventional civilities when he took his leave of the Panel.

Chapter 40

At just about the time Snoddy was delivering his shock treatment to the Panel Inspector Myles was making his way to the rectory. The Reverend John had made an impression on Myles. The man offended against the maxim of *a slot for everything and everything in its slot* which was a cornerstone of Myles' view of life and a given about the way the world basically shapes up. Any re-arranging that might on occasion be required he saw as minor restoration work on a temporarily errant status quo. When he was younger he had been fundamentalist in this belief, but his time with Stuart Stranaghan had taught him to be more accepting of the varying degrees of disarrangement and bedragglement that reality can get itself into. When confronted with characters such as the Reverend John he could persuade himself to put their perverse methods of percolating reality down to the strange late twentieth century craze for surrealistic distortion. He had not as yet come as far as to understand what would induce anyone to go down this road. Why any mature man, let alone one who clearly had some wisdom about him, would want to project himself as a with-it hippy beaming in from the nineteen-sixties remained a total mystery to him. One thought did occur: Could it be that the Reverend felt somewhat alien as an agent of the eternal values and needed something more obviously temporal to pass himself off?

It was a fine morning, crisp, with patches of frost on the path and the grass sparkling on the lawn as the melting frost turned to dew. The old house had an air of welcome about it, not as an asylum from the cold air, more as a homely extension of what was on offer in the garden. The ice-cream van jingle that came back to life when he pressed the doorbell brought a smile. He had forgotten all about the silly thing, but it did fit in terribly well with the thoughts he had just been having. This time the door was opened not by an eclectically clad cleric, but by a shabbily clad, but handsome woman in her middle forties smoking a cigarette. The cliché image of 'cleaning lady' immediately erased in Myles' mind's eye the actual features that the woman presented, but he was forced to refocus the moment she spoke.

"You must be Inspector Myles. My husband is expecting you. If you would follow me into the library?"

Without waiting for him to respond, she turned on her heel and led the way, throwing in a remark from over her shoulder about the frost and the damage it might be doing to her late-flowering geraniums. Nothing was said to announce his presence to the room; she merely opened the door, ushered him in and made off in pursuit of her own business, presumably something to do with geranium preservation. Inside, two figures got to their feet from the two tatty armchairs that had been positioned to capture what heat there was from the aspiring blaze in the hearth. The Reverend John came forward, arm outstretched, to greet his guest. The other figure, a young man of slight build with fuzzy hair and a decided stoop, remained by his chair with the air of someone at a loss to know what his role should be in the reception of the newcomer. When the Reverend introduced him he ventured only a fleeting glimpse at the Inspector's face. A third chair was pulled up and the three men installed themselves in front of the fire.

"I was anxious to talk to you, Mr Ross, to get some background on an organisation, The New Prometheans I believe it was called. I am told you were a member?"

Joseph muttered a perfunctory 'yes' and seemed content to leave it there. Myles was taken unawares; he did not expect the ball back in his court so soon.

"What can you tell me about the organisation? What was its purpose, what was it trying to achieve?"

Joseph gave a little glance to the side as if he were taking instruction from some invisible presence. Some kind of permission seemed to have been given as suddenly he started to articulate his words with an unexpectedly confident clarity.

"Prometheus was a Titan who stole fire from the gods and gifted it to men. Fire has two important characteristics; light and power. This is true both literally and metaphorically. Metaphorically, it is synonymous with the process of enlightenment, the ability of reason to take in the world, and the power follows on from that enlightenment to reshape the world. Historically, the Enlightenment was the wholescale rejection by men of reason of the authority of church doctrine and the overthrowing of the political and social dominance that emanated from that authority. Some of us think that modern society has come to a similar pass. The villain in this case is of course not the Church; it's the professional classes who have greatly exceeded the authority sanctioned by their expertise – lawyers who tell us what justice means, educationalists who determine what skills and values should be taught, senior policemen who decide what crimes should be investigated and which could be 'excused', and of course politicians who look down their noses at the values of their electorate. Can you imagine giving the bus driver the authority to decide where the bus should go?"

"So how did you propose to go about putting things right, as you saw it?"

"We held meetings to open eyes and spread the word, just like John here, when he gives his sermons."

"But you did more than that, didn't you? You did some … what shall I call it? … 'fieldwork' …, didn't you? Tell me about the 'fieldwork'."

Myles realised his mistake as soon as the words came out. He had been much too harassing. A look of anxiety took over on Joseph's face from the confidence that had grown as he laid out the Promethean position.

"I'm not sure what you mean. Do you mean the tests we did for Robby?"

A mere nod from Myles left him unaided. He had to make what he could of the original question.

"Robbie was always keen not to overestimate the power that reason exercises over our actions. There's no point, he said, in reaching a rational conclusion and not having the psychological strength to carry it through. So he made us do a lot of role playing. We didn't always know at the time whether or not it was a role play we were doing. That would have defeated the point. We had to believe we were really being asked to follow through on what our rational selves had dictated."

"I can understand that, but can you tell me what exactly was involved in these role plays?"

Joseph just looked blankly at him as if the question had not been asked.

"There were floggings. I know about them, but was there anything else?"

This question went the way of the first. Myles was getting desperate. He needed to find some way of provoking a response. A hunch came to him suddenly and he played it.

"You were involved in that big test that Robbie carried out, the one where he convened a jury to try a man for murder, weren't you?"

The 'yes' that came in a soft whisper from Joseph seemed somehow disconnected from the question. It was as if it was in answer to a slightly differently phrased question that he had been asking himself. Myles took his cue from the tone of the 'yes'.

"But you weren't just a member of the jury, you were also a member of the firing squad, weren't you, Joseph? Is that when you realised that you didn't want anything more to do with the Prometheans?"

This time the 'yes' was more brusque and more synchronised with the question. Myles gave it space to follow up on itself, but the Reverend John, seeing the mounting stress level in his ward, made a timely intervention.

"Joseph went through hell making that decision, Inspector, and he's gone through hell ever since living with it. Tell him, Joseph, what made you do it. Tell him. I know it hurts you to even think about it, but you need to confront those demons, not hide away from them."

Joseph took in several gasps of air in an effort to get his breathing under control. The clergyman reached for a glass of water that was sitting on a tray beside his chair and handed it to him. Joseph took hold of it, but seemed not to notice it in his hand as he squared up to the task of finding his words.

"I did it because I believed it was right. I saw the cruelty that that man had perpetrated and I wanted to rub it out. I couldn't do anything to make it 'unhappen', but I could at least eliminate what was left of it in the world. And what was left of it in the world was this man who had tortured and humiliated his victim and then just put him to death. Can you imagine the pain and terror Brown must have endured in his last hours, how he must have lost all his dignity as a human being – he probably even begged for his life. Maybe you can't, but I could, and don't tell me two wrongs don't make a right and all that sanitised wisdom – it's the wisdom of people looking for an excuse not to upset their own tranquillity. Well, I did a proper job on my tranquillity I'll tell you. I still think I was right, but that didn't stop me feeling I was wrong. One thing I did know – I could never do it again."

He paused and did take a sip of the water. The others might as well not have been in the room; it was himself he was really talking to.

"Don't tell me that that makes things all right, that it makes me a good person, because I listened to my conscience. I'll tell you what it makes me: it makes me someone who might as well not have a brain. What's the point of all the reasoning that goes into making a judgement and not having the moral stamina to follow through on what you've judged to be right? Dwayne Rodgers deserved to die for what he did. I thought it through and I'm in no doubt that I came to the right conclusion, and yet I fell apart when I followed through and did the dirty work that my reason demanded. Worse than that – it turns out I didn't even do that dirty work, I only thought that I had, and that's all it took to reduce me to a quivering wreck. I'm pathetic!"

So Wright had lied. There could be no doubt that this was the same charade that he had taken part in and yet he'd said he didn't know any of the other participants. Myles' mind was focused on this revelation, when suddenly the name 'Dwayne Rodgers' jumped out at him. He had come across that name before. Where was it? Yes, he remembered, it had cropped up in a report he had read, and it wasn't Wright's report, he was sure of that. It was in Stranaghan's report, that was it. That was the name of the murder victim he had found in a barn following up on an anonymous tip-off. There was definitely something wrong here. It couldn't possibly be a coincidence that the man who had been 'executed' by Snoddy's jury should suddenly turn up as a cadaver at almost exactly the same time. The two things simply had to be linked. And yet neither Stranaghan nor Wright thought to make the link? What was going on?

"Tell me, Joseph, at what stage did you become aware that the 'execution' wasn't for real?"

Joseph brightened at the question. It was much more comfortable to get back to hard facts.

"Robbie let me stew for quite some time – a couple of days at least. Of course that was part of the experiment. He wanted to see how I stood up to the psychological pressures. Yes, I remember. It was the day after Inspector Stranaghan came to see me. The Inspector had me convinced I was going to be arrested for murder. I hadn't realised Robbie had roped him in. I didn't know he was part of the role play. I tell you, it was one of the worst experiences I've ever had waiting for that squad car to come and pick me up."

"Inspector Stranaghan? *He* came to see you?"

This was getting worse by the minute.

"Yes, and he got me to write a full confession. He told me Robbie had set me up. He convinced me that he was trying to pin the murder on me and that the only way I had to avoid a long prison sentence was to turn Queen's evidence against Robbie. I fell for it hook, line and sinker. He got me to write a full confession covering everything that had happened. I signed it and he went off with it."

"But he didn't actually arrest you?"

"No, he said that a squad car would come and pick me up. That was the last I heard from him. No squad car ever appeared. I was petrified. I couldn't understand what was going on. And then Robbie came and told me that the whole thing was a charade."

"What did you do after that?"

"My nerves were shot. I wandered around for a few days. I didn't know where I was or what I was doing. I do remember sleeping rough on the streets. I couldn't face going back to my flat. It was too painful. Eventually I got fixed up in a hostel and they got me a job at a garden centre. That's when I met John here. He took me in and got me back on my feet. There was no question of me going back to my studies. I couldn't see any point. Why would you bother filling your head with thoughts and ideas if all you're going to do is abandon them the minute reality kicks in? I simply didn't believe anymore in the whole 'thought' thing. John helped me; he helped me to see a kind of light. It isn't what you would call the light of reason. It's different. It's a light that shines into you, not out on the things you're trying to see. But it's much better than being stuck in the dark and looking out."

211

Joseph was much calmer now. He went on to talk about his relationship with Justin Wright and how he had leaned on him as a support figure, something he was now ashamed of. Relying on the strength of others, he now saw, was no way to assert the strength of your own convictions, the very opposite in fact. What had started out as a painful confession was now taking on a cathartic glow as Joseph toured the battleground between reason and conscience. The Reverend John was unfailing in his support. "Better to aim at honest decency than heroic virtue", he said. "The path of sanity is always underpinned by humility and there is no shame in following it."

As he left the two men, Myles had much to think about. Joseph was clearly telling the truth, at least the truth as he saw it. Of that there could be no doubt. But how *could* this be the truth? Could Stuart Stranaghan really have consented to be part of Snoddy's game? What could possibly have induced him to do that? The question spun round and round but failed to find anything passable to fit into. It was only after frustration had succumbed to defeat that his thoughts turned to the nature of the threat that had been made to Joseph. How could pressurising the unfortunate into a confession by telling him he had been betrayed by Snoddy have any bearing on the so-called experiment? Snoddy seemingly wanted to test the pressure a normal healthy conscience would put on the rational self, but this would not show that; it was pressure of a completely different sort.

Justin Wright was now no longer a lone figure in Myles' dock. However regretful it was, a second seat would now be needed.

Chapter 41

The hiatus left by Snoddy's departure from the room was quickly filled by a flurry of indignation from Hugh Savage who had deemed the situation serious enough to warrant a flamboyant flinging down of his pen on the table before him.

"That's the most outrageous cheek I have ever witnessed. That man is never a socialist. He is an affront to everything our Party stands for. He spits in the eye of our long and proud tradition of progressive liberalism and he laughs at us for standing shoulder to shoulder with the most vulnerable members of our society. Who the hell does he think he is? And what makes him think he could ever be acceptable as a Labour Party candidate?"

Margaret Millership was quick to take up the chord with a litany of transgressions she had noted against the fundamental principles of penal reform, the Christian faith in the powers of rehabilitation, the wonderful system of justice that had been developed over centuries and had become the model for the rest of the world. This 'pipsqueak' seemed to think he knew better and we should turn the clock back and go all 'Old testament' with eyes coming out for eyes and teeth for teeth. She declared herself 'lost for words'.

Schinski could see that help was urgently needed, but it needed to come from a source other than him. Freddie Douglas had been primed to oblige. Unlike the others who had remained seated during their outbursts, he rose to his feet. It was a slow and deliberate act, designed it seemed to allow him to take in the faces of his fellow judges, for his gaze held the stage for several significant seconds before words came to his lips.

"I fully understand the strong feelings that have been

expressed by my two colleagues here. Mr Snoddy has been outspoken in his criticism of some of the ideas and sentiments which this great Party of ours holds dear. But just pause for a moment and try and take in what he was telling us. First of all, he was reminding us who this Party is supposed to stand for. It is the Labour Party and it's called the Labour Party because it is charged with representing the worker. Do you not think he may have a point when he tells us that our memories need jogging on this score? He is not wrong about the way we put the ideology of internationalism before the interests of the British working man when we supported the globalist interests of big business in its advocacy of mass immigration. It was the working man who had to pay the price, as Mr Snoddy rightly pointed out, as, I remind you, did the previous candidate, who no one would accuse of not being on the socialist ticket.

"As for education, are we really happy that we have been getting it right as a party? One of our aims was to get more and more people into university. It seemed a good idea at the time, but what has the actual benefit been to those young people we encouraged to go? Better paid jobs? No, not a bit of it, just more young people having their hopes raised, only to have them dashed. The number of proper degree-level jobs was never going to rise accordingly – they just stayed more or less the same. What increased was the number of graduates doing jobs they didn't need to pauper themselves to get. There's a nasty little statistic that no one in the Party wants anyone to know: social mobility has actually decreased in the decades since academic selection was abolished. And which party was responsible for that? The nasty Tories trying to keep the working class in its place? No, it was ourselves, at least the enlightened selves among us, those very same people who claim to be the champions of those at the bottom of the pile. It shouldn't have been beyond their intelligence grade to predict what was going to happen. It stands to reason that the precious diplomas and certificates that enabled bright youngsters from working class backgrounds to compete with their better-heeled middleclass rivals would lose their oomph, and in the absence of a reliable means of identifying true merit, employers would be left with little option other than to fall back on the bad old ways that public examinations were brought in to eliminate.

"The thoughts he brought to social justice I found particularly interesting. He's absolutely right: the legal establishment *has* become a law unto itself … if you'll pardon the pun. *It* makes the rules and the rules are zealously locked away and kept out of the reach of the unwashed laity. It is seen as something close to sacrilege for us even to voice an opinion about them. The length of 'a life sentence', for example, is a matter no longer to be decided by the Almighty, it's now subject to the whims and wisdom of the judiciary. And as for the police, their job you'd think is to look after us law-abiders as we go about our business. But you'd be wrong; you couldn't have failed to notice the fixation of the higher ranks with enforcing the rules of political correctness. Why would any policeman harbouring hopes of promotion waste his time putting burglars, muggers and drug dealers behind bars when there is so much more professionally lucrative work available? Even worse, the few real criminals the police actually take the trouble to catch are almost invariably let off. They might be given a caution, and if that fails to do the job, a second one and even a third one. And you can count on them being supplied with a right-on social worker to make excuses for them. Occasionally they receive a fine, and if, as invariably happens, they don't pay it, they're fined again. Again they don't pay and again they're let off. They may be given community service; they don't do it, and they're let off again or given bail. When they're on bail, they often commit further offences, but they're not locked up; no, they're given bail again. It's a complete farce, the whole thing.

"No, comrades – Mr Snoddy has told us some home truths

about the way the political class has let down the very people they are here to look after. We politicians have taken our eye off the ball and got sucked into a liberal bubble that distorts the light and prevents us from seeing what's happening in real time. I think we should be grateful to Mr Snoddy for this wake-up call. He will certainly get my vote, and I hope some of you at least will have the guts to admit that he has got a lot of things right that we in our Party and many in other parties have been getting very wrong."

No sooner had Douglas sat down than Max Fischer jumped to his feet – it would seem that Douglas had started a trend. Schinski did not know what to expect. Was this a leap of indignation or had Dr Greenfield done his work and brought his fellow Germanist onside?

"The other night I bumped into an old friend and we talked about things I don't often get a chance to discuss these days. Few of you – if any – have heard of Christoph Martin Wieland. He's an eighteenth century German writer. Among many of the things he wrote was a satire called 'Die Abdiriten' ('The Abderites'). He subtitled it 'A Very Probable Story'. In it the people of Abdera are so hell-bent on establishing their cultural credentials that they attack anyone who has the effrontery to dissent. One evening they get very irate when criticism is voiced during a production of one of Euripides' tragedies. How dare anyone challenge the genius of the great Euripides? But they are left without any wind in their sails when it turns out that man voicing the criticism is none other than the great tragedian himself! Further down the line the Abderites get smitten by religion – which in their case takes the form of adoration of the common frog. A total ban is imposed on any activity that might interfere with the life cycle of this reptile. The wellbeing of the frog is placed above any other consideration. The city and the surrounding countryside are hostage to the fortunes of the frog. The more bog-like the environment becomes, the more

216

hospitable it is to the frogs. Gradually over time the city degenerates into an enormous swamp and sinks slowly into the sea.

"That satire was written nearly three hundred years ago, my friends. Have we really learned anything since? I doubt it. Are we not guilty of exactly the same follies? – Everyone trying to outdo the other in their adherence to orthodoxy? No one able to stand back, look at the big picture and see where their devotion to the communal myth is taking them?

"As I listened to our young friend just now I couldn't help thinking of us and all the rest of this Party of ours, in our togas with the scrolls of ancient wisdom in our hands propounding the orthodoxies that have been handed down from the mists of the time of Kier Hardy. The question I think we should all be asking ourselves is: Would we recognize Kier Hardy if he came among us now? Or would we, like the *Abderites*, hound him out of the Party for challenging remedies to the ills of the world as it used to be?"

Schinski banged the table in approval and sprang to his feet. He fully endorsed the sentiments of the last two speakers and was conscious of how well the analysis offered by Snoddy overlapped with the excellent contribution made by George Sinclair. As well as this common ground, there were enough significant differences between the two men to offer the Executive Committee a rich choice of candidate. As he spoke, his eyes remained firmly focused on Nathan Roberts. Roberts returned his significant smile. The old Marxist's vote was in the bag.

Hugh Savage and Margaret Millership continued to protest but they were the only dissenting voices when Reggie Whitehouse, the outgoing MP, formally proposed that George Sinclair and Robert Snoddy should be the names to go forward for final selection.

Chapter 42

It was just going to be an impromptu celebration, the message on the answer phone confirming the venue had said. There would just be the two of them, Eardley and himself, and they would be delighted if he could join them. Most of the others were up north at the constituency, but a nice meal, some quality claret and a bit of what *you garrulous Irish* call 'craic' would do justice to the occasion. Stuart could guess what the celebration was in aid of. He had no particular desire to share in Snoddy's triumphs, but as he couldn't bring himself to say no to the prospect of an evening in the company of Bruce Greenfield, he found himself on the top deck of a bus on his way to *La Belle Epoque.*

It was a bleak kind of evening. The light was on its way out but the darkness had not yet fully established itself. The light emitted from the shop windows and the neon signs above them had not enough contrasting night to outshine, but the promise was there of spirited resistance when the denizens of the dark finally gathered their forces and imposed their worst. His mind went back to an evening in his childhood when he was being taken by his beloved Aunt Jean along the brightly lit area of Ballymacarrett in Belfast. It was on the far side of the river from where he lived and he remembered the notion he formed at the time that the people in this part of the city most likely had ways of banishing the dark – hearty things like drinking and chatting and singing in pubs – that the Presbyterians on the north side shied away from. It had nudged him towards becoming an anthologist of urban illumination – every new sign that the thoroughfares of Belfast could muster, especially if it was one that flashed, he saw as a stepping stone to the metropolitan illustriousness of a New York or a London. How naive, and how utterly crass, he thought now, but it is good to be reminded that in the past we were not always as we are now in the present. It should be a lesson to us to be more charitable in our judgements, yet somehow it doesn't work like that. We look on our former casts of mind much in the way we think of our pre-literate and pre-numerate perception of the world, as something for us to be taught out of. It was an insight that had come to him many times before, but his stubborn reluctance to embrace it brought another Presbyterian image from his past to mind, the would-be convert and the eye of the needle.

The bus left him off a few streets away from the restaurant. It was beginning to drizzle. Umbrellas were being hoisted and coats buttoned up. He dug in his pocket for the Breton cap he had taken to wearing. He had always hated caps, but now his thinning hair made them a necessity in cold air. The prospect of meeting up with Bruce Greenfield invariably inspired anticipation of good chat and cerebral stimulation, but the doubt always lurked that the man was more of a good companion than a good friend. As Snoddy's former schoolmaster he had been on Snoddy's side during the investigation at St Jude's, but, to be fair, he did warn the Inspector against making an arrest. At the time he appeared to be acting more in Snoddy's interests than in his, but in the event it proved to be wise counsel which, had he taken it, would have spared him much grief. And again, Greenfield's word had proved reliable when he had urged him to trust Snoddy over the Justin Wright business. By accepting to exercise the choice that Snoddy had given him he had severely compromised himself and was totally at Snoddy's mercy. Greenfield had assured him that Snoddy would not exploit his position. Snoddy could easily have used it subsequently to blackmail him, but he hadn't. And if truth be told, the erstwhile upholder of the law was not altogether unhappy that two guilty men were serving sentences for crimes they didn't actually commit. There were plenty of crimes they had committed for which they were not serving sentences. The murder – and he did consider it murder – of Dwayne Rodgers was a totally different matter however. He couldn't bring himself to apply the same logic to it. Rodgers had been behind the murder of Francis Brown. Of that there was no doubt. It was a brutal murder inspired by the blackest sadistic instincts. If the state had condemned Rodgers to die for what he had done, he would have had no qualms whatsoever, but Snoddy's crowd had no right to step in and do the job the state had cravenly failed to do. He wasn't being consistent, he knew that. If he could bring himself to condone the incarceration of two technically innocent men, why all his misgivings over Rodgers' killing? He had wrestled with this over and over again, and the answer that kept peeping out at him from behind the shadows was not a flattering one. When you got down to it, the difference that really mattered to him was not, as he would have liked to think, that one involved the taking a human life and the other only the deprivation of liberty, but that one involved *doing* something wrong and the other simply *allowing* something wrong to be done. It was pathetic really; he was clinging to the spurious innocence of the non-vegetarian who feels free to curl his lip at the barbarity of the butcher. That was the downside of an evening with Greenfield; there would be no escaping an uncomfortable face-to-face with his moral confusion.

Eardley had ordered champagne to toast *'new beginnings'* in Bury West. It was explained that Snoddy was far from home and dry, but by all accounts had a more than even chance of being selected as the Labour candidate for the constituency.

"We've struck gold', Eardley explained, "We found Robert an agent who can make things happen. We thought it was a long shot at first, but this man has done his stuff. He has managed to persuade them up there that Robert is saying the kind of things they need to hear if they're to get their party back on speaking terms with its own grass roots."

"So what exactly is he hoping to achieve if he gets himself elected?"

The question was brusque, closer to aggressive than he had meant it to be. Eardley however seemed not to notice.

"It's hard to say exactly what can be expected. In itself his election would be a small thing, but it might be the first of many small things which in time could become a very big thing. I watched a documentary recently about bridge-building. It described how they get the enormous cables that hold the bridge up across between the two towers; they just feed little wires across, four at a time, and, when they have tens of thousands of them in place, they wrap them round in one huge bundle. Patience is the name of the game."

"I don't think that's what Stuart meant, Matt. I think he wanted to know what was on Robert's wish list."

Stuart's nod of agreement gave Greenfield the go-ahead to take over the answer.

"Robert thinks, and on this I do agree with him, that the whole political debate has become too 'precious' – it's as if everyone is playing badminton with a shuttlecock immersed in a PC solution that must be kept from falling in the dirt and making contact with all those nasty germs. They bat this around and that around and keep everything in the air. All goings-on are well above the head of anyone whose feet are planted on the ground. The important thing to know about germs though is that the only way to beat them is to join them. If you keep avoiding them for long periods allergies develop. In the end you become allergic to all forms of organic reality and the only place you're safe is in an oxygen tent."

Greenfield was warming up. He took his companions on a conducted tour of *the post-war graveyard of elephants-in-the-room*, tracing the graph of the increased severity of response to any mention of the un-PC. Disapproval for a considerable time had remained at the level of mild condescension – *silly Billy* –

but then it took a leap to righteous derision – *nasty swine* – and from there before you could say 'Gollywog' we found ourselves in a world of hate speech and thought law – *Nazi pig!* When he switched his attention from politics to the arts the old boy became even more voluble.

"Conceptual art, now there's a thing, gentlemen. The illuminated elite decide what it is and the rest of us go along with it or risk being frozen in the primordial frost of pre-enlightenment. Any collection of everyday objects can be anointed as art provided the magic is performed by someone with a licence to practice; the arrangement can mean whatever the artist says it means. Alternatively, it can mean what you, the viewer, want it to mean. Alternatively again, it might just be a clever ruse by the initiates to confuse and expose that terribly old-fashioned bourgeois need, felt only by the naive of course, to make sense of the world. The would-be disciple is on a hiding to nothing. Even crass subservience to the whim of the artist earns him no credit, since these great ones will not be denied their muse-given right to reconfigure their interpretations as the mood takes them, from day to day, from hour to hour even. Yet still undeterred, the toadying cultural aspirants cling on to the smock strings of their heroes in the forlorn hope of crumbs from the high table, or should I say blessed bread from the Eucharist?"

The talk bubbled in similar vein through the starter and most of the main course. It was only after the decision to go for a third bottle of the excellent *Brunello di Montalcino* that Greenfield brought up the subject of Myles.

"So you had a visit from your old sergeant, Stuart – a fine young man, a good heart and quite a good brain to go with it. How is he? You tell me he's been promoted."

Stuart's antennae were immediately activated: Had he been invited here just to provide information about Myles' enquiries? It was perfectly reasonable for them to want to pump him, but it did put a dent in the sense of inclusion he had been encouraged to assume.

"Yes, he's a Detective Inspector now. As I told you on the phone, it's Justin he's investigating. The top brass, it seems, aren't too happy about his account of the case. I don't think there's much to worry about though. I can't see the investigation getting very far as long as everyone is discreet."

Greenfield smiled thinly.

"I passed the news on to Robert of course. As you can imagine, he has other things on his plate at the moment, but he pointed out that there is one weak link in the chain, a chap called Joseph Ross. From what he says, if young Myles gets to him, there's no telling what worms will crawl out of the can. Matt here got one of his people to make some enquiries as to Joseph's present whereabouts. He traced him to a garden centre. He had worked there for a time after his breakdown, but he had lost that job and nobody could say where he had gone to. What he did find out however was that a police Inspector had been there the day before asking the same questions."

He looked to Stuart in expectation of reassurance. But assurance was the last thing Stuart was able to offer. This was serious. He had told Myles he had had no direct contact with Joseph. He knew it was a mistake at the time, but he couldn't get round it. Not only would Joseph make a liar of him, he would tell Myles all about the phoney arrest and the confession he had got him to make. There would be no question of him being able to talk his way out of that one. He could feel the sting of panic mounting in his head. The best he could do in response to Greenfield was a perky: 'We can only hope that Myles isn't a better detective than your man.' It was a faint whistle in the dark. Myles was a ferreter. He knew how to get in among the roots of things. He would get the job done.

Chapter 43

As there was only to be a fortnight between the selection of the two candidates and the final nomination, a process of getting to know the candidates was instantly set in motion. The main features of this procedure were an informal interview with the two wives or partners and a formal dinner at which both men would be expected to make speeches. This, it was thought, would give the Panel a chance to assess their social skills, an essential part of the armoury of any MP wishing to twist arms and slide things under doors. The sexist lobby had *concerns* about treating spouses as appendages, but when it was pointed out that the principle also applied to husbands of prospective female MPs and same-sex partners of gay and lesbian applicants, they found themselves able to come to terms with it.

Eardley and Greenfield accompanied Naomi on the train on the Wednesday morning. They were met at Manchester Piccadilly by a more than usually animated Robert Snoddy. His animation took years off him. The look of caution, if not suspicion, that normally shadowed his face gave him the air of a man quite happy to have his youth behind him. But today he was in the full bloom of juvenility. Even Greenfield who had known him as a thirteen-year-old marvelled at the transformation. A taxi was summoned and the party headed off to the hotel in Brown Street that Eardley had on good authority was the best in Manchester.

At dinner they were joined by the very glamorous Francesca Bergman who was already in Manchester as an adviser to Snoddy. She took her seat at the table next to Greenfield who engaged her in a discreet tête-a-tête. When asked how she and Robert had been getting on, she replied that she found him stimulating company, even if a bit headstrong. The only serious point of contention between them had arisen over the tone he should take in his interview with the Panel. They were both agreed that boldness was what was needed, but they couldn't agree on what that entailed. Snoddy saw it as taking the bull by the horns and going on an all-out attack on the Labour establishment. Francesca thought that the odd dollop of scepticism scattered here and there would be enough, for the present at least. Greenfield was quick to pick up on this.

"So you thought he went too far, Francesca?"

The expression that appeared on Francesca's face betrayed a certain embarrassment that her remarks had provoked such a candid question.

"Let me say that I understand perfectly where Robert is coming from. For a very long time the political elite have been living in not so much a fool's paradise as a paradise free of what they consider fools. They've been pontificating on all matters political and moral and recent indicators are that ordinary folk – the people they are so fond of patronising – have had a bellyful of it. Robbie wants to get into Parliament to turn things around, so why not start, he says, the way he means to continue? The Party needs to listen to what he has to say if it wants to survive. Fine, but he doesn't have to be heavy-handed about it, a light touch is all that is needed at this stage. The cure must never come over as more painful than the symptoms. It's not for no reason that doctors use words like 'oscopies' and 'ectomies'; they know they need to gloss over the bloody business of sticking things down throats or up rectums, cutting flesh open and severing organs from innards."

Snoddy was at the other end of the table and was not privy to this exchange, but he was aware that he was the subject of most of the dialogues that were going on. Unusually for him, he seemed happy to be more talked about than talking, but the leopard hadn't really changed his spots and it was not long before he stirred himself and, in a voice loud enough for general consumption, said to Eardley who was sitting next to him.

"You know what really pisses me off about that shower? They take such pride in being on the *good* side of the Right-Left divide. It's their *I-got-invited-to-the-party* glee. You know they're thinking: 'Where's your invitation? You don't mean to tell me you haven't got one! You poor thing! ' It's all so transparent. And then, when you get down to what it is they actually believe in ... When I was a kid, there was an animal charity that got you to sponsor endangered animals in the third world. You could adopt a chimpanzee or a panda or a snow leopard. It was always something that was sure to appeal. I never remember a snake or a crocodile or anything like that being in need of a leg-up. It's not quite the same, and yet the pattern is similar, with these Islington socialists; they adopt minorities – ethnic groups, down-and-outs, immigrants, preferably the illegal ones, anyone with an addiction, and all those forced by *the system* into a life of crime. What about the herds of ordinary, boring wildebeests or zebras, the ones who put in an honest day's grazing and ask for nothing more than to be allowed to get on with it and raise their young free of the attentions of rapacious neighbours? Not interesting enough. They are merely the victims of the victims – too far down the need chain to bother with."

Greenfield whose state of merriment had received the say-so of several malts raised his glass and proposed a toast.

"To Robert, the new breed of knight-errant! May he sit comfortably astride his gallant wildebeest as he launches at the fairy castles of the great and the wannabe-good. Of one thing we can be sure: the presence of the beast and its earthy ways is going to cause something of a stink at Westminster. Allow me to repeat the encouragement given by Apollo to Ascanius, the son of Aeneas, who had just used his bow for the first time in battle and been blessed by Jupiter with a victory – *Macte nova virtute puer sic itur ad astra.*

Snoddy smiled in acknowledgement and, as everyone raised their glasses, added a not-to-be-taken-too-seriously *aut ad inferna*.[5]

Naomi joined in the jollity with an equally self-mocking expression of gratitude to Greenfield for choosing to describe Robbie's venture as a 'launch' rather than a 'tilt'. She took hold of her glass and, extending her long elegant arm extravagantly upwards towards the ceiling, proposed a new toast to *Don Roberto*. This produced a noisy farrago of simulated outrage and hearty appreciation. No one heard the knock on the door of the little private room which the celebrants had been allocated and no one noticed as the door was opened and a slight figure emerged apologetically from behind it. It got to just behind Snoddy's chair before its presence was registered. Everyone assumed it to be a waiter and took little notice.

"I'm sorry to disturb you, Mr Snoddy, but may I have a word?"

The voice was soft, the voice a waiter might well use to explain some minor hiccup in the kitchen, but Naomi picked up on the look of concern that immediately appeared on her partner's face. Nothing further was said. Snoddy simply stood up and followed the newcomer out of the room. It was only as they were leaving that Francesca recognised the man. She had accompanied Snoddy to the interview and had been present when the Chairman came to conduct the applicant into the interview room.

"That's Trevor Windsor," she blurted out, "the Chairman of the Selection Panel. What on earth is he doing here?"

It was some ten minutes before the answer was forthcoming. Snoddy reappeared, drained of all his earlier jollity.

"There has been a development. Someone has been at their work. Cameron Brown has launched an appeal against the

---

[5]   Be of courage, young man; thus is the way to the stars ... or the way to hell.

decision of the Panel. He is alleging that there was a breach of protocol and demanding that the decision be reviewed."

He paused to allow the collective annoyance to catch up with his own before continuing.

"That was the Chairman. He came to break the news to me in person. He thinks Brown may have a point. Technically, the Panel were not entitled to follow through on the set questions. They should have allowed the candidates to develop their answers in their own way without interference. The protocols are clear on that. So the Panel will have to be reconvened to decide on whether the whole thing needs to be re-run. They may even decide to stand down and allow a new Panel to take over. Any nominations they make must be seen to be free of the judgements they made on the back of the first interviews."

Chapter 44

The emergency meeting of the Panel took place the following evening. Trevor Windsor showed all the symptoms of a man torn between defiance and compliance. The general tone of his voice resonated resignation, but his eyes showed flashes of sprightly anger. Schinski had always thought of him as someone who had never been anything other than middle-aged and 'stable', but those flashes made him realise that there was a man who had been a boy lurking under the persona.

He looked around the table at the other faces. He was looking for Judas' faces, ones that were trying too hard to conceal their pleasure or ones that weren't trying at all. Margaret Millership toppled effortlessly into the latter category. She had been greatly annoyed at the insensitivity of the Panel in not giving the Committee *a gender choice* and was clearly delighting in the punishment that had been meted out. Hugh Savage on the other hand had adopted a glazed look. He obviously did not trust his theatrical talents to affect fraudulent responses, he was settling for a simple ban on all ventures in facial subtlety. Funereal solemnity was as much as he would allow himself. The other faces displayed a wide variety of response: regret at their own ineptitude, frustration that the process had to be rewound, and resentment at being at the beck and call of bureaucratic procedures and not being credited with the sagacity to conduct matters as they thought fit.

Trevor Windsor proffered his resignation as chairman for having failed in his responsibility to ensure that correct procedures were adhered to. The offer was summarily rejected. His exoneration gave everyone a welcome opportunity to express something warm and positive. They all knew that Trevor was a natural chairman; he never foisted his own opinions on a meeting, or if he did, he orchestrated it in a truly chairman-like way; he would simply solicit the opinion of members he knew would accord with his own at a point in the discussion when it would carry the most weight. As conductor of the orchestra he never stooped to play an instrument himself. No, there could be no question – Trevor Windsor should remain in the chair.

Having made this sliver of progress, the meeting felt itself in better shape to take on the question of its own legitimacy. Margaret Millership took the floor and went on at some length on the need for the 'revised' selection to be made free of the *contamination* that the lapse in procedures had necessarily occasioned. The only thing to be done was for the Panel to recuse itself. The logic was impeccable, but no one seemed keen to follow through on it. The Chairman was obliged to fill the shifty silence with an overblown acknowledgement of the clarity with which the case had been presented. His tone was concessive, but he was clearly at a loss to come up with something to go with the 'but' that he obviously wanted to add. He scoured the faces around the table, looking for someone to step up. Paper was shuffled, noses were blown, throats were cleared: no one met his eyes. In desperation he was about to turn to Schinski. Derek was a good man in a crisis; he always came up with something. But before he could, Freddie Douglas stepped forward.

"I think we are being a bit too legalistic about all this. Okay, we made a mistake, but we are willing to acknowledge it. It's a procedural point and we are willing to answer it in terms of our procedures. That should be the end of it. We have been appointed as a result of a democratic vote to carry out the task of selecting two candidates for the Executive Committee to look at and comment on before we make the final decision. If we have to go back to the Committee and recuse ourselves, the Committee will have to come up with a completely new Panel, made up, may I say, of members whom it did not initially choose to place its confidence in, and the whole business of drawing up a new set of questions and conducting the interviews will have to be gone through again. A lot of time will have been wasted, time that should be spent on the campaign trail and the only people who will benefit from all this will be the Tories. No, I say we carry on as we are."

This was met with the kind of approval that seeks to portray itself as reluctant. The meeting could see the logic of what had been said and would obey it, but it still felt honour-bound to respect the integrity of the opposing view. Head must carry the day over heart, however painful that may be. Margaret Millership should not and would not be denied her right to feel aggrieved, certainly not by those whom the decision was hurting every bit as much as it was hurting her. When unsure of itself the collective mind is a much less strident agent of self-assertion than the individual one.

Having neutralised the Millership disgruntlement, the meeting proceeded to the question of how to salvage the situation. Hugh Savage forsook his scribbling for a moment to propose that the interviews be re-run the following weekend with the five questions being simplified. The candidates should simply be asked to express their views on each of the five areas and given a maximum of five minutes to address each one. Any candidate who was unwilling or unable to attend should be excluded from the contest. The proposal had the merit of both simplicity and efficiency. It seemed to find general favour and was edging smoothly towards formal acceptance when Schinski took the floor.

"Mr Chairman, if the thing must be done, then I agree that the Honorary Secretary's proposal is a sensible one. But I think we shouldn't be too hasty. We came to a collective decision. We did so after due consideration and the additional questions that the candidates were asked were prompted by no more than a desire for clarity. If we had not heard what one of the candidates said, would it have been out of order to ask them to repeat it? Would that have constituted a breach of the rules? It would after all have given the candidate the chance to improve on his performance the first time round. That's the kind of nonsense you end up with when you lose your trust in common sense. What really concerns me here is the interference from upstairs. We came to a conclusion that the top brass don't seem to have taken kindly to, so they ask – no, they tell us – to think again. This is exactly the kind of thing that is turning the Labour Party into a stooge of the London elite. I forget which of the candidates made the point – I think in fact it was both of them – they said that we've lost touch with our grass roots, we treat them as bigoted fools for not accepting what their intellectual betters set before them. The *useful idiots* aren't even allowed to chew on what they're given; they're simply required to swallow it. Well, I think it's time for a bit of hunger striking."

Scarcely had Schinski regained his seat when Reggie jumped up. Throughout the whole process of finding his successor the outgoing MP had been remarkably subdued. It was as if he had accepted to personify the fading of the light. But now suddenly, brimful of animation, the Reggie of old was back in his bones.

"That was well said, Derek, and by God it needed saying. What have we let ourselves become? A load of Nancy boys, all PR shit in our heads and no guts in our bellies. Let's do what Derek says, let's take the bastards on; let's find out what they're made of. When I started off in this game, I talked to real people with real problems and I did what I could for them. Nowadays, these new MPs with their fancy talk and their fancy ideas don't listen to anything their constituents say. No, it's they that do all the talking: they tell the constituents what their problems ought to be and then go off and pretend to act in their name. So the poor bloke with neighbours that make his life a misery or with children who are being targeted by drug dealers at school is supposed to feel proud at having an MP who makes 'a principled

232

stand' for all the right-on things: gay marriage, transgender recognition, better dole for the work-shy and cushier prison conditions for the scum that infest his neighbourhood? No, ordinary folk don't see their politics as an exercise in virtue signalling. They just want the kind of politics that makes life more bearable for people who deserve a more bearable life.

"I say we tell these London types where they can stick their finicky rules. We are in the business of choosing an MP to represent us, and we'll bloody well decide who to choose and how to choose."

This was the Reggie that some of the older heads around the table had known in years gone by, the Reggie that had been elected as a young firebrand to represent Bury West all those years ago, in the days when he didn't have to rely on the inertia of habit to get himself elected. The outburst produced a warm smile on Trevor Windsor's face that eerily exposed the hollowness of all the fabricated chairman-smiles that everyone had got used to seeing on it. Windsor was happy to allow enough time for all the 'well-saids' and 'here-heres' to run their course before coming in.

"I admire the spirit of what you are saying, Reggie, but the fact remains, we'd be playing a very risky game if we defied HQ on this. They have the letter of the law on their side and the financial clout to squeeze us dry. It sticks in my throat to say it, but they hold all the cards and I can't see how we can avoid having to do what we're told."

Noises of grudging consent passed like a dirty hanky around the table. The transition from oomph to hangover was striking in its suddenness. For Margaret Millership of course the weather had turned back to fair. She spoke in hushed tones, at pains to pay all the respect due to the sad loss of autonomy, but *had to agree* with the Chair that discretion was the better part of valour. Emboldened by her own persuasiveness, she went so far as to venture the thought that there would be little point in the Panel revisiting their decision if that decision were to remain the same. At least one of the candidates should be replaced, preferably both, if HQ was to be convinced that they were acting in good faith."

Reggie Whitehouse exploded. He jumped to his feet, nearly knocking over his chair. Had they not been on opposite sides of the table, no one present would have ruled out a physical assault. As it was, the elderly MP settled for a thunderous thump on the table.

"Go to hell, Ms Millership, and take the rest of your kind with you! I've had it up to here with the claptrap that pours out of your backside. We've been putting up with your kind of bilge for years. Hold your tongues. Don't upset the sisterhood. Those were the orders. Well, stuff that! I'm all for the brotherhood, me. When you think someone's talking rubbish, you look them in the eye and you tell them what you think. You've got to be prepared to take as good as you give. You don't whine about it afterwards. And you don't get big daddy at HQ to fight your battles for you. It was you, wasn't it? It was you that got HQ to raise this stupid quibble. You want your woman in. You don't give a damn about the Party. The only thing you're interested in is the sisterhood."

There was a shocked silence. Everyone was used to this kind of raw frankness from Reggie when talking one to one, but in open meeting, never. Schinski was quick to grasp where the old warrior was coming from. For more years than anyone could remember Reggie had been the MP for Bury West. In a sense he and the constituency had become one and the same. But now with all this focus on the seat and none on the man, he must feel like a patient in a care home – everyone talking about him as if he wasn't there. He needed to assert himself; everyone should be made aware that he still had blood in his veins. The relief of impending retirement had loosened his tongue, but he really ought not to be playing so carelessly with his prospects of becoming a peer. Margaret Millership, jolted out of the stride she had been confidently proceeding in, simply stared in open-eyed disbelief. Before she could reconfigure, Schinski seized the opportunity to intervene.

"Come now, Reggie. Margaret here, perhaps more than any of us, knows what it feels like to be on the receiving end of the whims of the bully-boys at HQ. Our society needs watching when it comes to decisions between men and women and she's quite right to make sure blind eyes are not turned. Unless she thinks that this Panel has been guilty of this, I am quite sure that the Maggie Millership I know would not only accept the judgement of this Panel, but would be prepared to stand up for its right to make that judgement. I do think it was very astute for her to point out that a mere rerun of our procedures will not satisfy our critics. We are being told, gentlemen, that we have come to the wrong conclusion. It is that autocratic attitude of the high command that we must address, not the petty quibble that is the excuse for its expression. The alternative, as Margaret quite rightly points out, is to crawl under the blanket and let them run the show."

It is hard to accuse someone of damaging your furniture when he has done so in the act of saving your life. Schinski had clearly misrepresented her position, but he had rescued her from the pillory that Reggie had clamped her in. She hardly owed him full-blown gratitude, but indignation would be even more inappropriate, so she settled for a stoic smile at her champion and a venomous glare at her assailant.

Schinski had of course a natural ally in Nathan Roberts, with his man, George Sinclair, being under just as much threat as Robert Snoddy. Revolutionary change is never far from the Marxist mental horizon and Roberts was not slow to summon up the juices of insurgency. He proposed an open campaign of defiance, full press disclosure of the attempts to intimidate and subvert local democracy and, if necessary, mass resignations.

This did not go down well. Worse than that, the extremism it propounded was in real danger of swinging the meeting back to a position of abject compliance. The Chairman seemed inclined to try to edge them towards some kind of face-saving gesture that would allow them to concede defiantly. It was time for Schinski, if not to show his hand, at least to show that he had a hand.

"Smoke-filled rooms," he proclaimed, "that's where these decisions get made . . . or unmade. I propose we send a message back to HQ expressing our disappointment at their interference and a polite, but firm request that they reconsider their position. In the meantime I will don my oxygen mask and my goggles and see what can be done in the smoke."

The proposal pandered to indecision's natural instincts. Events might well come to the rescue. And in this case the undecided did have a champion in the shape of someone with a track record of producing rabbits out of hats. It was passed with only one abstention, Margaret Millership seemingly feeling the need to compromise between the long-term needs of her cause for allies and the immediate demands of her dignity.

Chapter 45

Graham Myles' first instinct after the revelations by Joseph Ross was to seek higher counsel. He had not been a detective inspector for very long and had grown comfortable in the understudy role as sergeant. He was sharp when it came to suggesting improvements and amendments to a line of enquiry and adept at digging out evidence. These were the qualities that had secured his promotion, but they were the skills of an apprentice, not of a master. Here it wasn't a question of re-working and refining. The challenge was quite different: he needed to come up with something to fill a blank page.

He could not bring himself to think the unthinkable, that Inspector Stranaghan, the senior officer he had most admired, could possibly be involved in anything shady. Two facts had come to light that pointed clearly in that direction. Firstly, there was the remarkable coincidence of the mock execution being carried out on Dwayne Rodgers and then the body of that same man miraculously turning up, and with wounds consistent with what he might have received had the execution been for real. In his report Wright had failed to identity Rodgers as the man on trial. There was no way that could be dismissed as a minor oversight. In the light of subsequent events it was pure dynamite. Clearly it was not an act of omission. But what good reason could Wright have had for trying to suppress it? It established a clear link to Snoddy, and wasn't that the whole point of the undercover operation? Could it be that there was nothing *mock* at all about the execution? Was that when Rodgers had actually been killed? Had Wright gone rogue and switched sides?

But what was Stuart Stranaghan's involvement in all this? Could he have been duped by Wright? If he hadn't known that

Rodgers had been the victim of the execution, he would have had no reason to smell a rat. But surely the details of the case would have aroused his suspicions? He went back and read through Wright's account of the mock trial. No, Wright had kept everything very general. The few details he did give were at variance with Joseph's account. Based on that, Stranaghan wouldn't have had any reason to connect the two. But then there was the other thing, this 'confession' that Stranaghan had extracted from Joseph. He had made no mention of that anywhere in his account of the events. Worse than that, he had denied ever having had any direct contact with Joseph. Why would he do that? Did that mean that he and Wright were in it together? Had they both gone over to Snoddy?

He struggled with these questions longer than he knew he ought to, before deciding on a course of action. He would not confront Stranaghan with accusations and demands for explanation; he would play the fool, seek guidance and see how far his former boss was prepared to play along. It was a strategy that gelled with his feelings as much as with his cunning.

It was nevertheless only by an act of willpower that he got himself the next morning to Stranaghan's front door His next step, if he followed protocol, should have been to go and get a detailed written statement from Joseph. It would have been both easier and proper for him to do things in that order, but something told him he should give his old mentor a chance to explain himself before the whole thing became formal and untouchable.

The sight of his former sergeant on the doorstep set off something akin to a storm in Stuart Stranaghan's head. It is strange how suddenly a face can slip from benign to sinister once the background is darkened – a smile can turn into a leer, eye contact an invasion of the soul and small talk a smokescreen for ill intent. The saddest thing is the question it raises as to why you had never seen the face in that light before. How could you ever have been gullible enough to read the smile as genuine or the look as benevolent? It is like looking back at photos of youthful faces after you have seen the damage age has wrought on them and wondering how you could ever have been taken in by the assurances they gave of permanence.

He took the visitor into his 'den'. (Curious that, it was the first time he had consciously thought of it as a 'den', a place of sanctuary). The two men installed themselves in the two comfortable armchairs, both of which faced diagonally towards the desk. That way, they were not confronting each other, physically at least. Myles immediately spotted the row of shields on the wall. Stuart had made a collection of the coats of arms of the various establishments that he and his family had been associated with. They formed an impressive display along the wall above his computer desk. His old school crest with its Latin motto, *labor ipse voluptas,* was brought down for inspection. Myles needed help with the translation – *Work itself is pleasure –* although Stuart favoured the freer version – *Work is an end in itself.* His being in charge of the small talk somehow made it less potent and Myles less perfidious. It was impossible however not to treat it as a charade. He couldn't believe that Myles had the slightest interest in what he was saying. He was tempted to say something totally nonsensical to see if it would go unnoticed, but he managed to keep things going on half-hearted power.

It wasn't long however before the talk petered out and Myles got round to his gritty business.

"I made a discovery yesterday that I'm having trouble getting my head round. Did you know that the object of the trial and execution that Wright took part in was Dwayne Rodgers?"

The look in Myles' eyes left Stuart in no doubt that the emphasis was on the question that was being asked rather than information that was being given. He was not being given the option of a non-committal response. He could deny it of course. That was the obvious thing to do. But it could take him into

239

water that he would drown in. He played for breathing space.

"Who told you that?"

It was unclear whether this came over as evasive or as an expression of surprise. In his response Myles' face gave nothing away.

"I have a witness who was involved in both events, and he tells me it was Rodgers who was on trial. He was able to give me details of the charges and those details fit perfectly with the court records of the Rodgers' trial. Everyone involved knew it was Rodgers who was being tried. Did *you* know this?"

The *witness* had to be Joseph. And if it was Joseph, it was hardly conceivable that he wouldn't have told Myles all about the confession. He had been right not to deny that he knew that it was Rodgers.

"Yes, I did know. I knew that it was the Rodgers' case they had role-played."

"Why then was that not in Wright's report? You read it. Didn't you ask him why he made no mention of it?"

"We both thought it might look odd."

Myles gawped in histrionic incredulity.

"You're right about that. It looks more than odd; it looks downright suspicious. Are you asking me to accept that it was a mere coincidence, a man being put on trial and sentenced to death in a make-believe scenario and that same man turning up as a real-life cadaver? My God, the place where the body was found and the wounds he died of were practically identical. And you, as senior officer, you allowed these facts to be suppressed?"

This was not the way Myles had intended to play it. He had hoped that his old boss would have some easy way of explaining what had happened and contrive to make him feel ashamed of the doubts he had harboured, but he was disappointed and he was angry at being disappointed. For his part, Stuart was not surprised by the blows his former sergeant's questioning was landing on him – they were no heavier than what he had been dreading. What had taken him unawares was the aggressive tone. That, for some reason, he had not expected. And yet, why ever not? He had no appetite for matching aggression with aggression. He would come as clean as he needed to come.

"You're right of course. I should have insisted on all the facts being disclosed."

"We're not talking here about some detail that should have gone into a report. That fact is a complete game-changer. It implicates Snoddy, and possibly Wright too, in Rodgers' murder. Don't tell me you didn't see that?"

The look that this solicited from Stranaghan was suggestive more of disappointment at the question than embarrassment at the answer he was about to come up. It was as if the apprentice was being slow in the up-take.

"That's precisely why I kept it quiet. But it wasn't Snoddy I was protecting; it was Justin."

"And why would you protect him? If he was involved in the killing, why should you want to protect him?"

"Look, if I'd thought for a moment that he had done the killing I'd have had no hesitation in shopping him. But he was innocent. Snoddy had sussed that he was an undercover policeman and this was his way of getting rid of him. He had set the whole thing up and created a scenario that would have convinced a jury that Justin had murdered Rodgers."

"What makes you so sure that Wright was innocent? It's not unheard of for undercover men to go feral. And don't you think it's significant that he is now working for a newspaper that's owned by Matthew Eardley, who is, need I remind you, the paymaster of The New Prometheans?"

The long pause before Stranaghan replied was surprisingly unflustered. Again it was as if the tutor was giving the student time to catch up.

"I know because Snoddy told me."

"Snoddy told you?"

"Yes, he gave me a choice. There were two weapons used in the killing and he had got Justin's fingerprints on one and Gary Burrows' on the other. He left it to me to decide which one he should allow the police to find. He called it the *Barabbas Choice*. He had me over a barrel. Given my options, it wasn't a difficult choice to make. It was a no-brainer. It had to be Burrows. I couldn't let Snoddy ruin Justin's life, could I?"

Myles had been on automatic pilot, asking the questions that the answers provoked but without feeling the full impact of the punch they packed. This answer however dealt a blow that couldn't be so lightly ridden. He looked open-mouthed at the man he had admired as the embodiment of all his hopes for himself as a detective. No other reaction could have shamed Stuart more. A very cruel silence ensued before Myles' thoughts could reconnect with his words.

"But you didn't mind ruining Burrows' life, did you? He was innocent too."

This was a lesser blow than what the silence had threatened.

"Innocent? You've got to be joking. Okay, he mightn't have killed Rodgers, but he was as guilty as hell of the murder the courts couldn't get him for. Justin, on the other hand, has never killed anyone. If *you* had been faced with the choice, what would *you* have done? Would you have cast a young inexperienced officer, a man you have thrown in at the deep end, someone you have a duty of care to, would you have cast him to the wolves? Would you really have put your allegiance to the police force above your sense of justice and decency?"

"But you were a policeman and your first duty was to uphold the law."

"I could see that. Why do you think I resigned from the force?"

This, in an aberrant way, was not what Myles wanted to hear. Having discovered that Stuart had lied, he wanted to dig deeper into the wound and confirm that the man was a complete fraud who had been deceiving him all along. That way contempt for the charlatan and shame at allowing himself to be taken in would have joined forces and opened up a clear line of sight. But this *was* the Inspector Stranaghan he knew and admired. The man *had* acted with honour; he had put his obligation to a comrade above his own professional ambitions. And integrity had come at a heavy price – it must have cost him, and not just financially, to give up on his career. But what if his sacrifice had been misplaced, what if the man he had covered up for *was* in fact guilty? The story about Snoddy and the *Barabbas Choice* had a ring of truth about it. It was exactly the kind of thing Snoddy would do. But it was also the kind of bluff he might have run if he and Wright had been in it together. The whole business rested on that question: had Stranaghan been taken for a ride by the two of them? Had he sacrificed his career and his integrity as a policeman to protect someone who had totally betrayed his trust? That was the question he must focus on.

The parting of the two men was stiff. Myles said nothing of his intentions beyond making it clear that he would be back with more questions after he had made further inquiries. Stuart did not seek clarification. He was surprised and relieved that no immediate action was to be taken. The paucity of words and the sadness in the faces of both men however did register a great cooling of warmth.

Chapter 46

Like many of the great and the good Lord Dooley had the luxury of being able to surround himself with people of *sufficient discernment* to endorse the sense he was cultivating of his own greatness. Professionally, he was able to lord it over minions whose talents, should they dare to exceed his own, could be shunted to the back office, or in extremis, the broom cupboard. His friends by contrast were drawn from a coterie of modestly talented individuals more easily impressed with the baubles of his political status. He had allowed his speech to remain untutored, this to show the strength of his ties to the ordinariness of his origins. Coincidentally, it also served to underscore the heights to which he had risen, the broad span of his soul and the hard-headedness of his view of the world. He was well on the way to *perfecting* himself, plugging all the gaps that might let in the chilling air of self-doubt.

Schinski had a long wait before he was admitted to the venerable presence. He had come as the official messenger of the Selection Panel, Trevor Windsor having been more than happy to delegate the job to him. As he sat in the plush waiting room he distracted himself by trying to anticipate the line that Dooley would take with him. Would he play the hard-pressed high flyer making the effort to attend to the trivial business that had brought the visitor or would it be the good sport, magnanimous in victory over a hapless opponent deserving of nothing more than his piteous condescension? There were other possibilities, but these were the two that Schinski could best envisage. In the event, his lordship found his own way of getting the best of both worlds. When the door was opened and he was summoned, Schinski was confronted by an energetically polite PA who advanced towards him, hand outstretched.

"Lord Dooley sends his apologies. Unfortunately, due to pressure of work, he cannot spare the time to see you, but I will do my humble best to fill in for his lordship."

Schinski grinned. You had to admire the old bugger. He belonged to the body of leopards that don't change their spots. They can be the most frustrating obstructers of plain sailing, but they can also be the most colourful characters in the cast of life. Today Schinski was of a mind to appreciate their virtues.

"I'm sure you would do your best, young man. And I'm sure you've less reason than most for being humble, but I'm equally sure that Lord Dooley would like to find out at first hand the steps he needs to take if he is to keep his political career afloat."

The young PA seemed about to add another layer to the veneer of courtesy he was intent on pattering out, but then, only a few words into it, he took in what Schinski had just said and stopped himself. Schinski didn't wait for any further reaction.

"I tell you what I'm going to do. I'm going to go back into that room and wait while you go and fetch your master and tell him what I said. I'll give him ten minutes and if I don't hear from him in that time, I'm out of here. I can assure you he won't like what I'm going to do next."

With that he turned back into the waiting room and made an elaborate process of installing himself in the easy chair he had just vacated. The PA simply stood and stared. There was no way for him to recover the control he had assumed would be his. His dignity reached its nadir as he pulled the door meekly to and made his disappearance behind it.

The closed door did not remain in a state of quiescence for long. Sounds of agitated movement suddenly became audible from behind it before it was burst open by a red-faced monster with flashing eyes eagerly in search of a prey. Schinski had not been aware before of the uncanny resemblance that his lordship bore to Jimmy Cagney. Belligerence was clearly their point of convergence.

"What the hell do you mean coming here and delivering threats? I'll have you thrown out on your ear."

Only the New York twang was missing. Schinski did not have to force a belittling laugh.

"Calm yourself, my lord. I haven't come to bury Caesar. I've come to offer him my services. If your butler, or whoever that young man is, got the wrong end of the stick, then it's him you should be riled up with, not me."

This plea of innocence was delivered with a sardonic grin that had the predictable effect of further stoking the fires of Dooley's indignation. He blasted off another tirade of invective. This Schinski simply ignored. Instead, he got to his feet, pushed past his aggressor who was stood in the doorway, and invited him to come and join him in his own office. The invective did not abate, but that notwithstanding his lordship did as he was bid. Curiously, despite the eccentricity of the circumstances, the two men seemed to be in thrall to some wired-in ordinance for conducting business and took the seats that convention decreed, Dooley behind his desk, Schinski in front of it. This seemed to act as a corrective to Dooley's anger; it was as if it had been reprimanded by the reinstated protocol. Schinski waited until the last embers were petering out before he began.

"Lord Dooley, you have tried to exert undue influence on our Panel. You have picked up on a minor procedural point and are trying to use it to force us into rethinking our decision. That just simply won't do. I have been instructed by the Panel to convey its response to you. Our decision stands."

Dooley took this more calmly than might have been expected. An arrogant smile passed over his face. Anger in mid-combat is for those who fear defeat; Dooley did not see himself as being among their numbers.

"You and your little Panel will do exactly as you are told. It's

246

not me you have to answer to; it's the rules and the rules need to be obeyed. I would have thought that would have been obvious, but if you can't grasp that the first time round, maybe we need to think again ourselves, maybe these kinds of decisions should be made by people who can get their heads round ideas that the average ten-year-old could cope with."

Buoyed by the resonance of his own voice, he went on:

"If you can't keep to the rules and you can't see the importance of that, what confidence can we have in your judgement as a whole? How can we possibly believe that you will show any gumption when it comes to picking a parliamentary pig from a parliamentary poke?"

"You mean we poor peasants should know our place and content ourselves to do your bidding? Sorry, have I got something wrong? Didn't I think that the Labour Party was the party for ordinary Joe Soaps like ... well me anyway, not you of course."

Dooley's anger showed signs of a second flare-up, but Schinski forestalled it.

"I'm sure neither of us would want to do anything that would be damaging to the Party. And I can assure you that's exactly what you would be doing if you persist with this procedural nonsense, not to mention the damage you would do to your own career. Let's put our cards on the table. You have all the weight of HQ on your side and a plausible excuse for bullying our Panel – a good hand, the equivalent, would you say, of two pair or even a full house?"

Wary of this concession, Dooley launched a pre-emptive attack on the 'but' that was looming.

"Whatever it is, it's a winning hand. You can huff and puff as much as you like, but you'll end up doing what I tell you. You talk about the good of the Party. I'll tell you what's good for the Party. It's getting people like Cameron Brown on board. We live in a celebrity culture. Hasn't anybody told you? Give them a celebrity show, and the punters come out and vote in their millions for the all-cooking, all-dancing and all-singing contestant that takes their fancy – they love it and they love the things they associate these celebs with. We simply want them to put the Cameron Browns of this world and the Labour Party into the same mental block. Okay, it's not high-minded politics, but it's the politics of the age. It's what works, and that's the only thing that matters. Bums on seats, parliamentary seats, that's what it's all about. I'd have thought you of all people wouldn't have needed to be told that."

Schinski had never been one to dive deep within his inner self in search of any stray strains of idealism that might be lurking there. It hadn't occurred to him that there would be any to be found. And yet now he caught himself feeling something akin to disdain for this piece of cynical pragmatism from a fellow realist. The irony was not lost on him, but he was not to be distracted.

"You didn't let me finish, my lord. Don't you want to know what I have in my hand? Look, I have it here."

He slipped his hand in the side pocket of his jacket and, slowly withdrawing it, brought a slim package into view, which he placed between them on the desk.

"Do you know what that is, my lord?"

Dooley's curiosity was roused. Indulging it would lose him the initiative, but it was not to be denied. He made a vain effort to cover it up.

"What nonsense have you come up with now?"

"Tell me. What do you think of when you hear the name Richard Nixon?"

Schinski was in his element spinning out his little game. But Dooley was in no mind to play along. An answer was not forthcoming. Undeterred, Schinski continued as if addressing a third party.

"Most people, without thinking, would have come out with

'Watergate'. It's the obvious answer. But it's not a good answer, is it? It's the kind of answer any Tom, Dick or Harry would have blurted out. The question is: what would a Lord Tom or an Earl Dick or a Duke Harry have come up with? You know what I think? Or maybe you don't care, me not being a lord and all that? Well anyway, I think their lordships might have said ... 'Tapes!'"

In the pause before the word 'tapes' was uttered Schinski cast a significant glance at the package on the desk, nodding his head as if he were in agreement with himself. It took a minute before half of the penny dropped with Dooley.

"Are you saying that this package contains tapes? What the hell are you talking about?"

"Do you remember our first meeting, Lord Dooley, the one where you came and tried to bribe me into supporting your candidate? Well, I felt so honoured by your attentions that I thought I would record the scene so that my future grandchildren would know what lofty circles their granddaddy moved in. But then I thought, maybe Lord Dooley would like a copy too, not for the same reasons of course, quite the opposite in fact. He might want his grandchildren to know how low he was prepared to sink for his Party, how he was prepared to deal with low-lives like me and compromise his own career in an otherwise noble cause. He might even want the wider public to know ... It's a CD by the way, not a tape. Would you like me to play you a snippet?"

Dooley rose to his feet and lunged forward, propping himself with both hands on the desk in the manner of an angry bear about to strangle a rabbit. He was a small man, but well-built and for a moment Schinski feared himself at risk of physical assault. But the desk, which prevented any further advance, seemed to bring home to the would-be assailant the futility of his aggressive impulse. The fierceness faded from his eyes and he slumped back into his chair.

The battle was over. Schinski could see that he had won. But he wanted to win well, and winning well meant not crushing his opponent and pushing him into seeking the solace of mutual destruction.

"Lord Dooley, let's stop messing about here. It's unfortunate that you and I have found ourselves on opposite sides of this particular fence. Neither of us is anybody's fool. We have much in common and I can envisage us being able to work together in the future, should our interests coincide. I think we'd make a good team. I certainly have no desire to damage your career. If you drop your objection to the decision of the Panel and keep your word and make sure old Reggie gets his peerage, then I'll consider that I owe you one. You needn't worry about these recordings either. If Reggie gets his peerage, the last thing either he or I would want would be for them to get into the public domain."

Dooley was not used to losing and his natural inclination was to be bad at it, but his propensity for obedience to the practical outweighed all else. This Schinski was a smart operator. And what he said about the CD also made sense. Maybe the two of them could work together, or alternatively, maybe he'd get his chance to get his own back some time. In any case, when you lose a battle you minimise the losses. That's the smart thing to do.

As he made his way home Schinski was flushed with his success. The Lord Dooleys of this world were worthy opponents. A victory over them was worth ten over the plods that sat around the tables of the committee world. But triumphant though he was, he could not take all the credit. When he got home he raised a glass to Terence Cooper.

Chapter 47

When Justin Wright heard that Inspector Myles was on Joseph's trail he decided he must get there first. He had been told of the failed attempt of the man Eardley had sent, but his own inquiries at the garden centre met with more success. Eardley's man had been unlucky; the manager had been out delivering an order when he had called and so hadn't passed on the details of Joseph's departure. When Justin appeared, he was there to tell him the same story he had told to Myles, pointing him unto the same path to the Reverend John's rectory.

Justin had been up north covering the story at Bury West, so his arrival at the rectory didn't take place until the day after Joseph's interview there with Myles. The Reverend John was less than pleased at this further source of harassment of his ward.

"Joseph is in a very vulnerable state. I really think he should be left alone. He has told me all about you. He saw you as his friend and allowed himself to become quite reliant on you. It's really important for him not to be brought back to that state of dependency."

"But I think I can help. He thinks I betrayed him. Surely that was an important part of the reason for his breakdown. If I can assure him that I am still his friend, wouldn't that help him to put it all behind him?"

The Reverend thought for a moment. There was possibly something in what this man was saying. This indeed might be a way to lance the boil. Okay, he'd give him Joseph's address. He could only pray that he was doing the right thing.

Joseph's bedsit bore an unhealthy resemblance to the one he had had in Oxford. It was dingy and depressing – the kind of hovel old Fagan might have lurked in, except that it was not big enough to accommodate the urchins. The single-bar heater positioned in the middle of the room was the sole relief from the general gloom. Joseph had greeted his appearance at his doorstep in a manner that could best be described as under-whelming. His surprise, such as it was, was almost instantly neutered and chalked up under 'things-that-happen'. Justin was 'admitted' rather than invited in and offered a stool by the heater.

When Justin asked how he had been, he got only a shrug-of-the-shoulders reply, the type that says, 'You'll need to come up with better questions than that if you want to engage with me.' Under the pressure, Justin told him about Lizzie's disappoint-ment at him not keeping in touch. The two had been quite close at Oxford. Maybe that could help break the ice. But that too was met with determined indifference. He was getting slightly desperate now. For want of anything better he tried the Reverend John.

"The Reverend John tells me you have found faith. I'm really pleased for you. I know how important it was for you to find some set of ideas to live by."

Joseph's face suddenly thawed.

"No, you've got that wrong. It's not a set of ideas. It's an insight into oneness. Philosophy is analytical; it deals in nuances of difference. That's what's wrong with it, that's what makes it antithetical to the nature of truth. The philosopher tries to divide truth up into a network of propositions which one day will produce a comprehensive picture of the human condition. But the whole thing is wrong-headed. It's like trying to learn to swim or ride a bicycle by reading physics textbooks. John helped me to see that. Descartes got it all wrong. It's not *Cogito ergo sum*. It's the other way round."

There were sparks here of the old Joseph that had enlivened those Oxford tutorials. Justin was keen to fan the kindling.

"So, you've become a Christian. I must say, that's the last thing I would have expected."

Joseph shook his head in disapproval. Exasperation with those who couldn't keep up was another of his Oxford traits.

"No, I wouldn't describe myself as a Christian. Well, I would actually, but then I wouldn't describe Christians as Christians. All that nonsense about the resurrection and the symbolic sacrifice of divine goodness as a magical penance for all the human evil in the world is just like the Ptolemaic system that was used to explain the movement of the planets – very clever, certainly, but more interested in its own cleverness than in re-examining the premises it was based on. Jesus was a very wise man who understood important things about the human condition that others either missed or ignored. He doesn't need all that divine mumbo-jumbo to merit a following."

The 'thaw' was in full flow now. Joseph described in detail how the Reverend John had rescued him, how they had talked into the small hours and how he had been weaned away from the questions that had been setting his *psychological agenda*. (This was a term that Joseph seemed to set great store by). His Damascus moment had come when, on the Reverend's recommendation, he'd read 'War and Peace'. In Pierre Bezukhov, the main character, he'd discovered an alter ego, a kindred spirit, a fellow seeker after truth. Bezukhov had explored every avenue of discovery – hedonism, philosophy, Freemasonry – but it was the bond he formed with a humble Russian peasant when he'd been taken prisoner by the French that changed his life. This simple peasant was the embodiment of Schillerian naivety;[6] he wasn't someone to stand back and make mental templates of nature and the world, he *was* nature, albeit only a small part of it, and he instinctively accepted that he – and the whole of mankind for

---

[6] Reference to Friedrich Schiller and his concept of Naivety as a direct perception of reality, in contrast to what he called the 'Sentimental', which filters reality through the prism of thought and sentiment.

that matter – wasn't at the centre of nature's concerns. He simply got on with being alive, savouring the good and enduring the bad that came his way and eschewing any expectations of them balancing each other out.

It was so good to see Joseph come alive again. Thus it was with more than a tinge of self-loathing that Justin, having judged the moment right, brought the conversation round to the Myles' visit. The link was as smooth as he could make it, but the shunt did not pass unnoticed. Joseph hesitated and clearly struggled not to obey his instinct and bring the interview to an end. He recounted the meeting he'd had with Myles in stop-start flurries of words that focused on the facts naked of comment or commentary. There were no highlights. Everything came through as if he were a machine talking to a machine. Justin tried to press him to describe Myles' reaction to the 'confession' Stranaghan had got him to write, but he hadn't been aware of it provoking any reaction at all. Myles, he said, had been very sympathetic. He seemed to understand what had driven them to take part in Rodgers' execution – the sheer evil of the man, the horrible sadism of the way he'd murdered Francis Brown.

Justin had come expecting to hear the worst, and this was it. Yet somehow it still came like a bolt out of the blue. How were he and Stranaghan to talk their way out of this? How were they to account for the incredible coincidence of the man they had condemned and executed, but only in make-believe, actually turning up riddled with matching real-life bullet holes? There was only one straw he could see to grasp at.

"Did the Inspector get you to make a written statement?"

Joseph looked surprised.

"No, why should he have done that?"

"Look, Joseph. Okay, the whole thing that you and I took part in wasn't for real. We didn't actually kill anyone. But somebody did."

"Yes, and they're both serving life sentences for it. So what?"

"Did it not strike you as odd, Rodgers' body turning up like that just after we had 'executed' him? Do you not think that any reasonable person might conclude that that was too much of a coincidence?"

"So what are you saying? Do you think Robbie was lying to us and that we really did kill Rodgers?"

"No, I don't think that, but I'm convinced he had a hand in Rodgers' death and planted the evidence that convicted the other two."

The look of haunted horror that this produced on Joseph's face was truly alarming. His face remained frozen as his brain struggled to process the ramifications of what it had taken in. Justin felt the need was urgent to take him in hand and face him in the right direction.

"I'm going to be completely up front with you, Joseph. You and I were – are – friends. But Inspector Stranaghan and I are also friends. The Inspector thought that Robbie was trying to set me up, and he was doing his best to protect me. That's why he got you to write that confession. He wasn't going to arrest you; he was going to use it to stop Robbie pinning Rodgers' murder on me. In the end he did a deal with Robbie. Robbie made him choose between Burrows and me. He had both our fingerprints on the two murder weapons and he could arrange for either one of them to fall into police hands. So, you see, if this Myles fellow can prove that it was Rodgers that we tried and executed, the whole thing will blow up in our faces. I'm relying on you to make sure that doesn't happen."

Joseph stared as into the distance. His brain was close to catching up with what was being said. It took a few seconds for the catch-up to complete.

"But surely," he stuttered, "it's too late. I've already told the policeman that it *was* Rodgers we shot ... or thought we shot. There's nothing I can do."

"Yes, there is. You didn't make a written statement. There's nothing down on paper. All you have to do is to tell Inspector Myles that you got confused, you read about the Rodgers' case afterwards and you superimposed the events you read about on your memory of the role play. It's a common enough phenomenon. Real life memories often get confused with things that you've pictured in your head. Okay, he mightn't believe you, but he'll simply have to lump what you tell him. And that's all that matters."

Joseph made as if to contradict what he obviously saw as an unpalatable conclusion, but he stopped short before any words came out. Old habits die hard, and Joseph's long established allegiance to logic was not something he could easily dismiss. He did not want Justin to be right on this issue, he did not want to take on the burden of another lie, he just wanted the whole nightmare of the past, of his failure to bring his feeling and his thinking together, he wanted it all to go away and leave him in peace. What right had Justin to come and put all this pressure on him? This man claimed to be his friend, but was he really? He had done nothing but lie to him all along; he had come to Oxford as a student, but he wasn't a student; his real job had been to spy on them and get them all locked up. How could he say he was his friend? He owed Justin nothing. He had every right to be angry with him. And suddenly for some reason he began to feel the better for being angry with him. A string of expletives came out of nowhere in his head. In one rabid movement he was on his feet knocking over the flimsy chair he had been perched on.

"You're a f...ing c..., Justin. Get the f... out of my house. I want nothing more to do with you. You can go to hell for all I care. If that f... ing policeman comes back, I'll tell him too where he can go. Now, get out and leave me alone."

The screeching voice and the violence of the movement took Justin completely unawares. He had never heard Joseph even swear before. His first instinct was to stand his ground, but he thought better of it. Any attempt to dampen down the fire that was raging behind those eyes looked a poor prospect. There was nothing for it but to do as he was told and beat an undignified retreat.

Chapter 48

Once the Panel received confirmation that HQ's objection had been withdrawn the go-ahead was given for the formal dinner at which the two candidates were to be offered the opportunity to put their wider personas on display.

Naomi was an elegantly beautiful woman; with her long auburn hair and deep brown eyes that offered warmth and at the same time teased with mystery, she needed little adornment to persuade beholders that they were being given a glimpse of empyreal reality. On this occasion the adornment was not lacking either; the full-length evening dress of rich purple that she wore showed off just enough of her figure to allure, but not enough to suggest that she valued her sexuality above her gifts as an all-purpose person. She came over as much more than a coveted trophy wife, some superficial beauty whose anti-male defences had been breached. The casual way she seemed to look on her own physicality extended the scope of the qualities needed to win her, which in turn reflected favourably on the charismatic power of the rather gaunt figure by her side. The effect was further enhanced by contrast with the rather dumpy Mrs Sinclair, hardly a credit to her husband's powers of attraction.

Snoddy himself felt like a fish out of water. He hated this kind of social ritual where you are expected to smile, mouth platitudes and avoid giving expression to anything cerebral or emotional that doesn't come with a designer label. Women were so much better at this kind of thing – even intelligent women like Naomi. Somehow they saw no shame in saying what they would never dream of thinking. In fact they took pride in maintaining the greatest possible tension between the two. It was a mark of their skill and their savvy. He knew that it was something he must become at least passable at if he was to have a career in politics, but for the moment he would draw as much as he could on Naomi's dazzle. He chuckled to himself as he remembered a line from the Bible. *No man cometh unto the Father, but by me.* Yes, he could get away with a minimum of social prattle if he could seem grand and aloof enough to merit such a magnificent conduit. He could certainly do aloof much better than he could do chatty.

The part of the evening that Snoddy dreaded most was the inevitable encounter with his opponent. Naomi had warned him of the necessity for gracious charm, a firm handshake and a convincing display of good nature. Snoddy shuddered. The degree of insincerity that a show of sportsmanship places on people hell-bent on winning demands a level of self-control equal to the effort of suppressing a sneeze when there's pepper in the air. Sportsmanship is only appropriate when the contest is over; you can acknowledge your opponent's superiority or sympathise with his pain in defeat, but wishing him well before the contest has begun is pure humbug. Did he really have to do humbug? Fortunately, George Sinclair seemed to feel the same way. There was a handshake and there was a smile, but Sinclair, more used to this kind of occasion than Snoddy, looked him in the eye and, the smile changing to a grin, declared that he was going to beat the hell out of him. Snoddy warmed to this immediately; it was an acknowledgement that they were the only two people in the room who were there in full earnest. He had in any case been predisposed to like his rival. He had heard of him from his father who had the habit of reading out selected passages from The Morning Star over the dinner table to a wife who cared nothing for politics and a son whose limited understanding allowed him only to feel admiration for the reader. In later years that admiration had waned; its decline was a great loss to the father and was felt almost as strongly by the son. There is something enriching about admiration. Like love itself, it enhances those who feel it even more than those for whom it is felt.

Snoddy had given a great deal of thought to the speech he was required to make. He enjoyed the kind of wit that preys on the incongruities of streaky thinking and misdirected action, but there was a cruelty in that which he knew he must avoid. Funny stories were decidedly out; they were just not his thing. In the end he had turned to Greenfield for advice. 'Tell them a story', the old man had said. 'Tell them something that moved you when you were young. The most significant moments of everyone's life take place in the first decade or so. After that we simply put finishing touches to the impressions we have formed. Tell them something that turned you into who you are.'

Sinclair was first to speak. He was a seasoned after-dinner speaker and had a wealth of stories to draw on from his colourful past. Names that had been in the headlines were given flesh and bones and brought to earth as fellow strugglers in the maelstrom of events. Even opponents were humanised and given some of the best lines to deliver. All those used to hearing Sinclair in full ideological assault on the iniquities of American sponsored capitalism were being invited to look more kindly on the source of the invective, not some angry mechanical monster but a man steeped in irreverent empathy with his fellow creatures. It was a masterful performance. And there was a very empty hole waiting for Snoddy to fill when he sat down.

When the applause had subsided, Reggie Whitehouse, who had been given the honour of acting as master of ceremonies, was fulsome in his praise for 'the old bugger who during most of his tenure as the MP for Bury West had been a pain in the . . .' He paused in mock panic before settling on the word 'neck. He then turned to 'the young whippersnapper' from Oxford and called on him to share his thoughts with them. Snoddy rose modestly to his feet putting on as good-natured a smile as he could muster.

"Ladies and gentlemen, like all of you who have listened to George here, I am left in awe at the wealth of experience and the depth of humanity that this man has allowed us to glimpse. My own slender hopes are pinned on some clever publisher snapping him up and redirecting him to write what would be one of the most entertaining autobiographies of the present age. That might distract him and get him out of my hair. And believe me, I would throw away my razor and grow enough hair for him to get out of, if he would take up the offer.

"Obviously, I don't come with anything like the existential pedigree that George has shown us here tonight. But I do believe in the progression of human culture; no generation starts from scratch; each generation feeds on what comes down from the previous ones. It's nature's way of putting old heads on young shoulders. When the heads match the shoulders you're in trouble. Young heads on young shoulders is a sure recipe for folly. And with old heads on old shoulders all you get is talk and no action. Well, you can all see my head. Does it look young to you? You know why I shave it? I shave it because my hair is in the advanced stages of waving goodbye. Hardly an action to go with a young head, is it?

"To be serious though, a lot of what is in this head of mine I owe to my father and my grandfather. It is the values they lived by that have guided my political thinking. Both of them were active trade unionists. Indeed, they both served as shop stewards and regularly took time off work at election time, giving up a precious day's wages, to campaign for the Party. There was a story my grandfather told that has stayed with me as something almost biblical. But I will avoid the temptation of beginning it with: 'And it came to pass that ...'

"It was in the thirties. My grandfather – we called him Pap – he had just come out of his time as a pawnbroker. I love that expression. In our more prosaic parlance it means: he had just completed his apprenticeship. That meant of course he would

261

have to be paid the full rate. The proprietor of the shop didn't think much of that, so he gave Pab his cards and like millions of others Pap found himself on the dole. It being the thirties, the prospects of getting a job in Glasgow were none too bright. He tried his hand at everything – labouring, odd-jobbing, even shoe-mending and barbering – you name it, he tried it. But these jobs were only fill-ins; none of them lasted. A close friend of his had a young brother, Lewis, who was just out of school and had landed a job as an apprentice engineer on a ship sailing out of Falmouth. The young fellow was only fourteen and had never been out of Scotland, so Pap being at a loose end, the parents asked him to accompany the boy to Falmouth. Pap thought he would seize the opportunity to see if he could get himself a job on a ship. He had no appropriate skills, but he thought there might be jobs going in a galley. No such luck; when he got there, he discovered that all the galley hands were Chinese, and surprising as it may seem, Mandarin hadn't been on the curriculum at his public elementary school.

"To make matters worse, the whole away-from-home experience was proving too much for young Lewis; he was desperately homesick and begged Pap to take him back with him. Pap had been given just enough money to get himself back up to Glasgow, but he couldn't just leave the young lad. If they cut out food, there would be just enough to get them both back. It was the dead of winter and the snow was on the ground. They had to change trains several times and at one station he described how they warmed themselves in front of a blazing fire in a waiting room as the snow fell outside. I wasn't there of course, but it's an image that has worked its way with lifelike clarity into my memory. The two of them gradually made their way back up north. In Carlisle I think it was, they booked into a cheap boarding house – it was their last twelve and six pence. I always remember the way father told the story – for it was from him that I heard it. The landlady asked if they wished to have supper. The look on their faces must have told her how much effort they were putting in to come up with a 'no', for before they did, she smiled and assured them that supper was included in the price. Father's face always took on his version of that smile when he told this. Pap suspected that the price wasn't really included; it was an unassuming act of human decency.

"Eventually they made it back to Glasgow. To my knowledge Lewis never ventured south of the border again, but the idea had been spawned in Pap's head that he might chance his arm at wangling a job on a ship as a fifth engineer. He had a cousin, George Stirling, who was a first engineer. When asked for his advice, Stirling reckoned Pap had a fighting chance of bluffing his way; he gave him a few tips, lent him a couple of textbooks and wrote him a false reference. He applied and, lo and behold, a week or so later a letter landed on the hall floor with the offer of a job on an oil-tanker.

"It was hard-going at first. When one of the engineers asked him to go and fetch a particular tool, he would go off, wander about a bit and come back and say he couldn't find it. He had to put up with a lot of stick – ''Bloody Stupid Jock' was the only phrase that cleared the censor when father told the story. Next time of course Pap would know what a whatever-it-was looked like and what it was for. When the war came, granny insisted on her new husband leaving the sea, but the experience he had gained stood him in good stead, for he was able to get work in the shipyards on the Clyde. He worked his way up and by the time he reached retirement he had established himself as the top milling machinist in the tool room.

"There's nothing mind-blowing about this story. There's no heroism in it, no wondrous happenings, no righting of wrongs. It's the ordinariness of the story that appeals to me – the warmth in it, the ingenuity and self-reliance, the instinctive dismissal of self-pity; these are the things that have come down to me – the sense that generation had that, despite being all in it together, they were each responsible for finding fixes for their own problems. I will always be grateful to Pap for the legacy he has left me, the indelible imprint on my mind of what it is to be a dignified human being. That's the kind of man our Party should be looking out for. What really worries me is that that kind of man is now seriously threatened with extinction; he is desperately in need of rescuing.

"You don't need to look to see where that threat is coming from. You'll find it lurking in the shadows under the glitz of the good-time culture. Look closely and you'll see global capitalism beavering away to steamroller us all into one-dimensional consuming cretins, moral and political zombies. I will not labour the point, but just look at the kind of adverts that appear on our TV screens night after night and ask yourselves: 'Is this the kind of thing that should be addressed to a grown-up such as my grandfather?'"

He bowed his head and sat down. There was silence from the audience as if in disappointed expectation of more to come. It was difficult to say whether the ripple of applause that followed, tentatively at first before it acquired enough strength to produce momentum, was an expression of courtesy belatedly catching itself on or the impact of what they had heard taking its time to work itself through.

Chapter 49

The state of resolve in which Myles had managed to ensconce himself in the course of his encounter with ex-Inspector Stranaghan was buttressed by ramparts that gave little promise of durability. They seemed formidable enough when he kept his thoughts focused on the gash that had been cut in the heart of the justice system – a senior police officer conspiring with a criminal organisation to subvert both the police and the courts, and two men banged up in prison on trumped-up evidence for a crime they didn't commit. But then niggling doubts would materialise like little rivulets in the mortar. Why was it more important that these men should be in prison for something they didn't do than them not being in prison for something equally awful that they did do?

Then there was his old Inspector. Stuart Stranaghan was one of that rare breed of fellow creatures that come to your aid in moments of despair, not by anything they do, just by the assurance they provide by their presence in the world. Should he really pursue the case against him? What Stranaghan had done was wrong certainly, but it was done for the best of motives. The loyalty that a leader owes to those he leads is one of the moral canons that the modern conscience seems all too happy to neglect. Stranaghan was surely to be admired for doing the right thing, even if that also happened to be the wrong thing. Had it been Graham Myles rather than Justin Wright that he had acted to protect, would there have been any question of him looking to charge him with subverting the course of justice? Of course not, so ...? But then again, that was the whole point surely. It wasn't Graham Myles he had acted to protect; it was Justin Wright. And who was to say that Wright was innocent? Maybe

Stranaghan had been wrong about his protégé. All the evidence pointed to Wright having gone rogue. Joseph Ross for one certainly believed at the time that the execution was for real. They had only Wright's word for it that he had clocked it as a charade. The whole business of Snoddy presenting Stranaghan with the so-called Barabbas Choice might just have been a clever way of compromising him and getting him to call off the investigation. Wright could well have been in on it. It got him off the hook, didn't it? And just look at what followed; he quit the force and got a job working for Eardley, the sponsor of the very organisation he had been tasked with bringing down.

These thoughts ebbed and flowed over all Myles' other doings, gumming him up a state of mental and emotional inertia. He had a couple of days leave due to him, so he decided to take them and give himself some breathing space. He somehow imagined that the change of the physical landscape would cause a reconfiguration of the mental pieces he was grappling with. It was a forlorn hope. Distance doesn't always make the mind go clearer, but it does at least have the merit of putting an interval between the decision and its execution. The hiatus had the desired effect of reducing the angst element of the decision-making process, leaving him freer to side with his rationality. He would go ahead and get a detailed statement from Joseph. That wouldn't commit him to anything. Depending on how things panned out, he could make use of the statement or he could simply tear it up. At least he would be doing something. Persisting in doing nothing was beginning to diminish his sense of himself. Once he was in possession of the statement, he would be in the driving seat, even if he wasn't sure what exactly it was that he was driving. Yes, that's what he should do and he would do it first thing when he got back.

The morning rituals – washing, dressing, having breakfast – had the effect they usually have of *de-nebulising* the plan of action for the day and ushering it into the realm of the palpable.

The mutation was abetted by the crispness of the air and the thin coating of hoar frost that lay on the garden lawns. Sunlight made sporadic darts through the white cloud that hovered just high enough overhead as not to be mistaken for mist. Myles experienced the feeling of invigoration that comes with the sense that everything around is in a state of incipience. He used an old-fashioned street map to make his way to the address he had got from Joseph. It led him through a series of short streets lined with houses with little token gardens, few of which were in receipt of any attention. It was as if the owners had started with the best of intentions by planting a bush or a shrub but then had lost interest, leaving the poor specimen to fend for itself in a wasteland of bricks and mortar. When he got to Joseph's street even this botanical tokenism had been abandoned; two terraces of houses squared up to each other with nothing but the bare flagstones of the pavement and the patched-up tarmac of the road between them. There were no parked cars either, since the thoroughfare was barely wide enough to allow for two-way traffic. The door to Number 17 was a sorry sight; the paint – a nauseating lime green – was peeling at the edges and the bottom board was showing advanced signs of disintegration; large splinters of wood had broken off, eaten away by the damp and the slaters. At the side there were two bell pushes each bearing the name of the occupant. Joseph's was the upper one. Myles pressed hard. It was impossible to tell if it was ringing, although the little light did go out when the button was pressed, so something had to be happening. He tried several variations, pressing hard, holding the button down, using a staccato action, but still no response. He stood back and looked to the upstairs window for any signs of life. The curtain wasn't drawn but there was nothing to offer any promise of occupancy. He then tried the bell of the lower flat, but here again there was no response. There was nothing for it but to give in to defeat.

After a coffee in a run-down diner a few streets away he

thought to see if the Reverend John had any information on Joseph's whereabouts. He tried the home number he had been given but got no reply. It wasn't going to be his day. For want of any alternatives he made his way to the rectory; it was likely that he would find the Reverend in church or at least find someone who knew where he was.

Even before he got to the lich-gate he could hear the mellifluous sounds of the church organ. If any God did exist, that surely, he thought, must be the register He would speak in. None of that horrible tininess or twanginess of a born-again brother, he'd settle for the reassuring gravitas of an old-fashioned paterfamilias anytime. He was surprised though to find that it was the Reverend himself at the organ; he would have put down him more as a guitar-strummer than a Bach freak. The creak of the church door as he entered was not enough to perforate the resonance and the play went on for several minutes before coming to a climactic end. Myles favoured a cough over an ostentatious clap as his method of registering his presence. The Reverend John turned round, clearly startled by the presence of a third party. The church was in the gloom of a wintry morning and he could not make out the figure making its way up the aisle. For some uncanny reason he assumed it to be Joseph. (Myles was no more than marginally the taller and stouter man). It was only when Myles was within a few yards that he recognised the visitor.

"Inspector Myles ... What brings you here?"

The pause between the realisation and the enquiry showed definite traces of disappointment.

Myles explained that he needed to see Joseph but had been unable to raise him.

"I wondered if you would have any idea where I could find him."

The Reverend dismounted from his pedestal and walked right up to Myles before replying.

"Look, Inspector Myles, do you really need to speak to him?

I'm very worried about him. He rang me late last night. He was in a terrible state. He'd been drinking. It was hard to make sense of what he was saying, but he seems to have had a visit from that man Wright. I don't know what passed between them, but whatever it was, it really got to Joseph. He was right back to where he was when I first met him.

"I was so alarmed I went round to see him. When I got there he was totally out of it. He was slumped over a chair and I found two empty bottles of vodka on the floor beside him. I took off his shoes and got him into bed and waited around for an hour or so. But he was out for the count. I thought it would be safe to leave him. I had a prayer meeting to conduct here first thing this morning and was intending to go round to see how he was. But, to be honest, I felt I needed a quick shot of Bach to keep my courage up before I went. You say he didn't answer when you called this morning? That doesn't surprise me. With that amount of vodka in his system I'd be surprised if he surfaced today at all. Come over to the rectory. I'll grab a coat and we'll go round and see what's what. I have a key. Joseph gave it to me the last time he was laid up with depression so that I could come and go."

Joseph's flat was just over a mile from the rectory. In the course of the twenty minute walk the Reverend attempted to give the Inspector an insight into Joseph's mental state.

"Depression is a form of addiction", he declared. "The alcoholic looks to the next drink to rescue him from the pit he is stuck in. The gambler is convinced the next bet will undo all the damage done by the previous ones. Similarly, the depressive looks around for something substantial in his life to assure him that he's is not living in an empty void. But in all three cases the 'cure' only serves to provide more fuel for the ill. When you're depressed the last thing you should be doing is looking for something worthwhile to pull you up. It may seem the obvious thing to do, and it's what people tell you to do when they're

269

trying to help. But it doesn't help. It's just the same as with that extra bet or that extra drink, you only succeed in adding another layer to the big bubble of nothingness that engulfs you. Worse than that, when the bastion you hoped you could count on lets you down, you've edged a step closer to the pit of despond. You must ride out the storm ... no, that's completely the wrong image ... you must embrace the debilitating powers of the doldrums and reduce yourself to the point where there is nothing left for them to have power over. Then, and only then, do they release you and leave you free to re-engage with things of substance and value and take sustenance from them. I've learned that over the years, but believe me, that doesn't make it any easier to deal with."

Much of this was lost on Myles. He was one of those fortunate creatures whose take on the world had never suffered any distortion greater than what comes through the lens of anger, jealousy, fear or just simple boredom; in consequence he tended to look on depression as one of these simply overindulging itself. He could sympathise with Joseph only to the extent of acknowledging that he was suffering, but as to the pain itself, it was merely a matter of fact that was needed to balance the equation. What he couldn't understand was what was stopping Joseph from just walking away from his demon. The Reverend on the other hand clearly could. He was all too well acquainted with the demon and was driving himself to act on his Christian conviction that in sharing the pain of others you get to dilute its effect.

The key was inserted in the lock and the door gave a shudder as it disengaged from its frame. Myles followed the clergyman up the dark, narrow staircase and into the bedsit. All that he was aware of at first in the murk was the general state of clutter and disorder and a sickly-sweet smell that filled the air. The Reverend had been calling out Joseph's name, but suddenly stopped as the two men caught sight of the figure lying spread-eagled across the bed. A leg and an arm were dangling over the edge. The head, with a nasty gash on the temple, rested on the pillow at an unnatural angle to the rest of the body. The Reverend recoiled in horror at the pitiful sight, but Myles had been in such situations before and, following his training, checked for a pulse. There was one, but it was faint.

The ambulance took about ten minutes to arrive. As they waited, Myles looked through the clutter of things on the floor by the bed side. There were two large one-litre vodka bottles, both empty and an assortment of medicine jars, one of which was marked 'Diazepam'. The other names were not familiar to Myles. There was also a notebook which he picked up and flicked through. It was a seemingly random collection of thoughts and observations, each marked with the date they had been entered. The last entry was in the form of a short poem. Myles showed it to the Reverend who, to the detective's surprise, chose to read it aloud.

> *How can we smile in a world of men*
> *Whose mouths, o'erstretched, have been slit with pain*
> *And now lie gaping like gutted trout,*
> *Their entrails emptied, their life run out?*
> *Whom can we love on this earth of ours,*
> *Where friendships pall and sweetness sours,*
> *Intrigues slap and flirtations tease*
> *Our hearts, puff-punctured like toasted cheese?*

Tears welled up in the Reverend's eyes and his voice clogged up as he read. Myles was not unmoved, but his sympathy ran to no more than the onlooker's respect for the feelings of the affected. His own thoughts were already turning to the consequences this turn of events might have for his investigation.

There was room in the ambulance for only one of them to accompany the victim, so Myles deferred to the Reverend and

271

stayed on in the bedsit. There might be something to be found that would shed some light. He went about his work methodically, but the search proved fruitless. There were no signs of the recent presence of a third party. There were several unwashed cups and plates in the sink, but they were obviously the accumulation of at least a day's indifference to household duties. The only mail was an electric bill and a catalogue for menswear still in its plastic rapping. The bookshelves were packed mainly with foreign books with titles that meant nothing to him; the English ones were all philosophical or religious. The only author Myles recognized was C S Lewis, but they weren't the Narnia books he had read as a child, they were two tracts entitled *Mere Christianity* and *The Problem of Pain*. Flicking through them, his attention was drawn to two passages that had been heavily underlined.

Aim at heaven, and you will get earth thrown in, aim at earth, and you will get neither.

This made some sense to him, but he couldn't make anything of the second.

Friendship is unnecessary, like philosophy, like art. It has no survival value; rather it is one of those things that give value to survival.

His puzzlement did not engage him for long. The Reverend had left him the key, so he locked up and made his way back to his hotel, where his car was parked.

The A&E coughed up the usual assortment of broken down human specimens, refugees from the whirlwind of life. It was always the faces – not the spluttering coughs and retching, not the bandages nor the wheelchairs nor the plastic crutches, not even the thinly disguised whiff of urine and vomit – it was invariably the look of stoical non-expectation on the faces in the waiting area that pierced his defences. He wondered if the souls queuing up at the gates of hell would look any different. When you're in a queue, it's a natural instinct to want to get to the top of it, but in such an instance can you really go with that instinct? The tension totals out as a lifeless nullification. That's what registers itself on the faces. The triage nurse directed him to a small so-called family room close to where Joseph was being treated. There he found the Reverend pacing up and down and clearly doing battle with his feelings.

"Any news?"

The clergyman, oblivious to Myles' arrival, was startled by the inquiry.

"No, they haven't said a word to me. They seemed to know what they're doing and just went about their business."

The temper of the reply suggested a mind reluctant to re-surface from the murky depths it was delving in. Myles could see that he was being drawn back under, so he left him to it and, somewhat shame-facedly, turned his attention to the coffee machine. He had his own thinking to do.

When he had set out that morning to get the statement from Joseph he hadn't been able to make up his mind what to wish for for his former boss. He wanted to nick Wright, if there was something to nick him for, but as to how that would affect the man he still had so much regard for, he chose for the moment to keep well to the back of his mind. He would get things to happen and then allow himself to be driven by the way they configured themselves. It was a way of turning the actions he might take into extraneous happenings and relieving himself of any responsibility for their eventual outcome. It wasn't a thought-out strategy, just an instinctive reaction. It was a pattern of behaviour, he now realised, he had followed on many previous occasions, but this was the first time he had been fully conscious of it. The last thing he wanted to do now was to engage in a series of mind-numbing what-if exercises. He would simply wait and see how the cards would fall.

The wait was over before his coffee cup was empty. The door opened and a young Indian doctor entered, his face primed for sympathy, and declared that despite their best efforts the patient had not recovered consciousness and had slipped away. There would of course be a post mortem and possibly an inquest to establish the exact cause of death. When Myles mentioned the gash on the temple and asked if there might have been foul play, the young man cleared his throat before replying that it wasn't for him to say, but at the moment it did look as if the patient might well have taken his own life.

Chapter 50

It was generally accepted that both of the candidates had acquitted themselves well at the formal dinner. Snoddy's youth, underlined by the sexual allure of the gorgeous Naomi, could just as easily have weighed in against him as for him, but his story of his grandfather's experience in the hungry thirties had proved the perfect counterweight and allowed him to bask in the light of both worlds. A full account of the evening appeared in the local press. Written by Justin Wright, it tilted, as one might expect, more to the Snoddy's side than to Sinclair's. But much greater impact was made by a magazine article featuring *the woman in the up-and-coming man's life*, with glossy pictures of Naomi at her most alluring as well as a glowing account of her academic credentials, a first at Cambridge followed by a PhD at Oxford. Little mention was made of Snoddy, but the implication was clear that anyone capable of attracting such an Amazon must be of a special breed. The article was unattributed, but it had in fact been penned by Francesca Bergman.

The next stage in the selection process was to be a head-to-head debate between the two pretenders. After much discussion, and in consultation with the candidates, it was agreed that the two should give their thoughts on the question: What is socialism for? Each man was to be allowed five minutes for an opening statement to be followed by a free-for-all at which the committee would be permitted to stoke the fire with questions of their own.

The toss of a coin determined that Sinclair should kick off. The main thrust of his address was an appeal for the Party to get back to its roots.

"The determining feature of any man's identity is the way he earns his living. That is what determines who he is and what he is. It is also what establishes his political identity. The Labour Party was formed to represent that political identity. Its mission was to fight for workers' rights and promote causes that worked in workers' interests. There could be reasonable disagreement over the merits or otherwise of given causes, but the criterion that must always be applied by a party such as the Labour Party is whether, or to what degree, it serves working class interests. For some reason however the modern Labour Party seems to have developed a blurred vision of that mandate and has tied itself up in all sorts of causes that have nothing to do with the lives of the common man. If I join a pigeon fanciers club, I don't expect the leadership to speak for me in matters that have nothing to do with pigeons. Similarly, when I vote for a party to represent my economic and political interests, I don't expect the leadership to go off on all sorts of liberal tangents, let alone focus on such issues and neglect the job they were put there to do. Gay marriage, transsexual awareness, gender quotas, global warming, foreign aid, nuclear disarmament, pro-Europeanism – these are all subjects that are open to proper debate, but they do not belong among the core beliefs of a party devoted to the interests of the working class. Socialists may well choose to side with liberals on many of these issues, I've no problem with that, but what I do have a problem with is the insistence that our members must all sing from the liberal songbook. What happened to the socialist songbook? The saddest thing of all is that many amongst the leadership of our party don't know the difference; they think that that *is* the socialist songbook."

It was now Snoddy's turn. He had a grin on his face as he rose to speak.

"I'm sorry, but it looks as if I'm going to have to disappoint you, ladies and gentlemen: I agree with everything my worthy opponent has said. The Labour Party has become the Liberal Party in overalls. The only thing is that the overalls are fake;

they're too clean and much too tasteful. The psychology is easy to understand. Our Party was formed to take up the cudgels on behalf of Labour in its struggle with Capital. That was, and still remains, a noble cause. But in its determination to fight this good fight, it has developed a compulsion to see all issues in these terms. It's in constant search mode for victims and villains and noble errands. The poor, the weak and the sick-in-mind are the good guys and the prosperous, the strong and the conventionally minded are all agents of the dark force. It's a classic case of 'seek and ye shall find'. A blind eye is turned on everything that might subvert this narrative. It wouldn't do if we discovered that many of the poor were poor because they were too idle to work or if some of the weak were weak because they were too easy on themselves. And woe betide anyone judgemental enough to prescribe sickness-in-mind from a vantage point of bourgeois conventionality. No, we of the left much prefer to gorge on tall tales of capitalist giants and social casualties. The trouble is: if we keep on crying wolf and lamb, who will take us seriously when a genuine case comes up?

"But that's too easy a point to make. The more pressing problem is the effect this narrative is having on the class we are pledged to represent. We are encouraging them to think of themselves in a way that is inimical to their development as human beings. To be frank, what we are doing is helping to infantilise them. What's more, in so doing, we are playing into the hands of the very forces that we should be resisting. George was right to make the point that it is the primary business of the Labour Party to focus on the struggle between Capital and Labour. I couldn't agree more. Where I suspect we would disagree is in the topography of the battlefield. Traditionally, this has been on the shop floor. The employer wants to wring as much out of the worker as he can get in return for as little as he can get away with paying him. I am not saying for a moment that that has ceased to be a flash point, but what I do say is that

that is no longer where the crucial clashes are at. Capitalism is at a very different stage to where it was in the early days of our Party. As Marx himself said, the capitalist system is confronted with a fatal contradiction. It is a system designed for the employer to exploit the worker, but to the extent that it succeeds in this, it also cuts off its own air supply. It needs the masses not only to work in its factories; it also needs them to buy the goods that those factories produce. Impoverished workers make for pretty hopeless consumers. Therein lies the contradiction and, according to Marx, the inevitability of the collapse of the system. The great man however underestimated the system's capacity for adaptation. Thanks to automation and the supply of cheap labour from the Third World, capitalism became much less dependent on the masses of the First World as its source of labour. These workers could now be released from their bonds as full-time working trolls and given the time and means to work in their new role as consumers. Their job is to shop. Everyone must fill as many baskets as possible, eating to the point of obesity and drinking to the edge of oblivion, acquiring new outfits for every week of the year, keeping their house interiors fashion-sensitive, and defying the grim reaper with as many 'holidays of a lifetime' as they can fit in. Of course, if they don't have enough to fund all this, it is their duty as consumer-proles to borrow at exorbitant rates whatever their credit rating qualifies them for.

"What is our Party's response to this? Does it have a response? No, I don't think it does. Worse than that, it aids it and abets it and gets on with fighting yesterday's war."

As he resumed his seat, a look of confusion seemed to light on Sinclair's face. This was ground he was unfamiliar with, but thankfully, there was something to take issue with in that closing remark.

"So you think the whole business of fighting for higher wages and better conditions is yesterday's war, do you? You should try telling that to people with families on the minimum wage? Or do you think we should forget about them, them being yesterday's people and all that?"

This generated a murmur of approval that went round the room. Snoddy's heckles instantly rose. *Why were people so bloody stupid? Did they not hear what he'd said?* He had to make a considerable effort to disguise his annoyance.

"Of course I don't. I stated quite clearly that the fight for a better deal for the working man is still an area where we need to be active. I was appalled at the attitude our Party took to the swamping of the labour market with cheap labour from Eastern Europe. While the Party top brass preened themselves with their impeccable internationalist credentials, the ordinary plebs in this country had to put up with having their wages depressed, not to mention the bullets they had to bite in housing, health and education. Now, that really was a case of treating them like yesterday's people. As if that weren't enough, we even threw in a few insults; if they complained, we called them racists, xenophobes, or plain bloody stupid. Could you get a better example of lyrics that belong in the liberal songbook?

"No, I wasn't dismissing the need to address the problems of the people at the bottom of the pile. What I was trying to do was draw attention to a newer phenomenon that is affecting much greater numbers of people, one which we in the Labour Party have been slow to acknowledge, understandably so, since in a way we have been suckered into advancing its progress."

Seeing a chance to sideline Sinclair in the debate, Schinski stepped in, expressing fascination with this 'innovative analysis of the contemporary political scene' (He had gone to some trouble to come up with this wording) and inviting the speaker to expand on his ideas. Snoddy was happy to oblige.

"There is, in my view, irrefutable evidence that we have slipped into the market mindset in relation to our voters. What the customer wants, the customer should get. It seems a straightforward enough maxim to follow. It certainly is one that goes down well at election time. But is it a maxim that a parent or a doctor or a teacher should follow, in other words anyone who has a deep interest in the welfare of the people he is dealing with? If a child wants more sweets, should it been given them? If a patient wants to stuff his face and smoke his lungs out, should his doctor refrain from doing that terrible thing and being *judgemental*? And what about a pupil who plays truant from school and spends his days playing games on his i-pad? Should the education authorities take a live-and-let-live approach? Of course, what you will say is that the examples I have chosen all involve children or vulnerable adults. True, but does that mean that political parties don't have a duty of care to voters? Should they not strive to shape the political landscape in a way that is likely to be in the long term interests of those who vote for them? If all we are interested in is their votes, then by all means give them what they want. That's what successive Labour administrations have done – relaxation of the curbs on gambling, extended opening hours for clubs and pubs, turning a blind eye to the use of illegal drugs. As a party we used to view such activities as the opiate of the masses, now we strum along in harmony with the commercial tune.

"But that is only the tip of the iceberg. In education – something our Party once regarded as an equal partner in the two-pronged attack on class privilege – we now sip with the money-changers. We have edged surreptitiously away from the notion that education is there to transform and enrich the learner's experience to one where it is called on merely to confirm him in his satisfaction with his own, in many cases miserable, set of thoughts and feelings. A great frown wrinkles the liberal brow at any attempt to fill heads with knowledge and insist on rigour and discipline in the classroom. And in the best children's party tradition every student comes away with a gift-wrapped package of degrees and certificates that flatters them into thinking they are educationally blessed."

This was not an area Sinclair would have chosen to cross swords on, but he desperately needed to register a voice. He was quick to spot that *umbrage* was there to be taken and seized his opportunity.

"I'm amazed at this young man's arrogance. He comes along here, having fiddled about for a few years with his pals playing mind games in Oxford, and has the effrontery to tell the working man what he should be doing with his hard earned wages. And then he informs us that only people like him can tell if a degree is worth the paper it's written on or not. I take it, Mr Snoddy, that you've given your own degree the thumbs up? Now, why should that be, I wonder?"

Sinclair, a past master at playing an audience, allowed the scathing indignation to feed rapaciously off itself before turning back to the '*grown-up*' question of how to support those at the bottom of the economic ladder.

"Don't be fooled by these side issues that my opponent is trying to introduce. When it gets down to the nitty-gritty, our members want one thing from us and that is to put a stop to capitalist exploitation of labour. When I read in the glossy magazines about the life styles of the privileged rich, about their yachts in St Tropez, their villas in Beverley Hills, their fancy clothes and their shameless wantonness, I take out an old cutting I have. It tells the story of a widow in Grimsby. Her husband was lost at sea. He worked for a fishing conglomerate. She got a measly £50,000 in compensation to fend for herself and her four kids. The company argued in court that the man had not followed the health and safety procedures and so it could not be held responsible for the accident. The £50,000, they claimed, was an act of charity!"

The old tunes are the ones that go down best and Sinclair was a past master at playing them. Snoddy had been bold in his attempt to draw the fight unto less familiar ground, but the old warrior knew that where the heart was the brain would follow. Intervention was urgently required. Schinski rose to his feet.

"What strikes me is how close the two of you are to each other. Both of you can see how our Party has moved away from its working class origins to embrace a form of liberalism that has more of a place at a Hampstead dinner party than a working men's club in Bury. I think you are being a bit hard on your young rival, Mr Sinclair. He does not have your distinguished war record in the fight for workers' rights, but surely he has a point when he says that we mustn't allow our enthusiasm for better material conditions for our people blind us to the fact that we might unwittingly be doing the capitalists' job for them."

This met with several nods of approval, but before sitting down Schinski cast a petitioning look at Freddie Douglas. The appeal was answered.

"I'm sure we all share your enthusiasm for the ongoing fight against privilege, Mr Sinclair, but I for one am fascinated by the analysis offered by Mr Snoddy. What you are saying, Mr Sinclair, is not incompatible with what Mr Snoddy is saying, and what Mr Snoddy is saying offers new insights into the pernicious influence of Big Business on the lives of ordinary people. I think we should be grateful to this young man for breathing some new life into the debate. God knows, our Party could be doing with some fresh thinking."

Schinski's 'hear, hear' generated at first a half-hearted, and then a self-confident chorus. Snoddy was encouraged to expand on his thoughts on how the 'juggernaut of capitalist consumerism' could be resisted. Thus given the floor, he was able to take aim at a variety of standard bogey targets and add vapours to the mounting suspicion in some minds at least that George Sinclair, worthy though he was, might indeed be yesterday's man.

Chapter 51

The Reverend John's reaction to Joseph's death took Myles by surprise. As someone committed to proclaim the hollowness of death's denial of life, he might surely be expected to take this sad little suicide as a glancing blow. Not so, the man took on a look of utter devastation. Joseph, he explained as the two men sat over a coffee in the hospital canteen, had become for him the embodiment of innocence and its will to good. To see it so cruelly crushed was a blow that cut to the very core of his faith. He didn't blame God – God wasn't a him or a her, or even an it or a them – but it did bring him to doubt the standing of the membership of goodness in the executive of life. He knew of course that Christ's teaching promised it no standing. It denied it in fact, but the crushing of vulnerable goodness and the beauty that went with it was something his whole being rose up against. It made him doubt the scriptures; if the Disciples felt as he did, could it not be that the whole Christian claim for metaphysical triumph in the face of physical defeat was no more than an escape route out of despair?

"Poor Joseph was inspired by the vulnerability of innocence in the world and tried to oppose the evil that threatened it, but the same innocence that was within him, the innocence that called on him to champion the weak of the world, reviled those very actions that he forced himself to perform on its behalf. The thing that broke him of course was that damned charade. He really believed at the time that he had been party to the death of that despicable creature Rodgers. He had been so horrified by the sadistic cruelty of the crime that Rodgers had committed that he felt that he owed it to everything he believed in to pull that trigger. He couldn't live with the paradox that his action let out of the box. It didn't really help when he discovered that he hadn't in fact killed anyone. A vital crack had been exposed in the lining of reality. I tried to get him to stop looking at it, but, as you see, I failed. He was just like a moth that couldn't say no to the insistence of the light."

Myles made little contribution to the dialogue. He could see that the Reverend was in need of an ear rather than a voice and he was happy to take on the role. He had a blank about people such as Joseph. Okay, he could see that they were genuine and he could even see the logic they used to get themselves into the state they were in, but for the life of him he couldn't see why they took the thoughts and feelings that drove them so seriously. Why not just disengage, let the cog wheels keep turning by all means, if turn they must, but uncouple them from the drive shaft and get on with the ordinary experience of being alive. When the two men left the hospital and went their separate ways, he felt relieved to escape from the asylum and get back to the sights and sounds of the everyday. Presently a new thought formed in his mind. What if the Reverend had got it all wrong? Was it not at least as likely that Snoddy's crowd had got wind of what was going on and had decided to silence Joseph before he spilt the beans? It would make much more sense. They hadn't bothered with Joseph up till now, thinking him a naive fool, but then when a policeman comes and questions him, they realise how harmful his evidence could be to them. But who could have told them about his visit to Joseph? Not the Reverend certainly. Joseph himself? Possibly, but unlikely; surely the last thing he would have wanted was to put himself back in the firing line of memories that haunted him. But wait a minute, what about Naomi Ballintyne? He had asked her for Joseph's contact details, hadn't he? She would have told Snoddy and more than likely he would have gone round to check up. When he heard what Joseph had said to the police, he realised he couldn't afford to leave him around to repeat it in court.

The thought had started out as a fragile, foetal thing somewhere in the shadowy depths of his consciousness, but gradually its definition was sharpening and it was well on its way to establishing itself as a self-confident entity. No sooner had it reached the point of conviction however than another embryonic notion launched itself on the same course. What about Stranaghan? He hadn't mentioned Joseph by name to him, but the Inspector would have had no trouble identifying the source of his information. He would probably have alerted Justin Wright and it could well have been Wright, and not Snoddy, who had plied Joseph with the lethal concoction of booze and drugs. Yes, that was certainly possible. He couldn't see Stranaghan being party to this. That was surely out of the question, but the Inspector had a blind spot as far as Wright was concerned; he might have passed the information on without knowing what it would lead to.

He decided not to confront Stranaghan immediately; he would do a bit of snooping first. He went back to the bedsit, but the follow-up was no more productive than the initial inspection. As an act of desperation he tried the neighbours. Bedsit land, he knew from experience, is barren ground for information; urban nomads take little interest in the doings of their fellow transients. After several buzzes followed by a couple of vigorous raps on the door of the bedsit across the landing, a dishevelled figure appeared. It was male, young and clearly disgruntled, demanding *what the f ... anyone wanted with him at this ungodly hour.* (It was 8.30am) *No, he didn't f ... ing know anything about his neighbour across the way. No, he hadn't heard any of the comings and goings of the night. He had been out of it.* Then, remembering that it was a policeman he was talking to, he retreated to a U-rated version of his being out of it. He had been up the previous night finishing an essay and he was catching up on his sleep. Myles came away with the testiness that always rose in him when he had to deal with 'those bloody pampered brats of academe'. It was the one time his awareness of being a payer of taxes with no say over how his money was used always peaked.

As he approached the door of the ground floor bedsit, the one directly under Joseph's, a middle-aged man was in the process of putting a key in the lock. At his side was a spaniel whining for him to hurry up and let them both in. At Myles' 'Excuse me, sir' the man turned round and smiled as if in gratitude for being addressed so politely. Myles had not got very far with stating his business before the man joined in with a descant of acknowledgement.

"So that was it! Right! It must have been that terrible row he had the other day, two days ago it was. That's what drove him to it! He was shouting like a madman. Ordered the man out, he did. I tell you, I thought the two of them would come to blows. Mind you, Joseph Ross you say his name was, Joseph wouldn't have stood a chance. The other guy was a much bigger man – a rower or an athlete of some sort, I'd say"

"You actually saw him, did you?"

"Oh yes, I went out on to the landing and saw him coming down the stairs."

"He was a big bloke, you say. Did you see his face? Was his head shaven?"

"Oh no, he had a fine mop of hair, blond I think, but in this light it of course it's hard to say. But, yes, I think his hair was at least dirty fair."

"Anything else you noticed about him?"

"No, but I was able to make out one thing Joseph shouted at him. He called out something like 'And I thought you were my friend' and called him by his name. It sounded like Houston, but I don't think it was Houston."

"Could it have been Justin?"

"I couldn't be sure, but yes, that could be it."

Chapter 52

The day after the constituency debate the following article appeared in the Manchester Herald.

Labour Party sources have revealed to this paper that the contest for the nomination to stand for the Bury West constituency in the upcoming bye election has hotted up. It is a two-way fight between George Sinclair, a traditional hard-line socialist with a distinguished record of service to the trade union movement, and Robert Snoddy, a young academic and writer known for his forthright views on social issues.

At first sight it would seem a standard clash between the traditionalist and the progressive wings of the party. Sinclair certainly fits the profile of a stalwart of the Left; he is renowned for his uncompromising stance on industrial relations and has been unrelenting in his criticism of the Blairite wing of the Party. His opponent however does not fit the Blairite mould. He shares Sinclair's hostility to the drift towards liberalism in the party, declaring it a betrayal of the party's grass roots. He cites as an example the party's unrelenting support for immigration from Eastern Europe. This, he is convinced, undermined the bargaining power of British workers and put considerable pressure on public housing, health and education, burdens that fell on the shoulders of the working class, not the liberal elite, who, conversely, benefited from the cheap labour it provided. This, he claims, was no isolated case; it was typical of the way the party has for years been cosying up to its liberal masters at the expense of the people it should be representing.

He regards it as the raison d'être of the Labour Party to act as a watchdog on the devious doings of big business. He makes an interesting comparison between the way the EU move the workers of Europe around the continent like pawns on a chessboard and the coercive forces of capitalism in the nineteenth century when rural communities were uprooted to man the factories in the new industrial cities. The social problems to which this upheaval gave rise were of course not the concern of the factory owners then, any more than the squeeze on housing and health and education and the subsequent drain on the East European countries as a result of EU insistence on 'free movement' are now. It was revealing, he said, how the language of liberalism has been used as a tool against those who have stood by the grass roots on these issues. Gordon Brown's infamous put-down of the woman who expressed her concerns over immigration should have been the nadir of the socialist love-in with liberalism, but the fact that it wasn't is a shame Mr Snoddy insists the Labour Party must do all in its power to live down. He details how liberalism is continuing to be used as an instrument of capitalism. Big business has persuaded us to define ourselves by what we can afford to consume. Where once it exploited us by overworking us, it now degrades us by demanding that 'we shop till we drop'. It has denuded us of our dignity. He uses rather colourful language to make his point: 'We live', he said, 'in a cultural sweetie shop, a paradise for five-year-olds with no adult voice demanding a halt to the great gorge on the goodies.'

Many in the constituency are very excited by what Mr Snoddy is saying; others less so. Whether or not he is chosen to fight the seat will be decided in the coming days. We will know then if the Party is willing to take his sobering message on the chin. These are certainly interesting times for Bury West. Will it be the beginning of a major shake-up in British politics? Only time will tell.

As Justin read it, his pride in it sat uneasily with his doubts over its pretentions to impartiality. Why hadn't he included some fleshed-out details of Sinclair's political record? It was never intended that the piece should be even-handed, but it could have had more of a smile on its face as it dug the dagger in. Francesca was not going to be pleased. He should of course have run it past her before submitting it, but he was pressed for time and had allowed himself to get carried away with how well he thought he had summarised Robbie's position. '*If you want to make your opinion count as a journalist, you need to present it in a pickle of the opposition's choosing.*' How many times had Francesca told him that! No, she was not going to be pleased.

Just then his mobile rang. How could Francesca have got so quickly on the ball? He had expected a bit more breathing space than this. But it wasn't Francesca, it was Stuart Stranaghan. No formalities, straight in.

"I've some very bad news, Justin ... Joseph is dead."

The leap from where his thoughts had been to this bombshell was too much for Justin's mind to make with all its faculties on board. The information made it across, but the feelings were left in limbo.

"Joseph's dead? How? Did he have an accident?"

"No, it looks as if it might have been suicide. But Myles isn't so sure; he thinks there might be more to it. Listen, Justin, where are you? We need to talk about this. Can we meet up in Oxford?"

The question passed Justin by.

"Holy God! He committed suicide? The poor bugger!"

There was a distinctly strangulated sigh before his speech picked up again.

"It's my fault. I pushed him too hard. He went all weird on me, but I never thought for a moment ..."

"You need to calm down, Justin. We really need to get together on this. I've booked myself into the Premier Inn here in Oxford. Can you come?"

This was met with the kind of silence that normally signals a rummage for excuses, before the surprisingly business-like reply came back.

"I'm in Manchester, but I'll borrow a car. I'll be with you about eight."

Chapter 53

Myles had been reluctant to confront Stranaghan at his home. It was bad enough being his former junior, but being his guest as well was a burden he didn't need to bear. The Rambler's Rest, a pub within walking distance of Stranaghan's house, was the venue the two men decided on when Myles made his phone call. He gave no specific reason for the meeting, but made it clear that it was a matter of some urgency. Despite, or perhaps because of the peal of alarm bells juddering in his head, Stuart did not press for details. He would know the worst soon enough. There might even be a best to the worst.

At their last encounter Stuart had put the same case to Myles as he had put many times to his conscience. His actions had been dictated by his concern for the young officer who, he had every reason to think at the time, was being set up. He had put him in the firing line, so, as his superior officer, he had a duty to protect him. That for him was the bottom line. His experience of the law in action inspired little confidence. He was only too well aware of how often it fails to get things right; despite the confidence it has in itself, it isn't always able to drill down to truth through all the layers that randomness and human connivance envelop it in. Worse than that, it clings to the mantra that it's better to be wrong for the right reasons than right for the wrong reasons. This somehow has been elevated to the central tenet of its liturgy. The question of what are the right reasons and what are the wrong ones is invariably resolved on the basis of what obeys and what offends the legal modus operandi and all its venerable ancestry stretching back up into the mists of heaven. Snoddy was certainly clever enough to exploit the rules of the judicial game. He had demonstrated that at his own trial. Yes,

Snoddy would have pulled it off all right and Justin would have gone to prison. It was only when it was too late that he realised Snoddy was playing games with him; he had no intention of shopping Justin, he had come to see him as one of his own. It was he himself, the senior policeman, that Snoddy had in his sights, and the senior policeman had fallen for it hook, line and sinker.

He could of course pull the plug, confess his involvement, put the pressure back on Snoddy and get the convictions of Burrows and Wilson declared unsafe. But for what? Burrows and Wilson were the scum of the earth. What did he care if they rotted away in prison; he had seen so many of their sort acquitted for crimes they most certainly had committed, and had had to stand by and watch as the judiciary preened itself on its noble defence of justice. What did those pompous asses care about the little people they had condemned to live cheek by jowl with the fiends they were letting loose? Their allegiance was solely to the Law. And if anything calling itself justice begged to differ and went its own way, it was dismissed ipso facto as a fake and a fraud.

If he did make a confession, what would the consequences be for him and Heather? It was unlikely that he would go to prison. It would be hard to pin him down to an actual crime. After all, he didn't know for a fact that Snoddy's mob had killed Rodgers and planted the evidence against the other two. He had no way of proving that the conversation where Snoddy forced him to decide who the finger should be pointed at had taken place at all. Snoddy could claim – and would claim – that he was making it all up. It was all a question not so much of what he had done as of what he hadn't done. He might not face a criminal charge, but he would certainly lose his pension. And the media – they would make damned sure that he and Heather were put through hell, and at the head of the pack would be the very same tabloids that never tire of exposing the absurdities of

291

the criminal justice system. At the end of it all Snoddy would be free as a bird. The courts would be *solemnly* unable to lay a glove on him.

When left to itself, the default expression on Myles' face was one that gave full recognition to the vexatious nature of the human condition, so there was nothing specific to be read from the gravity of his countenance as he approached Stuart's table. Dispensing with the formalities, he blurted out the news of Joseph's death as soon as they had taken their seats. This was something Stuart had not been expecting. He had only met Joseph on that one occasion when, not to put too fine a point on it, he had *bullied* him into making that confession. He had felt a bit guilty about that, but in the end no harm had been done and he had left it to Snoddy to sort things out with Joseph afterwards. So Justin must have leaned on him too, and clearly he had leaned too heavily. But Myles wasn't happy to leave it at that.

"What makes you so sure that Wright is squeaky clean? Did you know he was with Joseph the night before he died? And that there had been a blazing row and Joseph ordered him out of the house? Did you know that?"

Stuart's look told him that he certainly did not know.

"You tried to protect Wright last time. You gave up your career for him. Did it never occur to you that he was in cahoots with Snoddy and that he might have had a hand in the real killing? Even if the so-called execution was all smoke and mirrors, (and how do we know it was?) that still doesn't mean he had nothing to do with the murder. The anger and the disgust he had for Rodgers didn't suddenly just go away. If they were strong enough to get him to join the firing squad, why do you assume they weren't strong enough for him to do the actual killing? It's clear from what you told me that someone from Snoddy's organisation carried out the murder, why could that not have been Justin Wright?"

"That's absurd! Justin was being set up. It was obvious."

"So obvious that it turned out that he wasn't? You were wrong about that, weren't you? Snoddy knew he had turned Wright. And he had, hadn't he? Wright was his man now, not yours. And he was using Wright to get at you."

"But Justin didn't know that. When I saw Justin at the murder scene, he was wandering around like a stray dog, he had no idea what was going on. Snoddy had sent him there so that I could find him. If I had been doing my job, I would have arrested him. What would Snoddy have done then? He couldn't have got Justin out of that."

Myles was about to come up with a counter, when suddenly the full force of what had been said struck home.

"You met Wright at the murder scene? You didn't tell me that! You mean to say you were given a tip-off, found Wright with the body and you didn't report it? And you still think Wright had nothing to do with the murder? What the ... blazes were you thinking of, sir?"

When it was put like that, it certainly looked bad, that he had to admit, but the putting of it is not always the way of it. Over the twenty odd years he had been a detective he had learned to trust his instincts. Experience is hard won. It gives you the faculty to sniff and feel and taste the things that the brain can only see and hear. And with the brain come the words. Words are the intellect's best workers, but they are not always obedient servants, all too often they get uppity and turn the tables on their master. No, Myles was wrong, Justin was telling the truth; that night in the barn when they found Rodgers' body his whole being gave off innocence and bewilderment. He couldn't have faked that.

It is strange how unpredictable sharp-wittedness can be; there are occasions when it is prepared to concede ground to experience, but more often than not it takes sadistic delight in tramping all over it. The young in particular are prone to disdain when confronted with anything that strays outside the jurisdiction of their cleverness. Now and then however, even with them, the mellow tones of experience find a way through the high-pitched haughtiness of rationality. Despite his comparative youth Myles had a lot of 'old school' in his veins and was not closed to doubts about the dominion of his reasoning. While he was confident in his mind that the force of argument was with him – he was surprised and, curiously, disappointed at how poor a fist Stranaghan was making of defending himself – a voice in his head persisted in whispering warnings that the ground he had seized could well turn out to be fallow. There was no question of him allowing Stranaghan's instincts to dictate; he would keep faith with what his own brain was telling him. He did however make terms with those faint whisperings of wariness; he'd give Stranaghan time to talk to Wright. Wright was likely to be more open with his old boss than with him. It was a risk and there would be a loss of momentum, but it might well turn out to be worth it. If Wright said anything to cause Stranaghan to doubt him, it would be a complete game-changer, Stranaghan would be on his side then and he would know the best place to dig for evidence.

Chapter 54

Schinski was puzzled. What on earth was Snoddy playing at? If he was so hell-bent on getting himself into Parliament – he certainly had no scruples about using blackmail to get there – why in God's name was he risking everything by peddling a line that was bound to stir up serious opposition? Why not simply keep his head down, stay in the middle of the road and leave it to the likes of him to twist all the necessary arms and bend all the necessary ears? That meeting last night could have gone very badly; it could have been a total disaster in fact. It had required all the agility he could muster to put a gloss on it. But how long that gloss would last was anyone's guess. Rhetorical intoxication generated in the heat of a meeting can be very short-lived. Snoddy must be persuaded to tone things down. The two men needed to meet.

He made an early start, being anxious to catch Snoddy alone before he set about his day's business. When he inquired at the hotel lobby he was directed to the breakfast room. As he entered, Snoddy and Naomi were rising from the table and taking their leave of Eardley and Greenfield who were still in mid-breakfast. Naomi was first to spot him and greeted him with a solicitous charm that was a clear cut above good manners.

"Mr Schinski, how very nice to see you! I hear you did sterling work last night. Robbie tells me you are a real treasure. Well, actually he doesn't. Not given to effusive language is my Robbie, but you did get credited with 'knowing your onions', and in Robbie speak, that means he greatly values your services."

She laughed and looked towards her partner for confirmation. Her smile went unreciprocated. Snoddy merely explained that he and Naomi were having to leave to do an interview on local radio. It was Francesca Bergman's idea. She thought it would be too pushy at this stage to focus on him, so the interview was to be about Naomi; it would delve admiringly into the relationship between an intelligent and ambitious woman and a successful partner.

"It's all part of the crap, Schinski, but where there's crap, there's votes, or so I'm told."

The remark was not accompanied by the smiling appeal for understanding you'd normally expect. Clearly it was his own feelings of repugnance that were uppermost in the Snoddy mind. This did little to reassure Schinski that the message he had come to deliver would stand much chance of getting through. Nevertheless he pressed Snoddy for a time when they could meet. There was a decided dragging of the feet before the would-be MP found a gap in his diary later in the day.

"Now that you're here, Mr Schinski, why not join us over a coffee and give us your thoughts on the progress of the campaign thus far?"

The invitation was issued by Eardley. The tone was congenial, but not without a hint of the mandatory. Schinski was happy to accept. This offered a chance to bend the ears of those better placed than him to make what needed saying palatable to Snoddy. He sat down and an extra cup was called for.

"Well – Derek isn't it? – how do you think things are going?"

"I would have said very well, until last night that is. I don't understand why he chose to ruffle so many feathers. He practically dismissed the efforts of the Party to raise wages, he rubbished the Party's policy on education and he opened up all the old wounds on Europe. There was no need for any of that."

Greenfield, who had said nothing up till now, reached Schinski the coffee he had just poured for him and casually asked, "Has Francesca ever spoken to you about golf, Mr Schinski?"

Schinski simply blinked in surprise and Greenfield continued,

"I'm not a golfer myself, but she tells me they have such things as doglegs. As I understand it, when you play a dogleg you can be forced to go for a difficult shot in order to have any chance of reaching the green with your next one. The safe shot is not an option if you want to get your par."

"I do play a bit of golf, as it happens. What you say is perfectly true, but I don't see the relevance. Mr Snoddy is not playing a dogleg. All he needs to do is hit the ball straight up the middle of the fairway. He doesn't need to dice with the rough."

Greenfield smiled and took a sip of his coffee.

"I think you play a different game from Robert, Mr Schinski. You go for your par, but you see a par won't do for Robert. He's looking for a birdie. That's Robert all over."

The smile faded and his face took on a more earnest look.

"You think he's more likely to end up with a bogey, don't you?"

Eardley interrupted before he could answer.

"You must excuse Bruce, Derek. He can never say no to an analogy. What he is saying is that Robert is not in the business of winning the nomination at any price. He aims to get it on his own terms. He wants to have a free hand to pursue policies that are dear to his heart and not let himself be compromised by easy-sounding clichés that could come back to haunt him. He's thinking ahead. He has no interest in being a party hack and following the party line whatever it happens to be. He wants to shake up the party and get it moving in a radically different direction. That's what this is all about. And that's why we need you. If Robert were only interested in becoming a run-of-the-mill MP, there wouldn't be a problem. He has the brains, he's not short of connections and there's ample financial means at his disposal. No, he's aiming much higher and, to achieve those aims, he has to build up a platform that cannot later be swept from under his feet."

Schinski was somewhat taken aback. He had simply assumed that getting into Parliament was all it was about for Snoddy; he had never thought to ask himself why he aspired to do this. To his mind, one goal was as good as another; the bit that mattered was getting a plan down on the drawing board and overseeing its implementation. That was the fun part. In a sense he had appropriated the project; he was enjoying the campaign a hell of a lot more than Snoddy was. Okay, he had been press-ganged at the outset, but he had long since burgeoned from a reluctant conscript to a fully fledged and committed professional. Snoddy's cause had become his cause, but now he was hearing that what he had taken to be the *end* was in fact just the *means*. This needed some reconfiguring.

"That may well be, but if he pushes too hard he won't get in. It's as simple as that. For God's sake don't let him knock any more party sandcastles down."

This produced a good natured chuckle from both men.

"Do you mean to say," asked Greenfield, "that he has to sign up for the kind of taxation policy that every Labour government since the War has come within a whisker of bankrupting the country with? ... or a foreign policy that says to the enemies of this country, 'Look, we won't do anything to defend ourselves, but if you attack us you'll be letting yourselves down terribly and history will show you up for the nasty sorts you are?'"

"Stop your bantering, Bruce. I don't think Derek wants Robert to go quite that far, do you Derek? Rest assured, Derek, we both know what you're saying. Robert has an agenda; he wants to change the Left's mindset on the kind of people it should be trying to stand up for. This affects the issues that should be prioritised. The greatest failures of the party, as Robert sees it, have been in criminal justice and education. It's in these areas above all others that the party has let the working man down. He'll settle for trying to put that right. As for the rest, we'll try to make sure he's as good as gold and keeps his mouth as shut as you deem necessary."

As he was leaving the breakfast room, having been promised a meaningful tête-à-tête with *his client* when they met up later that day, he was overtaken in the front lobby by Eardley, who put a friendly arm over his shoulder and led him into the empty bar area.

"I wanted a quiet word with you, Derek. You've a right to know how you stand in all this."

He gave Schinski a look that indicated that both men knew what was coming next. This simply added to Schinski's confusion. Eardley noticed.

"Well, we did get off to a rather uncivil start, didn't we? – all that unpleasantness about Mr Cooper and that little scam of yours. Tell me, why did you do it? Now that I've seen you in action, I wouldn't have thought it was your style at all."

Schinski was gratified by the question. The more he thought of that whole business, the more he loathed the image it created of his self. It wasn't just that Cooper was a decent bloke and had been treated very shabbily – the assault on him by Bailey's thugs was a total disgrace. All that was bad enough, but the thing that really got under his skin was the sheer amateurishness of it all. It was small-minded both in its conception and in its execution. He was better than that, and it gladdened him to hear that Eardley thought so too.

"No, you're right. It wasn't my finest hour. It would be easy to blame Reggie. I could have said no, or I could have come up with something a bit more subtle. But when you've been riding along in the back seat as long as I was with a big, powerful MP at the wheel, it takes a while before it dawns on you that it's you who should be in the driving seat."

This brought a knowing smile from Eardley.

"Okay. Let's both put the past behind us. Let's draw up a new arrangement. No more threats of what we'll do to you if you don't do for us. I'll be frank with you, Derek. I've been impressed with your work and I would like you to work for me when this thing is over. I can see that you're a real artist; you take an artist's pride in doing a job well. Whether we win or lose this nomination, I know you'll have given it your best shot. If you work for me, I'll give you more challenging commissions than you'll ever get working for that union of yours. Money will not be a problem. What do you say?"

Schinski's habit, acquired over years of wheeling and dealing, of inverting the correlation between the eagerness he felt and the enthusiasm he put on show came under such strain as to produce only the slightest of hesitations before, with a grin that spread broad across his face, he clasped the outstretched hand of his future employer.

Chapter 55

If Myles thought he had sown any serious doubts in the former Inspector's mind about Justin's innocence, he was wrong. As far as Stuart was concerned, the meeting with Justin was a council of war with one thing on the agenda – how to find a way out of the pit they currently found themselves in.

Myles was now in possession of two facts that could damn both men. The first was the unpalatable coincidence of Justin taking part in role-play involving the execution of a man who just happened to turn up dead a matter of hours later. The second was even more damning; how could he have been stupid enough to let it slip that he had found Justin at the murder scene? And how were they to get round the fact that none of this information had been logged by either man. The only saving grace was that Myles could produce no material evidence beyond what he had been told by Joseph and Stuart. He had nothing in writing. He couldn't use in a court of law anything Joseph had said – it would be mere hearsay. And if Joseph dug his heals in and denied all he had already confessed to, since he wasn't under caution, none of that would count either. Against that, now that Myles knew what stones to turn over, questions could be asked that might lead the two of them into inconsistencies glaring enough to convict Justin of murder and him of conspiring to pervert the course of justice.

Their best hope lay in the influence Stuart might be able to exert on his erstwhile junior. Myles had a deep sense of decency and an obvious respect for his former boss. That might count for something, but the man was also a firm believer in the primacy of due process. Just before he and Stuart teamed up in the initial investigation into Snoddy case he had made himself very unpopular at his local station for shopping a colleague accused of abusing a suspect. This was hardly an encouraging sign. He was younger then of course and wetter behind the ears. He had rubbed up against a lot more of life since then. Experience is the cholesterol in the dream-flow of the idealist; it clogs up the arteries and stops visions of perfection getting through to the head. Any hopes they might have must rest largely on that. But for such hopes to have any prospect of running, Myles needed to be convinced that Justin had no part in the Rodgers murder. How to do that was another thing; there was no obvious way, short of getting a confession from Snoddy. And that wasn't going to happen. The only strategy Stuart could come up with was for Justin to come clean with Myles: no more pretending that he'd twigged that the whole execution thing was a put-up job. Give Myles full sight of all the anger and outrage that had driven him to sign up for the firing squad. Let him see all the decency and humanity behind his actions. Yet at the same time make it clear that he wasn't for throwing himself on Myles' mercy, that what he was saying was off the record and would be denied if he was questioned about it later. If he had read Myles correctly, respect would carry more weight with him than compassion. It wasn't a wonderful plan, but it just might work.

Justin was less than convinced. He could see that as long as it remained off the record there was little to be lost by this confessional gesture. It would get a pretty obvious lie out of the way and keep it from contaminating his overall credibility. Whether it would weaken the Inspector's resolve was another matter, but he took comfort in Stuart's guarded optimism. Stuart had worked with the man and Stuart was good at reading people. If *he* didn't think it unreasonable to run with it, it had to be worth a shot. He would get in touch with Myles and seize the initiative on this. Better to jump into the puddle than to be pushed into the mire.

As it was too late to go back up north after the confab Justin decided to spend the night at home. With all the toing and froing he hadn't seen much of Lizzie of late and tonight of all nights he was in need of the support and reassurance that only an other-half can give. It was just after eleven when he got to the flat. Lizzie was clearing away a few dishes from among the exercise books that were strewn in their usual fashion across the kitchen table. Her surprise at seeing him turned almost immediately to a delight that seemed all the more genuine for coming second in line. He refused her suggestion of a cup of coffee; instead he went to the drinks cupboard and took out the near empty bottle of whiskey and a couple of glasses. Lizzie looked on in renewed surprise, but compliantly took her seat beside the glass he had poured and placed on the table.

"A hard day, was it?" she asked.

Justin evaded her gaze. He felt himself at one of those pivotal moments when you know that the shape of feelings and attitudes will be set for good and all by the words that you are about to use. It is not a feeling of power, quite the opposite in fact; it's the terror of letting go of the steering wheel.

"Joseph is dead!"

The words came out by themselves. Lizzie didn't seem to take them in. This gave him a second chance at rephrasing what he had said. But again all he could hear himself saying was a repeat of 'Joseph is dead.' The look of slightly forced attention she had adopted when she had sat down suddenly collapsed like scaffolding in front of a building. Her face contorted into a horrifying grimace. It was a long moment before words came out of her.

"How can he be dead? Was it a car accident? No, it couldn't be – Joseph didn't drive. Did someone knock him down?"

It was exactly the way he had reacted himself when Stranaghan had told him. But that look on Lizzie's face … He dreaded the next bit, the suicide bit. She was not going to take it well.

"It was suicide, Lizzie. Joseph took his own life."

When horror runs out of steam it invariably turns into misery. Usually there is a decent interval between the dying of the one and the emergence of the other, but in this case the transition was dramatic. Tears instantly flooded down Lizzie's cheeks to the accompaniment of the sobs that seemed to be pumping them out. Lizzie had known Joseph before she met Justin. They were never an item; their relationship was more that of a brother and sister. Justin knew it went deep, but he hadn't realised just how deep – after all she had made no attempt to keep in touch with him after he had abandoned his studies at Oxford. Within a few minutes the sobbing abated and the tears became a trickle. Joseph, refraining from adding further details to the news, maintained a respectful silence. In the end it was Lizzie who broke it. But it wasn't Justin that she addressed – he might just as well not have been there – it was just the surfacing of a monologue she had been conducting in her head.

"So, it finally got him, did it? That effing bastard Robbie should be locked up. He used poor Joseph as a guinea pig for his sick experiments. He knew Joseph was weak. You'd have thought that would have put him off. But no, that was the very reason he used him in the first place. He was hell-bent on seeing how far he could push someone as weak as Joseph. Well, now he knows, now we all know. It's high time the authorities knew as well."

An instinct had warned Justin to expect the unexpected when he passed on the news, but that did nothing to lessen the impact. His own sadness at Joseph's death was heart-felt. Joseph had been like a younger brother to him, a dear soul in need of protection. Joseph had looked up to him as a counterweight to the pressure that Snoddy was putting him under, or to be more precise, the pressure that Snoddy was pushing him to put himself under. In a curious way Joseph was the incarnation of the old philosophical dichotomy of mind and matter. He had lumbered Justin with the responsibility of being his *praegustator*, his food tester – if Justin was seen to give the same ideas that shaped and refined themselves in Joseph's head the authority to dictate *his* actions, that gave the green light for Joseph to make his own leap from word to deed. It was not a role that Justin had sought, but he had not taken it lightly. Anything he had encouraged Joseph to face up to, he had faced up to himself. The *volte face* he had made from undercover policeman to volunteer for a vigilante firing squad was by any standards a much more radical leap than the one Joseph had made from the will-o'-the-wisp phantoms of the mind to the blood and guts of rooted reality. And, unlike Joseph, he had had no one to look to for support. He had been willing to stand up on his own for what he instinctively knew justice required of him, without the backing of the law, indeed in open defiance of it. In doing so he had helped Joseph through that same barrier. He hadn't forced him; he hadn't even tried to persuade him. If Joseph chose to follow his lead, that was his affair. Just as it was up to him how he dealt with it afterwards. As it turned out of course, the whole firing squad thing was only a charade; they hadn't really executed anyone after all. Surely that should have let Joseph's self-doubt off the hook? Seemingly not.

The same instinct that made him wary of Lizzie's reaction to the news of Joseph's suicide had warned him off telling her earlier about the encounter he had had with Joseph. He now realised what a mistake that had been; he should have told her, for telling her now was going to sound like a confession of guilt. Yet the longer he put it off, the greater the damage was going to be – he knew that. Better to get it over with now. He tried to sound casual, but his attempt was pitifully inept.

"I didn't get a chance to tell you, but I went to see Joseph a couple of days ago."

Lizzie tweaked her head to the side in a familiar gesture of incomprehension.

"You did what? How did you know where to find him?"

"I did a bit of digging. It's part of my job after all. I tracked him down to an old vicarage. He had made friends with the vicar there who helped him through his breakdown."

"You should have told me. I'd have gone to see him. How was he? Did he seem suicidal to you?"

Justin dreaded the effect the revelation he was being cornered into making was going to have.

"He had had a visit from that detective inspector who came here asking about him – I think it was that that pushed him over the edge. He had given the inspector a full account of all that happened, and I mean all – the confession that he'd made to Stuart, and of course he told him that it was Dwayne Rodgers that our phoney little firing squad thought it was blasting to kingdom-come."

A look of disgust suddenly disfigured Lizzie's face.

"So you lost it with him, did you? Did you use your fists? Or did you just tell him what a pathetic little weakling he was? How could you, Justin? Didn't you know that boy worshipped you? He was in love with you. Or are you so macho that that never even occurred to you?"

This charge was outrageous. Lizzie had got it so wrong. He was ready with a retaliatory riposte … but that last bit, she might be right about that, it really hadn't occurred to him. Nothing came out of his mouth; he simply gaped in fading disbelief. Lizzie seemed to take this as an admission of guilt and was clearly surprised and alarmed that in her grief she had inadvertently hit on a narrative that was closer to the truth than she had ever really suspected. This fuelled further accusations, which she hurled at him in the hope, no doubt, and expectation that they would be perfunctorily dismissed.

"It wasn't like that." Justin protested, but not defensively. His voice had taken on tones of reflective calm. "I was not angry with Joseph, but he got very angry with me. I've no idea why. We were talking quite calmly. When he told me what he'd done, I simply said what was done was done. All I asked of him was to make sure he didn't make a written statement. If there was nothing down in writing, what he'd said to the inspector couldn't be used in court. He could simply deny it all. Then, all of a sudden, out of the blue he got really het up and ordered me out of his house – just like that."

Lizzie allowed time for this to sink in. Justin waited expectantly, unsure of what direction her mind would go off in. After what was too long to count as an interval, she got up, stared almost absent-mindedly at him and left the room. It was as if a tomb had been sealed.

Chapter 56

It was while he was shaving the morning after his meeting with Eardley and Greenfield that Schinski had a visitation from the angel of truth. As always, it came in a cloud of the blindingly obvious. Sleep must have been incubating it and the new day had enticed it out into the light. Declan Nolan – that was the man he needed to speak to ... if he was still alive, that is. And he would need some money, about ten grand – that should be enough.

A quick phone call to Matthew Eardley secured the funding. Eardley obviously wanted to know what the money was for but seemed happy enough to settle for an assurance that a plan was afoot that stood every chance of giving Snoddy a winning lead. How Schinski envied Eardley such immunity to financial *angst*! Next, a series of phone calls established that Nolan was indeed still in the land of the living and kicking about, divorced from his wife but wedded to the bottle, in a council estate in north London.

The sun was shining as, some hours later, Schinski drove into the estate. The shabby houses and the littered streets depressed the spirits but in a strange way seemed to lessen the feeling of menace; it was as if this was all there was to the negativity of the place and that the drug-dealing, the drunkenness and the violence that it was purported to sponsor could well be merely figments of bourgeois extrapolation. The cacophonous sounds of a cluster of youths in hoodies outside a bookmaker's put this new optimistic scepticism under strain, but then that too could be dismissed as a case of his middleclass sensibilities getting ahead of themselves. The games we people play with our intellectual does and don'ts, Schinski mused.

It was with some apprehension that he left his car to its fate outside the maisonette that his satnav had assured him was his journey's end. The green area in front of the building was freshly mown; it produced a semblance of neatness but at the price of exposing nasty patches of dog dirt amid all the weeds and moss that had ousted the grass. The front door had doubtless seen better days, but it was hard to imagine how the ancient painter could ever have been able to stand back and look with pride on his work. There being no sign of a bell, he knocked. A loud bark, followed by a series of lesser but more enthusiastic woofs, quickly morphed into a snarling beast on the other side of the frosted glass. The animal made several sorties back into the room where his master was presumably to be found, before a distorted figure appeared in the glass, muttering admonishments to the dog's eagerness. When the bolts were undone and the door was finally opened, Schinski's eyes were fixed exclusively on the dog which was being restrained by the collar in mid-lunge position. The owner too was focused on his keeper role and without as much as a word to the visitor dragged the dog back and closed him in what looked like the bathroom. When he returned he was out of breath and clearly not pleased at having been put to such trouble.

"Well, what is it?"

The Irish brogue was as thick as stew; the 'it' had the hint of an echo on its 't'. Schinski smiled; this was his man.

"You'd be Mr Declan Nolan? My name's Schinski, Derek Schinski. I'd like for us to have a chat. I've a proposition I'd like to put to you."

Nolan was a man in his late sixties or early seventies. There was enough in his stature to suggest he had been solidly built in his younger days, but he cut a pitiful figure now with his thin, unkempt hair, unshaven chin and a shirt that gave telltale signs of having been slept in. His eyes were the most run-down Schinski could ever remember seeing; definition of pupil and iris had blurred into a smudge. They were the eyes of a man who had lost any keenness he might ever have had to look on anything new. They did manage a squint at the stranger, but the spark of curiosity failed to find kindling; he simply turned on his heel and muttered something to the effect that Schinski should come in and shut the door behind him.

Schinski did as he was bid and followed 'his host' into a room at the end of the narrow hallway. Like the proprietor, the room had seen better days, and to judge by the predominance of teak and the cheap excuse for an ersatz fireplace, a soulless electric heater unit in a teak surround, those days would undoubtedly have been in the seventies. Nolan flopped down on one of the armchairs that flanked this unlovely sanctum and invited Schinski to take the other. A half-empty whiskey bottle and a half-full whiskey glass nestled on the little coffee table beside Nolan's chair, adding their pennyworth no doubt to the accumulation of white rings that had been allowed to deface the wood. Nolan picked up the glass and sipped, more, Schinski suspected, for the pleasure of not offering one to his guest than for the need for reinforcement of the spirits.

"Well, what do you want? Are you another of those fucking reporters that turn to old ground when there isn't enough blood left for them to suck from the current bunch of anaemic shysters?"

"No, I'm not a reporter, but I do know where you're coming from: too many college boys, too much hair pulling. Whatever happened to the good old-fashioned punch in the gob? But of course that wasn't quite your style, was it? You were more of a bullet-in-the-head, a bomb-under-the-bonnet man, weren't you?"

Nolan, who had adopted a sprawling position in his chair, suddenly tensed and sat up, but just as suddenly relaxed and resumed the sprawl. Another sip of the whiskey reinforced his recovered apathy.

"No, I was pretty free with the old fists in my time, that I admit, but the bomb and the bullet now that's something I left to others. The gift they said I had for the gab was all they wanted from me. Jesus knows, there were few enough with the balls to come out and talk the talk when one of their operations went bottoms up. Anyway, that's all piss down the Grand Canal. What's this proposition you're talking about?"

"Before we come to that, tell me, why did you have the big fallout with Geordie Sinclair? You and he were bosom pals, weren't you? He must have done something pretty awful to made you so angry."

Nolan's eyes narrowed to a squint.

"That's none of your fucking business! You were lying. You are a fucking reporter, aren't you? Get the fuck out of here before you feel the weight of my fist. You'll not do much sniffing around with the bloody nose I'll give you."

He made to get up, but once again his aggressive energies failed him and he slumped back into the chair. Schinski on the other hand did get to his feet and said in a voice that was firm and fearless but distinctly non-belligerent,

"I didn't lie to you. I'm not a fucking reporter, as you call it. To be perfectly frank, I couldn't give a tinker's curse why you and Geordie Sinclair stopped licking each other's arses. I just wanted to know how strongly you feel about your old buddy. I need to know if you'd be prepared to land him in the shit. If you have something on him that I could use I would make it worth your while. From what I hear, you're not a man to take Judas money, so I wouldn't insult you by offering you money if it was a friend I was asking you to shaft. That's why I needed to know how the land lies between you."

Nolan's eyes widened. There was a long silence before he spoke. Eventually words started to come from him, hesitantly at first and then with growing fluency.

"Geordie and I used to be close, real close. You don't make

many friends in our line of work; you make comrades and you make enemies, but there isn't a spit of difference between the two when what you're looking for is someone to help you believe you're worth something on this bloody earth. Politically, we were brothers: We were both Celts, we were both commies, and we were both republicans, although Geordie wasn't as strong on getting the English out of Scotland as I was on throwing the bastards out of Ireland. Mind you, he'd guts, he wasn't afraid to show his face at the big rally we organised just after the Brighton bombing and he stepped up when the reporters took agin me for saying that was exactly the kind of action that was needed to get the British government to sit up and listen. There were many on the left in this country that shared my view. They were falling over themselves to tell me so in private of course; they never had the guts to come out with it in public. No, true bill, Geordie was about the only comrade on this side of the Irish Sea I was ever able to call a friend."

"So, what did he do? It must have been something pretty dire."

Nolan looked blankly in front of him. Schinski might not have been there; Nolan was squaring his feelings with his own past self.

"It bloody well was. The fucking bastard ran away with my wife."

He paused as if to let the sadness catch up with the anger. But before Schinski could believe his good luck in finding such an explosive source of enmity between the two men, Nolan turned his anger on him.

"You've come here to get me to shaft him, have you? You thought you'd get this old bum to stick the knife in old Geordie's back, did you? Well, I *am* a bum, I'm no use to nobody these days, there's just me and the hard stuff. But me and the hard stuff, we know where we stand; I know the booze is not my friend, it's going to put me in the grave, but there's absolutely nothing personal in it. It'll do that to anyone who gets too fond of it. So you thought, that Irish bastard will do anything for a drink – that's what bums do, isn't it? Well, you can take your money and stick it up your arse, Mister. This bum doesn't need it – this bum has enough drink money to rot down his liver a dozen times over."

By way of a demonstration, he filled his glass up and sank three quarters of it in one gulp. The man was deep in the badlands where judgement drowns in the effluent of whim. Schinski knew better than to argue.

"I'm sorry, Mr Nolan. You're obviously a man who puts loyalty above everything else. I respect you for that and I can see how a man like you would take the double blow that you suffered harder than most. On the other hand I might be overestimating you. Maybe you think that by turning down my offer, you get to hold on to your entitlement to indulge your pain. Maybe that's what it's all about. If you shafted your old friend, you might have to call a halt to the wake."

He said this with no real hope of the words hitting their target. He was mistaken. Nolan suddenly became alert. His eyes cleared and his voice lost the slur of the drink.

"You're not as big an eejit as you look, are you, Mr Schinski? There might just be something in what you say. But you're missing the point. I know all about Geordie running for Parliament. What you don't seem to understand is I'm as keen as anyone to see him get in. I wouldn't dream of doing anything that might scupper that. It's bloody well time we got someone into that fucking whorehouse that might do a bit of good. Okay, Geordie's not about to start the Revolution. Jesus knows, you have to wonder if the people of this country will ever catch on to what's really going on and kick out the capitalist bastards that have been feeding them on tripe. No, Geordie's no Jesus Christ to be sure; he's not God's gift to socialism, but he might just make it as a poor man's Pope."

313

When he had beaten his retreat and secured a much needed pint in The Lion's Den, the aptly named pub at the corner of the street next to Nolan's, Schinski made a quick call to Eardley. He had to make do with voicemail.

"I'll not be needing that money I asked you for. The fish didn't bite, but I'd like you to send me round one of your reporters. I've an important job for him."

Chapter 57

The relationship between Schinski and Chief Superintendant Bailey had never been a close one. Reggie Whitehouse had been the less-than-honest broker between them. It was he who had come up with the scam in the first place and had brought the policeman on board. Bailey was well aware of Schinski's general antipathy towards him and in particular of his disgust at the bully-boy treatment of Terence Cooper. However he recognised in Schinski a sharper brain than in his friend Reggie and was keen to consult with him on the investigation into Justin Wright. The initial report he had received from Inspector Myles had raised questions about Wright's relationship with Snoddy; it certainly did not fit with his role as an undercover policeman. There were bound to be more slaters under the stone. He was intent on pressing Myles to step up his efforts, but Schinski urged caution. He assured Bailey that things were under control; they were well on their way to squaring their accounts with Snoddy's crowd and there was no need to open up a second front if hostilities could be brought to a bloodless conclusion. There was nothing to be lost however by letting his man continue to sniff around. *Knowledge boosts horsepower and a good throttle is just as effective as a good brake when you've sharp bends to get round.* If on the other hand the Chief Superintendant were to make too big a thing of the investigation he might find himself under pressure to act on the intelligence he received and that might not be in anyone's interests. Better to keep everything low-key. Chief Superintendant Bailey had a mind that normally ploughed in straight furrows, but he was astute enough to recognise good advice when he heard it.

Myles had expected to be under more pressure to report and

was relieved when each day passed without a summons for an update on the investigation. He developed the habit of composing reports in his head, some full-blooded in their detail, some clumsily aping the vacuity of the diplomatic communiqué. Should he commit the facts he had discovered to the mercies of his supervising officer or would he do better to hold off in anticipation of more auspicious revelations emerging? What he had come up with so far fell well short of an adequate basis for any kind of prosecution. It would certainly discredit the two police officers; it would probably cost Stranaghan his police pension and it might just be enough to render the convictions of Gary Burrows and Shane Wilson unsafe. But it would not achieve the big prize he quietly coveted, a successful prosecution of Snoddy. Wright was a more realistic target, but Stuart Stranaghan's cooperation would be needed for that, and for that to happen his faith in Wright would have to be shaken. The hopes of that happening were slender, but who could say? It was not beyond the bounds of possibility that Stuart's attempt to come up with proof of Wright's innocence would produce the converse result. Time must be given the chance to tell.

In the meantime he was at a loss as to how to move the investigation forward. He spent an entire morning poring over the reports that Wright and Stranaghan had submitted on the final days of the undercover operation. The narrative was littered with generalities and truisms. The prospects of accumulating enough evidence for a major conviction were rated as minimal. All indications pointed only to a low level of criminal activity, nothing more sinister than beatings and floggings, all of which were tightly controlled. It would have been perfectly reasonable to conclude, as Stuart had done, that an investigation producing such thin gruel was an unjustifiable strain on the police budget. Myles didn't doubt that, off the record of course, Stranaghan would also have tossed in the embarrassment of it coming out in court that a member of Her Majesty's constabulary had taken part in punishment floggings – all this negative publicity, and for what? No link was made between the operation and the arrest of Burrows; Burrows' name did not in fact figure in any of the reports. Nor, of course, was there any mention of Stranaghan finding Wright at the murder scene or of the statement Stranaghan had pressurised Joseph Ross into making. Things certainly did not look good for his former boss. Myles never for a moment suspected him of any active involvement in the Rodgers murder, but the man had clearly acted to prevent his protégé from coming under suspicion. No matter how pure the motives were, he was aiding and abetting a criminal act, an act of murder, if in fact his confidence in Wright was ill-founded.

Gradually the question began to form itself in Myles' head: Were things not in danger of repeating themselves? Was he himself not drifting towards a similar cover-up? He had sold himself the idea that it was in the interests of the investigation to get Stranaghan onside. That was undoubtedly true, but was it the real reason for the relief he felt in allowing him that room for manoeuvre? Was he not gambling too heavily on the hope that his friend would find a way of extricating himself from the fall-out if Wright were convicted of murder? Surely what he should do was simply go back to his superior, lay the facts before him and let *him* decide what was to be done. What was stopping him?

Strangely, now that he had allowed the guilty secret of his will to surface he found the powers of his rationality less encumbered and more confident in their operation. It was perfectly sensible for him to delay reporting back until he had something more substantial to offer than what had been said off the record. He was quite clear about that now – no shadows of conscience blurring the edges. As to what he wanted to achieve, three objectives identified themselves with the same clarity of outline: first, to nail the killer of Gary Burrows, whether that be Wright or

Snoddy; second, to quash the convictions of Rodgers and Wilson; and third, the one he had been unwilling to acknowledge to himself, to spare his old friend Stuart as much of the flak as he could without compromising his commitment to the first two. As things now stood, he would fail in all three if he jumped the gun and filed a report.

Chapter 58

Lizzie Partridge was angry and she was of a mind to indulge that anger. After her row with Justin she decided that if she spent the night in the same house as her husband she couldn't trust her rage not to fizzle out. She knew that from experience. She could never stay angry for long, even with strangers, but with people who were dear to her, her rage stood little chance of surviving the first overtures of reconciliation. She phoned one of her teaching colleagues, Ursula, and invited herself for a cosy overnight at hers. Wine was drunk and confidences shared while Lizzie privately gloried in the absence she had created and the hole it would make in Justin's configuration of their relationship. By the end of the evening she was proud of her achievement, but already the soft liberal voices calling for an end to hostilities were beginning to subvert her inebriated sense of triumph. Lurking in the shadows behind the rage she had been so keen to preserve was the terrible truth that Joseph was dead. Poor, clever little Joseph was no more. All his agonising over right and wrong, all that intellectual fizz trained on shades and niceties of meaning, all that bright hope that there were answers to go with the questions, all wasted, all lost forever, and with it all a dear boy who should have been content to be a mother's son or a sister's brother. The wine had done its work; she was too spent to wring any more fury out of her grief. She simply sobbed quietly and let sleep come upon her. In the adjoining room Ursula heard nothing. And if she had she would never have suspected her friend of being in the throes of mourning for a friend rather than vexation with a lover.

The two ladies had a largely silent, minimalist breakfast mostly on the hoof. There was much dashing around as lesson plans were hastily checked, files shuffled and last-minute additions made to to-do-lists. Frenetic activity has the curious effect of speeding up and at the same time bloating the interval between beginning and end. So it seemed long and it seemed no time at all before the two were setting off for school in Ursula's ancient Peugeot. Lizzie was not used to sharing her morning arrivals, the slight nausea at the first sight of familiar uniforms making their way school-wards, the despair of the will to impose any kind of order on the seething masses in the playground, both compounded by the dread of a day that would last so many more hours longer than these first few moments of panic. The lack of chat from Ursula served to confirm that the threat was indeed real and not just some unworthy phantom in her head. The echo that this produced of her dread was the very last thing she needed.

The day did not improve. Just when the early morning demons were dying back into the shadows she received a summons from Mrs Blackstaff, the headmistress, requesting her presence in her study at the beginning of the morning break. Normally a haven of calm in a choppy sea, the prospect of break was instantly disfigured into a dissonant siren emitting bleak blasts of low-grade anxiety. And she would not get that cup of coffee she now realised she so badly needed.

The interview, when it came, was neither as bad as she feared nor as good as the promise of the wanton optimism that swelled inexplicably out of nowhere at the last minute as she knocked on the study door. There had been a complaint from a parent. The mother of Louise Lazenby had taken great exception to a homework Ms Partridge had set her daughter. Her daughter – *could you believe?* – had been expected to learn fifteen items of French vocabulary by heart. *What kind of homework was that? Surely rote learning went out with the Ark? This was not the way the French learn French, and they should know, shouldn't they?* On a normal day Lizzie could have looked with no more than mild annoyance on the indulgence with which the Head was gracing this complaint, but today it was intolerable. Why was it that a display of aggressive ignorance in the guise of caring for an offspring's discomfiture should always take the pot? It was like attending the funeral of a serial killer and not being able to contest the grieving mother's insistence that he was really a lovely lad who made everyone laugh. Deep, positive feelings, however misguided, never fail to trump the detailed etchings of reality. She already knew that of course. How often had she tried to persuade Justin and, before him, Snoddy that that was the way of it? That did not deter her from launching into a defence of her action, but the weary *I-know-I-knows* from Mrs Blackstaff left her with nothing to push against. Her indignation ground to a halt. She left the study less at anger with the sloppy sentimentality of the parent than in sympathy for the hapless headmistress who had signed up to swallow daily doses of the same. In a curious way, by opening up a second front, the irritation helped lessen the pain she had brought to school with her and helped her edge more smoothly through the remains of the day.

When the bell finally rang for the end of school she was ready to face a return to the flat and an encounter with Justin. He wasn't likely to be home just yet, so she would have an hour or two to collect her thoughts and superintend her feelings. As a reflex she checked the mail in the hall. Justin tended to get more than she did, and sure enough most of it was for him. There was a lot of advertising bumph which she didn't even bother with, but among the other letters was a large A4 envelope with an assortment of amendments to the address. It was handwritten and addressed to her. Across the address in green ink and in large capitals was a very authoritative 'Not known at this address' and underneath that a scribbled note, 'Try number 37' She looked again at the original address. She would have known that handwriting anywhere. Those miserable little scratches were unmistakable. That was Joseph's scribble! She almost dropped the envelope. This was Joseph writing to her from the grave! It must have been one of the very last things he did before he died! In her eagerness to see what was inside she made to tear at the envelope, but then it struck her that she would be desecrating a coffin. Caution and passion made poor collaborators as the envelope was clumsily undone.

At the first reading she was too anxious to read ahead to fully take in where she was at. The only thing that came across loud and clear was the poor creature's self-loathing and his gratitude to her for having been his friend. There was no key piece of information in it to turn the received version of events on its head. Only when she came to read it again was she able to dwell on what was actually being said rather than what the next sentence might reveal. Shorn of the expectation she had had the first time through, the utter sadness of the writing came into its own.

Dear Lizzie,

I don't think I can bear it any longer. I tried to fly. I thought I could grow the wings for it, but they never sprouted. I'm just what I started out being, a miserable little hollow grub fit only for the compost bin. How stupid can you be! I dreamed the Nietzschean dream. I thought I could become a real man, someone worthy of having convictions. I thought I could forestall the bad faith that keeps weak men down and follow through on what my own brain told me to do. But then the doubt crept in: 'What if it's my brain that's lying to me? What if what my conscience is whispering in my head is a genuine warning against a Faustian pact that my reason is making with the devil?' Robbie and I talked about this. He told me that I was right to be wary of that. Reason must never be allowed a completely free hand, he said, it must be informed by one's humanity. The problem lies in sorting out the calls of the false conscience, the ones inspired by the fear of losing the approval of the crowd, from those that come genuinely from one's own gut feeling of what's right and what's wrong. He's right of course, but it doesn't sort the problem.

When I agreed to take part in that bloody firing squad I was pretty sure in my mind that I was acting in accordance with the pity I felt for Francis Brown and not merely in obedience to my rational notion of justice. My head and my heart were at one. Justin helped me a great deal in this. I could never really rely on Rob; he's too much like me. Justin is a good man. He doesn't let his ideas carry him away the way I do. He doesn't seem to live in fear of them turning out to be ghouls in Reason's clothing. He has his feet on the ground. And he felt that it was right and just to put that monster Rodgers down. That gave me the confidence to push myself into performing a truly authentic act, perhaps for the first time in my life.

But then things fell apart. Justin wasn't what he seemed. He was a bloody policeman. He had an agenda completely different from the one I had set so much store by. When that other policeman, Stranaghan, came to arrest me he told me Justin and Robbie were laughing at me all the time; they called me the 'noumenal phenomenon', the guy who couldn't hack it in the real world. They were right of course. I'm a pathetic sod of a creature. But Stranaghan never came back to arrest me, the confession he got me to write wasn't what it seemed either. It was only a way of getting leverage on Rob. He made a fool of me, but then I started to think that maybe what he told me about Justin and Rob laughing behind my back wasn't true either. I nearly convinced myself of that, but then, how would an ordinary police Inspector come up with a phrase like 'noumenal phenomenon'? That must have come from Rob; it's just the kind of phrase he would use. And if it came from Rob, Justin could well have been in on it too. But I clung on to the doubt – it didn't get rid of the sting, but it took the edge of it. I got close to believing in Justin again.

323

But then last night he came to see me and I realised he hadn't come as a friend, he'd only come because he needed me to do something for him. He was scared of me giving that Inspector Myles a written statement that would land him and his friend Stranaghan in the shit. He had no real feelings for me, he was simply using me. It made me think. You know where in Brecht's 'Leben des Galilei' Andrea says: "Unglücklich das Land, das keine Helden hat."[7] and Galilei replies:" Unglücklich das Land, das Helden nötig hat".[8] That says it all for me. I'm a double loser. I've lost my hero and it serves me right for I fucking well shouldn't ever have needed one in the first place.

Thank you, Lizzie, for being my friend. You were always there in the background for me. I hope you and Justin will make it through. Tell Justin he was right not to care about me. I'm a grown man and I shouldn't have needed him or anyone else to hold my hand. Rob called me a noumenal phenomenon. Well, I'm going to give it a go at being a phenomenal noumenon. It's all a big joke really, isn't it?

The letter was signed JFJ. This bizarre formality tarred it with a quasi official status, a bit like the declaration on a tax certificate. In a way that's what it was, a declaration of liability, a confession to the murder of an unworthy self.

Lizzie could not hold back the tears. Poor little Joseph! And it was so typical of him. Even in the throes of despair he hadn't been able to resist that final little play on words. His brain never stopped working, but neither did his heart. That was his tragedy; he wanted to serve both masters and he found himself out of his depth. She went over to the cabinet and poured herself a more than ample glass of gin. Memories came crowding back of the seminars and the endless discussions they had had in the Oxford

---

[7]   Unhappy the land that has no heroes
[8]   Unhappy the land that needs to have heroes –
Both quotes from Brecht's play 'The Life of Galileo'.

days, Joseph listening intently to what the others were saying before coming in with an inevitable 'But surely ...' and then proceeding to give his completely different take on the poem or the drama they'd been discussing. He would always start in this tentative manner, but as one idea mated with the next, his self-belief would grow and with it his assertiveness. By the time he had finished, everyone, if not won over, would at least be brought to feel uncomfortable with the thinness of the contributions they had made earlier. The strangest thing however was that Joseph never cashed in on this power he had to change minds. At the next seminar he would start just as hesitantly as before. It was clearly ideas, not people that he was contending with.

As the memories played through, a vague angst started to signal its presence in the darker regions of her grief. Little by little it edged forward and identified itself as shame. Despite all the histrionics of her departure the night before and the show she made of anger towards Justin, she knew in her gut that she had merely been making a gesture to her self-esteem. It was just a way of keeping her conscience from knowing that nothing was going to change. The truth was, she didn't want anything to change. That was the worst of it. She had been going through the motions just in order to be conscience-free in making it up with Justin. As for Joseph, he would of course be *honoured* with a toothless 'memorial' somewhere in their collective memory. How contemptible was that!

Chapter 59

He had been to these places before. The clang of metal on metal reverberating against the hard walls and concrete floors created an alien environment for anything as nuanced as human speech. It was how the earth must have been before stone and rock had been worn down into dirt and that dirt had given birth to life. The warder who accompanied him robot-like through the labyrinth of corridors and antechambers was a creature of the place. As they proceeded, Myles felt a mounting impatience to make contact with a human inmate, some specimen of flesh and blood; he needed reassurance that life had something left in its locker. He imagined that anything human, however unbeautiful, would do, but he hadn't reckoned with the sight that confronted him when he finally reached the interview room where Gary Burrows was awaiting him.

Everything about Burrows' appearance suggested disfigurement and distortion. Nature had not been kind to him in the first place, but what he had done by way of response came across as a calculated insult to the injury he had been dealt. Tattoos abounded like craters on the moon, the hair was an unnatural colour of yellow, but what appalled most was the facial expression. It wasn't rigidly fixed, it did allow for adaptation, but every form it took on was in sneer mode and clearly primed to block even the tiniest shimmer of human warmth passing either in or out. The sight of the creature was nearly surpassed by the sound of the creature. It was a minute or two before anything audible issued from it, but when the voice came into play it was firmly pitched in the high octave spanning sullenness and outrage.

Swallowing his reluctance, Myles made a start.

"I've come here to check out your version of events around

the murder. I've read the transcript of your trial and you maintained that you were, I suppose you could say, 'abducted' and beaten up by a gang of men who had offered to sell you drugs."

He paused and waited for a response. None came. Burrows sat back in his chair and moved his gaze to the right and left as if in search of something of more interest than what was directly before him. Myles was forced to re-boot.

"You said that, after showing you the goods, these people accompanied you to a cash machine, you took out £500, but instead of doing the deal they stole your money, beat you up and made off in your van."

Again, no response.

"The only bit of that story that you were able to substantiate was the cash withdrawal. You did withdraw the cash at the time you said. But the prosecution argued that that was also consistent with the case they were making against you. The three of you were in it together, you, Rodgers and Shane Wilson. You got the money to buy the drugs, you did the deal but then there was a falling out which ended with you and Wilson shooting Rodgers with the two Remington 700Ps, the ones that later turned up with your fingerprints all over them. You no doubt got them as part of the deal along with the drugs. You made off in the van but you were too keen to get away and you lost control and hit the ditch. You were forced to abandon the van, so you removed the drugs and reported the van stolen. But your luck was out. In the darkness and the confusion you missed a couple of packs and left them for us to find."

This did trigger a reaction. The eyes stopped darting to the side and bore down straight on Myles.

"If you're such a clever cunt, what the fuck are you doing talking to me? You already know it all. You and all them poncey lawyers think you know everything and you know fuck all."

At last Myles had something to work with.

"I *don't* know it all, Gary. That's why I'm here. I am trying to believe your story, but I need more help from you. Can't you give me anything that would make your account of what happened that night more convincing than the prosecution's version?"

There was some delay in the reaction. There was a visible weakening of Burrows' scowl, but only momentarily; the shutters were quickly slammed down again.

"That's supposed to be your fucking job. You've got the wrong man, but that doesn't matter, does it, as long you don't get any grief from your newspaper friends? They don't like it, do they, when you've nobody to feed to them? Dwayne was a right dick-head, but him and me was mates. We didn't have no falling out. He wasn't even there for fuck's sake. And Shane wasn't either. He was off his head that night, the stupid git. He's as thick as champ to start with, doesn't know his arse from his elbow, but when he's on the crack the bugger doesn't even know he has an arse or an elbow. Easy pickings he was."

"Okay, okay. Make it harder for us to stitch you up. Give me something, anything. If you didn't do it, who do you think killed your friend? You've had plenty of time to think about it. What do you think really happened?"

The expression on Burrows' face suddenly changed. His eyes turned inward. Myles had evidently pressed the right button.

"I *have* been thinking about that. Been thinking about fuck all else. It had to be them drug dealers. They were into guns, I reckon, more than drugs. Dwayne was always in the market for a good weapon. Always on about it he was. I reckon he was doing a deal with that crowd. Something went wrong – I don't know what, maybe it was about money, or maybe he got up someone's nose, he was good at that, who knows? There was some kind of bust up and the bastards shot him. They needed someone to pin it on, so they picked on me. When I think back on it, the price those guys were asking for them drugs was way too low. It was good stuff. They could've asked a lot more. It was a bit odd too the way they offered me the shooters, out of the blue like. That's not the way them guys operate. I reckon they just wanted me to handle them so that they'd get my fingerprints on them."

He said all this with a quiet calm, like a smithy forging some arbitrary shape out of the bits and pieces that had washed up from the depths of his memory. It was clear to Myles that this wasn't a man trying to sell him a line; it was a man trying desperately to make sense of the facts. Myles was keen to prevent the momentum from stalling.

"In your statement you said that one of the gang was a black man with a posh accent. Is there anything else you can remember about him?"

Rodgers greeted the question as one of his own.

"Yea, there was something about him. It wasn't just that he sounded posh, he looked posh, like one of them celebs. Yes, I remember, he wore one of them fancy scarves round his neck."

"You mean a cravat?"

"No, it wasn't like that. It was more like what the cowboys used to wear. The knot was round the side and it stuck out like, at the side of his neck. I remember thinking, that bastard fancies himself as the Sundance Kid. It was weird 'cause he didn't talk that way. He sounded more like one of them poncey guys that do the news on the tele."

A bell started ringing somewhere at the back of Myles' consciousness. He had come across a not dissimilar description somewhere before. Where was it? Maybe it was just from Burrows' own statement, but he had a feeling something he'd heard had prompted him to picture someone who dressed … like an artist, was it? He had it! He'd read it in one of Justin's reports. It was the way Justin had described one of The New Promethean facilitators. He'd check it out when he got back.

Having got the stone rolling, Myles decided to try his luck further and see if he could ferret out anything new about the Francis Brown murder.

"I'm very tempted to believe what you're telling me, Gary. I'll follow it up. I can't make you any promises, mind, but I'll do what I can. But you know, it would really help if you told me what you know about what happened to Francis Brown. I know there was bad blood between him and Dwayne. Was it Dwayne who killed him? You didn't want that, did you? Did you try to stop him?"

Burrows stared open-eyed at the lure before him. He was being offered the chance to pin the blame on a dead man who was in no position to make a liar of him. He could claim he'd tried to stop it. That's what this copper wanted to hear. It might get him off the hook. What wasn't there to like? Myles could see him hesitate. It looked like the hesitation of a man double-checking he has the keys before he leaves the house. Then, just as he thought he had him, Burrows' face contorted into a snarl.

"So that's what all this shit's about. You think I'm going to rake all that stuff up again. All that sweet talk about being my friend and getting me justice! What the fuck do you take me for? Since when do the likes of you give a monkey's about getting justice for the likes of me? Just go and fuck off!"

He sprang to his feet and had to be restrained by the two warders who had been present throughout the interview. When he thought about it afterwards, Myles had to admit to having mixed feelings about this final twist. On the one hand a can of worms that needed reopening had its lid still on, but on the other he felt relieved of a burden heavier than the one he already carried. He would really have hated having a personal duty to Burrows over and above the one he had to justice.

Chapter 60

Justin made his way home with the pride of a man who had earned his other dollar for another day. Archive research wasn't exactly his thing, but it went with the job and, just as with his marriage to Lizzie, he had to put his hand up for the sickness as well as for the health. It had all turned out well in the end, albeit more by luck than good judgement. He had scoured all the main newspapers for the entire month following the Brighton Bombing. There were plenty of venomous quotes to be found to match Morrissey's infamous expression of regret that Thatcher had been spared. The far Left were in full cry against 'the evil Tories'. The righteous outrage of the Left travelled with a moral visa that gave it immunity from any attack coming from outside its own ethical base. Anything not explicitly authorised on the moral visa was simply cold-shouldered. There was no question of balancing one good or one evil against another. Morality was monochrome.

Justin was shocked. He had been aware of the events of the time; he knew there had been a great strength of feeling during the Thatcher era, but this was different. This was more like the bloodlust of the Terror that followed the French Revolution. This coming together of the British far Left and Irish republicanism in a holy war against the centre and the right was enough to turn the stomach. He now understood why so many working class voters had swung to Thatcher in the eighties; there was too much acid on the menu their own leaders were presenting. But he was getting distracted. What had started out as a focused search was rapidly turning into a history-learning. He needed to get back to the task on hand.

When the name George Sinclair failed to materialise in

any of the leading nationals he had turned his attention to the local press. This made for heavier wading; the view from ground level provides too much detail to enable you to form a composite picture of the terrain. He concentrated on the northern papers and here reports on the miners' strike took up more space than the Brighton bomb. Sinclair's name popped up regularly in support of Scargall. He was quite outspoken, calling the Tories scum and advocating a general strike to put an end to right-wing rule once and for all. But this was standard fare for the time. In one interview however he was pressed on the implications of the miners' refusal to accept the legitimacy of a Tory government. Asked if that would not lead to the kind of dictatorship they had in Russia during the Stalin years, he replied that there could be no such thing as a dictatorship of the proletariat; the proletariat were the people, so how could the people dictate to the people? He went on to say that Stalin had been maligned by the right-wing press; he was a visionary who had led the revolution through turbulent times and provided the strong leadership needed to see it succeed in the face of capitalist attempts to undermine it. He refused to dignify the slanderous lies that had been put about to blacken the name of a great man. Justin licked his lips. This wasn't exactly what he had been looking for, but it would do for a start. There was in fact better to come. In the 21st October edition of *Socialist North* he gave an interview on the bombing. There in glorious black and white Technicolor he declared Thatcher and her cabinet *legitimate targets for any revolutionary movement forced to take up arms in the cause of social justice.* He was particularly venomous towards Norman Tebbit, the man *who had the gall to tell the unemployed to get on their bikes.* It was a good thing, he said, that the bomb hadn't killed him and his wife. Killing would have been too good for him. *Better he should have to live out his remaining years having to care for a woman confined to a wheelchair.*

Eardley was going to love this. Little wonder that, as he turned the key in the latch, he felt like a young boy going into school with a homework he had done the night before, one he knew that was a dead cert for an 'A' star. Thoughts of Lizzie and her tantrums of the night before had receded and finally faded in his mind as the day had gone on, but suddenly as he opened the door, they rushed back to the foreground. It was as if, having been shunted aside, all the thin layers of concern had plied together into a thick block that was now coming down on him with its full might. In an attempt to take some findings before exposing himself to her presence he called out her name. There was no reply. He tried the bedroom first, then the kitchen. Maybe she had left for good. Maybe in the unfathomable depths of her reasoning she had come to see him as a heartless beast. He could well imagine her accusations of him being too self-driven to be aware of his emotional illiteracy. He hadn't tried the living room as it was in darkness, but as a last resort he switched on the light and there she was, sprawled out on her back on the sofa with an arm dangling down almost touching an overturned gin glass on the floor.

"Good God, what has she done?"

The fear came at him with such force that it had to be spoken. For a moment he just stared in horror, but then he rushed over to the lifeless figure and started slapping at her face. It was something he had seen his father do when his mother passed out during her illnesses. The effect was instant. Lizzie's eyes flashed open, but not with the look of someone emerging from a deep chasm.

"What the hell are you doing? Why are you hitting me?"

Justin's relief was mighty, but almost immediately it was suffused with a feeling of his own foolishness. He had been watching too many melodramas.

"I thought something was wrong and I wanted to see if you were okay."

She twigged immediately the way his mind had been working.

"Ah, I see. You thought I was trying to top myself, is that it? Well, put your mind at rest. I'll not be burdening your conscience any more than it's burdened already."

That again! He thought she would have got past that by now. He had persuaded himself that last night in her grief she was entitled to some degree of latitude. But enough was enough surely. This really was too much.

"Listen. Lizzie. We've been though all this. I'm as sorry as you about Joseph, but I don't see how you can hold me responsible for his death. Joseph was in with the Prometheans long before I came on the scene. It was he who inducted me, not the other way round."

He dosed his exasperation with as much patience as he could muster, but the effect was counterproductive, patience seemed to have swopped clothes with condescension. Fortunately Lizzie didn't pick up on this as he feared she would the moment he heard the words coming out of his mouth. She simply bent down and picked up the sheet of paper that had been lying on the sofa beside her.

"Read that," she said. She said it with the assurance of someone who could see beyond the horizon. He took it from her and began to read. He hadn't quite got to the end, just to the bit, 'He had no real feelings for me, he was simply using me' before Lizzie, unable to contain herself any longer, let loose.

"You see what he's saying? He's saying that you are the reason he took his own life. He was just beginning to believe in you again when you came along and pressurised him into lying to that policeman. If you had left him alone Joseph would be alive today."

Justin had felt a wave of guilt pass through him as he worked through the letter, but when it was crystallised into an accusation and that accusation came from a source other than himself, anger suddenly sprang up to his rescue.

"That's rubbish, Lizzie. You're overreacting. I never laughed behind his back. I've no idea where the *noumenal phenomenon* notion came from. I certainly never used it. How was I to know how close he was to the edge?"

"Come off it. You knew how vulnerable he was. He gave up his studies, for God's sake. He was a born academic. He had a glittering career before him. He'd have been a don in no time. And he gave all that up! He talked to you. You knew what he was suffering and still you went and brought all his old demons back to life."

"No, you're wrong, it wasn't me who brought the demons back to life. It was that Inspector Myles. It was he who was pressurising him into making a decision."

"What decision? There was no decision for him to make, until you came along that is. All Joseph had to do was to answer the Inspector's questions and tell him what happened. He had no duty of care to Robbie or Stuart Stranaghan. They are the ones who would have been suffered had he told the truth. The truth wouldn't have hurt you at all. You'd done nothing criminal. What you did would have finished you in the police, sure, but that doesn't matter, you've left the police anyway. You weren't acting selfishly, I'll grant you that. What you did was put your other two friends first and throw poor Joseph to the wolves. And by God, didn't the wolves do their job well."

"Okay, maybe I could have been a bit more sensitive, who knows? But where are you going with this, Lizzie? What would you have me do? Or is it just a case of having someone to kick? Is that it? If that makes you feel better, okay, go on ahead."

There was something in that, Lizzie had to concede – but only to herself. Justin was right. There was no point in going on at him. He had been bloody insensitive, but hardly more than could be expected from a man. The real bastard, the one she really wanted to get at, was Robbie. He had treated Joseph in the most abominable way. And he knew exactly what he was doing. All that pressure just to see if the poor boy would break. He'd have shown more consideration if it had been a monkey he had been doing his research on. He must be made to pay. She didn't know how, but she would find a way. Until then, she might as well call off these hostilities with Justin. He had always been no more than a surrogate villain for her. She didn't really need a surrogate; she had a real one to kick out at.

She got to her feet, went up to Justin, looked into his eyes and, to his utter bewilderment, put her arms around him. He had no idea what had suddenly changed, but he was uncomfortably aware that there might be a lot more that had not changed.

Chapter 61

The scene was exactly like one of those life-style habitats you get in TV dramas about fashionable middleclass professionals – everything new, minimalist and designer-trendy, the type of bubble devised to make the viewers feel unqualified to enter but privileged to be shown. Of course, the viewers know that they will have the last laugh, for inevitably this paradise will become infested with messy human stuff and the seemingly superior beings that inhabit it will be shown to be just as unfitted for the dream lifestyle as they, the viewers, are. On closer inspection of this particular tableau one figure stood out as a troll among the avatars. His clothing was coarse – the tweed jacket was an affront to finery – and there had been no obvious attempt at conciliation between the colours, his light tan shoes standing out as the most villainous transgressor. At the other end of the spectrum was a tall elegant woman in her early forties. Her long black hair streamed down her back, giving off a sheen as it picked up the light. Everything about this woman evinced style and gracefulness. She wore an off-white skirt and jacket over a tastefully outrageous flowery blouse. The effect was enhanced by the polarity provided by the slightly ungainly satchel that draped from her right shoulder. The heels on her shoes were just high enough to show off her ankles and sexualise her walk, but low enough to make it clear that she was making not the slightest effort to allure. What was not least striking about her were her hands; they were femininely petite, but the long fingers with their well groomed, ovoid nails had a lithe quality to them suggestive of an agility in the use of the sort of buttons that could make important things happen, or not. The two were chatting amicably as they collected their coffee before taking their seats at the table that was already occupied by a group of four men and a second woman.

At the head of the table was the dapper Matthew Eardley. With his easy grace and the understated quality of his tweed he clearly belonged to the same executive elite as the beautiful lady who had just come to the table. When he had assured himself that she was comfortably installed he addressed the meeting.

"Thank you all for coming. As I indicated in my invitation, I think it's time for an up-date on the progress at Bury West. We are all anxious to know how it's going and no one is better placed to inform us that Francesca here. As you know, she has been up there advising Robert not so much on what to say – Robert is not one to be told that – but on when to say it and, more importantly perhaps, when *not* to say it. Well, Francesca, how's our boy been doing? What kind of marks have you given him?"

Francesca beamed an acknowledging smile as she extracted a file from her satchel.

"Thank you for that, Matt. I'm not exactly flattered by your analogy. I've never quite seen myself as a headmistress, certainly not a 'jolly-hockey-sticks', Joyce Grenfell type. I'm afraid I'd be too fond of the red ink for modern stomachs. Having said that, I'm minded to give 'your boy' a pass, although not with distinction.

"We always knew we were trying to insert a square peg into a round hole. The question was whether to do it by rounding the peg or squaring the hole. Robert is all for the latter. Up to a point I agree with him on that – but only up to a point. Fair enough, he needs to be true to himself. And it's true that he's at his most persuasive when he is expounding ideas that he really believes in. But he shouldn't try to convert the unconvertible. There are times when he needs to give the impression of being a little bit rounder. Let me give you some examples."

She placed a pair of heavy framed glasses on her nose and scrutinised the file before continuing.

"Here's one. An elderly lady said to him that she was proud to be a socialist because for all its faults the Labour Party was the party that came closest to Christian teaching. This wasn't even a question. He could have let it go. No, he weighed in and told her that the Christian church had allowed itself to slip into the sentimentality of the age. Being poor or disadvantaged didn't give anyone a pass when it came to taking responsibility for their actions. Welfarism wasn't the answer to anything, he said, it was merely a self-righteous hobby for patronising prats. The poor woman had no idea what he was talking about. She smiled as if she had got some version of the response she had expected to get. And who knows, maybe she clung on to that.

"There was another occasion when he was asked about the small number of working class children getting places at our top universities. Another opportunity, you'd think, to trot out a few well worn clichés about privileged private education and the underfunding of the state sector. No, too easy! Both feet in again. He said that funding had very little to do with it, it was a question of attitude and expectation. The working classes had been completely demoralised. He then proceeded to explain that by 'demoralised' he meant they had been robbed of their morals as well as their morale. They had been indoctrinated into the belief that they were victims and they had developed the expectations of victims, namely that nice things rather than nasty things should be made to happen to them. One of those 'nice' things was academic success. So the exams were dumbed down, practically every institution catering for school-leavers had been declared a university, degrees and certificates were bestowed by the bucket-load, and the magic target of a population that thought of itself as educated was in sight. Of course there is still some way to go; some universities still persist in thinking that there is a reality outside the subjectivist bubble. Thinking that the world is at your feet doesn't actually bring the world to your feet. He then asked the man if that's what he wanted; did he

339

want the top universities to join the bandwagon and sign up for the lie or did he want more working class children to be led through to become the measure of, if not all things, the things they could reasonably aim at. It was a fine speech, but again, was this the occasion for it?

"I must say however there are times when it's hard s not to say 'good on you, Robert'. One time a social-worker type challenged him about his views on law and order, trotting out the usual line about seeing things from the point of view of those who are tempted into crime and weaning them gradually off it. She cited the case of drug related crime. Helping people get off drugs, she said, would surely be a more effective strategy than criminalising their use. Robert gave her a look of wide-eyed approval and said that he agreed entirely and thought the authorities should take the policy of supplying substitute drugs even further and supply those inclined to violence with the means and skill to give their victims more humane injuries and deaths. This would mean drawing up a list of appropriate weapons and training all aspiring thugs and assassins in their use. If the criminal justice system can't stop people from killing or injuring their fellow citizens, wouldn't it at least be better if we focused our efforts on minimising the pain they inflict? He said all this with a straight face. The poor woman was taken completely unawares and nodded enthusiastically in agreement before she caught herself on. She obviously didn't do irony."

She took a sip from the glass of water in front of her on the table and allowed the humour of the anecdote to ripple through her audience, before continuing.

"There are a few areas which I advised him very strongly to avoid. We agreed that he should be as vague as possible about the economy. The Labour Party is not to be separated from its historical fantasies any more than a child is from its teddy bear or its comfort blanket. Any narrative that does not lay the blame for unemployment or low pay squarely on the employer class is a damp squib. It's as simple as that. You can cite other contributory causes, they'll let you away with that, but only provided you make it clear that you know who the bad guys are and you hate them just as much as any self-respecting socialist ought to. Robert and I talked about this a lot and on the whole he has been good about it, but has had one or two lapses. One time he went as far as to say some nasty things about the unions. He compared what happened in Germany after the war with the situation here. He pointed out that industrial relations were hampered here by the bitter rivalry between the unions whereas in Germany, where there were only a handful of unions, things went much more smoothly. The focus was on competing in the world market rather than haggling with employers and bickering over demarcation issues. This did not go down well. Robert must learn that people don't follow arguments, people pick up vocabulary; they don't have the attention span for syntax. Of course he *knows* this, but the problem is, he doesn't know it in his bones. I doubt if it will ever seep in that far."

This produced a wry smile on the face of the Chairman which just as quickly dried.

"So what are you saying, Francesca? Are you saying that Robert's not the man for the job?"

Francesca thought for a moment.

"No ... (it was one of those elongated 'noes' that harbour strong elements of 'yes') ... I'm not saying that. As I said before, we went into this knowing what the dangers were. Robert, God bless him, does not think like a politician. He believes that coming up with solutions is what his brain is for and he can't come to terms with the fact that voters mustn't be asked to stray too far out of their comfort zone. Comfort comes from the very clichés he is trying to destroy. It's a conundrum. He'd have a better chance of a successful political career if he left well alone. But if he did that, what would be the point of him getting elected? I'm treating the whole thing as an art rather than a science. There are no formulae available to us that can guarantee success, but there's every hope that we'll manage to tweak it."

There was one figure that did not join in the spirit of resigned optimism that these remarks produced around the table. That, rather surprisingly, was Dr Greenfield – he of the coarse tweed jacket.

"I don't think you've quite answered Matt's question, Francesca. He asked you if you thought Robert was the right man for the job. What you've told us is how you are coping with the fact that he isn't. If we could turn the clock back and revisit our choice, is it at all likely that we could have come up with a better candidate, given the constraints you mentioned?"

"That's a very hypothetical question, Bruce", she began, but then she paused as if the question she was about to dismiss was beginning to acquire more interest for her. "If I were honest I would have to say that it's a two-man job. Politics is about changing hearts and minds without their owners catching on that it's happening. Robert is the man to decide where best to travel, but I must admit I have grave doubts about him being the best man to captain the ship."

Greenfield gave a nod of acknowledgement to what suspiciously looked to have been his own fears. The others looked glumly on. The feeling of resignation had lost its optimistic edge. Eardley however, perhaps seeing it as his duty as chairman, refused to allow negativity to take hold of the meeting.

"Thank you, Francesca, for your frank assessment of our prospects. You have confirmed what we knew all along. Unfortunately Parliament only allows one MP per constituency. But come to think of it, maybe the solution was staring us in the face all along. Maybe we should have cast our net more widely and found ourselves a brainy, empathetic schizophrenic, someone with the capacity to keep his brain away from his tongue and his tongue away from his brain."

Chapter 62

As the members of the Selection Panel assembled in the upper room of the party offices the solemnity of the occasion seemed to drape from each of them like a great judicial gown. The hand of history had placed a noble burden on their shoulders, and although there were no witnesses present, the ghosts of Labour past and the embryos of Labour future were there to hold them to account. It was an occasion for polished shoes and clean underwear. Light-hearted conversation was permissible, but only as long as it knew its place. As befitted his chairman's role, Trevor Windsor led the way in this. Today he had been invested with honorary membership of the same order as the Speaker of the House or the Master of the Rolls. There was no personal pride in this, simply deference to the solemn weight that had been placed upon him.

All the members of the Panel seemed to be similarly up for the occasion. Hugh Savage was poised to take the minutes with the classic fountain pen his wife had given him as an anniversary present. Margaret Millership had had something done to her hair. Whatever it was, she looked less intimidating than usual. Reggie, on this, his last official appearance as the sitting MP, sporting a House of Commons tie, was obviously determined to underline the status he was today taking a further step closer to relinquishing. The effect however was more that of a first-former wearing his new uniform with a pride that no self-respecting older boy would ever be seen dead with. Nathan Roberts had donned a suit no one would ever have suspected him of owning and Max Fischer's beard showed signs of inter-ference from someone with serious aesthetic ambitions. Freddie Douglas was the sole tieless male. As an outsider and the

343

youngest member of the committee he, whether consciously or unconsciously, seemed to have assumed the role of tribune for the rising generation and settled on *smart casual* as his take on gravitas. Only Schinski and Johnnie Taylor looked to have made no special effort. Schinski always dressed quite formally, although not always with a tie, and Johnnie Taylor had a predilection for the businessman look, dark suit, white shirt, matching tie.

Coffee and perfunctory small talk completed, the party took to their seats around the table. Chairman Windsor opened proceedings with a few well whetted words. All present, he declared, had been entrusted with a great responsibility, one to be borne in the full knowledge that the future of the Party, indeed of the nation, depended on the skills and clarity of thought of panels such as theirs. Factionalism and petty ambitions should play no part in the decision they were about to make; they should draw on the wisdom their myriad encounters with life had distilled in their hearts and minds. He was sure that this panel would live up to the expectations placed on it by the Executive Committee and that Bury West would send a member to Westminster who would be a credit to the constituency, the Party and the country at large. Schinski was on the point of adding sotto voce, 'And the entire Papal see' to his neighbour on the right, but seeing that it was Margaret Millership, thought better of it. Some bubbles are best left unburst.

Windsor went on to outline the procedures to be followed. The two candidates would be brought in separately and given five minutes to address the meeting. This would be followed by a short question-and-answer session lasting a maximum of fifteen minutes. The Panel would then deliberate and a vote would be taken. On the flip of a coin it was decided that Mr Snoddy would be first up and Hugh Savage was dispatched to fetch him from downstairs.

When he appeared, Snoddy looked decidedly less flustered

344

than the Honorary Secretary who was taking it on himself to put the candidate at his ease. What could best be described as a captain's chair had been placed at the far end of the table facing the Chairman and Snoddy was invited to sit. Windsor, more practised in the patronising role than his inept Secretary, assured him in tones befitting an elder statesman that there was nothing to be nervous about; the committee merely wanted him to tell them as briefly as possible what message he had for the Party. Snoddy responded with a look that mocked the deference of his words of thanks. He then looked around the table, pausing very deliberately and taking in each face before he allowed himself to begin his oration. It was as if he was making sure that each was worthy of hearing what he was about to say. Then he began

"I don't know if any of you are familiar with H G Well's novel, The Time Machine?"

He conducted the same review of the faces of his audience, this time even more slowly and deliberately.

"Well, if not, let me commend it to you. It has much to tell us about where the world is and where it's going. With the narrator we go forward in time, something like 800,000 years, and discover mankind in a very sorry state. It has split into two races. The first, which he calls the *Eloi*, is harmless and wishy-washy, feeble in both mind and body; they live off the bounty of the land, happily singing and dancing, eating and sleeping, but with a great terror of the dark. They are completely incapable of taking any kind of positive action to meet their needs. The second race, the *Morlocks*, live under ground, they shun the light and only come out at night, and then only when it's moonless. They are an aggressive and brutal bunch but they provide what infrastructure is needed to keep the *Eloi* going. It's not a case of philanthropy however; their support for the *Eloi* is the support an estate owner gives to his game birds. They keep the *Eloi* for hunting and live off their flesh.

"It's a salutary tale of what happens when what are traditionally known as the feminine virtues part company from the manly ones and float off on their own. Take a look at modern political debate. What do you see? *(a brief pause)* I'll tell you what I see – I see *Eloi* and I see the fear that stalks them that they might encounter anything that smells of the *Morlock*. They huddle together in one great mollycoddle. You see it everywhere – we ban any form of expression that *might* cause offence to any group that, mistakenly or otherwise, sees itself as disadvantaged, we have an education system that discourages success for fear of exposing failure, a criminal justice system that treats offenders like victims and renounces the firm hand of justice in favour of the warm, self-satisfied glow of mercy. Our social security system, originally designed as a safety net for those who have fallen on hard times, has mutated into a fully fledged lifestyle support network – and what a miserable apology for a lifestyle it sponsors! The modern political arena is getting more and more like a Jane Austen drawing room, where nasty topics of common concern are not to be mentioned and certainly not in language that shows any tolerance of the Anglo-Saxon. It's funny how snobbery has been turned on its head – psycho- and socio-babble have taken over from the received language of the salon, the ban on Anglo-Saxon is not total; it is still permitted in expressions of contempt for the *Lumpenproletariat* who refuse to don the swaddling clothes, more the winding sheets, that the good people of the liberal persuasion wish to wrap them up in.

"Do we really want to turn the working classes into *Morlocks*? For that's what will happen if the political establishment doesn't change course. If exiled by their counterparts, manly virtues will not wither and die; in their isolation they will coarsen and become disfigured. The inventiveness of the provider will switch over to the service of Machiavellian self-interest, the courage of the defender of hearth and home will regress to the daring of the marauder, the fatherly insistence on

346

firmness and discipline will fossilise into a merciless stone-heartedness. And just as surely, the Eloi softness will slide inexorably into mental paralysis. Each pole needs the other to keep madness at bay.

"It's not just our politics; our whole culture is in meltdown. In so-called modern art we are invited to view 'meaningful' blank canvasses and paint being ridden over by an artist riding a bicycle or walked over by a passing chimpanzee. We get 'serious' music that sees melody as the enemy and novels that are oh so proud of themselves for not providing a good read. Our so-called high culture prefers to look up its own arse and syringe itself with awards and prizes that cover up the venereal symptoms of its incest. Meanwhile mass culture gets cruder and cruder, football, sex and violence, violence, sex and football. And what does the Labour Party, the party of the people, have to say about all this? Sweet Fanny Adams! Well, I think it's damned well time it did have a view.

"It should start by stripping down and remodelling our entire social security system, making sure that the little matter of the attitudes and behaviour of those in receipt of its benefits gets built into the system. How many times should the Prodigal Son be forgiven? That's a question we are not allowed even to ask. Why not? Because we might actually decide on an answer! And any answer short of infinity would expose us as human and not as members of the heavenly host. It's interesting, isn't it, that words like 'humane' and 'humanity' have been put right up there with 'god' and 'godly'. That's the folly that dares not speak its name. There's no doubt unconditional nursing and ministering can sometimes be called for, but the call should be answered with the head as well as the heart and the answer should certainly not be hijacked as a gesture in the ritual of moral preening.

"Moving on to education: Our Party has a lot to answer for here. We've meant well, but we've created a hell of a mess. We've gone along with the great wallow in selfhood that our state schools have shrunk education down to! Their constant obsession with *experiences that the kids can relate to* has condemned generations of deprived children to lifelong incarceration in their own dreary culture of the humdrum. Out of regard for stomachs weakened by their constant diet of junk food, the rich fare of literature, history, philosophy and the like is kept from them. You've got to be kind even if it means being cruel, you know. Don't these self-appointed saints see that education is about getting out and about in the world of thought, not sitting clinging to the cliché experiences you were born and grew up with? The brain must be stretched to and beyond the point where it begins to hurt. But students also need to become aware of their limitations and learn to be humble and in awe of the achievements of minds greater than their own. They might be disappointed with the talents they have, but at least they will find out what they are and build real lives around them. The joys of learning are great, but you don't get them on the cheap.

"Then we come to the Law, arguably mankind's greatest achievement. It is something man has created in acknowledgement of the fact that nature does not have the element of fairness in its DNA. The Law is there to correct that as far as is reasonably possible. So let me be clear, I in no way underestimate the importance of the Law. But that doesn't blind me to the fact that it has gone dangerously awry. Firstly, it has allowed its perfectly legitimate concern that innocent people should not become its victims to develop into a debilitating obsession, a cuckoo in the nest that stifles and steals the equally legitimate concern for getting justice for the victim. As a result the cause of justice as a whole is sacrificed on the altar of caution. Legal niceties are put before all else and justice is often manifestly denied in the name of … justice! When witnesses are intimidated, how do the courts react? Do they acknowledge the reality?

No, they simply ignore what is blindingly obvious. Any statements the witnesses have made earlier are simply set aside. This is outrageous! Criminals are being rewarded for compounding their criminality! A whole assortment of technicalities is invoked to rule out the most clear-cut evidence. But even more galling is the pride the legal profession takes in the 'cleverdickyness' of defending barristers at twisting the facts and obscuring the truth – and this from a squeaky clean profession that preens itself on its devotion to justice! The Augean stables are in sore need of clearing out.

"The second folly is contiguous to the first. Again, the whole emphasis is on the welfare of the criminal. The death penalty has been rejected as barbarous and its replacement, life imprisonment, the sop thrown to those who opposed abolition, has been watered down to the point where it has become totally meaningless. Yet despite this the name has been retained. Now why is that, I wonder? Why keep a sheep in wolf's clothing? The question surely answers itself: It's exactly what the early Christian Church did when it set about the task of converting; it used many of the same sites and symbols as the pagans had used. That way they could be eased into conversion without realising it. It's commonly known as 'pulling the wool'. The *bien pensants* don't want the truth to dawn on the public that they have given up on the very notion of justice and replaced it with the more motherly virtue of mercy. Murderers are released from prison to murder again, and many do. But the virtuous ones, the good people who have performed the act of mercy, do they share in the blame for the part they played in the loss of innocent lives? Not bloody likely. No, their consciences are clear and their commitment to virtue remains undiminished. Their courage will not fail them even in the face of death, the death of other people that is. Collateral damage in the pursuit of virtue!

"I could go on; I could tell you what I think of the state of

Her Majesty's prisons. Their governance has been passed like a bad smell from the government to the private sector and then – breathe it softly – from the private sector to the prisoners themselves. It's a classic case of a self-fulfilling prophesy – truth has caught up with the liberal view: our prisons don't work. The reformers have made bloody sure of that. But you only gave me five minutes. I think I have conveyed to you where my priorities lie and I hope I have persuaded you to give me the opportunity to set about the work which I feel this Party has been neglecting for far too long."

The entire speech had been given with barely a reference to the single sheet of paper before him. The fluency had stunned the audience whose comprehension of what was being said lagged somewhat behind. It took it a moment or two to catch up. When it did, it produced a collective gasp which, in the absence of other willing spokesmen, it fell to the Chairman to articulate.

"You seem very critical of our Party, Mr Snoddy. Are you quite sure that we are the people you wish to represent in Parliament?"

Snoddy nodded in acknowledgement of the legitimacy of the question.

"What do you do when a close friend goes off the rails? Do you say, 'To hell with him' and seek out new friends or do you try to help and get him back on his feet?"

"So you really think the Party is that bad, do you?"

The question came from Max Fischer.

"I'm afraid I do, Dr Fischer. I don't think it really knows what it's for anymore. It feels that as a radical party it behoves it to be angry and it listens to almost any group with a low-cost grievance to sell. Even when it's operating on its own patch (and that, I need not remind present company, is looking after the welfare of the average Brit), even here it picks the wrong battles to fight. Many of the leading politicians of our party behave as if they were in a fifties movie with the nasty Normans oppressing the thoroughly decent Saxon peasantry. It's all about booing and cheering."

Fischer beamed, seemingly in agreement.

"I'd be interested in your thoughts about human rights. Is that a cause our party should embrace, do you think? Or do you consider that another source of *low-cost grievances*?"

The question gained increased propulsion from Savage and Millership who both showed eagerness to share ownership of it. Snoddy made a point of showing awareness of their interest in the course of his reply.

"This is perhaps not the time or the place to enter into a philosophical discussion, but I must say I am deeply uneasy about the concept of human rights. I can understand how they came to be conceived. The horrors of Nazi Germany and Stalinist Russia needed some kind of moral response and in a post-Christian age divine authority could not be called upon. So what better than to establish a humanist creed? The trouble is, humanism must always base itself on what is human, but human rights have a tendency to soar into the stratosphere and sup with the gods. Like the gods, their dictate has become absolute, no hemming or hawing, no tweaking or trimming. Once something is accepted as a human right, that's the end of discussion, blind obedience becomes the order of the day. And just like the religious fanatics of medieval Christianity or the Islamists of our own time, the demand for conformity doesn't stop at deeds, it demands purity of thought. To any proponent of heretical thought it shows no mercy; it ostracises them, sometimes even locks them up. We haven't got to burning them at the stake – yet.

"No, I am a secularist in these things. I believe in *civil* rights, rights that every society is free to fashion for itself, and perhaps even more important, rights that are conditional on the citizen fulfilling his obligations as a citizen. This, I admit, does not provide a moral basis for judging societies such as Nazi

Germany or Pol Pot's Cambodia, but there are other moral arguments available for doing that. What's wrong with saying that such regimes are cruel and despicable and leaving it at that? Why do we insist on constructing a web of absolutes that ties us in knots and produces outcomes that defy the very decency we are trying to uphold?"

It was clear that Savage and Millership were less satisfied with this answer than Fischer, who gave a thoughtful nod. But before either of them could decide on the best line of counterattack Trevor Windsor called time on the discussion. The Panel, he said, would have ample time to consider the very thought-provoking ideas that Mr Snoddy had been good enough to treat them to.

Chapter 63

The Panel took a comfort break after Snoddy's departure. A couple of them availed of the toilet facilities while the rest headed in the direction of the coffee dispenser. Hugh Savage was quick to seek out Nathan Roberts and get his view of '*that performance*'. Roberts seemed amused rather than outraged.

"Well, what else did you expect? The man is no socialist. I could have told you that before he opened his mouth today. I'll say one thing though. He was honest. He didn't try to bullshit us and if we're daft enough to nominate him we'll have no one but ourselves to blame."

"Yes, I think you're right there, Nathan"

There was an affected note of hesitancy in Savage's reply designed to flatter the astuteness of the insight of the other man. It wasn't often these two men agreed. Savage was one of those who looked back fondly on the golden age when Tony Blair could do no wrong and Labour had become the natural party of government. The likes of Old Nathan here were having to lump it then, he and his cronies on the far Left were out in the cold, but at least they were in sight of the tent. The same couldn't be said of Snoddy, the man wasn't a socialist of any hue. He had just bad-mouthed the whole Labour movement. He obviously had nothing but contempt for all the moderate Left had achieved. He'd rubbished the advances in education. He was intent on undermining the very essence of the welfare state. What was that he said about the Party and grievances? You'd think they were pure figments of the Party's imagination, that there weren't myriads of people out there with real problems looking to the Party for help. And human rights, the man doesn't believe in human rights! And that same man proposes to go to

Westminster and represent a party whose very raison d'être is to look out for the underdog! No, the choice was clear. George Sinclair might be far too far to the Left, but at least he's of the Left and once he's in Parliament means will be found to rein him in. It might stick in his throat to say it, but George Sinclair would be getting his vote.

Derek Schinski could hear what was being said, but forbore to get involved. Snoddy had certainly taken the bull by the horns. If he were to get the nomination it was most definitely not going to be from under the radar. Bold certainly, but wise? It wouldn't have been Schinski's choice of tactic, but he could see some merit in it. A new broom is free of the dust and threads of the old floor, at least until it sets about its job. That was an advantage his opponent was certainly not about to enjoy.

When everyone was back in their seats Trevor Windsor ruled out discussion of the merits *or otherwise* of the first candidate until the committee had heard from his opponent. It was an exercise in comparison they were engaged in. That should be their sole focus. They were not there to decide what it was they liked or disliked about what either of the candidates said, the question before them was which candidate's approach they liked better, or indeed disliked less. After these words of wisdom from the Chairman the second candidate was summoned.

It was striking how much less old and experienced the venerable George Sinclair looked as he entered the room. One could imagine him as a sixth former walking down the examination hall to sit his A levels – not that he had ever done any A-levels, growing up as he did in an era before the myriad creeks and brooks of education had been homogenised into the long, straight, featureless canal that now all are compelled to swim along. After the formal invitation from the Chairman to address the meeting the aspirant put a nervous hand in the side pocket of his jacket and pulled out a little clump of crumpled papers which he began to speak from – it wasn't exactly reading, but there was enough reading involved to discredit any claim it might make to be even rudimentary oratory. This uneasy standoff between reading and speaking lasted only briefly however before the papers were abandoned and speech was given its head. The rich Sinclair tone gradually recovered itself and the gravitas of the old dog peeped through. Like all orators of the far Left he was at his most fluent when inveighing against the mores of the bourgeoisie.

"Let me begin", he said, "by telling you where I *don't* think the Party should being going. That won't take me long: we should head everywhere in the opposite direction from where Blair and his acolytes tried to lead it. Shallow people do a lot of harm when they elbow their way into positions of authority. And by God, weren't Blair and his cronies dab hands at that. They won a lot of admirers for how well they bobbed and weaved, but it's easy to bob and weave when you're not carrying any baggage, things like beliefs and principles. It's like what happens in rugby, isn't it Reggie? Fancy stuff pleases the crowd, but if all you've done is go sidewise and keep the ball, there's not a lot of point to it, is there? Of course for the likes of Blair that's what it was all about, wasn't it, retaining possession. Tory Cameron was exactly the same? A few tweaks to the buzz words and ... ABRACADABRA ... the colour changes from red to blue. Neither of them had a clue what they should be doing with the power they were holding.

"What's really sad is that they didn't have a clue that they were clueless. They would be genuinely hurt if you accused them of not having a moral compass. They were such proud ticket holders of the high moral ground. Look at what they achieved. They both took ownership of the great drive for European unity – no more European wars, no more petty nationalism and an open invitation to the population of Europe to come and share our tiny island. They didn't give a rap about old-fashioned things like the way folk talk and think, the things they value and the faith they hold. No, everyone would adapt to everyone else. Mind you, just who was to do the adapting and who was to be adapted to, was a question that was never asked, let alone answered. And they didn't stop there; they welcomed hundreds of thousands from outside Europe as well. What did they care if most of these were immersed in a culture that was unsympathetic to western values. Many hated our guts, and worse still, despised us when they discovered how gullible we were. The British working class was lectured and sermonised on the dangers of *overreaction* when this hatred of the infidel spilled over into isolated acts of jihad. A hell of a lot more righteous anger was directed at those who might *overly react* than at the perps themselves. Anyone naive enough to make, and voice, a connection between the atrocities committed by any of the new Brits and the open-door policy of the government was universally condemned as racist and profoundly un-British. Strange that, there was me thinking that the notion of Britishness had been cast aside as Old Hat.

"When I said 'universally' I mean of course in the only universe that really counts, the world of posh dinner parties and bourgeois chit-chat, where the great and the good hold hands around the table and talk their big hearts out about issues like global warming, gay marriage or transsexual toilets and swear red-wine brotherhood in the ruthless persecution of the nonconformist rabble. Every time I hear one of these sanctimonious prigs spout morality I think of Zsa Zsa Gabor – remember her and her pink poodles? Liberals have moral feelings the way the fashionable set have pets, something to show off, to feel cuddly about, but most important of all, something that looks on them with adoring eyes and tells them how wonderful they are. I'm more the peasant type, me. I like my morals to be out there in the mud and the wet earning their keep. They're working dogs, not pampered freaks living off the fat of other people's labours with a free pass through the shitty parts of life. Show me a liberal and I'll show you a moral hanger-on."

You could see by the sparkle in his eyes that Sinclair was in his element. He had spent his entire career working audiences and had mastered all the little pauses and mannerisms that make words come alive. He started his address seated, but somewhere, just after he had abandoned his notes, he had risen, almost unnoticed, to his feet and was now looking down on those who were to decide his fate. He took a theatrical sip of water to allow the audience time to look forward to more. Then, as his expression changed from a look confident of appreciation for what had been said to a more uncertain gaze towards some distant horizon, he proceeded.

"Well, I've told what I think the Party should *not* be doing. Let me come to what I think it should be doing. In all its doings it must never lose sight of the fact that it's there for one reason and for one reason only, and that is to look after the interests of the working class people of this country. I said 'this country', and I say it with no sense of shame. I believe in international cooperation – that goes without saying. Where the interests of the working people of this country are served by cooperating with the workers from other countries, I'm all for it. But if there is a conflict of interests I'm damned if I'm going to sacrifice the people I have been elected to represent for some great act of ideological showmanship. People have called me a Marxist. If by that they mean I share some of Marx's view on the nature of class conflict, then I accept the title. But if they mean I think 'Das Kapital' is a kind of Bible and that a true Marxist must follow its teachings like a true Christian follows the Bible, then I'm not your man. I do think that the history of the world is the history of class conflict, but I think that Marx underestimated the resilience of capitalism and its ability to adapt. The crude takeover of the means of production by the state wasn't a success – we saw that in Russia and to a lesser extent even here in

357

Britain. That doesn't mean that it would never be a success, but it needs to be done in a much more subtle way. Capitalism is only an evil to the extent that it gets in the way of history's advance towards socialism. But let's not forget, it was a positive force in its day; it took history forward and raised us out of feudalism. A true socialist programme does not require the full-scale abandonment of capitalism. That's a misunderstanding of the Marxist dialectic. What it needs to do is to select and retain all the sophisticated mechanisms that capitalism has evolved to run an economy and surgically transplant them into the new socialist heart. That would be true synthesis, that would be the authentic resolution of the Marxist dialectic and that is the work I'd be happy to spend the rest of my political life trying to advance."

He sat down with the air of a man bravely shouldering a great burden and scoured the faces around the table for signs of intellectual comradeship. Nathan Roberts got in first, banging the table in appreciation for what he described as 'a brilliant exposition of the socialist rationale'. Max Fischer was also appreciative. He commended Sinclair for not shying away like so many socialist MPs from the deeper questions of political theory – a *breath of fresh air in an empirical fog*. This was too much for the departing MP who was in no doubt that he was being got at.

"What I'd like George here to tell me is, when you strip away all this fancy waffle, what are you left with? I've had to listen to this kind of guff all my life, and I tell you one thing: I'm not going to saddle the House with another windbag. God knows, the last thing that place needs is more hot air. It's already up in the clouds with the stuff."

This produced a sarcastic chuckle from Sinclair, but before he could follow up, the Chairman came in with a more placatory rephrasing of the question. It was to the Chairman that he directed his reply.

"The first thing I would do would be to introduce a law making it mandatory for all companies to have equal representation of workers and shareholders on their boards. I would also tackle the problem of unfair competition. Cheap labour, sometimes amounting to slave labour, in many third world countries is stealing the jobs and depressing the wages of our workers and at the same time lining the pockets of capitalists, and not all foreign, many from this country as well. That's the kind of internationalism that must be challenged. Thirdly, I would replace personal tax with family tax. Too many mothers are being forced into work when they would rather be at home raising their children. This is pure daft, particularly when we are constantly being warned of the threat of technology to jobs in the whole of the Western World. I'm sceptical myself about this – political economists will do anything to get themselves in the limelight – but if there is to be a significant increase in the levels of unemployment, would it not make more sense to deal with it in a sensible way, a way that puts family life first? I will be campaigning for a doubling of the individual tax allowance for married couples and a rise in the threshold before they enter higher tax bands."

His face struggled to maintain an expression of a suppressed modesty. That Reggie's challenge had been well met was apparent to all, all that is except Margaret Millership who had not taken at all kindly to the final point. She got out what she intended as an opening salvo in the form of an accusatory inquiry as to the seriousness with which Mr Sinclair held this patronising view of women. Sinclair however was spared the burden of replying by the intervention of Schinski who 'was quite clear that Mr Sinclair had no intention of dictating to mothers and that, far from trying to restrict the choice open to women, he was proposing to extend them.' This was said through a friendly smile directed intermittently at the source and the target of the feminist ire. The smile however turned itself very deliberately off as Schinski's focused his gaze on his fellow jurors.

"I have another question for Mr Sinclair," he continued, "I was pleased to hear the emphasis he put on Britishness, how he would protect British jobs and look after British interests even if that meant breaking with the internationalist traditions of our Party. I fully concur, but I must say I am rather puzzled by this. Is this the same George Sinclair who condoned the killing of British soldiers in Ulster, who took positive delight in the attack on British democracy by the Brighton bombers? Is this benign figure sitting at the end of this table the same sadistic monster that wallowed in the suffering of a Conservative minister? Let me read to you what he is on record as saying.

'It was a good thing that the bomb didn't kill Tebbit and his wife. Killing would have been too good for him. Better he should have to live out his remaining years having to care for a woman confined to a wheelchair for the rest of her life.'

"This same man now proposes to go to the House of Commons and enter into civilised debate with the likes of Norman Tebbit. How can he have the gall to expect to be accepted by his opponents or indeed his colleagues in an establishment dedicated to the resolution of difference by argument and not force of arms? Of course anyone on record for describing Stalin as a maligned figure and not the monster that murdered millions of his own people is clearly at home with the wonders of double-think. I wouldn't count on the good people of Bury West being quite so comfortable with it."

This was said without even a glimpse in Sinclair's direction. You would have thought that Sinclair had been called as a mere exhibit, not someone there to be listened to. This had the effect of somehow delegitimizing the eruption of anger that ensued.

"So you've been doing a bit of muck-raking, have you, Mr Schinski? (There was a nasty stress on the word 'mister') That was a long time ago. People change; it's called getting older and wiser. I wonder you didn't dig out some of the things I said when I was at school. I've a couple of my old exercise books at home. You can look at them if you like. I'm sure you'd find a few things there to add to your collection."

Schinski turned back to him with exaggerated reluctance, the sort that is bred of distaste rather than concern.

"They would be of no interest to me, Mr Sinclair. I'm only interested in things you did and said as a political figure and as far as I know you weren't in a position to shape other men's thought and actions when you were a schoolboy. If you said a quarter of what you did about anyone other than a middle-aged, middleclass, white male you'd find yourself locked up and your career would be at an end. It would be called a 'hate-crime'. Well, parliamentary democracy doesn't work if one side treats the other with the contemptuous venom which you were not ashamed to put in the public domain."

"If you had taken the trouble to find out, you'd have seen that I have apologised for those remarks. I was wrong to say what I said and if Tebbit was here in this room I'd offer him an unqualified apology"

"So that makes it all right, does it? And no doubt you'd turn the tables on him and call him a moral pariah if he refused to accept that apology? What about throwing in a bit of penance? You could show how really sorry you are by doing something to put things right."

Sinclair looked genuinely puzzled.

"You could do what old-fashioned people used to do when they fouled up. You could resign. And think what a glorious resignation it would be – the first resignation ever that predated appointment. You could walk with your head upright out into the snow. You'd be right up there with Captain Oates."

Sinclair got back to his feet. His fists were clenched but they remained for the moment under constraint by his side. Eyes blazing, he turned to the Chairman.

"I will not be sneered at, Trevor. I've come here in good faith. I thought this committee was a serious body concerned with the future direction of the Party, not some crackpot historical research unit. But what do I get? I get this clown raking up things that belong in the past. Surely it's what I am and who I am here and now that you should be focusing on."

The Chairman had been taken unawares by Schinski's onslaught and was keenly aware of his failure to keep the meeting under control.

"You're quite right, Mr Sinclair. That's exactly what we're here for and I can assure you that you will be judged according on your record as a whole and not on a few ill-chosen remarks that you now quite clearly bitterly regret. Please be kind enough now to leave us to our deliberations."

Sinclair gathered his unused papers and left the room with the air less of a man about to be judged than of a juror in need of further persuasion.

Chapter 64

Trevor Windsor's many years of experience of chairing meetings had taught him the value of procedural punctuation. There are times when commas are required, short pauses to let a point sink home, or indeed full stops allowing greater time for mental digestion. Then there are situations which are best left in the air so that nothing has the opportunity to come crashing to the ground. His chairman's antennae told him that such a need had arisen here. He would dearly have liked to wind up the chapter. But unfortunately this was not an option open to him; all he could do was to end the paragraph and make as fresh a restart as the short interval would permit. He desperately needed a cigarette and he knew that Fischer would be dying for a puff on his pipe. The meeting would reconvene in twenty minutes.

Keen to avoid any suggestion of a conspiracy, which would inevitably arise if he was seen in a huddle with any of the other members, Schinski took himself off for a breath of air. The last thing he wanted was to encourage hard borders to spring up within the group. People have a strong herd instinct and fear isolation if left out of a faction. Schinski knew that Nathan Roberts was the only member that it would be impossible to recruit. The others could go either way and he mustn't give any of them the feeling that there was a plot afoot to manipulate them.

He had scoured the faces as he was delivering his diatribe against Sinclair. The findings were disappointing. What had made him think that they would be totally outraged at his revelations? He should have known better. The Party has always had strong antimilitary instincts. When it thought of the army it saw public schoolboys in officer uniforms, the other ranks as soulless, subservient lackeys that hadn't the wit to espouse the socialist cause. Anything connected with the British imperial past was a red rag to the bull of shame and self-loathing, and right at the top of the list was Ireland. Cromwell, you'd have thought, would be the darling of any antiroyalist, pro-people's movement, but no, the very mention of his name in the hearing of leftists is guaranteed to produce a venomous reaction. How could the socialist conscience forget the atrocities he committed against the Catholic Irish in 1649? By the same token, the Ulster Protestants, planted there centuries ago, were still looked upon as quislings of the British and undeserving of inclusion in the loop of any serious political manoeuvrings; there was a feeling, barely suppressed, that they could always do the decent thing and go back to where they belonged – three or four centuries ago. Schinski took little interest in Irish affairs but he was always bemused when he heard this line being trotted out by *Irish* Americans, the very people whose ancestors had supplanted the 'Native Americans' – it flashed across his mind every time he was tempted to think that politics had anything to do with rationality. Still, he had hoped for more outrage at the sheer viciousness of what Sinclair had said. He had three votes in the bag, his own, Reggie's and Freddie's. He only needed another two. It wasn't going to be easy though. Snoddy had done himself no favours. It is one thing to present yourself as a reforming prophet, but quite another to act like a new Messiah.

When the meeting reconvened the hiatus had worked its wonders; it was as if the diners had processed the heavy meal and were ready to eat again. Trevor Windsor opened proceedings with a short, cheerful speech that passed the raw experience they had just shared through a prism of sober recollection and expressed every confidence in the wisdom that *this band of veterans* would bring to their judgement. Each 'veteran' in turn was invited to share their take on what had transpired.

Margaret Millership, being the only lady present, was given

the first slot. She was very uncomfortable with Snoddy's views on human rights. The Party had a proud history of promoting the cause of human rights both at home and abroad. If these were eroded in any way, women would be the first to suffer. How could we criticise the way women are treated in certain parts of the world if we say that it's all just a matter for each individual society to decide? She wasn't happy with Sinclair's notion of treating the family rather than the individual as a taxable entity. It was all very well saying that this would give women more choice, but the realty was that it would put women back to where they were in the nineteen-fifties, locked in the nursery and the kitchen. Any final choice she would make between these two candidates would be on the basis of the lesser of two evils.

Johnnie Taylor, who had said little to nothing throughout the interviews, was next. He shared the previous speaker's concerns and was more than a little annoyed about the Snoddy's strong attack on the Party's record. While some valid points were made, the tone had left a lot to be desired. As for what Sinclair had said, he was quite simply appalled. Up to that point he had been quite sympathetic to Sinclair's candidacy, but he was not at all sure that such vicious sentiments were fitting for a would-be parliamentarian. Against that of course the comments were made a very long time ago. He hadn't made up his mind yet. He was keen to hear what the others had to say.

Freddie Douglas defended Snoddy's criticism of the Party. Yes-men were two-a-penny, he proclaimed. He was impressed by what Snoddy had to say about the Party being Labour in name only. He was greatly taken by the description of it as the Liberal Party in brown overalls. He agreed with Snoddy that it was high time for socialism to get back to its roots and get some honest oil and dirt on them. But it would be a mistake to see those roots as Marxist. He recalled the old adage of Harold Wilson that the Party owed more to Methodism than to Marxism. If George Sinclair had his way he would take the country back to the horrors of the sixties and seventies. Sinclair talked as if he had learned the lessons of state monopoly, but he for one wasn't buying it. For him the choice was clear: it had to be Snoddy.

The Honorary Secretary took the next slot. It wasn't clear whether it was his turn or not, but his indignation had clearly reached a level that demanded an urgent outlet.

"How can any member of this panel seriously think that Robert Snoddy has a smidgeon of socialism in his veins? He seems intent on destroying everything that we socialists hold dear. He has demonstrated that he has no compassion for the poor; he dismisses the benefits system as mollycoddling; he thinks state education should be more elitist and his idea of prison reform seems to be to murder the prisoners and call it justice. I'm sorry, but I don't think we should even be discussing this. The man's a fascist."

As he spoke he had half risen from his chair and when he finished, ostensibly exhausted by the emotional storm that had come upon him, he fell back into it, his eyes darting this way and that as if in search of something that would offer him a foothold out of his desperation. The dramatic effect was totally wrecked by a loud burst of affected laughter from Max Fischer.

"Forgive me, *mein lieber Hugh*, but you remind me terribly of one of my little grandsons. His mother took his favourite teddy bear from him. The thing had got quite filthy and was sorely in need of laundering. But all the little mite could think of was that it wouldn't be there for him to cuddle in bed that night."

There was bad blood between the two men. No one was sure how far it went back. But Savage was generally looked on as the injured party. Everyone was slightly afraid of this clever German who used words they were uncomfortable with and sentences that asked too much of their attention span. Most bystanders had the feeling that there but for the grace of God would go they. It was not an intervention that Schinski particularly welcomed.

Fischer was inevitably going to be too sadistic in his criticism.

He was not wrong. Fischer slalomed between scathing and offensive as he tore into the inability of *certain sections of the British Labour Party* to get *their tiny brain cells* around ideas that didn't come with pictorial illustrations. He himself had no problem with illustrations as such – just as he had no problem with people needing glasses or hearing aids – but he did have a problem when the illustration took over from the idea. And that was exactly what was happening here, he said.

"Press any button bearing the label – National Health Service, unemployment benefit, comprehensive education, prison reform, race relations – and you get an instant witch hunt for any hints of dissent. Every adjective, every verb, every noun is passed through the scanner and, irrespective of their context in the sentence, declared clean or unclean. Any trace of contamination and you're out. That is no way to conduct debate. That's the PR politics of Blair and Cameron. Snoddy is quite right to take us to a higher level."

Savage gave every appearance of being engaged in some kind of mental haka as slowly and deliberately he rose to his feet. His mouth contorted and his eyes flashed, but then, at what looked to be the eleventh hour, he turned square-on to the Chairman and appealed for a ruling on *the inappropriateness of this highly personal and overbearing attitude that Herr Fischer had introduced into the proceedings.* As the hapless Chairman, clearly anxious to elude the glare of expectancy that was bearing down on him, struggled to choose what line of response to take, Schinski intervened.

"Come now, Hugh. I know it may have sounded a bit over the top, but I'm sure Max here was not being personal. We all know Max. Max is a purist when it comes to ideas. He sees them like the rest of us ordinary mortals see people. When he comes across an idea being abused or ignored, he steps in to rescue it. He might not look like it, but Max is the nearest thing we have around this table to a noble knight. He feels it behoves him to rescue ideas in distress. I can assure you, Hugh, he does not see you as the dragon any more than he sees any of the rest of us as dragons; we are all just people who have the irritating habit of preventing him from getting at the dragon. We've all been there."

The speaker's good–natured smile got a more welcome response from Fischer than from Savage, although even he allowed a hint of sun to peep through the clouds.

"But let's get back to the business at hand. I'm inclined to agree with you Hugh that our Mr Snoddy is a bit of a maverick. And I can understand why you say he's not a proper socialist. I wouldn't go quite that far myself. I think he has a point when he says that the working-classes are being taken for a ride by the liberal establishment. The middle-classes indulge their noble thoughts from the comfort of their leafy suburbs and leave it to the plebs to deal with the fall-out. They get the glamour and excitement of riding the stallions in the big arenas, while the simple stable lads are left to muck out the stables. I think any socialist party worthy of the name would want to endorse that scenario. Maybe Snoddy has a point when he tells us we have been just a bit too keen on the grandstanding and a little too reluctant to get our hands dirty.

"I'm must say, I was finding it very difficult to decide who to cast my vote for. George Sinclair has a fine record of standing up for the interests of the working class. As a trade union leader myself I can appreciate the work he has done. When you think about it, (*This was directed back at Savage.*) he seems to be just as critical as Snoddy of the direction the Party has taken in recent years. But he couches his criticism in more familiar terms. Perhaps that's why we are not doubting *his* socialist credentials? (*Another glance in Savage's direction*) I thought he cut an impressive figure, but then I stumbled on the material I put before you earlier. I can't tell you how disappointed I was. That simply did it for me. I know ... I know he was a younger man when he said those things. An older, wiser man wouldn't have allowed himself to put stuff as crass as that on record. I don't doubt for a moment that he bitterly regrets saying what he said. But what I do doubt is whether he regrets thinking what he thought. I for one would not want anyone like that to be associated in the public mind with our Party, let alone our constituency."

Before he sat down he directed a final word to Nathan Roberts.

"I know one person in this Panel who will be even more disappointed than me. (*Eyes on Nathan Roberts*) Nathan has been a great backer of George Sinclair, and for all the right reasons. Both men are on the left of the Party and I'm sure, Nathan, you acted in good faith. I know you as a man of good instincts whose only interest in politics is to promote the cause of socialism as you see it. But I would ask you to consider whether that cause would be well served if we were to nominate a candidate who has made himself so vulnerable to what could easily become a press witch hunt? Would you really want to risk the entire left wing of the Party being tarred with the same brush?"

Roberts could see that he was being offered an honourable defeat. He could accept it with his judgement unsullied and live to use it another day or he could try to change the topography of the battlefield. He decided on the latter. He thanked Schinski for his *wise words of caution*, but there were times, he said, when wisdom and caution were a toxic mix. There was a new wave of militancy building up in the country. The younger generation were sick of caution; they wanted action and if they couldn't get it in Parliament they'd get it on the streets. They were crying out for the kind of leadership George Sinclair could give them. George was not one to weigh his words in grams. What he had said had been out of order, okay, but what did the voters, particularly young voters, want – a smooth charlatan like Tony Blair or

David Cameron or a man with fire in his belly and convictions that were shaped by his conscience?

It was a fine response and well delivered, too well for Schinski's liking. However it was not the final word. That was the prerogative of the departing MP prior to the matter being put to the vote. As Reggie rose to speak, Roberts, in a great show of nostalgic affection, reminded him playfully of his own youthful militancy, recalling an incident when the venerable member had been arrested for his part in an anti-government demonstration that had got out of hand. This achieved its intended purpose of undermining the main thrust of what the grand old warrior was about to say and gave a decidedly hollow ring to the warning he delivered of the dangers of electing someone lacking in respect for the primacy of Parliament and the integrity of political opponents. The speech did end however on a sterling note as he recalled his rugby playing days when he would 'kick the shit out' of the opposition on the pitch but be quite happy to share a pint and a yarn with them in the clubhouse afterwards.

The vote was called. It was a close-run thing. There were two abstentions, from Windsor and Taylor. The former took the view that in these circumstances it behoved the chairman to abstain. Taylor said nothing, but it was more than likely that he did not relish committing himself to a side when it was so unclear which way the wind was blowing. Max Fischer however did come on board and Snoddy sneaked through by four votes to three.

Chapter 65

After a night of disturbed sleep racked by images and imaginings coming at her through the prism of the storm raging in her head Lizzie woke up in a state of exhaustion. Justin had made an early start and was long gone by the time she had dragged herself to the bathroom and got her day underway. A little voice kept whispering to her that skipping school would be no wrong thing: the feelings she wanted to work through and the thoughts that needed forging into workable shapes surely had a higher priority than the relentless call to humdrum duties. Obligation however, once it takes hold and establishes itself as a full-blown sense, is a taskmaster that has a way of coating its demands in faith and love. She felt ignoble at even giving headroom to the thought of playing truant. Anyway, a day amidst the buzz of creatures revelling in their youth, blissful in their ignorance of the burdens of adulthood, might be just what the doctor ordered.

Her brain operated at stand-by setting as she went through the mechanical procedures of preparing breakfast – kettle on, dishes out, cutlery from drawer, milk from fridge, fruit from bowl. It was only as she was placing the cereal on the table that she noticed the presence of a large brown envelope. But she hadn't collected the post? It wouldn't have arrived yet. Then she remembered. It must be part of the other day's post. In her preoccupation with Joseph's *suicide note* she had forgotten altogether about the other envelope – this thick, slightly dog-eared one. She picked it up. It had the same message in the same green ink *Not known at this address* with the accompanying, *Try number 37* scrawled across it. She tore it open. There were between thirty and forty A4 pages, all handwritten in blocks of text with a date in the right hand corner of the space between them. It was a diary of some sort. Stuck to the top page was a post-it note. The handwriting was even more difficult than the slightly more carefully worked script of the diary. It said simply, 'These are some thoughts I've been having that you might care to read.' Lizzie started into the top page, before realising that chronologically they were in reverse order. She must start at the bottom.

It took her just over half an hour to work her way through the thirty-seven pages. It wasn't really a diary of events; it was more a chronicle of thought sequences with references to the events that inspired them. The chronicle began with some general musings on the criminal justice system and how undeserving it was of the dignity it bestowed on itself. Bitter comparisons were made with the pomp of deans and bishops wallowing in their 'institutionalised narcissism'. The Promethean notion of seizing justice back and putting it in the hands of the people was described as a 'Reformation for our time'. But the question loomed: 'Would the people be up to the job?' He started from the moral premise that it behoved anyone who believed in the justice of punishment that fitted the crime to be prepared to carry out the punishment themselves and not ask others to do the dirty work for them. He was committed to the philosophical notion of dialectic based on the synthesis of contradiction. The anger that inspired the desire for punishment received its legitimacy from the compassion felt for the victim. The negative and the positive must be fused together and the bond maintained. If either got isolated from the other, the result would be either brutality on the anger side or some form of moral sentimentality if compassion was given its head. In either case justice would be the loser. Numerous examples were cited of the post-war collapse of the synthesis, the Holocaust and the Soviet purges having produced almost universal horror of the very notion of punishment, giving birth to the conviction that all would be well if only we could get our wishing for it right.

All this ground was covered in the prose of rational calm, but as he went on to describe his difficulties in putting theory into practice when tasked with the distasteful business of flogging, the language changed; the sentences became more disjointed, there was a heavy reliance on adjectives that were obviously not quite hitting the mark. Snoddy, who had earlier been cited as a mentor, morphed into a thorn to his conscience. When he broke down at the first flogging before even having dealt the initial blow Snoddy had not been openly angry with him, but Lizzie could see that that didn't help, if anything it made it worse – Snoddy simply left him to drown in his own poor opinion of himself. It seemed however to have the desired effect. When he gathered himself together for a second go a couple of weeks later, he did complete all twenty lashes. He was physically sick afterwards, but Snoddy lauded his achievement. It was exactly what he had hoped for, he said: *the triumph of the will-to-justice operating in full view of the gaze of compassion.* He, Joseph Ross, had set an example and opened the way for all decent, justice-loving people to follow. The entries that followed showed that Joseph had taken great comfort from this, but his doubts persisted. He had no confidence that he would ever be able to repeat the *triumph.* He saw it as being like one of those tests conducted under lab conditions that establishes the feasibility of an outcome, but gives no guarantee of it being replicated in real life. Snoddy's response to Joseph's doubts did little to boost his sense of self-worth. It amounted to: 'If someone as weak and effeminate as you can do it, then anyone can.' The actual words that Snoddy used were doubtlessly less stark, but that was the meaning that Joseph was left with.

It was at this point that Justin's name came up in the journal. There was one paragraph in which Joseph offered his thoughts on the new man. He gave him an alpha double minus for brain power, admiring above all his *resistance to irrelevancies* and avoidance of *over-zealousness with detail*. This was a sore point for Joseph; he saw it as the pride of bourgeois intellect, but a barrier in the path to wisdom – hence the miserable malfunctioning of most of the professions. He also expressed a liking for Justin's preference for Anglo-Saxon English in discussion – ... *not one of those bloody idiots who talk in puffs of smoke*. The most telling passage however came in the form of a confession.

"It's daft I know, but I find myself thinking about Justin nearly all of the time. When he's not there I imagine how different things would be if he were. And I think of the future and how full it would be if I could count on him being a constant presence in it."

Lizzie recognised this immediately; it was exactly the way she herself felt about Justin. Poor old Joseph – he didn't realise he was in love. But it probably wouldn't have helped him if he had put that label on it. It might have made things worse if anything.

The events leading up to the mock trial and execution were described in great detail. Snoddy's tough-love approach continued to exacerbate Joseph's feeling of self-loathing. It was a double whammy: he loathed himself for not overcoming what he loathed about himself and the fact that Snoddy saw him as a test case magnified his failure and undermined his entire moral identity. He wondered if his brain was just a kind of gaming machine, of use for nothing more serious than distraction and entertainment. That's where Justin came in. He showed the way. He was the conduit between the world of cyber men and cyber causes and a reality where notions of what should be could live and thrive alongside feelings and emotions that were firmly anchored in flesh and blood. He had not a moment's doubt about the rightness of executing Dwayne Rodgers, a monster who took pleasure in torture and murder and whom the law in its self-absorption was prepared to let go unpunished. With Justin there to support him he was able to move from belief to faith and do the deed. It hadn't been easy – once again he had been violently sick – but he knew he had acted like a man. He had been neither a weakling nor a monster and he understood what Snoddy had been telling him all along about the importance of feeling pain at committing an act that in physical terms was so close to the brutal deed that had inspired it. Being right did not spare him from the dirks of conscience – the blows they rained on him were the price he must pay if he was to hang on to his humanity.

The visit of Inspector Stranaghan was described in equal detail. He gave a lengthy summary of the confession he had made and his feelings as he waited for the car to arrive and take him into custody. There was relief certainly when he later learned that Stranaghan never had any intention of arresting him and had extracted the confession just to put pressure on Snoddy. But there was still Justin's betrayal. That's what really knocked the stuffing out of him. The revelation that Snoddy and Justin hadn't in fact set him up and that the whole business of the trial and execution had been staged had come too late. He had been forced into seeing things from a disturbing angle and the horror stuck. All the efforts he had made to tame his mental demons had been for nothing. He had fought so hard to make *his word become flesh* only to find he hadn't made the transition out into full-blown reality at all. Even if Justin hadn't set him up or even instigated the charade, he wasn't the man he had taken him for, the trust he had put in him was tainted by the unreality of what they went through together. He needed to get out of Oxford and get away from all this empty mental stuff. He had been wrong to rely on other people to get him out of his head; he needed to do that himself. Something was urging him to get back to immerse himself in the sap of Nature. That particular paragraph ended with a quote from Wordsworth; he needed, he said, to rediscover:

> 'An appetite; a feeling and a love,
> That had no need of a remoter charm,
> By thought supplied, nor any interest
> Unborrowed from the eye.'

The pages that followed were full of the relief of the calm he experienced at first at the garden centre and then subsequently under the tutelage of the Reverend John. At the Reverend's suggestion he had read *War and Peace*. It had a profound effect and was a great inspiration to him. The great spirituality of the depictions of *Prince Andrei's* dying days touched his soul. In *Pierre Bezukhov* he saw a kindred spirit, a fellow seeker after truth who, like himself, had resolved to take a life in the name of justice. What made the deepest impression on Joseph was the encounter the aristocratic Pierre had in prison with the humble peasant *Platon Karataev*. This simple man taught the great intellectual not to allow his perception of the world to be choked in chains of finality, but rather to live in the moment and experience life in its all its *now-ness*. Following these revelations Joseph took to dabbling in yoga and immersing himself in the writings of Lau Tzu. The enthusiasm with which he embraced the new insights came across in the much more relaxed style of his prose; little observations took over from sweeping pronouncements, the sentences shorted noticeably, rarely containing more than a stray subordinate clause, the vocabulary became more tactile with scanter sprinklings of '-ations' and '-isms'.

But it was a case of calm before the storm. Justin's visit brutally uprooted all the tender plants that the Reverend John had helped him sow. He fell back into the perception that he thought Justin and Snoddy, the two most significant people in his life, had of him. All the things that had helped him recover were cast aside as make-believe, *pathetic mental pros-theses for an emotional inadequate.* The diary ended in a very dark place. There was no actual statement of intent to take his own life, but little reading was required between the lines.

Chapter 66

As she got to the end of Joseph's diary Lizzie's eyes welled up. There was no longer any question now of her going to school. She phoned through to the headmistress' secretary claiming a valiant defeat in a battle with a splitting headache. She then poured herself another coffee and sat for a good half hour staring vacantly at the breakfast debris on the table before her. Her mind kept circling over what she had just read, scouring the ground for somewhere to land and be busy with.

Joseph had been the victim of Snoddy's hopelessly unrealistic expectations of humanity. Snoddy wanted ordinary human beings to love the good and hate the bad and not let either emotion intrude on the territory of the other. He despised Christianity for its surrender to softness and its refusal to stand firm against evil. Emotional ostriches, that's what he used to call believers; the Church of England was the RSPSS, the Royal Society for the Protection of Sensitive Souls. And he'd laugh. She remembered that laugh, it was a cruel laugh. When they first got together she was excited by the mix of testosterone and high intelligence he embodied. He was never dull. He always seemed to be engaging with issues that the slumbering world was oblivious to. Ideas would come off him like electric flares. At the beginning it was the high voltage current that provided the frisson; she wasn't terribly bothered about *what* the ideas were; it was *how* they were – bright and new and fulminating with energy. It was only when the falling-in-love phase was over that she began to consider them for what they were. She had no problem with his political analysis; things needed to change, and society could do worse than move some way at least along the lines he was advocating. It wasn't the direction, it was the destination that she took issue with. Taking things from where they were all the way to where he wanted them was too big an ask for the human will over the human disposition. Snoddy wanted to de-infantilise society and turn it into something run by and run for what he called grown-ups, who for him were people who had come to the awareness that life is morally neutral and not in the pay of anthropomorphic fantasies. Society can take only so much moral sugar, he would say, but if too big a dollop is forced down its throat an allergic reaction will set in and the entire brew will be spewed up. A decadent society always ends up betraying the things it holds dearest. The only way to stop the slide is for us all to learn to live in the force field between the poles, softness and hardness, pity and retribution. That's what being grown-up is all about... How often had she heard him say that? It was a fascinating thought, but not a practical one, a philosophy for supermen perhaps, but not something for mere mortals. Certainly, it wouldn't be unreasonable to try to nudge society in that direction, slowly, bit by bit, without expecting too much – there is safety in numbers; if the crowd could be inched forward, the leap required of the will to bring the 'is' to the 'should-be' would become increasingly realistic – but to put pressure on men like Joseph to step outside the collective conscience and act in moral isolation, that was nothing short of criminal.

But she was still circling. Where was she to land? She looked at the diary. It was primarily a chronicle of thoughts and impressions, but it did cover events too, not least an account of the floggings that Joseph had been induced to take part in as well as that infamous execution. Snoddy's involvement in these events was evident. What would Labour Party headquarters make of that? Would they really want anything to do with a candidate who not only went about organising floggings but staged the mock execution of a man who – purely coincidently? – turned up dead a few hours later? She could show it to that policeman,

Myles. He'd know what to do with it. But she needed to be sure that there was nothing in it that would compromise Justin. The flogging, yes, but surely that would already be in his reports. If you're working undercover you have to be granted some latitude. You have to be convincing, after all. The big thing was the *coincidence* of Rodgers' body turning up just after they had simulated his execution. That's what they were so desperate for Joseph not to put down in writing. And here it was in black and white. Snoddy would have some explaining to do.

The thing that would really get Snoddy was if they could prove that he had allowed Stranaghan to decide who Rodger's murder should be pinned on. There was of course nothing about that in the journal since Joseph had no knowledge of it. But the phoney confession Stranaghan had got Joseph to write, there was plenty about that. How was Stranaghan going to explain that away? He could hardly pretend he just forgot to mention it, could he? If the pressure came on, the truth might well come out and then all hell would be let loose. Yes, she could a lot of damage with this document. Rob Snoddy was going to pay for what he'd done to Joseph.

Chapter 67

Myles was more than a little surprised to get a call from Lizzie Partridge. He had left a card with her, but hadn't entertained any real hopes of her using it. The two met at her request at The Parson's Rest, a quiet pub by the river. The weather was clement and they were able to sit out and catch the flavour of the day. Myles ordered a coffee, but Lizzie had a gin and tonic which she sank in as little as two or three visits to the glass before ordering a second. Myles was inclined to put this down to the grief she was obviously feeling at the death of her friend, but he quickly revised his view; nervous tension was what was at work.

She began the confab seeking an assurance from the policeman that nothing she said to him would be used against Justin. She had come here to provide him with material that could put *that cold bastard Snoddy* away, but she didn't want it used against Justin. He had done nothing illegal, he had made mistakes certainly, but she didn't want him being crucified for them. Inspector Stranaghan should never have put an inexperienced officer like Justin – he wasn't even qualified at the time – on such a difficult case. It was asking too much. She came out with all this in a flurry of words. It was as if she was trying to make things right by declaring them right. Myles tried to be reassuring while making the obvious point that he could hardly give an assurance before he knew what it was she was going to tell him. This seemed to cause her a problem. She stopped for a moment and thought before seemingly giving herself the go-ahead to continue. She followed through with a long and detailed account of the contents of Joseph's diary, interspersed with repeated visits to the chorus theme of Snoddy's heartlessness in pushing Joseph to his limits. Her tone became much more cautious when she came to the confession Inspector Stranaghan had extracted from Joseph. It was clear she had doubts about the preparedness of this detective inspector to act against the other, his former boss at that. Myles did his best to reassure her, but he did feel the pain of the sore point she had hit and wondered if he had made too light of it to convince. He heard himself declare that all personal considerations would be cast aside and he would do his job by the book. If Inspector Stranaghan had crossed the line he would have to answer to the courts. Lizzie looked at him full in the face. Those who knew her would have recognised the look; credibility nearly always depended less for her on what was being said than who was doing the saying. Perhaps it was the slight hint of pain in Myles' voice that convinced her – for most sharp-witted people the smoothness of the salesman only serves to belie the grainy texture of truth. Whatever the cause of her reassurance, she proceeded to confide the whole story of Stranaghan's encounter with Snoddy and the choice he had been pressurised into making. It made difficult listening for Myles, not because of the revelation – the facts were already known to him – but because there was now someone other than Stuart Stranaghan who knew that he knew. He had lost his authority over the story and now the reins were in her hands.

Before Lizzie handed the document over she repeated her demand for assurances that no charges would be brought against Justin. This time Myles could afford sincerity. He told her that she had done a good thing for her partner. Up until now he had been harbouring suspicions about Justin's part in Joseph's death. The journal made it perfectly clear that the unfortunate Joseph had taken his own life. The person who would bear the brunt of the follow-up would be Inspector Stranaghan; he was the senior officer and he would have to explain why he acted as he did in regard to Joseph's so-called confession. That in turn could put a lot of pressure on Snoddy and might possibly lead to his arrest and conviction for murder.

This was what Lizzie had come to hear. She was not one of life's doers and she had strayed a long way from the tracks of her normal mindset to do this thing. The further she had strayed, the stronger grew the feeling of uncertainty. Doubt that she might be compromising Justin kept popping up in the shadows behind the back of the pity she felt for Joseph and her anger at Snoddy. She had come to Myles the way people in dread of some terrible happening come to a priest, when need to believe trumps reason to believe. What Myles had told her was in no way unreasonable, but it did not account for the warm glow of faith she felt as she made her way home.

Myles left the pub with very different feelings. He had not mentioned the fact to Lizzie, but just a couple of hours before meeting her he had talked with Justin. Justin had called him. They had met, curiously enough, at the same pub. It must have been the couple's special place. Justin had been very forthcoming. He admitted that it was only after the whole thing was over that he discovered that the firing squad scene hadn't been for real and that they had only being firing blanks. At the time he thought they'd been using real bullets. It was clear to him that the law had failed in its duty to Francis Brown and he had been brought to feel an obligation to fill the void. Any other response to the opportunity that presented itself would have been a copout. He had no regrets; he would do the same again. He also volunteered an account of his meeting with Stranaghan at the murder scene. They were both sure at the time that Snoddy had sent him there for Stranaghan to find. It also lent considerable credibility to the ultimatum Snoddy subsequently presented to Stranaghan, the so-called Barabbas Choice. He owed a debt to Stranaghan that he could never repay for doing what he did for him. He begged Myles not to punish him for having been man enough to look out for his junior officer. The man had already paid the price with his career. He had no real need to resign; he could have spared himself that. He acted on principle. He had too much respect for the office to continue in it when he knew he had betrayed it. Why add further pain? A lesser man would have carried on as if nothing had happened. Myles himself had served under Stranaghan. Had he ever had a better governor, one with a deeper sense of duty to his men? When Myles asked him how he felt about two men serving long prison sentences for a crime they didn't commit, while the real culprit was standing for Parliament, Justin threw up his hands in a gesture of despair: Surely he must see that that was the whole point; Snoddy was trying to get into Parliament with the express purpose of changing the law so that no one would ever again be forced to go it alone and make the justice happen that the system actually preened itself on its failure to produce.

Justin was finding it hard going; he struggled to gauge the reaction he was getting from the Inspector. On the one hand he seemed to offer little by way of passionate objection to the points Justin was making, but there were precious few signs of sympathetic understanding either. Forced to the conclusion that it was all water off a duck's back, he changed tack. He didn't turn nasty and hurl accusations. He simply stood up and declared in a hardened voice, though one not devoid of warmth, that these revelations had been made in a collegiate spirit, but the Inspector should be in no doubt that he would deny ever having made them; he should expect no further cooperation from him.

Chapter 68

The strength that Myles had shown in resisting Justin's entreaties had been largely show. He was by no means immune to the arrows that Justin had unleashed but he had kept up a front of impervious self-belief. Beneath the facade bubbled a wobbly mass of uncertainty and indecision. He'd welcomed the move from monologue to dialogue; it had lifted his doubts out of the dark depths into fresher air.

Two things had changed following his interviews with Justin Wright and Lizzie Partridge. He was now in no doubt that Joseph Ross had taken his own life and that he was wrong to have suspected foul play. The account Wright had given him of his meeting with Stranaghan at the murder scene tallied exactly with Stuart's version of events and made perfect sense of what had subsequently transpired, the confession Stuart had extracted from Ross and the infamous Barabbas Choice Snoddy had offered him. It did not prove it, but he was now pretty certain that Wright had not murdered Rodgers either as part of the firing squad or later at the barn where the body was found.

The second new element was of course the diary. It was limited in its scope, but it did offer a written record of the confession and it did confirm that it was Rodgers who was on trial at the mock proceedings. This threw up a question that Stuart and Wright would be hard put to answer without compromising themselves: why there was no mention of either of these facts in their reports. His next step was clear: He should interview each of them, under caution this time, and then submit their responses along with his report to his superiors. It would then be for them to decide how to proceed.

There was an alternative; he could drop the whole thing.

Strictly speaking, his brief was simply to investigate any possible wrong-doing by Wright. It would be perfectly reasonable for him to say that he had found no evidence to suggest that Wright had done anything other than what was required of him to gain credibility as a member of the gang. He had discovered that Snoddy had tried to compromise him and that Inspector Stranaghan had taken the wise decision to pull him from the case. There was little doubt that Snoddy was up to his neck in murky dealings, but Stranaghan had always known this. That was after all the reason he had set up the undercover operation in the first place. But it had failed to come up with any evidence, it wasn't going anywhere and he was right to call a halt when he did. All of this was perfectly true. There would be no need for him to lie and Stuart would not be punished for standing by one of his men. On the other hand valuable, albeit not conclusive evidence against Snoddy would be kept covered up and two innocent men would continue to rot in jail.

He remained stuck in the doldrums of indecision for what seemed an eternity. He could imagine both outcomes and how he was going to feel if he made them happen. Each was just an avoidance of the pain the other would bring. The final outcome was one thing; the *next step* was another. Here there was a clear leader. It would be relatively easy for him to write a vacuous report; it would be just something between him and the page. He need take no notice of the party for whom it would be written, for he, whoever he was, wouldn't be in the room. At the very least there would be a decent time lag before he got to read it, at best he may never even get sight of it. A formal interview with Stuart on the other hand, that was a very different thing. He tried, but he simply couldn't see himself treating the man he had looked up to (and had good reason to go on looking up to) as a common criminal, subjecting him to an aggressive interrogation and picking holes in any answers that fell short of what he wanted. He simply had no stomach for that.

At times like this you look to the solid figures in your life for guidance, but for Myles that was a non-starter. It was no good asking himself what his mentor would do if he were in his shoes; he already knew the answer and that answer was precisely the issue. He thought back to the time when he had reported one of his fellow officers for using violence on a suspect. He remembered thinking at the time that he would be rewarded for doing the right thing, not in the sense of currying favour and advancing his own career, but simply by being taken into the bosom of the force and being accepted as a fully fledged member of the fraternity. It was only after he had done it that he discovered that there was no fraternity, at least not the sort he had envisaged. The force was headed by a collection of individuals whose notion of leadership went no further than using what power and authority they could muster to pursue their own agendas. High ideals did not figure in their thinking. His whistle-blowing was the last thing they had wanted; it reflected badly on the force and it made them uncomfortable to have someone in the ranks that couldn't be relied on to do the sensible thing and turn a blind eye. They took the disciplinary steps they had to take, but he was sure that on a personal level they looked more kindly on the miscreant than they did on him. He had expected the cold reaction he got from his fellow officers in the junior ranks and had braced himself to take what stick they gave him, but this moral void at the top left a deep wound. For a time he went into what was not unlike a state of mourning for the faith he had lost. It was his collaboration with Stuart Stranaghan that had pulled him out of it. Working with a man of his integrity was the antidote he needed to the institutionalised low-mindedness that had started to poison his view of policing.

These thoughts continued to circle like vultures until eventually a prey emerged from the shadows. What if he simply submitted the report warts and all, but did it now? Even with

Joseph's dairy, he had no proof of anything. All he had were awkward questions that Stuart really needed to have an answer for. Why not let the higher echelons make the decision for him? If he didn't carry out official interviews there would be nothing hard and fast to embarrass the top brass if they chose not to proceed. There was little likelihood of that, he knew, but it was the best he could do for his friend. He couldn't simply ignore his duty as a policeman. It was something vital to his sense of his self. He couldn't pick and choose when to follow it and when to pretend it wasn't there. That would make a total nonsense of it. Besides, if he ignored his conscience he would hardly be following the example Stuart had set him. Wasn't it Stuart himself who had taught him that when you acted morally you had to will that everyone faced with the same situation would act as you did? Who would want to live in a society where policemen got to decide which laws to apply? It would go against the whole notion of policing. So he would do what a policeman of his rank should do, report the facts to his superior officers and be guided by them. It wasn't exactly a heroic stance he was taking; there was cowardice in it, that he had to admit, but it was something he could live with.

Chapter 69

There were distinct edgings of urgency in Chief Superintendant Bailey's voice in the brief call, so Schinski dropped all and made his way to the café he had been directed to. He got there first and had to wait twenty minutes before the portly figure appeared. It was remarkable, Schinski thought to himself, how closely Bailey resembled those ineffectual police chiefs that every TV detective seems condemned to serve under. But he knew better than to fall for the fiction; Bailey was nobody's fool and bumbling was decidedly not what he did. He exuded impatience as Schinski went through the usual ordering rituals, making him feel like a literalist who was not getting the point of the meeting.

"I've received a report from the fellow I put on the Wright case. It looks as if that undercover operation Wright was involved in was dodgy to say the least. There was more left out of the reports of Wright and his Inspector than was put in. The two of them were up to their necks in the slimy stuff."

He went on to give the main outlines of Myles' report. When he had finished he looked across the table for a reaction. He was kept waiting. A lot of computing was clearly in progress in the Schinski brain. Finally a nod of the head and a smile of satisfaction suggested that the thinking had born fruit.

"It seems to me, George ... (He liked calling him by his Christian name – they both knew it was not an acknowledgement of friendship, more a pin to a balloon) It seems to me that you sent a man to catch a stickleback and he's come back with a big fat salmon. Wright and his boss were played by Snoddy. Okay, they broke the rules, but it was no big deal. Wright got a bit carried away, he tried, but he didn't really do anything. You can't lock somebody up for failing to do something that's against the law. As for Stranaghan, the guy was only looking out for his boy. Any good officer would've done the same, wouldn't he? (This was accompanied by a exploratory look for confirmation in Bailey's face) No, it's Snoddy that this puts in the shit."

Bailey looked doubtful.

"Not really. The only real hard evidence we've got, if you could call it that, is this diary of Ross's and it doesn't cover any of the stuff that touches directly on Snoddy. We've only got uncorroborated hearsay for the rest. We could of course put pressure on Wright and Stranaghan and get them to incriminate Snoddy. In fact I don't know why young Myles didn't just get on and do that."

"Maybe it's just as well he didn't."

Bailey looked puzzled.

"But surely if we can get to Snoddy we'd be off the hook. We wouldn't have the threat hanging over us that one day he might decide to double-cross us and leak what he knows about the Cooper business."

"Yes, but if we let this officer of yours go too far and get enough evidence to arrest him, Snoddy will have nothing to lose and he might as well just take us down with him. No, sit on the report for a while. Tell your man to hold back in the meantime and leave things to me."

Chapter 70

"You did what?"

Justin stared at Lizzie in utter disbelief. She had threatened to *get* Rob, and there had been real venom in the 'get', but he had never for a moment thought that anything as palpable as this would come of it.

"Did you not realise what this will do to me and Stuart Stranaghan and for that matter to us? Apart from anything else, how do you expect me to go on working for Matt Eardley, or more to the point, how do you think Matt Eardley will feel about having someone work for him whose wife is determined to destroy everything he and his organisation are trying to achieve?"

Lizzie was momentarily shaken by this. Evidently it was a side effect of her action she had neglected to colour in. She had been focused on the threat it might pose of criminal proceedings against Justin. She was sorry about Stranaghan; he had been a good friend to Justin, but she could live with the damage she would be doing to him; there was bound to be some collateral damage after all. She didn't see herself as an extension of Justin. She was his wife certainly, but why would any perceived fault line in her be assumed to extend to Justin? She never thought of herself as a liberated woman any more than a black American thinks of himself as a liberated slave. It was something that her whole being simply took for granted. A flush of anger passed through her at being forced back over this old ground.

"Matt Eardley doesn't employ me; it's you that works for him. Why should he expect me to live according to the company rules? And you, if *you* expect me to seek your approval before I carry out obligations I think I have to other people that I care about, I don't remember there being anything about an intellectual or emotional burka in the marriage vows. I wouldn't have acted if I thought what I was doing was going to land you in jail, but there's no way that's going to happen. So I saw my way clear to doing what I thought was right by Joseph and all the Josephs that might follow him."

"You can't be that naive. Of course Matt will see me as completely unreliable now. It's nothing to do with you being expected to be a good little wifey. The fact that we are close and that I'm likely to tell you things that people outside the organisation could use against us, that's what it's all about. Forget this feminist rubbish. Why does it always have to go back to that?"

This was greeted with a sullen silence. As is always the case with such silences, they cry out to be broken, inviting blows of even higher calibre than the ones that provoked them in the first place. Justin answered the call.

"And what makes you think you were doing the right thing by Joseph? Joseph believed in what he was doing. He believed in it so much that he drove himself over the edge. And what do *you* do? You do your best to undermine the very thing he gave his life for? Is that your way of honouring his memory?"

The attack was a tactical error. It gave Lizzie the opportunity to move away from ground her silence had shown she was struggling in.

"So you're turning his death into some grand, heroic act, are you? Like what the TV news people do when they're reporting a tragic death – the deceased is always puffed up as someone special, always someone kind, someone who made us laugh, someone with a grand past behind them or a grand future ahead of them. Wouldn't their death have mattered if they had been just ordinary, pretty dull, had never done anything special or were never likely to? They would still have been special to their nearest and dearest. Could it not just be left at that? No, let's be honest here – Joseph was no hero, he was highly intelligent certainly, but he was Mr Below-Average when it came to heroism. That was the whole point, wasn't it? Snoddy used him in the same way as those Islamist morons use suicide bombers. I can't forgive him for that, and neither, I think, should you."

Justin's defences were breached. She wasn't wrong about this – Snoddy had used Joseph – it wasn't the whole story though, there was a bigger picture. But he knew that he'd be wasting his time attempting to paint it for her. She was a creature of the existential. She never allowed her thinking to become a manipulation of digits and symbols. She didn't play chess, but if she had she would probably have consulted with the pieces before moving them to a different square. He'd say what he had to say anyway, but it would be his tone, not his words, that he would be relying on. But then suddenly it struck him that his anger had got pushed into the background. It was still there, but it wasn't calling the tune any more. Some little warning light had come on. If he wasn't careful, the two of them could talk themselves out of their marriage. He would not give in to her and act against Snoddy and the movement – that was out of the question – but he would try to limit the damage.

"Come on, Lizzie, okay you're right, he did push Joseph too far, as it turns out, but he genuinely believed Joseph would come through. If he had really thought otherwise he'd have backed off. He's not the monster you think he is. Why do you think he does what he does? He wants to make the world a better place, a place where justice can get back in the game."

He was driven to raise his voice to finish his sentence in the face of the fierceness of Lizzie's reaction.

"Not a monster? Not a monster? How else would you describe someone who wants to blot out the things that make us human? Rational minimalism, that's what he wants – no sentimentality, no softness, no inconsistency. God! How does he expect the world to follow him in that? We ordinary beings need our emotional rosaries and our mental bric-a-brac; we need myths to believe in and fairy tales to hold in reserve for dark nights too black to bear. That's what human beings are about, not Nietzschean superheroes giving their all to their will and nothing to the child within them."

This was grossly unfair – God knows, suppressing the childlike was the last thing the Prometheans wanted. But the counter-offensive he had ready and waiting had to be stood down. The risk was too great that it would bring the cauldron to boiling point. Instead, he simply gave Lizzie the saddest, most disappointed look he could muster and left the room.

Chapter 71

When Schinski got the call from Bailey he had been up to his eyes in directing the election campaign. He had graciously accepted the position as Snoddy's agent and had drafted in a small team to arrange public appearances and deal with the dull business of leafleting the constituency and organising the postal vote. At Snoddy's insistence the key position of press officer was given to Francesca Bergman who Schinski, meeting her for the first time, found a highly impressive figure. Justin Wright was acting as her number two; his job was to focus on the local press while she dealt with the nationals. The distinguished lady had also some useful contacts at the Beeb. Playing up the natural curiosity that by-elections always provoke in the Westminster bubble, she had talked them into running a short documentary on the event. The strain on her persuasive powers was considerably lessened by the interest in Snoddy's Conservative opponent who, as it happened, was the nephew of a former Chancellor. The young man had of course no chance of winning the seat, (The *my-father-and-his-father-before-him* voting instinct is rarely up for self-examination) but the press were keen to monitor the early toddler steps he was making in a career that might one day go on to rival the uncle's. Snoddy could not have hoped to have a more worthy opponent to beat.

Snoddy himself was doing only tolerably well. His doorstep manner was awkward. He didn't smile enough and when he did the effort was visible. When anyone raised an objection he was inclined to put them down with the same ferocity as he would a rival. He seemed incapable of taking the point that Francesca kept making to him that when there are no third parties around to witness the exchange of views it's more important to engage the person than to win the argument. Dr Greenfield, his old teacher who accompanied him occasionally on these door-to-doors, had a much better way with lesser intellects and did an excellent job on these occasions in keeping the temperature from plunging to freezing. On the positive side Snoddy's 'Spockean otherworldliness', as Freddie Douglas described it, did inspire confidence with some. Politics is not foremost in most people's concerns and just as they don't question the authority of a surgeon when they need an operation or an IT specialist when their computer is on the blink, all they look for in a politician is someone who seems to know what he's about. Schinski did wonder however how the Mr Spock line would fare in the bars and committee rooms at Westminster. But that was not his concern. His job was to get his man there. The rest was up to Snoddy. Nevertheless he couldn't escape a sense of impending futility: it would be a terrible pity if the fire cracker he had helped launch turned out a damp squib.

On his way back from his meeting with Bailey the weather turned nasty. The wind was up and the sky had darkened. As he got to the door of the constituency office he had a sudden change of mind. There was a pub at the end of the street. It was a run-down old thing, not the most alluring choice over the office but the only one on offer. It had the great merit of not being full of mission-focused people in the throes of their purposefulness.

The inside was just as dingy as the exterior. There were only four or five drinkers, all male and all pensioners. The barman was of similar vintage and gave the impression of having moved behind the bar solely to accommodate his mates, serving outsiders being a contingency he laboured to put up with. The small group huddled at one end of the bar eyed the stranger with a bizarre blend of indifference and curiosity. A couple of others, in a half-hearted effort to keep their heads above the slough of boredom, were throwing desultory darts. At the far wall a fire spluttered miserably in the grate. The Clean Air Act clearly had no writ here. Schinski ordered a hot brandy and when the landlord looked offended at his comment on the poor showing of the fire and positively outraged when he suggested that the coals could do with some reinforcement, he placed an extra fiver on the counter and declared that 'the good cheer was on him'. He went over to the table by the grate and awaited the delivery of the said cheer. When after a sullen interval the coal scuttle appeared, the contents were heaped with begrudging generosity on the dying embers. By the time they took to do their job the hot toddy was at work on the inner man.

Bailey's news had given Schinski much to mull over. There was nothing he liked better than working out strategies, deciding on what pieces to move and what strings to pull. Strategies require aims, but the aims were always of less interest to him than the how-to-get-to-them. He was a bit like an angler who didn't eat fish or an allotment holder who ate his greens only when his wife bullied him. But now a new kind of seed had sprouted tentative roots. What if this time he turned his attention to deciding on the terminus and not just on the route? As he sat there musing, taking the odd sip of his brandy and muttering the occasional word of correction or approval to what was going on in his head, he could have been taken for a wino from the streets come to shelter from the cold outside in the warm muddle of memory and fantasy. Nothing could have been further from the truth. Fantasy was not being indulged; it was being stripped naked and scanned for frailties that might be fatal should he choose to expose it to reality.

When the brandy glass was drained and the glow from the fire was beginning to fade, the nuncio of good cheer got up and took a very fulsome leave of the landlord and the paltry band of sanctuary seekers. No one deigned to respond, but that mattered not to him. He had broken through the thin coating of the present shape of things and viewed innards that might be made

397

to work in a very different way. There was a spring to his step as he made his way back down the street. It was late, but there were still a few stragglers from the election team in the constituency office when he got there. There were two phone calls he had to make.

The first was to Francesca. Could she please, as a matter of urgency, set up an interview with George Sinclair, and in it goad him into saying something really nasty about the constituency committee and its decision to abandon the legacy of the founding fathers – really nasty, mind, not something that could easily be forgiven and forgotten. If she failed to get anything really juicy, she'd need to spice up what she had. If he disclaimed it, it would only be his word against hers and the damage would already be done. Francesca was puzzled as to why he would want to do that; Sinclair was out of the picture now. What possible purpose would be served by antagonising him further?

"There have been developments, Francesca. The Panel might have pressure put on it to reverse its decision and I don't want them to have the easy option of falling back on Sinclair. We want them to be left with no other option than to stick by our man."

The second call was to Matthew Eardley. It went straight to voicemail. He left the briefest of messages: "Hi, Matt, we need to talk."

Chapter 72

Matt Eardley was a busy man. He had many fingers in many pies, but like all successful business magnates he had developed a highly sophisticated filter system that allowed only the most vital issues to come up to him for decision. That still made for a steady stream of calls on his attention. The ease with which he dealt with these was remarkable. He could be engaged in casual conversation one minute, receive a call, make a ruling and get back to the small talk as if he had never been away. There was decidedly something of the Pimpernel about him. Schinski noticed this at their first encounter and instantly felt both affinity and admiration. He had come across so many headless chickens in his professional life, all so proud of their conscientiousness and totally blind to the virtues of benign neglect. No, Eardley was a man he knew he could work with.

Schinski declined the offer of a brandy when the two men met in the lobby of the Bury Radisson. This was likely to be a tricky meeting and he'd need all his wits about him. Coffee would be fine. Eardley had chosen to fly up north and catch some of the flavour of the campaign rather than drag Schinski away from his duties as election agent. He was anxious to get an update on how the campaign was progressing and demanded a frank assessment from *the man with his ear to the ground*

"Now, none of that all-meaning, nothing-meaning blah that empty-headed politicians vomit up when they're forced to take a bite at a question."

Schinski hesitated before deciding whether Eardley really meant what he said. Often such remarks are just a way of asking for the blah to be well packaged. Concluding that Eardley did in fact want the truth, he expressed his reservations about Snoddy as a politician: If truth be told, a bit too short on that 'all-meaning, nothing-meaning blah', and a bit too long on the hard stuff, the stuff that people only want to be heard to say they want to hear. He expected Eardley to offer up something in Snoddy's defence, but curiously, he didn't. He didn't go as far as to agree, but his reticence left Schinski with the distinct impression that these thoughts were no strangers to him or perhaps not even at variance with his mental flow.

It was time to get on to *the other matter,* as Schinski ominously described it. He took Eardley through the latest developments, Joseph's suicide, the dairy, Lizzie's determination to bring Snoddy down, the pressure on Stranaghan to explain away the disappearance of the statement Joseph had made to him and the failure to record the fact of the very dead body of Rodgers, the man the Prometheans had pretended to execute, turning up within hours and with suspiciously similar gunshot wounds.

"You yourself were named in Joseph's dairy as having taken part in that trial, although not in the execution. It doesn't look good."

Eardley gave a concessionary nod, but almost absentmind-edly; already his mind was elsewhere computing permutations that might reconfigure the scenario. The first thing a good brain does when faced with a problem to solve is to pick out gaps in the data.

"Where did you get all this information from?"

Schinski smiled his best man-of-the-world smile.

"I have my sources. To be honest, I struck it lucky. A friend of a friend has a contact in the station Inspector Myles is currently operating out of and he got sight of the report he sent in."

Eardley didn't seem to feel any need to question this. He was already on to the next hole he wanted to plug.

"The thing I find odd is why this Inspector Myles hasn't

gone to town on Stuart Stranaghan. You say he hasn't cautioned him or got a formal statement from him. Do you have any explanation for that?"

Schinski gave a Gallic pout.

"Perhaps he feels that the whole thing is too personal for him to deal with. You must remember he worked with Stranaghan, the two men are friends. Maybe he's recusing himself. You don't get doctors operating on patients they're close to, do you?"

"Okay, I can buy that. Does your source have any idea who is in charge of the case? Who instigated it in the first place?"

"No."

It was a soft 'no', not one to suggest defensiveness. But it was succinct and unsupported. Never embroider a lie unless you really have to, was a maxim that Schinski never sinned against.

"Can you find out?"

"What do you have in mind?"

"I was thinking about that Superintendant – what's his name? Bailey, wasn't it – the one you and Whitehouse were running that naughty little scam with? He must carry some clout. If we could find out who was pulling the strings, he might be in a position to do something about it. We'd make it worth his while of course. What do you think?"

Schinski thought for a moment. When his reply eventually came out, it bore the hesitancy of something anxious to show that it had gone through the all the due processes of deliberation.

"I could ask him certainly. Yes, it might be worth a try, but even if he can do something there's always Lizzie Partridge I'm not sure she'd be prepared to let things drop. From what I've been told, she has the bit between her teeth. She's out to get Robert. She holds him responsible for Joseph Ross's death."

Eardley gave one of those smiles that come with a promise of ample collateral.

401

"Don't worry about that. You can leave Lizzie to me. I know her. She's a bright girl and she's devoted to Justin. She wouldn't want him compromised. I'll talk to them both. I'm sure we can come up with some sort of accommodation. You look after your end and I'll sort this one out."

This was not quite what Schinski wanted to hear. He'd have preferred to talk to Lizzie himself. Still, it was mission half-accomplished.

Chapter 73

Robert Snoddy's attitude to alcohol was unconventional. When he found himself in social gatherings where drink was the common currency he struggled to cling on to a positive view of his fellow humans. He never forgot something Greenfield once said to a fourth-former who had got himself drunk on a bottle of vodka purloined from the village supermarket. 'What do the half-witted do when they are at their wits' end? They move next door into the vacant half of their brain and gorge on in its banality.' He would tell himself he was overreacting, but that didn't help; it still left him with an overreaction to explain. Social drinking was an oxymoron for him: how could minds call on each other when they were so determined not to be at home? Asocial drinking was a slightly different matter; that was an indulgence you could allow yourself, sparingly of course, in the same way as you might take headache pills or cough mixture.

This was just such an occasion. It was with no sense of dishonour that he was settling down to an Irish coffee in one of the plush sofas in the lounge of The Grand Central Hotel. He had just had one of his now seemingly daily 'talks' from Francesca. She had supplied him with a 'script' and urged him, in the way a mother talks to a child, to stick strictly to it and not go off on one of what she witheringly called his 'dialectical safaris'. He flicked through the file she had left him with. It took the form of a series of standard questions followed by answers 'that would do no harm' – a kind of Book of Common Prayer, designed to keep on the right side of the zealous god of the Socialist Old Testament.

Question: Do you agree that the National Health Service must be protected from the creep of privatisation?

Line 1: Keep it vague: Where it makes sense, some minor jobs in the NHS can be contracted out – cleaning, catering, that type of thing – but the principle must be preserved that no one in need of health care in this country should be disadvantaged because of an inability to pay. We are rightly proud of our NHS and it is our duty to ensure that future generations continue to enjoy its benefits.

Line 2: Attack the Tories: The Labour Party is the party of the NHS. The Tories on the other hand cannot be trusted with a health system whose first duty of care is to the disadvantaged in our society. The Tories are the party of the rich, so the provision of medical care free at the point of delivery has no resonance with them. If they dared to have their way they'd privatise the lot. They've always favoured a system where money trumps need.

Line 3: Personal Anecdote: I remember a story my father told me. (*Always distance yourself from the source – makes it harder for anyone to check up on*) When he was a boy one of the neighbours had a son who contracted some rare disease (*Avoid being specific*) when he was visiting a relative in America. He was taken to hospital where the problem was diagnosed, but the insurance he had didn't cover the full costs of treatment, which were astronomical. So an appeal was launched back here in the neighbourhood and they raised enough money to get the boy home. An ambulance was waiting at the airport and rushed him to hospital where he underwent an operation that saved his life. That story has stayed with me ever since. It's one of the things that inspired me to enter politics and do my bit as a guardian of a system that protects those in need.

All the standard issues were covered in similar fashion. Any challenge to the affordability of increased public spending was to be drowned in a sea of invective against the rich or, alternatively, in a welter of examples of the tax avoidance stratagems *these bloodsuckers* hire expensive lawyers and accountants to come up with. It was categorically imperative to give a wide berth to all terms with the slightest whiff of bad breath: *Government spending* – bad, bad; *Public Investment* – good, good. *Tax reductions* – okay, but only if applied to the people at the bottom, otherwise to be referred to as *Government cuts!* Negative labels such as *thugs, criminals and vandals* were acceptable, and could even be qualified with adjectives such as *brutal, mindless* or *racist*, but only in cases involving either paedophiles or *right-wing extremists*; all other lawbreakers were to be referred to as *victims of the system*. The Right should never go unqualified; it should always be labelled *The Hard Right* or *The Far Right*. *The Poor*, or *The Underprivileged*, depending on the context, must always be credited with having *needs* and their *legitimate aspirations* should be juxtaposed with *the naked self-interest* of the bourgeoisie. The two great mantras, *social mobility* and *social equality*, should produce a quiver in the voice, but they should never be allowed to appear together in the same paragraph lest their antithetical nature be exposed. It wouldn't do if the public realised that the man-in-the-street, once he has worked his way up from the street to the leafy suburbs, must *de facto* be re-labelled as a *dog-eating-dog* transgressor against the core principal of social equality.

And so it went on. It wasn't really quite that bad, but Snoddy got so bored with its all-pervading blandness that he took pleasure in caricaturing it thus to Naomi. No doubt his Tory opponent had been supplied with a similar crib sheet. It was just like the esoteric conventions in tournament bridge: you bid hearts when you mean spades; you bid clubs when you mean hearts and spades; and you bid your opponent's suit when you don't have it. All good fun, but is that really what he was getting into politics to do? There surely had to be more to it. Maybe, just like bridge, once you'd won the contract you get to play your hand. Maybe after he had got all this verbal non-sense behind him at the hustings he'd get down to the real business of political change. How likely was that? Goethe's *Gesellschaft vom Turm*[9] had made a great impression on him when he had first come across the notion as an undergraduate. He had somehow imagined that that was what Parliament was really like, that the public posturing was just a front and behind the facade there was enough brain power and integrity to address society's ills. But the obvious question refused to go away. If he was right about this, why were wisdom and focus so reluctant to come out from behind the shadows? Why was there so little evidence that they were there? Why was the body politic still drowning in its own verbiage? Whenever his spirits took a dip the question drowned in its own despair, but when they bobbed back up he would tell himself that boldness was needed. The knot was resistant to traditional efforts of disentanglement. Like the Gordian knot,[10] it needed to be cut though. Maybe it was his destiny to do what Alexander had done, using the sharp edge of his words and the cold steel of his polemics. The public debate had been so muddled for so long and ideas so matted in their connotations that nothing short of dialectical violence would save it and give it back its access to reason. But would he himself be up to the task of landing this blow? The answer to that too floated up with the flow and down with the ebb. The Irish coffee was currently making a poor job of stemming the ebb.

---

[9]   The Society of the Tower – an elite group of enlightened intellectuals free of prejudice and self-interests who would run society on rational lines

[10] Reference to the legend that Gordius, king of Gordium, tied an intricate knot and prophesied that anyone who could untie it would become the ruler of Asia. It was cut through with a sword by Alexander the Great.Matthew

Chapter 74

After dispatching his report Myles had slipped into a strange semi-comatose state of not knowing what he was wishing for. It was only when he was called in and told by a very distant Chief Inspector Newbolt that he should return to his station and resume his normal duties that he realised that that was exactly what he had wanted all along. The top brass, he was told, would review the situation and decide what action, if any, to take. It was explained that since Stranaghan and Wright were no longer in the service no disciplinary action could be taken at that level. The question would be whether they had committed a criminal act or if the evidence they could provide against Snoddy would be enough to make a prosecution a realistic proposition. In any case it was a matter to be decided in consultation with the CPS. As far as Myles was concerned, all that mattered ... perhaps not quite all ... was that he was off the hook. His instinctive reaction was to pack his bags and head for home. But it was an instinct too ignoble to give in to. He had been given an honourable way out and he owed it to himself not to run like a scared rabbit. He had to face Stuart Stranaghan.

He had the distinct feeling of being a *brave* scared rabbit as he stood waiting for the Stranaghan doorbell to be responded to. It wasn't Stuart himself who opened the door; it was Heather, his wife. Her face visibly plummeted from expectation to aggrieved mistrust as she discovered who was at the door. She had to make an obvious effort to beckon him in. Her directions remained non-verbal until he was in the living room, at which point she managed a very dry 'I'll get Stuart' and left him, closing the door behind her. The brave-scared-rabbit feeling returned as he picked up the muffled sound of an animated female voice. It came in quick bursts, re-booting when it failed to produce any audible response. There then followed a prolonged semi-silence which he took to be the muted response, which evidently was refusing to be provoked into matching the pitch of the stimulus. Shortly after that the living room door opened and Stranaghan appeared.

Myles was anxious to get an instant reading of his expression, but there was no headline to be scanned. The face showed neither hostility nor supplication. There was no suggestion that he was confronting a man who wished him ill. The visitor, who had remained on his feet in what had felt like the 'waiting room', was beckoned to take a seat. Stranaghan himself took up a comfortable position in the armchair opposite and looked at Myles with warm but unsmiling eyes. He allowed a short silence to develop before he relieved the pressure on his guest to be the first to come up with words.

"What have you come to tell me, Graham?"

His voice was relaxed and, like his face, showed no trace of either anxiety or resentment. It was exactly what Myles suddenly realised he should have expected. The respect he had accumulated for this man was not idle hero worship; it had real roots and he felt diminished for not having being guided by it. He was uncomfortably aware of the tinny quality of his own voice as he responded.

"I have put in my report and it's all out of my hands now."

He cringed at his unprovoked defensiveness; it was all too clear that there were accusations buzzing in his own head that he was trying to parry. Stranaghan's benevolent smile in response seemed to confirm the transparency of his position.

"I see. You were between a rock and a hard place. I've been there and done ... well maybe not that, but certainly not what I totally wanted to do. The problem is in these cases, there's never anything one totally wants to do, is there? You'd like to do both things and you'd like to do neither thing, but you only get to

408

choose one thing and whichever one you opt for is the one that has all the disadvantages of not being the other."

He tried to engage Myles in the little smile that accompanied this observation, but Myles was too preoccupied with the pertinence of what had been said to appreciate the lightness of its formulation. In the absence of any vocal reaction Stranaghan continued.

"I was faced with an unpalatable choice. I could play it straight, report the facts as they presented themselves…or rather as they were carefully presented to me … and allow the law to take its course. That's what I should have done as a humble servant of the law, and as a policeman that's exactly what I was … a humble servant of the law. Mine was not to reason why, mine was but to allow the law to cast the die. Don't think that I didn't take my role seriously. As I've said many times, the law is arguably the greatest achievement civilisation has managed to come up with. It's man's bulwark against chaos and barbarity. But in order for it to work, it's got to command total obedience. You don't get to pick and choose the bits of it you like and ignore the bits you don't like. And yet that's exactly what I did. In making the choice I made I was blatantly betraying my duty as a policeman. I was putting myself outside the law and joining the outlaws. The very least I owed the law was to give up all pretence of being its servant. It's one thing to break the law; it's a far more serious thing to betray it. My resignation spared me from that at least."

This was again met with silence. It wasn't a contemptuous silence, the kind that withholds the honour of engagement, nor was it the kind of reticence used to put off admitting to the justice of what has been said. Myles' thoughts seemed to be working in parallel rather than in concert with what he had been hearing. Stranaghan resolved this time to see the silence through. When Myles finally did respond, the eye contact that he had been studiously avoiding was suddenly taken up, almost like an act of aggression.

"You called the ultimatum Snoddy gave you the Barabbas Choice. He gave you the choice of getting your hands dirty or keeping them squeaky clean. I suppose you don't think much of me. Pontius Pilate Mark 2, that's me, that's what you think, isn't it? Not only do I not defend my friend – who I know acted in good faith – I haven't even the guts to hand him over to the law. I left it to others to do the dirty work for me. That's exactly what Pontius Pilate did, isn't it?"

Myles' face contorted into a bitter smile as he said this. Stranaghan was at a loss to read it. There was real anger there. But who was he angry with? Was it with himself? Or was it with him?

"Well, I'm very sorry, Inspector Stranaghan, that I don't meet your high expectations" The pitch of his voice had moved up an octave. "You see, I'm just an ordinary cop. I'm a humble servant of that law you claim to hold in such high esteem, but, when it came to the crunch, you chose to abandon. I remember you once talked to me about the categorical imperative. I was impressed. I looked it up. You were quite right; you said it was Immanuel Kant who had come up with it. 'An action cannot be considered as moral unless the doer would will that anyone faced with the same choice should do the same.' That's why it's not okay for policemen to choose when to enforce the law and when not to. But if he does the honourable thing and resigns from the force, that makes it okay, does it? What kind of police force would that leave us with? Once you become a policeman you become a kind of priest, you put your personal feelings on hold and you enforce the law, end of."

At this stage Myles' voice was almost out of control. The eye contact he had initially made with Stranaghan had sharpened venomously for a time, but now it was morphing into a bitter stare locked on nothing in particular. That look told Stranaghan all he needed to know. He did not rush in to defend himself. Instead, he observed a respectful silence for what had been said.

The two men sat for some minutes before a word was spoken. It was as if they were both viewing the scene of a passing funeral. In the end it was Myles who broke the spell.

"I'm sorry, Stuart. I shouldn't have spoken to you like that."

Stranaghan nodded in a way that suggested reluctant agreement.

"No, Graham, it's not me, it's yourself you shouldn't have spoken to like that. Good and bad and right and wrong don't present in uniforms; they're masters of disguise, they swap clothes with each other, they even swap skins.

"Here you are, looking to do the right thing. You think that once you decide on what that is, you are committed to damning anything that thwarts it or contradicts it. Then you look at things the other way round and you find exactly the same thing applies. Whatever you do, you don't get to do in the knowledge that you are doing the right thing and none of the wrong thing. Don't be fooled by conventional moral rhetoric that bangs on about the supremacy of the law over all other considerations. Just listen to the brave words we hear so often from *men of honour* claiming how they would rather die than allow the writ of law to be compromised, and then fast forward a few years and see how the tune changes once they have done the unthinkable and concluded their shameful deals with the men of violence. No one knows better than an Ulsterman how this plays itself out. There's an argument to be made for such compromises certainly, but it's amazing, when the smoke has cleared, how unselfconsciously these men go back to the bosom of their cosy moral clichés and expect their renewed assertions of legal purity to be given credence. What's even more remarkable, by and large they are.

"So, don't get angry with yourself for not being able to square the circle. You've done what your gut instincts have told you to do. You're a decent man and those instincts will not lead you too far astray. It's people who abandon their instincts for

411

some ideological mantra who pose the real threat. I'll take my chances with whatever your masters choose to throw at me. I'm not just going to roll over, mind you. I'll fight them all the way. I'm just glad it's not you I'm going to have to kick in the goolies."

The smile that this elicited from Myles was one of those waiting for a hint of encouragement to appear. What his old boss had said had in a strange way been what he felt he should have known he would say. It wasn't something he would have thought out for himself, but it got him to a place he ought to have trusted Stranaghan to have taken him. He felt less bad about what he had done and a lot less bad about what his courage had failed him in.

Chapter 75

"Rumours? What rumours? What are you talking about?"

Trevor Windsor was a man of regular habits and was not used to being wakened up at one in the morning and confronted with threats to the smooth running of his morrow's agenda.

"You'll need to call a meeting of the Panel first thing in the morning. Everyone needs to be there. Make that clear. I'll contact Reggie and Schinski, and you and Hugh can deal with the rest. This is a game-changer, Trevor, and we've got to be on the ball."

"Hang on a minute! You say you've been hearing ominous rumours about Robert Snoddy, but what exactly is being said?"

"Listen, Trevor. Take my word for it. It's not something we want to get into on the phone. All I'll say is this: we may have to have a major re-think about our election campaign. Get everyone there for nine."

It was not a voice to brook any quibbling. The impatience it oozed was already plainly at tipping point.

* * * *

All the members found their way to turning up. Margaret Millership had had to delay her departure for a London visit and Reggie Whitehouse had had to withdraw from his regular weekly four-ball. Last to arrive was Freddie Douglas. It was he who had been the herald of impending grimness the previous night, so nobody had any clear idea of the nature of the doom that threatened. On his arrival he was descended on, but the Chairman insisted on everyone taking their seats and allowing Freddie an uncluttered floor. The expression on Douglas' face was grave, but half-hearted attempts to force through a smile bore witness to a desire not to milk the state of privilege the knowledge he had in his possession accorded him.

"I have asked the Chairman to call this emergency meeting, Ladies and Gentlemen, because of certain information that I have become privy to. I have it on good authority that the police are considering issuing a warrant for the arrest of our candidate, Mr Robert Snoddy."

Stunned disbelief passed like a wave along the faces around the table before giving way to a muddled flurry of questions. Douglas allowed free rein to the confusion as he took a sip of water. Then, almost magisterially, he raised his hand and asked for order.

"Whether or not the police will discharge that warrant I am not in a position to say at this stage. The charge, if charge there is to be, is a serious one. There is talk of our candidate being involved in a murder."

The communal gasp that this produced was again given its head before Douglas took back the reins.

"It's thought that he played a major part in the murder of a certain Dwayne Rodgers. Rodgers himself had stood trial for the very brutal murder of a young man named Francis Brown. The prosecution failed and he was acquitted, but in circumstances that inspired little confidence that justice had been done. It's believed he got off because the key witness against him had been got at. The police, it seems, have reason to suspect that Mr Snoddy might have taken it on himself to dispense the justice that the court had failed to provide.

"We have all heard Mr Snoddy's views on the subject of law and order, and indeed many of us would share in the sentiments that inspire them. But it's quite a different thing taking it upon oneself to play judge, jury and ... executioner. I'm not saying that that's what Mr Snoddy did. Indeed, the fact that the CPS is dithering on whether or not to proceed clearly shows that the case against Mr Snoddy is far from open and shut. Another point I feel should be borne in mind is the strong feeling against Mr Snoddy in certain sections of the police force; some of them are still smarting no doubt from the humiliation they suffered the last time he was put on trial for murder. It may well be that those forces are still at work and that an innocent man is being hounded for daring to challenge the sanctimonious narcissism of our justice system. As all of us here know only too well, the establishment can get very vindictive when its authority is put under scrutiny.

"But that's all beside the point. Whatever comes out of this, whether Mr Snoddy turns out to be guilty or innocent, whether the prosecution goes ahead or not, our first duty must be to the Party; we can't allow the good name of the Labour movement to be sullied by association. It pains me to say it, but I think there is no other choice open to us than to distance ourselves from Mr Snoddy and drop him as our candidate."

As he sat down the look he directed towards the Chairman seemed almost apologetic. It was unclear whether the apology was for the news he brought or for the fact that in his concluding remarks he had pre-empted the Chairman's role. The Chairman looked utterly rudderless and showed a strange reluctance to use his gavel to restore order to the meeting, which now, understandably, was in disarray. It fell to Schinski to cut through the hubble-bubble.

"This is indeed very disturbing news. Could I ask Mr Douglas how reliable his source is? It would be a complete disaster if we went down the road he suggests only to discover that the whole thing was no more than a vindictive rumour."

Douglas jumped back up to his feet.

"I cannot disclose my source. You will understand that. But I can say that I have not the slightest doubt as to its authenticity. As you all know, I was one of Mr Snoddy's greatest supporters and I would be the last to try to do him down. My first priority is the Party and I think the risk to the Party is too great. It's with the greatest reluctance that I propose this motion."

Margaret Millership, always quick to gauge the direction the wind was blowing, joined the debate earlier than her normal caution would have sanctioned.

"I don't think we should question the good faith of Freddie here. I believe him when he says Snoddy's candidature poses a real threat to the Party. I don't think we have any choice than to find ourselves a new candidate. I know that won't be an easy option. We'll get a roasting from the press and we'll have a lot of explaining to do. It might even cost us the election, but the alternative is quite unthinkable. A Labour Party parliamentary candidate arrested for murder! No, gentlemen, we can't take that risk."

Mutterings of approval were working up to a chorus as Schinski got back to his feet.

"Mr Chairman, I agree entirely that we must proceed with caution. Let's not allow ourselves to be panicked into a bad decision. If Mr Snoddy is prosecuted, then we are indeed up the creek without the proverbial paddle. But, as Margaret has quite rightly pointed out, if we drop Mr Snoddy we are landing ourselves in very hot water indeed. You might say we'd be right in the soup. Surely the only sensible thing for us to do at this stage is to hear what Mr Snoddy has to say for himself. I propose that the Chairman meet with Mr Snoddy. I think he should take Mr Douglas along with him. The matter must be resolved as a matter of the utmost urgency. Can I suggest that they meet with Mr Snoddy this afternoon and that we reconvene here this evening and make a decision one way or the other?"

Procedural delays always go down well with committees. They have the great merit of lending legitimacy to indecision. Like Mr Micawber, committee men live constantly in the hope that, if given a little bit more time, the authorised version of truth will eventually turn up.

Chapter 76

As the others drew breath after this new turn of events Schinski avoided involvement in the general consternation and called a taxi. He had arranged to meet Eardley that morning. They were to brief each other on the results of their inquiries. This new development would of course eclipse everything else.

There was an uncharacteristic glumness in Eardley's face as the pair shook hands in the lobby. As an *homme d'affaires* Eardley knew well the importance of *positivity* in one's dealings with people; it feeds hope and hope can graduate to confidence and confidence, especially when it is born out of fear of failure, bestows power on those who inspire it. That is the essence of the so-called confidence trick; it doesn't necessarily involve deception, but it does give influence greater clout.

The news of Snoddy's likely demise hadn't reached him. It was his encounter with Lizzie Partridge that was concerning him. He had tried to point out to her the dangers that her campaign against Snoddy might pose to her husband's career. He had been sure that this would prove an effective tactic. He had been careful not to be too heavy-handed and had even assured her that he, as Justin's present employer, had no thought of punishing him, but he couldn't speak for future employers. The newspaper world was not a place where memories were short and any mud that he would pick up would be sure to stick to him. And it was the wrong type of mud; mud acquired in anything that could pass as a liberal cause would count as something to be cherished like a duelling scar; it would go down as a case of youthful moral passion temporally getting the better of mature judgement, not a bad fault in a young crusading journalist. But any suggestion that he had answered a call from the Right would inevitably damn him as a fascist fanatic.

She had listened calmly to his argument and was willing to concede that he might well have a point. But Justin was a grown man, she said; he had made his choices and he must live with the consequences. What Snoddy did to Joseph wasn't just an unfortunate collateral effect that no one could have foreseen. Joseph had lost his life; he couldn't get another. If the worst happened and Justin lost his career, it wouldn't be the end of his world; there were other careers open to him. That was the bottom line for her.

"There was no reasoning with her, Schinski. She's determined to get her pound of flesh and the trouble is she knows enough to do just that. I don't understand the woman. Did she really have such deep feelings for Joseph? If he was so dear to her, why didn't she make any effort to keep in touch with him after he gave up his studies? Surely you don't put your marriage and your husband's career on the line for someone you didn't even take the trouble to keep in touch with. It must be Snoddy she's after. He must have done her some great hurt when they were an item. She's using Joseph as a pretext for settling the score."

This brought something close to a knowing smile from Schinski.

"Perhaps you're right. But I wouldn't be too sure. Clever women can be hard to read."

When eventually Schinski got round to breaking his own, even darker news Eardley's reaction was admirably measured. They had found a quiet unused bar in the hotel for their meeting. When he had heard the full account of the morning's events Eardley went over to the bar, poured himself a glass of water from the jug that had been left there and began to pace up and down the empty room. It was clear that his behaviour was inspired less by feelings he was trying to rid himself of than by ideas he was striving to seek out. Eventually he came up with a question.

"I was under the impression that this fellow, Douglas, was one of your men. If that's the case, what's he up to? Is he not supposed to be on our side?"

Schinski gave a pointedly grave nod of the head.

"Yes, exactly, it came as a complete surprise to me too. I haven't had a chance to talk to him, but I don't understand why he didn't at least give me advanced warning of what he was going to do. He's an ambitious chap. Maybe he thinks this is his chance to seize the nomination. Maybe he thinks that he'll get the credit for blowing the whistle and that'll make him the front runner to step in as a last-minute replacement. I don't know, but I'll damn well find out."

Eardley had clearly hoped for more from this line of inquiry. He continued as if his question had neither been asked nor answered.

"Can you think of any way at all of rescuing the situation? Would you be able to stir up any support for Robert? After all, it's going to be one hell of a setback for the Party if they take it on themselves to drop their candidate at this late stage. Surely you could take the line that they'd be running as much a risk dropping him as keeping him? Do you think you could get any of them to buy into that?"

Schinski thought for a moment before replying.

"It's possible, but I doubt it somehow. Obviously I can't count on Freddie's vote any more, and apart from Reggie I can't see any of them sticking with Snoddy. They're all scared and when people get scared they don't let their thoughts wander off on their own. To be perfectly honest, I think it might come down to a question of damage limitation."

"What do you mean by that? Either we get Robert elected or we don't. I don't see that there's any middle course."

Schinski smiled.

"I'm surprised to hear you say that, Matthew. There's always a middle course. I thought you and I were the kind of people who instinctively knew that. Leave it with me and I'll see what can be salvaged."

Chapter 77

"What exactly do you expect me to say, gentlemen? You come here and tell me that there's a rumour going around that I am about to be arrested for murder. You can't tell me anything about the source of that rumour nor indeed anything about the evidence the police are supposed to have against me. All I can say is that I've had nothing to do with any murder. But you're not going to be happy with that, are you? You want me to supply details, but in order to supply details I need to have specifics of what it is you want details of."

Windsor looked to Douglas for an answer to the point. This after all was Douglas' kite; he was the one who should be flying it. Douglas evidently was taking a different view and merely reflected the look of expectation back on the Chairman. It was an awkward moment, but he had chaired too many meetings to be at a complete loss.

"Tell us about this man Rodgers. What links did you have to him?"

Snoddy grinned; he had seen through the layer of chairmanesque assurance.

"Dwayne Rodgers was a sadistic murderer who our worthy judicial system had let go free because it was more interested in its own self-aggrandisement than in doing its job. As you know, I lead a research team operating in the field of law and order. We used Rodgers as a case study. We held a mock trial. We took all the evidence from the transcript of the real trial including information which the police had available to them, but were prevented by judicial rules from using. We wanted to see how a reasonable jury would have reacted if they had been put in possession of this evidence. As we expected, our jury recorded a guilty verdict. We then asked the jury what they thought the sentence ought to be. We insisted on them explaining the rationale behind their choice of sentence. If they had come up with say, twenty years, we wanted to know how they had arrived at that figure. There were some who thought initially that a life sentence – provided it was a full life sentence – would satisfy a certain logic, but the final decision – unanimous by the way – was for the death penalty. It was the only way both sides of the crime-punishment equation could be balanced. Then – and this was the most interesting element in the experiment – we put it to them that if they thought Rodgers deserved to die, they had no right to ask others to do the dirty work; they made the decision, so they should be prepared to do the deed themselves. We wanted to peel off the layers of sentimentality and armchair morality and see if there was any substance beneath. Saying someone should die is one thing; actually killing that someone is quite another. So we simulated an execution. We got an actor to play the part of Rodgers and we got the jury to form a firing squad, using blanks of course, but they didn't know that. They went through with it and our actor did a very convincing death. If by the way you are ever in need of his services I can put you in touch."

"And what exactly did all this prove, do you think?"

"It proves that modern society may still be capable of sustaining a system of justice that can withstand the emotional and moral weaknesses that our over-pampered sensibilities have lumbered us with."

"But then this fellow, the one you *pretended* to kill, turns up dead. A mere coincidence, would you say?"

Snoddy's grin widened.

"Well, maybe we do the gods an injustice; maybe they take their job more seriously than our judges do. Yes, there are some elements of coincidence certainly, but just think about the kind of life Rodgers led. He was a nasty piece of work and the people he associated with were just as nasty. He had a fall out with two of them, over drugs I believe, and they did the job society was too squeamish to do for itself. You can check the records; you'll find that a court of law – not one of our pretend courts – found Gary Burrows and Shane Wilson guilty of Rodgers' murder."

"Why do think then that the police are thinking of charging you for that murder?"

"You'd need to ask them. My organisation and I have ruffled a few feathers. Or maybe someone up there just doesn't like the Labour Party and is trying to throw a spanner in the works. If you panic and drop me as your candidate you'll be doing exactly what they want you to do. Have you considered the possibility of it being the Tories who started this rumour? They're no fools; they know the value of smoke and mirrors."

This was heading towards an outcome that Windsor dreaded most. He would have liked Snoddy to have come up with some revelation that would have made the accusation against him simply go away. He had never considered that at all likely of course. Suspicion is a clingy substance; once it latches on to its victim, it's pretty resistant to anything happening around it. Failing such a 'miracle', he had dared to hope that Snoddy's response would be totally limp and inept. That way at least, the decision to drop him would be clear cut, however awkward the consequences. He kept pushing in this direction, but Snoddy remained emotionally composed and rationally measured. The decision to deselect him was not going to make itself. In his frustration he turned his anger on Douglas. The man had been completely useless. He had hardly uttered a word through the entire exchange. He was the one who had opened this can of worms in the first place. He should have been the one to act as prosecutor. The Chairman should have been left free to play judge.

Towards the end of the interview Windsor thought to detect shades of threat in Snoddy's tone. If the Panel felt compelled to review his nomination, he had said, he too might have to reconsider his commitment and loyalty to a movement that ran scared at the first sign of the going getting tough. He might be forced to explore other ways of serving the cause that was so dear to his heart. The confident look in Snoddy's eyes as he said this suggested a lot more than a pre-emptive threat of withdrawal.

Chapter 78

Eardley's description of his encounter with Lizzie Partridge did not come as a revelation to Schinski. He himself had spent an hour in the lady's company the day after Eardley's fruitless efforts at bringing her round. He had made it his business to find out where she taught and had made the journey back down to Oxford in time to waylay her as she was leaving the depressing academic tenement. The two had not met, so he had to introduce himself. She recognised his name, having been kept sketchily informed by her husband of the doings up north, and accepted his invitation to a quick *restoration of the soul* in the local hostelry

She showed no obvious signs of surprise at having been intercepted in this way. The reason became clear in her opening remarks.

"Justin has told me all about you. You are Snoddy's fixer, aren't you, the man who wangled him a way into the nomination? Has Matthew Eardley sent you here to fix me? I can tell you, you'll have your work cut out."

This came with an I-dare-you twinkle in the eyes to which Schinski responded with a hands-up-I-give-in smile.

"From what I've heard about you, Lizzie, I wouldn't presume to do that. No, I've come to listen. I want to know exactly why it is you're so hell bent on crucifying Robert Snoddy."

Lizzie made a thorough check of his face before deciding on how frank she was prepared to make her answer.

"I want to *crucify* Robert Snoddy, as you call it – and I must admit, crucify is a good word, it's something Robbie himself believes in. Yes, I do want to take him down for what he did to Joseph and what he might do to other Josephs."

425

"Please explain. I have no trouble understanding how you feel about Joseph Ross, but I'm intrigued to find out what you mean when you say he should be punished for what he *might do*?"

This produced another sincerity sweep of his face. He had tried his best to make his question not sound argumentative. He was aided in this by the fact that his puzzlement was genuine. The *sweep* seemed to pick up on that.

"I think what was done to Joseph was dastardly. It wasn't cruel. Robbie is not a cruel person. He can even be kind and thoughtful and, to be fair to him, he's driven by a great respect for beauty and truth. He wants the best for people; he wants them to experience life in all its vitality and not be cowed into accepting the scraps that the patronising – he calls them 'matronising' – establishment allows them. Everything gets dumbed down – culture, education, religion, you name it. But, as he points out, the more germ-free life becomes, the more susceptible we are all to infections from the big, bad world.

"I understand all that and I can see that he has put his finger on something that matters. But he pushes too hard. He's determined to get us back to being what he chooses to call *a grown-up society*, a society of people strong enough to handle pressures from contradictory impulses of the brain. On the one side there's reason showing us the big picture and laying out clinically before us the scalpels we need to operate with to prevent the social psyche from throwing itself off a cliff or drowning itself in a swamp. On the other side of the brain we have all those healthy animal instincts that deal in smell and touch and taste and go all the way up to human warmth and compassion. If we sign up to reason and turn our back on our instincts we turn into monsters. But conversely, if we turn our backs on reason and focus exclusively on the things that make us feel good about ourselves and our fellow creatures we become infantile, more at home within our own skin certainly, but totally useless at

426

resisting the slide to the cliffs and the swamps. Robby is not content to nudge us a little bit this way and a little bit that. He wants a perfect synthesis; he wants pity and compassion to energise the instinct for justice and he wants reason to take it from there and go about its work, keeping that same compassion in its sights but not allowing itself to be thrown off course by it. It's too big an ask; the whole thing is predicated on a view of mankind that is totally unrealistic. Society is not made up of supermen; there are, and there will always be, a hell of a lot more Joseph Rosses than Robert Snoddys in the world, and thank God for that."

Schinski was impressed. More important, he knew he needed to show her he was impressed. It was one of those situations where words are the last thing you need. An inward look at the mark that what you've heard has made on you comes naturally in such circumstances and is instantly recognized for what it is. Schinski had to work to prevent himself from overplaying it. Evidently he succeeded, for Lizzie required little further prompting. She seemed almost anxious to unburden herself to him. She had been fighting a lone battle against her own doubts with only the shadows in her heart and head to counter the more substantial outside pressures that were coming from Justin and, more recently, Eardley. Common sense is something that by its very nature is predicated on there being at least one other person out there to endorse it. Without that endorsement it loses the potency of commonness and evaporates into the ether. This stranger seemed prepared to listen. It gave her an outside ear and, curiously enough, allowed her to listen to her own voice. The more she talked, the more confident she grew that there was *common* sense in what she was saying. She filled in the details of Joseph's diary, recounting the whole story of his attraction to the ideas of The New Prometheans and his emotional revulsion at following them through in practice, right up to the mock trial and execution. But she went further still and blurted out the story of Snoddy offering Stranaghan the chance to play God and decide who should take the hit for Rodgers' murder. This was a complete game-changer. Schinski pressed her for corroboration. There was nothing in terms of hard evidence that could be used, she said. There was no mention of it in the diary. All she had was what Justin had told her and he would be the last person to land Snoddy, let alone his friend Stranaghan, in the shit. She could understand that; Stranaghan had stood by him when he thought him to be in danger; he had gone as far as to give up his career for him. Justin wouldn't be the man she'd married if he welshed on the bond that that had created.

Schinski had come expecting an emotionally charged female hell bent on pursuing a personal vendetta with an ex-lover, using the sickening death of a defenceless friend to fuel the flames of anger and resentment. There might well have been elements of all that kick-starting her hostility, but there was a lot more to it than that. Lizzie, he could now see, was a thinking woman whose intellect was as much in play here as her emotions. In a strange way that made his task easier. Undiluted passion is not open to reason; it mistakes compromise for treachery and feels compelled to stand its ground however reasonable the appeal made to it. In fact, the more reasonable the appeal, the greater the compulsion to refuse it. He needed to know this before working out a strategy to rein her in. If she had turned out the way he had expected, he would have had to make common cause with her anger and come up with some form of punishment for Snoddy that would satisfy her and yet fall short of what would be lastingly injurious to his interests. Now at least he didn't have to share in her anger. Reasonableness would not be rejected out of hand.

Chapter 79

When the Panel reconvened to hear the Chairman's report of the meeting with Robert Snoddy there was one notable absentee. No one had been in touch with Derek Schinski since the morning's emergency meeting. The Chairman was naturally reluctant to make a start before he arrived. But as the minutes ticked by impatience mounted and he was left with no choice than to tap his gavel and declare a commencement to proceedings.

He gave a detailed account of what had been said – Snoddy's denial of any wrong-doing and his explanation of the staged trial and execution of Rodgers as a part of the psychological research he was engaged in. Freddie Douglas interrupted at this point.

"I was impressed by what he said about that. It was an excellent way of testing out what people think for real as opposed to what they think they think. People do love wafting about in their feelings and the hollow opinions they form around those feelings. He's absolutely right; that's exactly what children do. I thought it was a brilliant strategy. 'No Representation without Taxation' – that's what he's saying."

The others looked blankly at each other – what was the man on about? Only Huge Savage came back on it.

"You've got that wrong, Freddie. Jefferson's slogan was 'No Taxation without Representation.'"

Douglas sighed in exasperation.

"I know that. But Snoddy has turned it on its head. There's a price to be paid for having opinions. You have to earn the right to have an opinion; it's got to cost you something. The democratic process isn't just about phoning in and voting for something that doesn't touch on your life. It's not a reality show, it is reality."

He would have gone on, but the Chairman restrained him and reminded everyone of the business before them. Nathan Roberts was equally anxious to get back on track.

"How did he explain the coincidence of Rodgers turning up dead just after they had 'shot' him?"

"He didn't think it was such a coincidence. He pointed out that criminals like Rodgers live in the kind of world where violence is always lurking. And he told us not to forget that two men have been tried and duly convicted of his murder. Look, we could go round and round in circles here and get nowhere. We are not going to be in a position to know one way or the other whether Snoddy's so-called research is as innocent as he would have us believe. Is backing him a risk worth taking? That's the nub of the matter. There is a further issue: The man seems to have an unhealthy appetite for Old Testament justice. Is that something our Party wants to be associated with? We failed to pick up on this sufficiently during the selection process. Would it be better for us to see the thing through now that we've come so far, or should we put our hands up and limit the damage before the whole thing gets out of hand?"

Savage was in no doubt. They should drop Snoddy like a hot potato. He had always said that the man was no socialist and they should have the guts to admit they were wrong, even if it meant risking defeat at the election. Margaret Millership was inclined to agree, but the hesitancy in her voice betrayed a reluctance to jeopardise the election result. Max Fischer on the other hand expressed admiration for Snoddy's *conceptual acumen. A welcome change,* he called it, having looked on with sadness over the years at the steady decline in the intellectual weight of the Party's thinking.

"Its deepest roots have been systematically poisoned by ... sales talk, policies designed to pander to fleeting whims and opinions not worthy of the brain cells they took their life from. Maybe, just maybe, this committee has happened on someone offering a narrative that's a bit more viable than the newspeak marketing junk of our flash Blairites and, for that matter, the moth-eaten rhetoric of our dear old Commies and Trots. And, let me add, we should not be ashamed to admit that 'happened on' covers exactly what we did; we are where we are more through luck than judgement."

For all his intellectual gravitas Fischer was a poor judge of human reactions. A cannier man would have made sure of securing an ally before drawing his sword. But by focusing on what he was saying rather than who he was saying it to, he had managed to raise hackles on both wings of the Party. Huge Savage threw himself in the path of the bullet aimed at the Pinks and Nathan Roberts returned fire for the Reds. In an exasperated effort to calm things down, the Chairman called on the sitting MP to share the wisdom of his experience, no one in the room being better placed to gauge how Westminster was likely to react. Reggie had taken a very deliberate back seat in all the proceedings thus far, emulating no doubt the dignified silence that departing prime ministers officially adopt on the vexed business of selecting their successors. If truth be told, he had already moved on in his mind to the role he had cut out for himself in the Upper House – no more cheap words on deaf ears; he would limit himself to wise counsel, and it would only be on offer to those willing to coax it out of him. He waited until all the mutterings and counter mutterings had subsided before deigning to respond. Then, in very measured tones, he made a verbal tour of all the right things to say at such moments of crisis: avoid panic, take time to reflect, don't overreact, if you decide to jump make sure it's not into the fire. As for Westminster, he wasn't sure, but there could be no doubt that if things were to get as far as a criminal prosecution everything would blow up in their faces. Trevor Windsor was fulsome in his praise for the contribution. It had of course added nothing to the discussion – he had never expected anything else – but it had created the hoped-for break in the crossfire. The discussion could now proceed in a less fractious fashion.

"I think Reggie has hit the nail on the head. The issue comes down to how likely it is that our candidate will be involved in a scandal, whether it goes all the way to a criminal prosecution and at least gets so close as to arouse public suspicion that there is a case to be answered. That's what we have to decide on. If you think that that is a likely outcome – some might even say a *possible* outcome – then I think your vote must be, however reluctantly, to drop Mr Snoddy and find ourselves a new parliamentary candidate. But if you take the view that this is a ploy by our political opponents to panic us into making a bad decision that could well cost us the election, then your choice is equally clear. It's a matter of judgement, comrades, and unfortunately the buck stops with us. Reggie is right: we shouldn't panic and simply jump out of a hot frying pan. There might be worse waiting for us on the outside."

The weighting of these final words was not lost on the Panel. Could it be that the canny Chairman saw more danger in jumping than sticking? He was a man who would always plump for the safe option, everyone knew him well enough to know that. If he had come out and voiced an opinion, he would have been open to challenge and his opinion would have had no higher status than any of the others around the table. But veiled, and in the context of a judicial summing-up, the view, if view it was, was a much bigger beast. Had the vote been taken at that moment, it would have been hard to predict which way it would have gone. But just as things were moving towards a final resolution, the door opened and in rushed a very agitated Derek Schinski.

Chapter 80

Schinski was out breath from his frantic exertions to get to the meeting. He had had a very busy afternoon and had risked being late, even missing it, in order to fit in a visit that he felt he simply had to make. As a precaution he had phoned Freddie Douglas and told him to insist on getting the vote delayed until he got there, and failing that, to have it postponed. But Douglas was only to intervene as a last resort. He didn't want any suspicions aroused that he was up to something.

As he took his seat and sorted out some papers, the Chairman filled him in on the discussion thus far. He did so in the same style as earlier, one more befitting the bench than the chair, and again suggestive of the same disinclination for any form of *precipitous action*. Schinski listened almost distractedly as he shuffled his papers, nodding from time to time, but more in acknowledgement of the attention the Chairman was according him than as a token of like-mindedness. When Windsor had finished, Schinski gave a more distinctive nod of the head and looked around the table, pausing to take in all the faces. When finally he spoke, his words seemed to issue from a protracted sigh.

"I'm afraid I have very bad news for you, comrades. The situation is much more serious than it seemed. If no action is taken, it is almost inevitable that damning evidence will be produced against our Mr Snoddy linking him to the murder of Dwayne Rodgers. This evidence will not necessarily lead to a legal conviction, but it is strong enough to finish him off as a public figure."

The initial shock of this announcement took time to sink in, but as soon as it had bottomed out the stunned silence gave way to a raucous clamour for explanation.

"I am not at liberty to name names, but I've been in touch with a certain lady who is threatening to open this whole thing up. She was privy to information that would leave no one, no one outside a courtroom that is, in any doubt that Robert Snoddy was party to the murder. So, Mr Chairman, it's not just a public relations exercise we're talking about here. We have come very close, comrades, to foisting a *murderer* on the electorate of Bury West. The problem we are now faced with is not whether or not we should drop him – that now goes without saying – the problem is how we are going to stop the catastrophic misjudgement we made from getting into the public domain."

He paused to allow time for the question to be taken up and thrown back at him. He was not disappointed. Johnnie Taylor was the first to come out with it.

"Yes, yes, but how in hell's name are we going to keep the lid on?"

Schinski waited until the question had been echoed around the room. In his reply he lowered his voice almost to a whisper.

"As I said, I have spoken to this lady. She is a highly intelligent young woman and is very clear on what she wants. And what she wants is Snoddy's head. I'm not sure, mind you, she'd turn us down if we offered her the physical version on a plate, but she's quite prepared to settle for the political version. She will make it all go away if we terminate his candidacy. That's the deal."

"She might say that now," Hugh Savage exclaimed, "but can we trust her? How do we know she won't change her mind and drop us in it somewhere down the line?"

"She's very much aware that things could get very messy if she went the whole hog. Too many worms would come out of too many cans. She has a lot of spunk. If I'm reading her right, the same lady would pull the whole house down if she really needed to. But if we make sure she doesn't need to, we won't have a problem."

434

"So that's that then? Problem solved. We simply deselect Snoddy and the whole nightmare goes away? Is that what you're telling us?"

Schinski allowed the glance he gave at the speaker to morph briefly into a stare before softening it to a smile.

"Hardly, Hugh. If only things were that simple. Apart from the obvious problem of finding a replacement and selling our actions to the electorate, there is the other outstanding issue of how to sell our decision to the Snoddy crowd."

"What do you mean? Why should we have to answer to the Snoddy crowd, as you call them? What have they got to do with the decisions the Party makes? It's none of their business!"

"I'm sorry, Hugh, but I would have thought that was obvious. Snoddy has very powerful friends. His sponsor, Matthew Eardley, is a very rich man who controls large sections of the press. If he chose to embarrass us, he could do so at the click of a switch."

"Yes, but surely he could only embarrass us at the expense of his protégé. He's hardly likely to do that, is he?"

"Have you ever spoken to Eardley? He's a very hard man, and what's more, he's a man who's used to getting his own way. Snoddy may have been his protégé, but that doesn't mean he's his friend. And as protégés go, Snoddy is beginning to look like a busted flush. No, I wouldn't count on Eardley allowing any sense of loyalty to Snoddy to hold him back."

When Savage failed to come up with an answer, Freddie Douglas came in.

"So how do you think we should handle Snoddy?"

With all eyes focused on him, Schinski's face took on a reflective look. There was a smile lurking, but it was put by for another time.

"I've thought a good deal about that and I've decided that the best man to talk to was Snoddy's old teacher, Dr Greenfield. Bruce Greenfield is a wise old bird. It was he who got Snoddy up

435

and going in the first place. Snoddy is a very sharp cookie, but he has never completely broken free of his mentor. Greenfield's opinion still matters to him, and it matters a lot. That's why I went to see Greenfield this afternoon and that's the reason I was late for this meeting.

"We had a very productive exchange of views. He was perfectly aware of the danger posed by the lady I spoke about and was inclined to agree with me that the cause, which is as dear to him as it is to Snoddy, risked going down with the captain. I had a lot less trouble than I'd imagined getting him to agree to try to talk his man into doing the right thing and withdrawing his candidacy."

"So he undertook to do that, did he?" The Chairman was clearly struggling to credit such a triumph of hope over expectation.

"Yes, he did. But there will be strings. The main thrust of Snoddy's political ambitions was to promote his views on justice and education, but particularly justice. Personal ambition had nothing to do with it. In fact, Greenfield admitted to me that Snoddy himself had his own doubts about his suitability as an MP. He's an ideas man, and like most intellectuals he hasn't much time for the arse-licking and wheeling and dealing that goes on in politics. He was pretty sure Snoddy would play ball and step down without a fuss, but only if he is given a cast iron assurance that whoever replaces him will commit to the cause."

Margaret Millership let out a shriek.

"That's outrageous! Who do these people think they are? Are we going to let ourselves be dictated to by a bunch of non-elected nobodies? Let's call their bluff."

The defiance in her eyes was directed specifically at Schinski, but he declined to react. The lack of expression he contrived to produce on his face was a clear invite to others to answer her. Freddie Douglas was quick to oblige.

"Why on earth would we call their bluff? These are determined people. From what I have seen of Snoddy, he's not a man to play by somebody else's rules. I think it would be foolhardy of us to pick a fight with these people. We selected Snoddy ourselves, didn't we? I for one liked what he had to say. That's why I voted for him. And, I assume, most of you felt the same way. So what's the big deal about us choosing a like-minded replacement?"

Margaret Millership was not to be placated.

"It's not that. It's the arrogance of these people dictating to us what we should do. That's what I can't stand and that's where I think we should draw the line."

"Okay," Freddie replied, "Let's leave that aside for the moment. Let's think about who we'd pick if we didn't have that threat hanging over us. Let's remember we haven't time to go through all the standard selection procedures; we need to come up with someone who's already in the loop."

This was the chance Nathan Roberts had been waiting for.

"That's a no-brainer. There's only one choice to be made. It's got to be George Sinclair. He was our alternative candidate and now that Snoddy has fallen off the mantelpiece, he's the only one up there. Or is there something I'm missing?"

The confidence that his face exuded as he asked the question came too close to arrogance for his cause to be advanced by it. The naked triumphalism of it was begging to be shot down. Surprisingly, it was the Chairman who took it upon himself to do just that.

"I don't know if any of you have heard what Mr Sinclair has had to say about this Panel? He shared his thoughts with a journalist on ... what's the magazine called? ...' The Grass Roots', that's it. I've no idea who thought to send it to me, but I received a copy in the post this very morning. There's an article in it where Sinclair describes us in this committee as a bunch of losers; we are all lackeys of the system according to him, too thick ... thick, comrades ... too thick to see how we were being led by the nose by big business and global capitalism. 'A disgrace to the working class movement', that's what we are apparently. He was particularly nasty about you, Margaret. You aren't mentioned by name, but since you're the only woman on the Panel, I think you're the only one he could have had in mind in the reference he made to ... 'the unhealthy influence of Lesbians on the quasi-moral fantasies that have taken hold of the soul of the Party'. No, I'm sorry, Nathan, but I think we'll have to rule your man out."

Roberts exploded in a frenzy of indignation.

"This is bloody nonsense! Don't you see? You're doing exactly what this capitalist rag wants you to do. Did you never stop and ask yourself who's behind all this? Why would anyone send you this? And why would they not identify themselves? I've known George Sinclair for many years and I know that he'd never say such things ... to a journalist ... even if he thought them, which I doubt. Who wrote the article anyway?"

Sinclair put his reading glasses back on and scoured the relevant pages.

"It doesn't seem to say. That *is* strange, right enough."

"Let me talk to George and see if he has given any interviews recently. I think we owe him that at least."

The Chairman seemed to waver. His instinctive compulsion to be even-handed, ingrained over years of chairing meetings, was holding its ground against the will to be decisive and dismiss *this bloody Marxist* whom he couldn't stomach in the first place. Freddie Douglas once again came to his rescue.

"With respect, Mr Chairman, I don't think we can go into that now. We don't owe George Sinclair anything, any more than George Sinclair owes anything to us. I think it would send out the wrong message if we simply replaced the candidate we chose with a candidate we had earlier rejected. It would make it very difficult for us to persuade the electorate that we were a hundred percent behind him. No, whether or not he's been stitched up, as

Nathan wants us to believe, is now totally irrelevant. Our hands are tied."

This produced a chorus of hear-hears and a broad smile on the Chairman's face. But Douglas wasn't finished.

"I may be speaking out of turn here, Mr Chairman. I haven't had a chance to run this idea past him ..." He paused and looked inquiringly at Schinski. "... but I think we have the answer to our problem right here in this room."

Everyone's eyes followed the lead Sinclair had given them and lighted on Schinski. Douglas allowed just enough time for this to happen, but followed up before anyone else could get their voice in.

"In my view Derek Schinski is exactly the man for the job. I think you would agree with me, Mr Chairman: without him this committee would have struggled. Look at the way he handled things today, for instance. He is clear-headed, he can see the wood from the trees and above all, he knows what makes people tick. Another thing: He's not coming to the campaign cold. As Snoddy's election agent he has been right at the heart of it. He would give continuity; the press would not be able to accuse us of making a u-turn."

Chapter 81

The emergency meeting of the Selection Panel was not the only summit to take place that day. Seated around the magnificent mahogany table in Eardley's sumptuous hotel suite were Eardley himself, Bruce Greenfield, Francesca Bergman, David Compton, John Andrews, Walter Peters and Pascal Levy, with one exception the entire membership of the New Promethean Council. All had already been summoned for a strategy meeting scheduled for the following day, but it was decided that the much changed agenda could not be put off till then. The only member missing was Robert Snoddy. Although the hour was late – it was in fact nearly midnight – Snoddy had been asked to attend an hour later than the rest. After his interview with Schinski Greenfield had had a heart-to-heart with Eardley and the two men had come to the conclusion that there was indeed a bullet that needed biting.

Eardley opened the meeting and immediately called on Greenfield to give an update on events.

"This afternoon I had an unexpected visit from Derek Schinski. Matthew had already informed me, as he had you all, about what was going on, so it came as no surprise to hear that they were likely to show Robert the door. I asked him why he had come to me since he had already spoken to Matthew on the subject. He said he knew I was closer to Robert than any of the rest of you and that if I leave aside personal loyalties and see the good sense in what he had to say, then there was a better chance that the other members of the Council would do likewise. He didn't think there was any realistic chance of persuading the constituency party to stick with Robert. No purpose would be served by digging in our heels and trying to force it through. If we kept our eyes on the ball that really mattered, which was getting ourselves a voice in Parliament, then Robert had to be jettisoned. It wasn't all gloom and doom though. The Selection Panel were between a rock and a hard place. They'd need to come up with a replacement candidate that would be acceptable to the Constituency Party. That wasn't going to be easy. Time was against them. The election was only weeks away, and the last thing they could afford was a scandal. If Robert didn't play ball and kicked up a stink there was every chance they'd lose the election. That wouldn't be in anyone's interests, certainly not ours."

Eardley could wait no longer.

"Tell them what he proposed, Bruce."

Greenfield hesitated, showing an obvious reluctance to come out with his response, the kind of reluctance that in different circumstances might have been put down to modesty.

"He suggested that *he* should be our candidate."

Everyone looked at each other for assurance that they had heard right. Peters let out a guffaw.

"Who does this man think he is? Forgive me if I'm wrong, but is this not the man we had over a barrel? Does he not realise we could send him to jail at the drop of a hat?"

Eardley frowned. "I think we're long past that point now, Walter. I'm afraid he has as much on us now as we have on him. But in any case I think you're missing the point. I don't think he's trying to blackmail us. Yes, he's looking out for himself, but that's what makes him what he is. I've watched him at work. He's a very smooth operator. I had already offered him a job in our organisation, although I must confess, this is not what I had in mind."

"But does he really believe in what we're trying to do? As you said, he looks out for himself. He's a mercenary. How can we expect any loyalty from someone like that?"

Eardley nodded in sympathy with the question.

"Bruce and I had a very long talk earlier this evening and he

441

got me to see things in a different light. Say to them what you said to me, Bruce."

Greenfield, rather than being boosted by this, displayed symptoms of embarrassment at being put on the spot.

"I think we have greatly underestimated the significance of the death of the unfortunate Joseph Ross. As far as our project is concerned, we look on it as a bit of bad luck, a spanner in the works that threatens to bring our hopes of having a voice in Parliament crashing down. I'm not saying we are being callous, not at all. Most of you didn't know the young man personally, so his death could not register with you above the level of mild sadness. It was different of course for those of us who did know him. I know that, contrary to what Lizzie Partridge thinks, Robert himself was greatly upset by it. But that's not what I'm talking about.

"What I'm talking about is the threat this death poses to the very core of our project. We are trying to get a society that has been softened and sentimentalised to the point of puerility suddenly to grow up and throw away all the anxiety-busting fantasies it has been fed on for the last couple of generations. We want people to be able to look on moral decisions in terms of good versus good and bad versus bad and not expect always to only get the easy good versus bad decisions to make. We want people to be able to think at the same time as they feel and to feel at the same time as they think and to sustain the tensions that inevitably arise when they do both. That is asking a lot. What made Joseph Ross an important player in our project was that he excelled at both ends of the continuum. On the emotional side he was a sensitive soul, a gentle person with little anger in him. At the same time he had a first class brain capable of dealing in the most abstract concepts. He was the perfect subject to test our hypothesis on. So you see, Joseph's death is a much greater blow to our project than the blip it is now causing. We must even consider the possibility of it proving a fatal blow.

442

"We must re-think where we're at and whether it is possible to go as far we would like. I'm not saying that we should pack up and go home. Maybe Joseph wasn't the classic prototype. Maybe if we focused on people presenting a less extended model of the rational-emotional polarity we would get better results. I honestly don't know. One thing I do know, we should be grateful to Lizzie Partridge. Without her intervention we might have gone too far, and certainly too soon."

The heads around the table were beginning to drop. The reaction found a voice in Pascal Levy.

"You sound very pessimistic, Bruce. You sound as if you have lost faith in our cause."

Greenfield did not rush to contradict him. There was an uneasy pause before he replied.

"Pessimistic? No, I think I would say I've become more respectful of the difficulty of the task before us. I think we've been trying to decorate the house before we have it built. I've been talking about the dialectical tension between feeling and reason, but there's another force field which we have been less attentive to: the tension that inevitably arises between the individual's sense of right and wrong and the wider moral consensus. Think of them as planetary bodies. The smaller entity is pulled into an orbit around the greater, just like the earth and the sun. We have been focusing too much of our effort on shaping the individual conscience and then simply asking it to defy the laws of psychological physics and break free of the force of the moral consensus. We have been tackling the problem from the wrong end. What we should be doing is concentrating our efforts on finding ways to weaken the pull of the larger body.

"The more I think about it, the more I realise that this in fact was the path that Robert initially set out on. You are all familiar with the story of Robert being arrested and charged with the murder of his headmaster of St Jude's. You will have read the fictional account in his novel, but I was there and had firsthand knowledge of the forces at work. The head, dear old Bernhard Stevens, expelled Robert for an alleged sexual assault on one of the female staff. A not unreasonable punishment, indeed an act of clemency, you might think ... *but only If the assault had actually taken place.* But if on the other hand the lady had made it all up, she'd be the one deserving of punishment. The judgement that Stevens came to wasn't based on these considerations at all, it was based solely on expediency, and expediency for him was what caused *him* the least amount of hassle from the fewest amount of people. It was a perfect example of the way the amorality of *professionalism* has taken over leadership circles in our society. In the novel Stevens gets his deserts. No, I'd need to rephrase that – in his morally neutral world there are no deserts. He gets what's coming to him. Those who live by amorality die by amorality. He certainly didn't deserve to die for such a minor crime, but then he had no right of appeal to the very principle of justice that he himself had denied.

"I digress, but only slightly. Let's get back to this moral consensus. How do you get to change it? Its most formidable characteristic is its elusiveness. You can't pin it down, for the simple reason that the people who embrace it don't feel any requirement to live by it. The Left have de-privatised it and taken it into public ownership. An interesting development that – nationalisation twenty-first century style! All wrongs in need of righting have become the responsibility of government agencies. Moral virtue no longer requires individual sacrifice. Heaven forbid! That would be like the obverse of taking the law into your own hands. No, all you need to do to join the ranks of the angels of virtue is simply to sign up to the right politics and vote for a government prepared to do all the right things on your behalf. That gives you your get-out-of-jail-free card and leaves you unfettered to lead your life and act as you please in the greatly expanded amoral zone that that frees up. You can cheat on your wife, fiddle your expenses, do drugs, stab your colleagues in the back, anything – provided of course you tick all the right boxes on the official political affidavit.

"Shorn of the need for individual input, this 'nationalised' morality has nothing to keep it in check. It brooks no interference from anything outside itself. It is free to soar from virtue to virtue. Harmless idealism, some might say. No! That it most certainly is not; it's mightily dangerous! Faffing about out there in the ether, it might seem harmless enough, but it does impact on lives, not of course on the lives of the urban elite who embrace it; it's the lower orders who are left to cope with the damage it does to reality. Anyone who complains is told they are too stupid or too blinkered to see the New Jerusalem. This is what is normally described as 'brainwashing', but I think of it as a process not so much of clearing the brain of content as of infusing it with dye. Over a long period the dye is surreptitiously inserted into the public mindset. The aspirant middle classes are particularly susceptible. Every time they listen to their own inner voice, it shows up as a smear of guilt and shame and self-loathing. They end up 'brain-dyed', which is only a short step away from being 'brain-dead'. 'Aversion therapy' I think is what psychologists call it.

"Well, maybe it's time we started on a campaign of aversion therapy for the elite. Maybe it's not the murderers and rapists that the courts let off that we should be targeting, but the people who let them off. Not just them: all the great and the good, all those who have denuded the world of grounded and rooted virtues. Maybe they should be brought to suffer the debased reality that their moral delusions create. We need to find ways to put their self-indulgence at odds with this comfortable absentee morality that is so deeply ingrained. The House of Commons is not the forum for such a campaign, but we need members there to open channels for the message to seep through. A full frontal rational assault is unlikely to succeed at the stage we are at."

445

Somewhat fatigued by his effort, Greenfield sank back in his chair. Eardley took over.

"Thank you for that, Bruce. You have given us much food for thought. You always do. But, to get back to our more immediate problem, I'd like to ask Francesca here for her thoughts on these latest developments. She is our political expert and I think we should hear what she has to say."

The switch to another viewpoint was disingenuous. The whole time Greenfield had been speaking Francesca could be seen to be nodding in agreement.

"I suspect Bruce is right, we've been more than a little naive. I have a lot of respect for Robert; he is a deep thinker and an excellent analyst of political dialectic, but I doubt if he will ever cut much ice as a jobbing politician. When you asked me to coach him in the dark arts of politics I thought I'd be able to rub the rough edges off him. I tried, and to be fair, *he* tried, but after a time I felt not so much that I wasn't getting anywhere but that it was the wrong place I was trying to get to. The last thing I wanted was to turn him into a see-and-say-no-evil mannequin, but I fear that that's what my attempts to get him to curb the excesses of his very lively intellect were in danger of producing. He lacks the common touch. I've no doubt there will be a frontline political role for Robert to play sometime in the future, but this is not the time. We need people with the right skills to get in there and till the ground before it's ready to take the kind of stuff that Robert wants to plant.

"I think we might well have fallen into a trap that catches many people who pride themselves on having the vision to see where the world should be taken to; they think the means should be a mirror image of the vision. Our socialist friends are the perfect example of this; they see it as their mission to put money in the pockets of the poor. It's a noble vision, but how do they go about it? They simply go straight at it; they seize the money from the rich and pour it over the poor devils at the

446

bottom of the heap. They are genuinely amazed when this doesn't work. So they try more of the same. They tax their way down from the rich to the wealthy and the better-off and eventually get to the very fringe of the class they are committed to support. Does this work? No, in every country where it has been tried, within a decade or two, the poor devils at the bottom are still poor devils, in fact even poorer devils. Noble visions don't fly you to the Promised Land; you need boots on the ground and a good cobbler to make them stout enough to cope with the stony and very uneven ground of human psychology."

"And what about Derek Schinski, do you think he'd make a good cobbler?"

She gave an appreciative smile in acknowledgement of Eardley's adoption of her metaphor.

"I've been working alongside Derek for the past few weeks. He's shown himself bloody darned good at making shoes to fit feet rather than sitting back and expecting feet to fit his shoes. I doubt if he'll ever be a conviction politician. It's all just a great game to him. But I do think we could count on him to fight our corner – not because it's something he passionately believes in, but because it throws up a more interesting challenge, more peaks for him to climb, more markers for success. What has impressed me most about Derek is his ability to cope with the psychological chaos that confronts anyone intent on changing minds; he has a feel for when to push and how far to push, but above all he knows when *not* to push. Bruce talked about the need to narrow the gap between what people think and what they feel they are allowed to think. He's spot on there. Our ability to narrow that gap for them is where the fight for a justice system worthy of the name will be won or lost.

"Robert is much too inclined to call on the force of rational argument to do the job. That simply does not address the problem; reasoning itself is in the dock and it cannot simply talk its way on to the jury. He must learn the lessons of his own research. If he genuinely wants to gauge the capacity of people to see through the implications of the moral positions they think they hold, he must accept the evidence that he himself has garnished, however unpalatable it may be. The sad example of Joseph Ross cannot be dismissed as an aberration. Rational thought is in sore need of allies. To be fair, I don't think the point has in fact been lost on Robert. I've talked to Naomi and she tells me it has hit him harder than he lets on. He even admitted to doubts to her about his aptitude for the political front line, the very same doubts that he revealed to Bruce today.

"Everyday politics needs deviousness even more than it needs intelligence, Robert is quite brilliant at exposing the directionless meanderings that have been passing for political thinking in recent decades. In fact, I can think of nobody better able to unpick the irrational tangle of the contemporary moral catechism. With Derek Schinski there to act as front man we may well have hit on a perfect blend of the whereby and the what-for. '*Lente lente currite noctis equi*'[11] (As she said this her eyes were fixed on Greenfield). Yes, gentlemen, I would say the right outcome has been thrust upon us."

From the restrained grin on his face it was clear that Eardley had heard exactly what he wanted the others to hear.

* * * *

By a less than strange coincidence the Selection Panel of the Bury West Labour Party and the Council of The New Prometheans, within hours of each other, both passed motions approving Derek Schinski as the man to carry their torch to Westminster. A few weeks later the electors of Bury West did likewise and Derek Schinski entered on the career to which he was born.

---

[11]   Run slowly, slowly, horses of the night

Lightning Source UK Ltd.
Milton Keynes UK
UKHW011202151219
355424UK00004B/91/P